TESSA HARRIS read History at Oxford University and has been a journalist, writing for several national newspapers and magazines for more than thirty years. She is the author of nine published historical novels. Her debut, *The Anatomist's Apprentice*, won the Romantic Times First Best Mystery Award 2012 in the US. She lectures in creative writing at Hawkwood College, Stroud and is married with two children. She lives in the Cotswolds.

Facebook: Tessa Harris Author
Twitter: @harris_tessa
www.tessaharrisauthor.com

D1025738

Beneath a Starless Sky

TESSA HARRIS

ONE PLACE. MANY STORIES

HQ
An imprint of HarperCollins*Publishers* Ltd
1 London Bridge Street
London SE1 9GF

www.harpercollins.co.uk

HarperCollins*Publishers*
1st Floor, Watermarque Building, Ringsend Road
Dublin 4, Ireland

1
First published in Great Britain by
HQ, an imprint of HarperCollins*Publishers* Ltd 2021

Copyright © Tessa Harris 2021

Tessa Harris asserts the moral right to be
identified as the author of this work.
A catalogue record for this book is
available from the British Library.

ISBN: 9780008444983

MIX
Paper from
responsible sources
FSC™ C007454

This book is produced from independently certified FSC™ paper
to ensure responsible forest management.

For more information visit: www.harpercollins.co.uk/green

Printed and Bound in the UK using 100% Renewable Electricity
at CPI Group (UK) Ltd

For Catherine, with thanks and love

'. . . *Only when it is dark enough can you see the stars.*'
Martin Luther King Jr.

Prologue

Munich, Germany

1940

Tilting her silver head towards the gramophone player, the old woman listened to the shellac seventy-eight crackle into life. As the needle scoured out the music, Fred Astaire's voice rose, crooning from the grooves. *Dancing in the dark, dah dah dah dah dah* . . .

A smile twitched her lips. It didn't matter that she couldn't understand the foreign lyrics. Fred Astaire, in his white tie and tails, would scoop her up in his arms and whirl away all her thoughts of despair.

Outside, the city slept under curfew. The only distant sound came from armoured trucks and lorries that rumbled relentlessly along the main highway, taking men and machines to war. Inside, in her dark and damp apartment, its windows blacked out, the old woman was left rocking in her one remaining chair. All the others had been burned in the *kachelofen*, the huge, green tiled stove in the corner.

Dancing in the dark, dah dah . . . The song was a welcome distraction from contemplating her own mortality. It made her think of her daughter. Of happier times. Lilli had given her reason to hope; slipping out of Munich unremarked by the authorities just two days before, she'd left behind the travel papers for her and her granddaughter. The plan was to escape to Switzerland with the little girl, asleep now in the next room. They would both be safe there – safer – until Lilli returned. But nothing seemed to go to plan in war.

When the music's blue notes made the melancholy return, the old woman stroked the black cat on her knee. It was better fed than her.

Starvation could be the possible cause of her death, and if not starvation the cold – if she made it to winter. Or, of course, she might even catch diphtheria from her little granddaughter. That was the most likely cause at the moment. The child had been suffering for several days, although her fever had broken a while back and there were signs of improvement, she still remained weak. Now, however, the old woman herself was feeling a little flushed, her throat was sore and her old bones ached even more than usual.

There was, of course, another way she could meet her end, although she constantly tried to push it out of her mind. They could come for her. Some of her friends had already gone and she doubted she would ever see them again. When faced with the thought of either starvation or hypothermia, diphtheria seemed much more preferable. Dying in a camp would be the worst, but however death came, she prayed it would be quick.

As it happened the old woman was spared the indignities of nearby Dachau and at least her end, when it came, was swift, if rather brutal. She was fortunate, too, in that she was alerted to her executioners' approach before she actually saw them.

When they came that evening, their heavy tread echoing up the stairwell and their thick voices bouncing off the walls, she would not have heard them over Astaire's serenade at first. But the cat did. It heeded them all right and leapt off her knee. In

2

the few seconds between being alerted to her killers' advance and their knock, the old woman knew exactly what she had to do.

Scrambling into the bedroom as fast as her creaking legs would carry her, she lifted the child from the bed where she slept. In the bathroom there was a small chest where towels and sheets were kept. She laid the little girl on one then covered her loosely with the rest.

The pounding fists and the shouts that followed a second later were momentarily silenced as, nervously, the old woman opened the door. When she saw the four of them – an army officer and his three soldiers – standing there, smelling of leather and gun metal, she tried to swallow down her fear, but it caught hold of her throat and snagged her voice.

'Yes, sir? How can I help you?' she asked, feigning innocence, as if she had no idea what could possibly have brought these men to her door.

The officer was short and stocky with a long, raised scar on his face, as if someone had drawn a line in pencil from his left cheekbone to his jaw. Another smaller one marked his chin. His eyes were obscured by the peak of his cap when he spoke.

'Where is she?'

'Who?'

'You know who, you old Jew. Search the apartment,' he ordered.

His men stormed in. They split up: each stomping into a room. The old woman could hear wardrobe doors opening and slamming, drawers flung to the floor, china smashing on the tiles. *As if my daughter will be hiding in a vase*, she thought to herself.

While his men were wreaking havoc in the other rooms, the officer's eye was caught by the gramophone player. The disc was crackling incessantly as it pirouetted on the turntable. Stalking over to it, he lifted the stylus and grabbed the record to read the label. The old woman remained still, watching the fury march across his face. Suddenly he jack-knifed his leg and cracked the disc in two across his knee, cursing loudly.

'Fred Astaire!' he cried, flinging the shards to the floor. 'Records are *verboten*!'

One by one the soldiers returned from their forays shaking their heads. Again, the officer narrowed his eyes. 'You have one more chance. Where is she?'

The old woman also shook her head. 'I don't know who you mean,' she replied.

Without a word, the officer reached into his holster and pulled out his Luger. An image of the old woman's daughter filled his vision. He'd always wanted to possess Lilli Sternberg ever since he'd first set eyes on her all those years ago. There'd been something maddeningly mesmerising about her. She'd driven him frantic with desire, yet whenever he'd come within reach of her, she'd slipped his grasp. Once again, the intelligence had come through too late. She'd be in Lisbon by now. With the former King of England and his American wife. If he couldn't have what he wanted, her mother must pay. Even before the old woman had time to react, he pulled the trigger. An ear-splitting crack filled the space between them. His victim clutched her chest, made an odd gurgling sound and fell. Death did, indeed, come swiftly for her, as she had hoped.

The silence that followed the shot didn't last long. It was pricked by a needle of a cry coming from one of the rooms.

'What was that?' growled the officer.

His men froze, their heads switching involuntarily towards the thread of high-pitched sound. Without warning the door from the bathroom was opened by some unseen force. Hands were clamped around rifles on high alert until, from out of the room, dashed a black cat. It leapt over the crumpled body that lay on the threshold without stopping to sniff the pooling blood, and darted straight past the soldiers and down the stairs.

The officer cleared his throat, re-inserted his Luger into its holster and tugged at his jacket. As he worked his jaw in silent rage, he cast a final glance around the room. What the old woman had said was true. Her daughter wasn't there. His bird had already flown. In his gut he had known it before he came to the apartment looking for her and shot her mother instead. Lilli Sternberg was long gone.

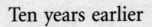

Ten years earlier

Chapter 1

Munich, Germany

1930

Smoke. Not just the smoke from a stove. It tingled in her nostrils. This smoke smelled different. Acrid. Harsh. Lilli Sternberg's quickening heart sounded an alarm as she rounded the corner into Untere Grasstrasse. When she lifted her gaze to the rooftops, she saw the sparks of a thousand fireworks join the stars to fill the black sky.

Fire. Suddenly cries cut through the cold air and a man careered past her at high speed. Before she could move out of the way, he clipped her shoulder and sent her spinning. She staggered back against a wall. Shaking the shock from her head she heard someone nearby shout a warning and she looked up just in time to see a blazing beam hurtling towards her. There was no time to react. It crashed to the ground just a few metres away. She screamed. And then she saw more flames.

'Get back! Get back!' yelled a fireman.

'My father. The tailor's shop! Is it . . .?' But her cries were lost in the confusion.

At least two shops along the street were alight, tongues of orange flame licking clean the bones of the bunched-up buildings lining the narrow street. There may have been more ablaze, but the firemen were keeping onlookers well back. Just before her way was barred, Lilli thought she could make out a few men forming a human chain along the street. They were passing buckets from the water hydrant at the end of the row.

The heat was starting to sting her hands and face. She decided to retreat, narrowly avoiding the shower of molten sparks exploding across the cobbles. The roar of the blaze filled her ears and the thick smoke seemed to suck the breath from her lungs, making her cough.

The flames had already risen to the upper floors. Shattered glass from windows carpeted the narrow road below. A fire engine blocked the street and a solitary jet of water arced up through panes, dampening down the blaze and making it hiss in protest. Lilli could tell some of the adjoining shops were beyond saving. Was her father's workshop one of them?

Lilli felt her legs melt beneath her. Already exhausted from hours of rehearsals with Madame Eva at the *Académie de Danse,* her feet were badly blistered, too. But she knew she needed to return home as fast as she could. She was worried about her father. What if he was inside his shop when the fire started?

An icy blast whipped around her legs and ripped through her lungs like a knife as she ran. Despite her pain, she struggled through the back streets of Giesing, stopping now and again to catch her breath and swallow down the agony in her feet.

Past the old doors plastered in posters and the boarded-up shops she went until she came to the run-down apartment block she called home. The stairs up to the fourth floor seemed even steeper than usual. The shock of what she'd just seen weighed her down. She felt sick with worry with each step that she took. What if her father had been stitching with the sewing machine? He wouldn't have heard the crackling flames. He had a cold, too.

It would have taken him longer to smell the smoke. For the first time in ages she found herself praying to a god she didn't believe existed. *Please, let him be safe.*

As she reached the first landing something darted out in front of her. She veered to avoid it, only to realise it was Felix, the block's black cat.

Just then a child's voice called down. 'Well, if it isn't the movie star!' A small face squeezed between the spindles of the staircase. 'Did you know your vati's shop is on fire?'

It was Anna Kepler, the dentist's daughter, an eight-year-old who often spied on people on the stairs. Her teeth were held back by steel braces. Lilli only wished her tongue could be. Angrily, she powered up the last remaining flights of steps, barging past the girl, cursing under her breath to burst into the apartment, gulping for air.

'Vati! Is he here?'

Her mother, Golda, was sitting hunched on the threadbare sofa. Wrapped in a shawl, she was cradling a cup of coffee in both hands.

'Oh Lilli!' cried Golda. 'Praise be!' A plump hand reached out to grasp her daughter's. Lilli rushed to take it, the room filling with the stench of acrid smoke in her wake.

Their neighbour, Frau Grundig, the one Lilli called the Ram because she wore her braids coiled around her ears, was by her mother's side.

'At last!' cried the Ram. 'It was a good of you to turn up,' she mumbled sarcastically. She disapproved of Lilli, suspecting her of fooling with boys when she told her parents she was at the academy.

'I'm sorry, Mutti, rehearsals ran late and Madame Eva . . .'.

'Madame Eva! Madame Eva!' mimicked the Ram.

Ignoring Frau Grundig's taunts, Lilli turned to her mother. 'Vati! The fire! Where's Vati?' she croaked.

'He's safe, praise be,' replied Golda, raising her eyes heavenwards. 'The Almighty took care of him.'

Golda was a heavy woman, with large, dark features. Like a sturdy piece of mahogany furniture, her frame was thick and serviceable. She moved in a cloud of resignation. Fire, flood or famine: because she believed they were God's will, she accepted them all without complaint. Her daughter did not.

'I came as soon as I could but . . .' The words still struggled to escape Lilli's gritty throat. She was careful to avoid the Ram's gaze as she spoke. It was true that she'd been kept late rehearsing *Giselle*. She'd been chosen to dance the leading role in this year's gala performance. But if her parents ever found out she also worked as an usherette at the cinema after classes some evenings, she'd be in deep trouble.

'Where is he?' Lilli asked, her dark eyes searching the room.

'Seeing what the Almighty will let him save,' replied Golda with a shrug.

Leon, Lilli's younger brother, sat by the *kachelofen* in the corner, feeding logs to the hungry giant stove. He was four years younger than her, but he had the mind of an adult. He said little, but thought a lot, preferring to bury his dark head in books rather than play sport. Up until then he had been content to watch events unfold, but he suddenly broke his silence.

'You put too much faith in the Almighty, Mutti,' he told his mother, finally prising himself away from the big stove.

'Leon!' Frau Grundig took it upon herself to scold him, too. 'If he were my son . . .' she began, but she was childless and everyone else's child, it seemed to her, behaved badly.

Golda lurched forward in her chair. 'Leon! Wash your mouth out with soap and water!' she cried.

Leon skulked across the room, his hands thrust deep into his pockets, his eyes cast down. Golda slumped back into her seat, shaking her head as she watched her son leave.

'He's angry,' she muttered on a long sigh.

Lilli agreed. She looked on politics as something that happened to other people, like being run over by a bus. Leon, on the other hand, thought all his family's problems were caused by politicians, who stirred up hatred against them. Her brother would not act. Not now at any rate, but Lilli feared that the day would soon come when he and his synagogue friends would do something foolish.

'The people who did this . . .' Golda carried on, staring into her coffee.

'People?' butted in the Ram. 'You think the fire was started deliberately?' Frau Grundig leaned forward, her ample bosom bulging over the top of her old-fashioned dirndl. A scandalised look puffed out her face. 'How do you know?'

Golda shot a savvy glance at Lilli before she replied. 'We can't say for sure but . . .'

'I'm afraid we can,' came a voice from the doorway. Jacob Sternberg stood bowed on the threshold, covered in soot. For an instant he reminded Lilli of the actor in the new American talkie *The Jazz Singer*, whose face was painted black. Her father gave a resigned shrug.

'A star with the word "*Juden*" was daubed on my shop door the other day,' he told them.

'Oh!' Frau Grundig's hands flew up to her face in an exaggerated show of empathy. 'Who could do such a thing?' she asked disingenuously. She knew as well as her neighbour about the recent spate of arson attacks on Jewish premises.

Golda stemmed her tears. Lilli could tell her mother wanted to cry, but, as ever, her pride ensured she did not. 'The usual thugs, with nothing better to do, I suppose,' was all she would say.

'The fire service was already there when I arrived,' Jacob told his small audience. 'They did their best, but . . .' His voice trailed off in defeat.

'They have their work cut out tonight,' butted in Herr Kepler. He was the dentist from the third floor. He stepped into the apartment uninvited, an unlit pipe clenched between his uneven teeth.

'What do you mean?' asked Jacob, wiping the soot from his spectacles with a handkerchief.

'The synagogue is ablaze, too.'

'How can this be?' asked the diminutive Frau Kepler. She'd followed behind her husband, making the sign of the cross as she spoke.

An annoyed Frau Reuter piled in, too, with one of her four small children on her hip. All the commotion had apparently woken her little ones.

Despite the difficult circumstances, Golda suddenly remembered her duty to her visitors. 'You will take coffee?' she asked the Keplers and Frau Reuter.

'My children have been woken up,' Frau Reuter replied testily, jiggling her infant on her hip, as if it was patently obvious she did not have time for a coffee.

Before the others could answer, however, the sound of heavy footsteps echoing up the stairwell brought a halt to the conversation. Lilli was only relieved that Leon was out of the room when the door was flung wide. Herr Backe, in his brown storm trooper's uniform, a swastika band on his left arm, paused on the threshold to survey the gathering. For a moment there was an uneasy silence. None of the residents liked the lodger who shared the Sternbergs' apartment.

'Sieg heil!' he barked suddenly, raising his right arm in an abrupt salute. An arc of spittle went flying through the air.

A few months ago, the gesture had made Lilli giggle. Now she and her mother swapped uneasy glances. He was as a cuckoo in the nest and a buffoon, but, as her father pointed out, he was the one whose rent money was putting much-needed bread on their table. They were wary of him and his ways, but they put up with him. Only Herr Kepler responded with a half-hearted salute that was more of an embarrassed wave. The others bobbed their heads in reply.

'Herr Backe,' acknowledged Jacob.

By day Hans Backe was a bank clerk, but by night, after attending one of his weekly National Socialist Party meetings, he seemed to transform into someone quite loathsome.

'Frau Sternberg. Herr Sternberg.' The lodger returned the greeting before pivoting on his heels towards his room. His uniform made him look bigger than his cheap clerk's suit did, thought Lilli. She hated him.

Everyone waited for the sound of the door to click shut, but the damage was done. The unwelcome interruption seemed to bring the gathering to an early close, as if a shadow had just passed over the room. No one knew what to say – not safely – so the Keplers, Frau Grundig and Frau Reuter just smiled politely, and did what any good German citizen would do. They bid the Sternbergs '*Guten Nacht*' and left.

Chapter 2

Later that night, in the corner of the small, high-ceilinged room she shared with Leon, Lilli washed the soot from her face and hands in a bowl. A poster of Greta Garbo, curled at the edges, hid a damp patch on the wall.

The evening's events had cloaked the agony she'd felt in her swollen feet. Now, however, she moved over to the bed and, sitting down, held her breath as she slid off her shoes. Leon watched transfixed as he saw that the blood from her toes had seeped through her woollen stockings. Gently Lilli peeled them off to reveal feet as purple as plums. At the sight her brother winced.

'Why do you do that to yourself?' he asked, as he watched his sister wipe the dried blood from her toes with a damp cloth.

'Dance through the pain,' she replied. It was what Madame Eva, the academy's principal, always said. She would often pinch her pupils, too, if she felt they were slacking. Lilli lifted the corners of her mouth in a shallow little smile, as if to signify her wounds were no great hardship. 'Some things are worth suffering for,' she added wistfully.

Reaching for a towel, Lilli suddenly thought of the ten-metre high billboard at the road junction on her route to the cinema where she worked. It was advertising a new American film called

Lights of New York. A beautiful actress looked wan in the arms of a handsome man. Amid the flaking plasterwork and shabby warrens of streets of her home city, the new talking films from America beguiled her in a way that ballet, and great ballerinas like Pavlova and Alicia Markova, could not.

'That'll be you, someday,' Oskar, the broom boy at the cinema, had told her. Poor Oskar was in love with her, she knew that, because he often paid her sweet compliments. A lot of men did.

'What things?' Leon, his dark brows knitted in a frown, snapped back. He was testing her, she could tell.

Gently she towelled her feet. 'I would put up with anything to get out of this place. I know you would, too,' she told him, trying to keep her voice as low as her frustration would allow.

Leon snorted and folded his arms. His sister had dreams, he knew. He nodded in agreement, even though he had no inkling about her plans for a new life in America. Nor of her earnings from the cinema. While he was ranting and railing against his parents, the government and the world, Lilli was filling her shoe box under the floorboards with banknotes. It was where she hid her money – the money for her ticket to Hollywood.

'But this is your home, Lilli,' he told her. 'What about Mutti and Vati?'

Lilli shook her head. 'I don't intend to be spat at in the street for the rest of my life.' She turned towards the mantelpiece. 'No, I intend to escape.'

A large white gilt-edged card took pride of place above the empty fireplace. It was an invitation to the eighteenth birthday ball of one of the students at the academy. She reached for it.

'And this,' she told Leon, waving the invitation gleefully in the air, 'could be my passport to a better life.'

Lilli had never regarded Comtesse Helene von Urbach as a close friend. If she was being truthful, she didn't even consider her a good dancer. She may have had flaxen hair and large blue eyes, but her legs were on the thick side and her movement was at best contrived and at worst downright wooden. The fact remained, however, that she was having a ball at her father's *schloss* just outside the city and Lilli was invited. She had decided to accept. Surely it would be rude not to? Helene's widowed father was not only a count with his very own castle but a high-ranking officer in the *Reichswehr*, the German Army, and commander of the Seventh Division. Some unkind pupils – Lilli wasn't among them, of course – believed if it wasn't for his money, Helene would have failed the academy's entrance exams. As it was, Madame Eva had found a place for her in the chorus of *Giselle*, to dance the part of an ethereal Willi, a sort of spirit. Lilli thought she suited the part. She'd always found her rather aloof – the way she hung around in her shadow, staring at her, but saying little. Nonetheless, Helene had invited Lilli to her ball, and she had decided it would be foolish to turn down an opportunity to mix in such circles.

Lilli took a deep breath as she pictured herself being whirled around the general's ballroom in the arms of a dashing young officer to the strains of Strauss. Her face broke into a wide smile at the image of chandeliers and Champagne. The embossed script gave the date in December, just four days after the performance of *Giselle*. She held the invitation to her breast for a moment and sighed at the thought of all that romantic glamour.

Leon rolled his eyes at his big sister. 'Your head is full of silly dreams,' he told her.

'No, Leon,' Lilli corrected him, pointing to her temple. 'My head is full of plans. Big plans. There is a difference.'

Chapter 3

Captain Marco Zeiller sucked abruptly through his teeth as he watched the razor-sharp blade slash through the other officer's flesh. Captain Kurt von Stockmar, however, did not flinch. He stood his ground and, less than a second later, the blood began to flow; a curtain of crimson falling down his left cheek.

Marco was there at von Stockmar's invitation, although at the time of acceptance he wasn't entirely convinced he really wanted to witness the strange ritual. A group of officers from his regiment had left their battalion's barracks in the northern suburbs of Munich to drive out to a small gymnasium a few kilometres away. Marco had no plans, so, largely out of curiosity he'd been persuaded to join them. Now he was very much regretting his decision.

Von Stockmar and his opponent had been fencing at arm's length, standing more or less in one place. Around thirty other men were clustered around them in a ring. Marco had kept his distance, choosing instead to watch from one of the raised seats at the back of the hall. The aim, he knew, was to hit the unprotected areas of your opponent's face and head. Flinching or dodging were forbidden, but enduring the resulting injury stoically was applauded.

At the sight of the cascading blood, the rest of the men leapt to their feet, cheering, like hounds baying at a kill. Marco, however, remained seated. There was something rather disturbing, he found, about the whole spectacle. It reminded him of stags locking horns in rutting season, fighting it out to the bitter end. Of course, he'd heard about these fencing matches before. They were more were like duels. It was a tradition – a noble one, apparently – perpetuated by the sons of aristocratic Germans and dating back almost a century. Supposedly, the practice taught men to endure pain without wincing, cowering or recoiling. And now Captain Kurt von Stockmar was on the receiving end of a particularly unpleasant encounter. His wound continued to bleed profusely.

Marco's instinct was to go to his fellow officer's aid, or at the very least offer him a towel so that he could mop up the blood. But no. He knew he must be happy for him. Von Stockmar had just won another 'bragging scar' and he would wear his disfigure-ment with pride. It would heal into a badge of honour – a visible scar that proved his resilience and endurance.

The other men surged forward, not to help, but to congratu-late their injured brother. This latest slash wasn't von Stockmar's first – there was already a much less spectacular, horizontal one on his chin – and he'd clearly stated he hoped it wouldn't be his last, either. But from the colour of his face, or rather lack of it, it seemed to Marco that von Stockmar himself might well be horizontal very shortly. He was clearly on the verge of fainting. Yet losing consciousness was also the ultimate sign of weakness.

Marco didn't care for the squat, cocky officer; he didn't even admire him. Yet he found himself willing him to remain standing at the very least. That was when he suddenly remembered he had brought his hip flask with him. Reaching for his belt, he heard the schnapps slosh around inside.

'Von Stockmar!' Marco stepped forward into the melee, brandishing his flask. '*Prost!*'

He took a swig himself then handed it to the wounded man,

whose wan face lit up for a second before taking up the offer. Tilting back his head, von Stockmar downed the liquor as if it were water. He staggered a little then coughed loudly, choking on the fiery liquid. His friends laughed and patted him on the back again. They'd been in his fraternity at university in Berlin. They were all bound by blood.

Just why von Stockmar had invited Marco to witness this ritual scarring – because that was what it was: a bizarre way of proving one's masculinity and bravery, like a rite of passage in an African tribe – he was not entirely sure. He supposed, however, it might have something to do with rumours of his own recent promotion.

Von Stockmar was jealous of him and had been since cadet school, when it soon emerged that Marco was better than him at everything: shooting, mathematics and communicating with his men. The rivalry turned to jealousy and had been left to fester like an ulcerous sore ever since.

There was also the matter of Marco's parentage. He was not what von Stockmar and his friends might call of *wholly acceptable stock*. His mother was Italian. Not only had he inherited her brown eyes, olive skin and good looks, but her Roman Catholic religion, too.

Von Stockmar handed back the flask to Marco. The schnapps had certainly revived him. So much so, that he began to pose enthusiastically for photographs, surrounded by the rest of his noisy fraternity. The blood that had poured down his left cheek had since dried, but the caked-on rivulets created an interesting dark fretwork on his skin. The photographer's shots would no doubt provide a much-prized souvenir of the day's events. Marco turned away.

'So, was it all too gory for you?' von Stockmar quizzed as he sat opposite Marco a little later.

They were in the *bierkeller* next to the gymnasium. A huge, celebratory tankard, overflowing with foam, presented itself to the newly wounded officer. A few of the other fencers crowded round on the benches by them. Each of their faces bore their own scars of various lengths and jaggedness.

'Gory?' Marco repeated. His unblemished face broke into a smile. He knew von Stockmar was playing a game with him, trying to make him appear weak in front of his friends. 'No. I'd say it was curious, more than anything.'

He took a gulp of beer from his own tankard then licked the froth from his upper lip. Cruelty and blood were no strangers to him. As a boy, he'd witnessed a convoy of half-starved refugees fleeing their homes during the Great War. He would never forget seeing their broken bodies and their haunted faces from the window of his mother's limousine as they sped to safety after the Battle of Caporetto. Since then he had grown up despising violence for violence's sake.

Von Stockmar, his left cheek now showing signs of swelling and inflammation, tried to contort his lips into a smile, but found himself defeated by the growing pain. He pointed to the wound. 'This blood is pure German,' he said. 'You would not understand. After all, your mother came from a nation of ice-cream sellers and opera singers.' He searched the faces of his friends for appreciation and garnered a few laughs and several nods.

Instinctively Marco shrugged. He'd been told it was a very Italian gesture – true Germans never shrugged – but there were many traits he was proud to have inherited from his mother. Tolerance was one of them. He was used to such insults and would not rise to the bait.

'Perhaps you are right,' he replied calmly. 'I need to fight for a cause, not for needless scars.'

Von Stockmar snorted a laugh and shifted on his bench. Looking around for support he said: 'You want a cause, then we will show you one, won't we brothers?'

A few choroused their approval. Another clenched his fist and banged it on the table, before letting out a belly laugh.

'Oh?' Marco would let them play their games. He knew their sort.

Von Stockmar's eyes were smiling as he nodded. 'We are off to the Brown House tonight, to hear Herr Hitler speak. You should join us.'

The officer sitting next to Marco slapped him playfully on the arm. '*Ja!* Join us,' he echoed.

Marco suddenly pictured the Brown House. It was the grand mansion in the centre of Munich that had recently been refurbished. It now served as the new headquarters of the National Socialist German Workers' Party. And of course, everyone had heard of this Herr Hitler, too: an unpleasant little politician with a big ego. There'd been much talk of him – most of it unfavourable – over dinner in the officers' mess, and how he'd had managed to gather his own personal army of storm troopers around him. In their brown shirts and big boots, they were little better than hooligans who fancied themselves as soldiers.

Marco shook his head. 'I do not care for the man, or his politics,' he replied bluntly, while still managing to raise a polite smile.

Von Stockmar swapped glances with his friends. 'But he promises to rip up Versailles – the treaty that has brought our great nation to its knees!' he protested.

'But surely he also threatens us, the army?' countered Marco, making certain his voice remained measured. He had little appetite for political debate. 'He would take power from our hands. You know the generals are uneasy.'

Von Stockmar's eyes flashed and a large vein pulsed in his forehead.

'He will make Germany great again,' he replied, his pale skin starting to flush.

'*Ja! Ja,*' exclaimed several men in unison.

In Germany, Marco knew that Germans always put their country first.

In Italy, it was family.

Buoyed by such enthusiasm, von Stockmar straightened his back and issued a rallying cry. His arm flew up. 'It's time to rise up and be the masters of our own destiny once more!'

The other officers cheered, but Marco merely sipped the beer from his tankard. His failure to respond was meant to diffuse the situation, but instead it seemed to antagonise it. Fury spread across von Stockmar's already inflamed face and his jaw shot out defiantly as he rose from the bench. He delivered his parting shot as he glowered at Marco from above.

'My dear fellow,' he snarled, 'that pretty face of yours is a sign of cowardice and the time is coming when such weakness will not be tolerated.'

And with those words von Stockmar stormed out of the building, followed by his own small army of narrow-minded men. Marco remained silent but unsettled. This new breed of politics troubled him.

Chapter 4

'*Nein. Nein.* Lilli! Giselle is dying of a broken heart, remember!?' Madame Eva Schwarzkopf shook her head vigorously, clapped her hands impatiently and clicked her tongue. The reprimand echoed around the walls of the *Académie de Danse* and made Lilli slide to an abrupt halt. She'd already caught her teacher's frustrated expression reflected in the floor-to-ceiling studio mirror. As she sashayed forward, she braced herself for one of Madame's famous pinches.

'I need more emotion from you,' cried her teacher. 'Your lover has deceived you.'

The pinch didn't come. Even so, Lilli wanted to protest. No one would shed tears over pimply, gangly Jens, who partnered her as Duke Albrecht. Besides, how could she act like her heart had been broken when it hadn't? Not yet. It was difficult for her to imagine what it must be like to love and lose the light of your life. After all, she was only eighteen. Her heart had ached at the sight of Josef, the rabbi's son, and it had yearned for a better life for her parents, far from the regular slurs and attacks they suffered, but so far it had remained intact.

November was always a busy month at the academy. Rehearsals for the annual Christmas performance at the prestigious Cuvilliés

Theatre in the city centre were well underway. The production had become a highlight of the Bavarian social calendar, attracting those with power as well as privilege. It also served to enhance the academy's reputation for excellence. In the demanding lead role, Lilli was required to give so much more of herself than she ever had before. She knew she must rise to the challenge. The rewards could be great. The lead dancer in *Swan Lake* a few years back landed a permanent position with a professional ballet company.

Taking a deep breath to steady her body Lilli stared at the floor as Madame Eva repeated her demand for 'more emotion'. Madame was right, of course. She wasn't dancing her best. The attack on her father's shop had unsettled her and hunger was making her stomach growl. Was it any wonder that after eight hours of rehearsals her whole body was exhausted and racked with pain? She longed the day to be over. Yet she still regarded it as an honour to be singled out to stay behind after classes had finished for the day. The great Pavlova wouldn't complain, and Markova never winced. Nor would she. Each pirouette, each plié had to be faultless. *Dance through the pain*, she reiterated Madame Eva's mantra. *Dance through it.* She placed her feet in the first position, tilted her head, lifted her chin and held out her arms in a gentle arc.

Mademoiselle Schultz, the pianist, a big woman with a frizz of orange hair, lifted her large hands over the keys as Lilli imagined how Giselle might have felt after her betrayal by the lying Duke Albrecht. She adopted an appropriately melancholy expression as, once more, Madame Eva clapped her hands and ordered: 'Again!'

Chapter 5

At long last the day of the performance of *Giselle* arrived – the day when every movement Lilli had rehearsed a thousand times over had to be exactly perfect. She'd felt the pressure mount even more last week when Madame Eva delivered the exciting news that an American talent scout would be in the audience. He was always on the lookout for exceptional dancers, she'd said.

'And you can be exceptional, if you put your heart into it,' her teacher had told her in one of her more generous moments.

Lilli Sternberg would be *exceptional*.

On arrival at the Cuvilliés Theatre, Madame Eva showed all the principal dancers onto the stage. Lilli thought her legs might buckle beneath her when she saw the sheer scale and beauty of the auditorium, its golden rococo tiers rising like some giant wedding cake into the roof.

Later in the dressing room, Lilli sat on a plush-topped stool, staring unblinking into the mirror. Thick black eyeliner accentuated her dark eyes and crimson lipstick slashed across her pale face. Her black hair was slicked back and her high cheekbones were rouged. She was no longer Lilli Sternberg. She was Giselle.

Around her all the other girls were chattering nervously, tightening waistbands, adjusting bodices, ribbons and headdresses.

Most of them, including Helene, were Willis – the ghosts of maidens who'd been betrayed by their lovers. They were swathed in white, their skirts made of delectate diaphanous material that reflected the light. Nerves were frayed as they elbowed each other, checking their make-up, dusting their faces, sending powder flying through the air. The smell of grease paint melded with lavender spray and every now and then a disconsolate wail would rise when one of them found a mark on their costume or a ladder in their tights.

The atmosphere was hectic, feverish, just how it should be, just how Lilli loved it. Suddenly she felt Madame Eva's hand on her arm. Her instinct was to pull away, but instead of pinching it, her teacher gave her a gentle squeeze.

'Remember there is a special guest in the audience tonight,' she said. 'The talent scout I mentioned – he has just arrived.' Madame was as close to excited as Lilli had ever seen her. 'I know that you will be a wonderful Giselle,' she added, looking into her pupil's eyes.

'I will try and make you proud,' Lilli said, even though a thousand butterflies of self-doubt were fluttering in her stomach.

So many people were depending on her to make the night a success. But her thoughts were centred on just one man in that vast auditorium, the man who had the power to change her life forever. It wasn't just the academy she was dancing for; it was her own future. Most of all, she couldn't let herself down.

Captain Marco Zeiller arrived at the Cuvilliés Theatre to find that all Munich's highest society was gathering at the venue. This production of *Giselle*, General von Urbach had explained to his officers, was under his patronage. All proceeds were to be donated to a military benevolent fund. They were therefore *encouraged* to attend. Marco, however, had not needed any such encouragement. He enjoyed the ballet and had heard great things about the academy's version.

Daimlers and Mercedes were queueing outside the theatre, disgorging the great and the good. Puffed-up majors and colonels from other regiments rubbed shoulders with politicians and city burghers, while their womenfolk eyed each other with the jealous zeal of beauty pageant contestants.

Marco made his way up the steps and inside the grand foyer. A young man in red and gold livery handed him a programme. He opened it and scanned the names. The general's daughter, Helene von Urbach, was at the top of the list of the chorus. He pictured the young woman who so often accompanied her father on official engagements and wondered if his commanding officer had insisted her name be first, or if the principal of the ballet school had just thought it politically expedient.

His reservation was in the third row of the stalls. It was a good seat near the central aisle, where he had a passable view of the audience as they flowed in a steady stream to take their places. As the orchestra tuned up in the pit, more elegantly dressed people took their seats. Marco would swear there were more metres of velvet in the gowns of the ladies than in the stage drapes. The atmosphere was electric. It reminded him of when his mother first took him to the opera house in Venice. He must have been no more than twelve. They'd watched a performance of *La Bohème* and, ever since, he'd fallen under the spell of opera. He found the power and the passion of the music and drama far more exhilarating than von Stockmar's sadistic duelling. And, as the lights dipped and a hush dropped like a veil over the audience, he was glad to be reminded of that same surge of anticipation he'd experienced as a child. Then the magic began.

Chapter 6

Lilli waited until the chorus had all left the room before she stood to do her breathing exercises. As she filled her lungs inhaling deeply, a thrill of excitement rippled through her. No longer was she posing in front of the bathroom mirror or being teased for having dreams by Leon. This was real and the feeling elated and terrified her in equal measure.

If she danced well, she might be spotted by the talent scout from America. A new world of opportunities would beckon. Buoyed up by the prospect, she was just about to head for the door when something in the corner caught her eye. Someone was lurking in the shadows.

'Helene!' she cried, her pulse made to race even faster. 'I didn't see you there.'

The count's daughter, dressed in her costume, was standing timidly in an alcove. Her eyes were lit up as she stared at Lilli in admiration.

'You look like a real star!' she said softly, mesmerised like a child in a sweet shop. Even though they rarely spoke to each other, Lilli imagined the only reason she'd been invited to Helene's ball was because she was the production's prima ballerina. Their backgrounds couldn't have been more different and yet the general's daughter seemed to admire her as a dancer.

Lilli, still recovering from her shock, managed a smile. 'How kind of you to say so,' she replied. 'I don't mind admitting I'm a little nervous.' That was an understatement. Her nerves were as taut as violin strings.

'You will be magnificent,' replied Helene.

From the doorway, a voice was heard to call: 'Five minutes.'

Simultaneously, both girls looked at each other.

It was almost time.

From the moment she stepped out on stage, Lilli's Giselle was mesmerising. Watching her dance, the audience seemed to hold its breath in a sort of sacred silence. She captivated their emotions, causing them to soar and fall with her as the tragic love story unfolded.

Marco was immediately entranced. He had never seen such grace and emotion in a dancer. The way the ballerina portrayed Giselle's vulnerable innocence made him immediately want to protect her from all the evils that lay in wait. He already knew the story, but still he was angry when Giselle's guileless heart was stolen by the charming young Duke Albrecht. When the nobleman betrayed her, Marco, like most of the rest of the audience, it seemed, also felt slighted on her behalf.

When it was time for revenge, the sinister Willis wreaked havoc. The corps de ballet was suitably terrorising, and Marco dutifully trained his eyes on his commander's daughter, Helene. But it was Giselle that had cast her spell over him. So much so that even when she wasn't on stage, he was thinking about her, wanting her to return to see her dazzle and enchant once more.

Giselle's duet with the repentant Albrecht was so sublimely realistic that Marco even felt a pang of jealousy as the young duke held her in his arms. He wished it could be him instead. But it was the death scene that brought tears to his eyes and when he looked around, he could see that he wasn't the only one to be profoundly moved by the performance of the prima ballerina.

As the final curtain fell, the applause was deafening. People leapt to their feet, their hands clapping high in the air.

'*Bravo! Bellisima!*' The calls of adulation rang around the theatre. Orchids and single roses landed at Giselle's feet. Marco wished he had brought a rose to throw, too. His eyes flitted to the programme, scanning the pages for the name of the lead dancer . . . *Lilli Sternberg.*

'Lilli Sternberg,' he said to himself as he stood to applaud her along with everyone else in the theatre. Lilli Sternberg had captured his heart, dazzled him and mesmerised him with her grace and her beauty. From that moment on, he belonged to her.

Marco looked on, while Lilli curtsied, trying to compose herself, her eyes ablaze with the adulation she was receiving. Moving with grace as though she was still part of the dance, she gestured to the other dancers and to the orchestra, who also received great applause.

A moment later a huge roar erupted from the crowd as a small, elegant woman, whom Marco realised must be the principal of the dance academy, took to the stage. Helene handed her an enormous bouquet which she cradled in her arms as the audience fell silent once more. Holding her back straight and with her eyes twinkling above the footlights, Madame Eva thanked the performers for their hard work and the audience for their support.

'But most of all,' she continued, 'I must thank our patron, without whom none of this would have been possible.' She paused, shielding her eyes to search the grand boxes of the tiers high above her. 'I am talking, of course, of General Count von Urbach,' she declared, gesturing to the tall, broad man with a hooked nose and hooded eyelids, who stood to acknowledge the audience below.

Marco turned to watch his commanding officer wave majestically, drinking in the thanks and admiration. Seeing him perched high up in his box, brought to mind a large bird of prey, surveying its helpless quarry. Marco joined in the applause. It was only polite. But for him, there really was only one star of the show and that evening, he made up his mind to meet her.

Chapter 7

It was like being carried on the wings of angels. As the applause rang in her ears and the love and appreciation of the audience permeated the auditorium and soared high into the air, Lilli felt herself suspended. It was as if her body was lifted from the stage, hovering ecstatically in mid-air.

The moment the curtain rose she'd transformed herself. Gone was any self-doubt that had troubled her before. She'd shut the door on all her negative thoughts. For those three hours she was Giselle. She lived her, breathed her, died her. She danced on air with a grace and fluidity that cast a spell on the audience. Her solos were sublime and her death scene left many in tears. Even Jens danced his best, while the chorus, dressed in their lavish, layered costumes, barely put a collective foot wrong.

This was what Lilli had worked so hard for; this was why her muscles ached and her feet bled. This was what her happiness, now and in the future, depended upon. And then she remembered what might, or might not happen in a few moments' time, and she came down to earth. Bending low to pick up more stems that had landed at her feet, Lilli dared to look out onto the audience again. But beyond the glaring foot lights, and the sparkle of jewels as they glinted, she could see very little. So she prayed that somewhere among the blur of faces, and the mayhem and the noise, there would be the talent scout Madame Eva spoke about.

'You were wonderful!' Helene called out. She was waiting for Lilli in the wings when she finally came off stage.

The lights had momentarily blinded her and she squinted into the gloom as someone handed her a towel. She wiped the sweat from her brow then slung it around her neck as she headed back to the dressing room.

Madame Eva was there to praise her performance again. Marsha, a Silesian girl in the troupe, followed behind her in the low-lit passage. She was laden with an armful of flowers.

Lilli ran the gamut of congratulations from the dancers in the corps once more as she passed through a tangled landscape of net skirts and discarded stockings. The excited squeals and inter-mittent wails had subsided to a low hum, like worker bees going about their usual business. It was then she heard a familiar voice.

'Here she is: our wonderful ballerina!' It was Golda. She and Jacob and Leon crowded round.

'We are so proud of you,' her father told her, kissing the top of her head.

Golda took both her hands in hers. 'You have made us so happy,' she said, tears streaming down her plump cheeks.

Even Leon came forward and hugged her. 'You were very good,' he managed. He handed her a bouquet of flowers that Lilli knew the family could ill afford.

'Yes, you were,' echoed an unfamiliar voice.

Lilli turned to see Madame Eva with an uncharacteristically wide smile on her face. She was accompanied by a gentleman.

'Lilli, this is Monsieur Raymond. He's from the American talent agency I mentioned.'

Monsieur Raymond was not at all how Lilli had pictured a talent scout from an American agency to look. For a start he wasn't American, but French. And all agents smoked cigars, didn't they? With his perfectly-fitting tailcoat, he looked more like a foreign ambassador than one of those sharks she'd seen in films, who always cheated their – mainly female – clients. She also knew that to get anywhere in a stage career, you needed one.

Lilli's pulse had barely slowed, before it shot up again. 'Pleased to meet you, sir,' she said, dipping a curtsey.

For some reason Monsieur Raymond seemed amused. He chuckled. 'Charming,' he said with a smile.

Lilli wasn't sure if she liked being described that way. He made her feel like a puppy or a kitten.

'You danced well, mademoiselle,' he went on. 'Very well,' he added. Lilli tried to steady her breath as she waited to hear more. *There had to be more, surely?* But it was to Madame Eva that Monsieur Raymond turned next. 'I will call you,' he told her, adding coldly, 'if I think there might be a place for her.'

He emphasised the word *if* and Lilli suddenly realised it was the biggest word in the world. In her mind, she'd already been on a ship bound for America, sailing off to stardom. The heart that she'd held so tight in her chest only moments before, the one that had pounded with excitement and leapt for joy, suddenly fell to the floor, and with it went her hopes and dreams. All Lilli Sternberg wanted to do now was cry.

Chapter 8

After the performance Marco stood in the foyer of the theatre, watching the audience file past him as he listened to snatches of their conversation. Even though he'd never met Lilli Sternberg, he felt a certain affinity with her and took a vicarious pleasure in hearing people praise her.

'Giselle was superb!' said one woman, a tiara in her white hair.

'Light as a feather!' remarked her companion.

'She'll go far,' said another.

'Who was she? Von Urbach's daughter?' asked a crusty old military man.

'Good lord, no. Some Jewish girl, I believe,' replied his friend.

Marco frowned. Giselle was not 'some Jewish girl.' Her name was Lilli Sternberg. She should not be dismissed so disdainfully; as if she didn't matter, as if her hard work and her talent could be written off in a single, callous phrase. He fought the urge to step in and defend the woman whose grace and beauty had won his admiration. He said nothing, but continued, instead, to look out for his commanding officer. He thought it only polite he should congratulate him on the evening's undoubted success.

General von Urbach appeared a little later, towering above the well-wishers who surrounded him, lapping up praise for the 'marvellous' performance, even though he had put no effort into it himself.

Almost half an hour had passed since the curtain fell when, finally, some of the dancers started to emerge from backstage to be reunited with their proud families. Many of them still wore their stage make-up and the girls kept their hair knotted in neat buns. Helene was one of them. Marco watched as she approached her father. Von Urbach kissed her on both cheeks and lifted his mouth into a mirthless smile; his eyes remained cold.

As there appeared to be no sign of Lilli, Marco decided now was a good time to make the general aware of his presence.

'May I offer my congratulations on an excellent evening, sir?' Marco said with a bow. He turned to Helene immediately and bowed. 'Comtesse Helene.'

'Ah Captain Zeiller,' greeted von Urbach. 'I'm glad you could come. You have met my daughter?'

Helene flashed a coy smile and held out a hand to be kissed.

'I don't believe I've had that pleasure, sir,' Marco replied courteously, taking her hand.

Instead of smoothing the introduction, however, the general seemed rather preoccupied. His hooded eyes were fixed on the other side of the foyer. Marco followed his gaze. This time, Madame Eva appeared to be in his sights. A few metres away from her, Lilli Sternberg suddenly appeared.

'Excuse me, my dear. I shall leave you in Captain Zeiller's capable hands,' he told his daughter. And with that, Marco watched his commanding officer fly off in the dance principal's direction. He only wished he could take off with him and land nearer to Lilli.

'You like ballet, Captain Zeiller?' Helene asked, emerging tentatively from her shell. Marco turned around to see her piercing blue eyes were trained on him.

He nodded. 'I do and I very much enjoyed tonight,' he told her. But sensing more was expected of him he added: 'Congratulations on your splendid performance.' He knew he must sound stilted and his words rather hollow. They didn't come from his heart.

'You are very kind,' she said, her eyelashes fluttering. 'Thank you.'

Glancing behind her, Marco could still see Lilli. She'd moved slightly further away from Madame Eva and was being congratulated by a succession of admirers. He dearly wanted to join the queue, but Helene was clearly keen to engage him in conversation. It would be rude not to humour her.

'Giselle was very good, wasn't she?' he remarked, forcing himself to focus his straying eyes on her.

'Yes. Yes, she was,' she agreed.

Realising he sounded a little too keen to praise another dancer, he added quickly: 'But, as I said, so were you, Comtesse.'

Helene lifted her shoulder coquettishly. 'It was a shame I could only accept a part in the chorus,' she began. 'I've been so busy, organising things,' she told him, suddenly sounding bolder, 'I simply couldn't take on a more demanding role.'

'Really?' replied Marco, trying to sound interested. 'What have you been organising, may I ask?'

Absent-mindedly, he'd walked into her trap. 'My eighteenth birthday ball next week,' she volunteered, then seemingly hurt, she pouted. 'I thought it would be the talk of your officers' mess.' An image of a child bragging in the playground suddenly sprang to Marco's mind. He was unsure how he should reply. It was clear the general's daughter was trying to impress him in her own, juvenile way. A slightly uncomfortable silence hung between them for a moment as he wondered how he might extricate himself from this young noblewoman's clutches. Undeterred, however, she resumed her ramblings about her party, either unaware or unmoved that Marco's attention was now occupied by General von Urbach, who was just about to pounce on his prey. While the young officer's eyes returned to Helene, his ears did not.

'Ah, my dear Eva,' said the general. 'An excellent evening.'

Madame Eva inclined her head as she allowed her patron to peck her hand with his lips. 'I am glad you enjoyed it, General.'

She knew from the tone of his voice to wait for a barb.

'And I must congratulate you on your bold choice of the lead role.'

'Bold?' she queried. 'How so?'

The general shrugged before showing his talons. Planting a smile on his face so that passers-by did not suspect his intention, he went in for the kill. 'We'd have got bigger donations, if you'd chosen Baron von Klaus's daughter or La Comtesse de Veille's,' he told her bluntly. 'I thought it would've been evident.'

Marco found himself bristling indignantly. What was the general suggesting? He was aware that buying your way into enviable government positions was the way of the German republic these days, but had bribery reached the ballet, too? Madame Eva, he could tell, was caught off guard by his comment. She switched back her head. 'Or your own, General?' she retorted, waving at a former student who was passing. 'It's obvious Fraulein Sternberg is exceptionally talented. She is simply my best.'

Von Urbach curled his lips in a smirk. 'I agree she is good, but she is also a Jew,' he hissed between clenched teeth. Marco noted the way the general's hooded eyes kept sliding towards Lilli. 'And the Jews are running this city, this country,' he told her, his expression suddenly switching to a smile to acknowledge an old acquaintance.

Madame Eva's lips also twitched. It was clear to Marco she knew how to handle him. 'And a good job, too. Who would tailor your suits, dear General?' she teased, lightly brushing the lapel of his tailcoat. With her riposte deftly delivered, she glided on.

Yet again Marco had heard vicious slights levelled at Fraulein Sternberg simply because she was Jewish. He cast her a longing glance as the more broad-minded members of the audience continued to offer their congratulations. She remained smiling graciously and offering her hand to the many gentlemen who wished to kiss it.

'And so you see, Captain Zeiller, it will be a wonderful evening,' Helene said. For the past few moments, she had been droning on about her imminent birthday ball, although the details had been lost on Marco.

'Fascinating,' he said, suddenly aware that he had no idea what the young woman had been telling him.

'Yes, isn't it?' Helene was delighted by his reaction.

'Indeed,' he replied absent-mindedly, his attention having been otherwise engaged by Madame Eva and now by Lilli Sternberg. There was something about her. The way she moved; the way she held her head. Her smile, too. It wasn't wide, more reserved, as if she was holding something back. Suddenly he wanted to be the person to make her smile, broadly, wholeheartedly, to make her let go of whatever troubled her. Even make her laugh.

'Well, then you must come,' cried Helene.

Marco's eyebrows lifted. 'Come? Where?' he replied abruptly, forcing himself to engage with the general's daughter once more.

'To my ball, of course!' She was virtually squealing with delight. 'I shall see that an invitation is sent to your quarters immediately.'

Marco felt a twinge of panic, realising too late he'd fallen, yet again, into this young woman's trap.

'How very kind of you,' he replied, trying to muster what little enthusiasm he could. The prospect of an evening in the comtesse's company filled him with alarm. He imagined himself sinking into deep mud, ensnared by her childish wiles. He had to break free. Lifting his head, he directed his gaze beyond her. This time, however, he found the object of his desire was gone. He scanned the thicket of bodies. The crowd had thinned, but of Lilli Sternberg, there was no sign.

'We shall meet again very soon, Captain,' said Helene, reminding Marco of her presence, fluttering her eyelashes wildly at him.

'We shall, indeed,' he replied with a shallow bow. Reluctantly, he kissed her outstretched hand and then retreated from her clutches as quickly as was seemly. He wanted to continue his search for Fraulein Sternberg.

Marco's eyes swept around the foyer, just to satisfy himself Lilli wasn't there. Defeat was rarely an option for him, so he began wondering how he might engineer a meeting even as he was collecting his greatcoat and cap from the cloakroom.

The night was cold. Cold enough to snow. Several limousines were waiting outside the theatre, all with their engines running and Marco scanned the cars for his own. Liveried chauffeurs were helping their passengers embark, and as he made his way a little further down the street, he spotted his driver standing by his car, smoking a cigarette.

'Linz,' he called.

The cigarette was hurriedly stubbed out as Linz opened wide the car door with one hand, while saluting with the other. Safely inside, the captain settled onto the back seat for the homeward journey.

The ballet had been wonderful, and the evening only slightly marred at the end by the general's persistent daughter, but what made it most memorable, of course, was Lilli Sternberg. It irked him that he hadn't managed to congratulate Giselle in person – that he'd let her get away without telling her how amazing he thought she was. As he journeyed back to barracks, he relived the evening's magic in his mind and filled his head with thoughts of the beautiful dancer on stage.

In fact, he was so busy thinking about her that when he noticed, among a straggle of workers wearily tramping home on foot that night, a young woman in a thin coat, carrying a cloth bag, he'd looked twice. With her lean body braced against the bitter wind, she was trudging along the side of the highway with an elderly couple arm in arm and a gangling youth in tow. They were headed towards the poorer area of the city. There was something about her that made him wonder if she could be . . . but no. He was deluding himself. The beautiful dancer, who had so enraptured

41

her Munich audience, the girl who had just stolen his own heart, would never be allowed to walk home on a night such as this. She could not be his Giselle. His driver drove on.

Chapter 9

Lilli was forced to put on a brave face. She had to act as if she wasn't frustrated and disappointed at being ignored by the talent scout. After all, acting was what she did. The only concession Madame Eva made to last night's performance was that lessons began an hour later, so back at her desk in a dingy academy classroom, the following day, once again, Lilli wore her mask.

'Oh, Lilli, you were superb!' exclaimed Leisl, a petite girl with a kind face.

'Yes,' agreed her friend, Ursula, clapping her hands. 'Bravo!'

Even the pianist with the orange hair, Mademoiselle Schwartz, congratulated Lilli on her way into class.

Their praise meant a lot, it really did, but not as much as a message from Monsieur Raymond. Had he thought her performance so outstanding that he could offer her a contract? Had she performed well enough to be a contender for his agency? If he had, surely he would have engaged her on the spot, for fear she might be snapped up by one of his rivals. Or was she just confusing real life with the plots from the Hollywood movies that continually filled her head?

When Madame Eva finally arrived in the classroom to give a full assessment of the production, she didn't look at her star pupil at first. Lilli took it as a bad sign and her stomach clenched with nerves.

The principal's post-performance reports were always like military debriefs; she made copious notes on every scene, commenting on every sloppy jeté or shoddy pirouette. True to form, most of the points she made about her pupils were negative. Claudette *missed her cue*, Jens's Duke of Albrecht was *too heavy* and Ursula – well, words failed her. Yet her many and varied criticisms were occasionally tempered with positive ones. Leisl was *light on her feet* and Helene, well Helene *did herself proud*. Most of her praise was, however, saved for Lilli.

'Fraulein Sternberg was an example to you all,' she told the class. 'Her hard work and dedication paid off.'

All eyes turned to Lilli, as she felt the colour rise in her cheeks. She thrived on praise, like a flower in sunshine, yet she needed more. Madame's generous words were all very well, but Lilli wanted to be certain that it was leading somewhere. Had Monsieur Raymond been in touch? Was this what Madame Eva meant when she said her dedication had paid off? Lilli stared blankly ahead of her, her back remaining rigid, her eyes to the front, like a combatant awaiting to be awarded the highest military honour and trying not to burst with excitement. She sat still as her teacher continued to heap on praise, but at the end of her speech came . . . nothing. There was no mention of Monsieur Raymond or his agency in America.

'Madame.' Lilli waited until the end of the class when all the other pupils had left before asking her teacher outright. 'Madame, did Monsieur Raymond . . .?' She broke off, knowing she need say no more.

Madame Eva smiled – something she didn't do very often – then she shook her head. 'He told me he enjoyed the performance, but that was all.' Her voice was measured and Lilli could take no hope from it. It was impossible for her to hide her disappointment.

44

'There will be plenty more opportunities,' added Madame, seeing the despondent look on her pupil's face. Lilli wasn't so sure.

Weighed down by disappointment, she traipsed to the cloakroom at the end of the day to collect her coat and hat. Laughter was coming from around the corner. She recognised it as the sound of what she called 'the gaggle' – a group of giggling rich girls who stuck together like geese. They were students whose fathers didn't have to scrimp and save to pay the ballet school's tuition fees. Lilli sometimes envied them with their designer shoes and bags and the way their chauffeurs always drove them to the academy for lessons. She couldn't even afford the tram.

Helene wasn't usually included in the group, but her forthcoming ball seemed to have made her the centre of attention all of a sudden. She stopped dead when she saw Lilli and smiled.

'Ah, Lilli, everyone is talking about what they will be wearing for my ball.' She looked around her, as if making a show of her newfound sisters who surrounded her. 'Have you chosen your gown yet?'

Lilli smiled back, but only with her eyes. After the Cuvilliés, the day had been such an anti-climax. Her dreams of a Hollywood contract had come to nothing. It had been ridiculous to harbour such a fantasy, she knew that now, but still she felt deflated and so wrapped up in herself, that she'd completely forgotten about the party.

'Yes, I have,' she replied enigmatically, not wishing to elaborate because she knew she could never compete with the other girls' sequins and lace. Their ballgowns were probably made in Paris and their beautiful shoes in Milan. Some might even own tiaras. Her *choice* was limited to one, but at least she did have a gown, one made by her father. Jacob had stitched it from two different fabrics in complimentary shades of blue. No one would ever guess they were remnants from commissions he'd undertaken last year. He'd saved the leftover material to create something special for his daughter, '*should the day ever come*', he'd told her with a gleam in his eye. So now that day had come and, as luck would have it, the gown was saved from the ravages of the workshop fire.

Helene tilted her head and nodded. 'I can't wait to see it,' she said. 'I'm sure it will be . . .' She searched for the right word. 'Interesting.' And with that she and her little coterie walked away, talking excitedly as they went.

Lilli sighed as she reached for her coat. Perhaps she was being churlish, she told herself. Helene had been kind enough to ask her to her party and she had accepted the invitation. She'd suffered a massive disappointment, but she would just have to pick herself up and train even harder. She would *dance through the pain*, as Madame Eva would say, again and again, until someone with Hollywood contacts took notice of her. And in the meantime, there was this glittering ball. She thought of the music and the lights, the glitz and the glamour, and suddenly felt fortunate to be going. It would be a welcome diversion for her; take her out of herself, allow her to escape into a different, fabulous world, if only for one night. Helene's *schloss* would be like the set of one of those Hollywood films that thrilled her so much. The thought suddenly cheered her and for the first time that day, there was a spring in her step.

Chapter 10

The arrival of a black Mercedes at the down-at-heel block in Giesing set the neighbourhood into a frenzy. Shutters creaked. Faces appeared at windows. The matchmaker, Frau Weber, the aged widow from the top floor, and Frau Kepler both emerged from their respective apartments like figures from a Bavarian clock. The Ram soon joined them, followed by Frau Reuter, a listless child on her hip. They stood on the landing, waiting for Lilli to leave for the ball.

Inside the Sternbergs' apartment, Jacob's chest swelled with pride to see his only daughter looking so beautiful in the creation he'd lovingly made for her. It may not have been an extravagant gown with huge skirts made from reams of damask and organza, but his design was more modern and understated. The fabric was moulded to Lilli's elegant figure and fell in soft drapes to the floor. The midnight-blue bodice set off her colouring and the sequinned headband he had stitched made her eyes twinkle.

Lilli had piled her dark hair up on top and Golda had presented her with a pearl pin to hold it in place. It, along with a pair of pearl droplet earrings, had once belonged to her grandmother.

'Thank you so much, Vati,' said Lilli, standing in front of a full-length mirror in her parents' bedroom, smoothing the dress.

Jacob chuckled as he tugged at a strap and stood back to admire her once more. 'You shall go to the ball, my Cinderella!' he announced.

Golda, standing close by, clapped her hands in glee then lunged forward and cupped them round Lilli's face.

'My grown-up daughter,' she cried, as if it was only yesterday that she was feeding her with a spoon.

Leon stood back from the excitement, but even he had a half-smile on his face. He was happy for his sister. 'Beautiful,' was all he said, but his sister knew the compliment was meant. She gave him a peck on the cheek.

At just before eight o'clock Lilli emerged onto the landing to a waiting huddle of women, all eager to see their very own princess.

'Oh! She looks heavenly!' gasped the Ram.

'So elegant,' agreed Frau Kepler, standing next to her.

'She will make some Jewish man a good wife,' agreed Frau Weber, shouting down from the top floor where she was propping herself up on the stair railings.

Lilli looked up to acknowledge their presence and gave them a wave, before hugging her mother.

'And remember, Cinderella, home before midnight,' teased Jacob, escorting his daughter down the stairs.

A beaming Herr Grunfeld opened the main entrance door for Lilli and bowed as he gestured her outside. Glancing up into the darkness, she could see the silhouettes of a few people pressed against their windows, hoping to catch a glimpse of 'Herr Sternberg's daughter, the ballerina'. For a moment, that same elation she had experienced just after *Giselle* charged through her chest. Once again, she was the centre of attention. Once again, she was about to perform.

The limousine pulled away from the apartment block just as the first flakes of winter snow began to fall. Lilli was driven out of the city and into the wooded outskirts where Schloss Urbach rose from among the dark pines at the end of a long driveway.

The snow fell thickly as the car sped through high gates, framed by two side wings, and over a bridge to the main castle beyond. Lilli knew it had been in Helene's family for generations and was even more imposing than she'd imagined. With its turrets and gargoyles, it would not be out of place amid the pages of a Grimm story book.

The chauffeur helped Lilli from the limousine. A red carpet had been rolled out on the steps and she joined a long line of guests, mainly couples, who were filing through a magnificent studded door into a vast hallway beyond.

Gothic grandeur was all around her. It was the stuff of little girls' dreams – and nightmares. Once more, a thousand butterflies were dancing in her stomach. This was how she'd felt before she went on stage before *Giselle*. Why did she always feel she was on show? This would be another performance and she felt she must dazzle. She knew she didn't belong in Helene's world of castles and candelabra. Her father had been joking when he'd called her Cinderella, but tonight that was who she really was: a poor girl in sophisticated, aristocratic company.

The oak-panelled walls of the cavernous space were decked with silver suits of armour, shields and swords, as well as huge portraits, but pride of place went to an enormous Christmas tree. Lilli guessed it was the height of three men and its branches sparkled with tiny candles and silver and gold ribbons.

Beyond the hall she caught a glimpse of the ballroom and heard snatches of an orchestra playing a waltz. The women reminded her of the ones she had seen in the audience at the Cuvilliés. Many of them were prim and haughty, with feathers in their hair and jewels round their wrinkling necks. They seemed to be accompanying younger women – Lilli presumed their daughters, – acting as chaperones. Lilli soon realised why when she cast her eyes about the reception and saw that there were plenty of young male guests entering the party. She assumed that they were all officers from Count von Urbach's division, whose barracks were nearby. Wearing the grey dress uniform of the Reichswehr, they could not fail to look at the very least, smart, and, at their very best, dashing.

As Lilli progressed towards the ballroom, marvelling at her glittering surroundings, a servant at her side cleared his throat. She was standing at the top of a short flight of shallow steps. Before her lay the ballroom; men were whirling ladies round the dance floor, while clusters of guests huddled together talking and smiling politely.

'Your calling card, Fraulein,' he asked, holding out a silver salver.

Lilli shot him a puzzled look. His request suddenly reminded her, once again, that she was out of place – that she neither belonged among these people, nor amid this splendour. She was the daughter of a tailor. Of course she didn't have a calling card. Even the gown she was wearing was homemade, yet still she refused to be intimidated. Reminding herself that she, too, could put on airs and graces when necessary, she decided to prove that a Jewish girl from Giesing could be every inch a lady, too. Straightening her back and lifting her chin, she simply told the servant her name. He raised a brow but a second later she heard 'Fraulein Lilli Sternberg' repeated in a baritone voice.

This was it. She had been announced. There was no going back now. Lifting her skirt slightly Lilli began her descent to she knew not where; she was launching herself off a cliff in the hope that someone might catch her. Fortunately, Helene was there at the bottom of the shallow steps leading down to the ballroom when she landed. The general's daughter had obviously been looking out for Lilli and from somewhere amid the silk and taffeta confections on the dance floor she suddenly appeared. Wearing a pale pink beaded dress, with a diamond and pearl tiara on her flaxen head, Lilli was shocked by her transformation.

'Helene, you look lovely!' It was as if someone had waved a wand at the awkward and uncoordinated pupil of the academy and magicked her into an elegant young woman, the perfect match for a dashing young officer who would, no doubt, be promoted in double-quick time. Lilli almost envied her. Not because of her looks, but because of the way her future was mapped out clearly before her. Her journey would be comfortable and, above all, predictable. She would want for nothing in life, except, perhaps her freedom.

'So do you,' replied Helene, smiling serenely. 'And your dress is very . . .' She searched for a word to describe the unconventional gown. She settled on 'different.' And in a well-placed stroke, she succeeded in making Lilli feel inadequate. All the other women were dripping in jewels, while their gowns were incredible creations, elaborate and shimmering with huge skirts that touched the sides of doors when they walked into rooms. Her father had done his best for her, but her dress was very plain by comparison. Nevertheless, she shot back.

'I prefer to call it fashionable,' said Lilli, her head held high.

Helene twitched a smile and, offering Lilli her arm, she said: 'Come, let me introduce you to some of my friends.'

The ballroom was bigger than the entire studio at the academy. Three glass chandeliers twinkled like clusters of stars from the ceiling and portraits of austere warriors adorned the walls. The same straight-backed Bavarian officers were to be found on the dance floor, too, as if they had just stepped out of the elaborate gilt frames for the evening. Some wore monocles, others regimental swords. Some both. The older men were weighed down by medals; the younger ones – it seemed to Lilli – were buoyed up by their own self-belief, or was it arrogance?

General von Urbach was Commander-in-Chief of the Reichwehr's Seventh Division. His father and his father before him had also been in the army in the days before the Great War. It therefore followed that his only child – his daughter – was duty-bound to marry one of his own officers to continue the long and noble tradition. Naturally only the most promising and highest-born young men were invited to the comtesse's birthday ball. And, true to her word, Helene introduced Lilli to someone – her cousin, Captain Kurt von Stockmar.

51

He was a short, broad man, who wore his fair hair shaved just above his ears to accentuate his angular jaw and made a long, fresh scar on his face even more noticeable. He clicked his heels noisily before kissing Lilli's hand.

'Kurt, you must meet my friend,' she said. 'Lilli danced the role of *Giselle* the other night.'

Von Stockmar raised a brow. 'Ah, yes, Fraulein . . .'

'Sternberg,' Helene told him.

'Sternberg,' he repeated, narrowing his eyes. He was still smiling, an odd, slanted smile, but Lilli suspected, especially when he repeated her name once more as though it stuck in his gullet, that he balked at her Jewishness. Her heritage made her enemies wherever she went these days.

'She is a wonderful dancer,' continued Helene, as if Lilli were not by her side.

'Quite so,' von Stockmar conceded with a nod. A fellow officer had persuaded him to watch the production. 'A fine performance,' he added grudgingly.

Despite the champagne – it was Lilli's first taste of it and the bubbles made her nose tingle – the conversation remained as stiff as the captain's army dress collar. At least *Giselle* formed common ground between them, she thought.

'Fraulein Sternberg is a star of the future,' Helene continued.

Lilli could feel her cheeks flush with embarrassment and lowered her gaze to the floor.

Von Stockmar nodded, although it was clear he lacked conviction. 'I am sure.'

An awkward pause allowed Lilli's eyes to meander over the sea of uniforms and gowns. It was then that she saw General von Urbach himself approaching. He was not alone. A handsome young officer was at his side.

'My dear,' he addressed his daughter playfully. 'I believe I have found one of your adoring fans – Captain Marco Zeiller.'

The soldier stood, a little sheepishly, it seemed to Lilli, at his commanding officer's side. She'd seen him swooped upon by the general almost as soon as he'd set foot in the ballroom. Now she realised why. Helene seemed extremely eager to see the young man. From her manner it appeared they were old acquaintances.

'Captain Zeiller,' Helene's whole face lit up. She held out a gloved hand. The young officer dispensed with the ubiquitous heel clicking. Instead he simply bowed, took Helene's hand and kissed it.

Lilli looked on. There was something different about this officer, she thought. For a start he stood at least half a head taller than most of the men in the room and his dark hair, although slicked back with oil, betrayed a natural wave. His skin had a sort of golden glow to it, while all the other men's seemed more like strudel pastry. His large eyes were brown, not blue or green like most Germans. But it was his smile that Lilli found so captivating and, judging by the blush on Helene's normally pale face, she felt the same way.

'At your service, Comtesse,' he declared.

Helene, still flustered by the officer's attentions, turned to Lilli. 'Captain Zeiller is an admirer of the ballet,' she explained.

It was then that the officer's gaze locked on to Lilli. His brown eyes suddenly flared, and Lilli couldn't help but wonder if the glint in them was because he recognised her from the ballet. His intense look sent a shock through her body.

'Fraulein Sternberg,' he murmured, cutting through the heat of the moment. Even the way he said her name sounded intimate.

Von Stockmar flexed his nostrils. 'You two know each other?'

'I don't think . . .' Lilli began. She would surely have remembered if she had been introduced to the Captain before.

'Giselle,' Marco said simultaneously.

'You were at the Cuvilliés?' she asked.

'Your dancing was exquisite, Fraulein Sternberg.'

'How . . .?' Lilli frowned. She suddenly felt quite light-headed.

'Your name was in the programme.'

'A detective as well as a soldier, eh?' remarked von Stockmar snidely.

Captain Zeiller shrugged at the other officer's remark and turned his attention back to Lilli, 'But you must have been exhausted after such a demanding performance,' he said earnestly.

'Madame Eva, our teacher, tells us we must dance through the pain,' Lilli replied, looking at Helene.

'She always wants her pound of flesh,' she agreed.

Just at that moment, a portly, older officer with bushy whiskers appeared at Helene's side.

'May I have this dance, dear Comtesse?' he asked.

Lilli saw Helene's face fall for a second before she recovered and drew her lips into a smile. 'General von Schwaab.' A refusal to dance with her godfather would be taken badly, yet an expression of despair gathered on her face as her eyes flitted first to the captain then back to the elderly man. Lilli understood. It was as if Helene was sensing that in her absence, she might lose her debonair escort. Captain Zeiller was her prize and she wanted to hold onto him or face ruining her own party. She hesitated, her gaze flitting from one man to the other.

'Come, my dear,' von Urbach suddenly intervened, hovering above the huddle. 'You wouldn't want to disappoint your godfather, surely?'

Helene forced her lips into an unnatural smile. 'Of course not, Father,' she replied.

'Comtesse,' the captain replied with a gracious bow. 'I must surrender you, I fear.'

From Helene's barely-disguised expression, it was obvious her parting from the young officer was agony. The look she flashed Lilli was a warning shot. It told her to stay away from him until her return, but it was in vain. The fight for Captain Zeiller's attention was over before it had ever begun.

Lilli watched Helene take the old general's arm and throw another anguished look back at her gallant soldier. When Lilli turned again, she saw Captain Zeiller's focus was already on her. She threw him a nervous smile, which he returned. He was looking at her very differently from how he had regarded Helene. His presence seemed to fill a vacuum that their hostess had created. Lilli turned her head, not knowing how to react, but there was something exciting about him that drew her to him. It was as if he understood just how she was feeling. Yet, instead of being unsettling, his gaze seemed to stir something inside her. She looked back and in that moment a connection was made. Given oxygen to breathe, the smouldering spark would most surely flare into life.

Chapter 11

Now there were the three of them – Lilli, Marco and von Stockmar – on the edge of the ballroom floor. All around, guests were making idle chatter, sipping champagne, enjoying each other's company. Before Captain Zeiller's arrival, it had seemed as if Lilli had landed on some distant shore and been told to leave immediately by its inhabitants. Now, however, in his presence, she felt different. Yet still she felt something wasn't right. A charged silence had suddenly settled between the two men, as if they were both poised to say something.

Von Stockmar broke first, firing a comment at his fellow officer that came with the anger of an accusation.

'You never mentioned you knew my cousin.'

Marco, unruffled, replied: 'I didn't. We were introduced at *Giselle.*'

'Then you obviously made quite an impression on her.' He was watching Helene dance stiffly with her godfather, throwing anxious glances back their way at every turn.

Marco smiled and shrugged. 'I feel very fortunate to be invited to the comtesse's ball.' As he spoke, he caught Lilli's eye, making plain the reason he thought his fortune had changed – for the better.

Von Stockmar also caught his fellow officer's expression.

'I'm clearly making this a crowd,' he announced, shooting a baleful look at Marco.

Lilli felt the colour bloom in her neck. She found the remark awkward, but Marco reacted decisively.

'We can't have you feeling out of place,' he said to von Stockmar, slapping his fellow officer lightly on the back. 'We shall leave you in peace,' he continued and, turning to Lilli, he offered her his arm. 'Would you do me the honour, Miss Sternberg?'

Von Stockmar's eyes now narrowed as Lilli tilted her head and silently took Marco's arm, her stomach fluttering at his touch.

'Excuse us,' said the captain confidently, but just as he passed, von Stockmar grabbed his other arm and leaned towards his ear.

'You do know she's Jewish,' he whispered from the side of his mouth.

Marco leaned back and forced a smile. 'Thank you, my friend. I hope you enjoy the rest of your evening, too,' he replied, a guileless expression on his face.

'Is everything all right?' asked Lilli, aware that words had passed between the two men.

'Everything is just wonderful,' Marco reassured her as he escorted her onto the ballroom floor, leaving von Stockmar quietly seething on the side lines.

Strauss played and they danced three waltzes in succession. There was little chance to talk above the music so they simply smiled at each other as they whirled around the ballroom floor. At the end of the third dance another officer asked Lilli to mark her card for him. But she didn't have a card and Marco told him that she was fully engaged for the whole evening. She opened her mouth to protest, but thought better of it. She felt comfortable with him and suddenly found herself reluctant to dance with anyone else.

Marco was light on his feet and whisked her effortlessly around the ballroom floor. To her delight, he was particularly good at the polka and she heard herself laughing at being spun around like a top. Afterwards they stood to one side, recovering their composure as a liveried servant offered them Champagne.

'You dance well, Captain,' Lilli said, taking a tentative sip from her glass, the bubbles still tickling her nose.

'I was partnered by the best,' he replied. 'Ballroom as well as ballet. Is there no end to your dancing talent?' he added playfully, raising his glass to her in a toast. 'To Giselle.'

'Giselle,' she said.

As they stood surveying the rest of the dancers, Lilli caught sight of Helene, still playing the bountiful hostess, conversing with an elderly couple. She almost felt guilty that Marco had chosen her over the general's daughter. Almost.

'So what do you plan to perform next?' he asked her, drawing her back to him.

Lilli gave a little shrug. After *Giselle* she'd been so hopeful of being scooped up by the talent scout and making a new life in America that she hadn't given any thought to her future in Munich.

'I shall remain at the academy as long as I can,' she heard herself saying, even though the notion depressed her. The idea of working even more hours at the cinema to pay the fees was doubly disheartening.

'So, you plan to dance professionally?'

'Yes,' replied Lilli. 'But not ballet.'

'Oh?'

The Champagne was emboldening her. 'I want to dance in musicals. In the movies.'

Marco's eyebrows lifted. 'The movies? Of course, yes. That's what they call films in America, isn't it? They have sound now, too, don't they?

'Yes. Talkies,' she said and they both laughed simultaneously.

'I said you were a star. You could be a talking movie star!' He was beaming broadly.

Lilli laughed again. She had never met someone who had such an effect on her before. Or was it the Champagne? 'That is my dream,' she told him, feeling as if anything were possible in his company.

Suddenly Marco was serious again. 'Dreams can come true,' he told her. 'But you have to be willing to pay the price to make them happen.'

Lilli knew he was right, even though she detected a slight bitterness behind his comment, as if he, too, had once had dreams that remained unfulfilled. Unsaid words suddenly crowded into her chest. The unexpected delight of finding someone who understood her, was even more intoxicating than the Champagne.

Now and again as they stood talking a guest would approach, wanting to engage Marco in conversation. Whenever they were interrupted, he showed himself to be good at small talk.

'A pleasure to see you, Frau Rath.' 'I trust your children are well, Comtesse von Schell.' He made the right polite enquiries about sons and daughters, or postings in the case of his younger friends. He was charming and courteous, introducing Lilli to everyone as a prima ballerina, which although true in part, was certainly not the whole truth.

'I am a ballet student,' she reprimanded him gently when they had a minute to themselves.

He shook his head and smiled. 'You are a star,' he told her, then added: 'In my eyes, anyway.'

She tapped him playfully on the arm. Her first glass of Champagne had gone straight to her head and she suddenly realised that perhaps she was being too forward. She'd heard of men like this captain before: charming and debonair, yet devious. They would declare undying love, take advantage of a girl then discard her like a plaything. And yet, something was telling her that Marco wasn't like that. True, there was bravado in his smile, and his flirting was outrageous, but behind the façade lay something else, something deeper, and it was drawing her further into his orbit.

When more officers came to ask Lilli for a dance, she decided she really should, if only for appearances' sake. She'd noticed conversations going on behind extended fans. Old dowagers were frowning at her and Marco, so she agreed to dance with two others; one a retired major and the other a subaltern with bad breath and clammy hands.

Marco was waiting for her when the subaltern took his leave.

'Shall we find somewhere a little quieter?' he suggested and together they seated themselves on a chaise longue at the far end of the ballroom.

'So what about you, Captain Zeiller?' asked Lilli, sipping more Champagne. 'You know a lot about me. Now it's your turn.'

His broad shoulders lifted in a shrug and he lowered his gaze in thought. 'I have taken an oath to serve the Fatherland and, if necessary, to sacrifice my life for Germany,' he told her, seemingly without conviction. 'My future lies in the army.'

Lilli frowned. 'You sound as though you are not happy being a soldier,' she said, then immediately regretted being so candid. The Champagne had loosened her tongue, making her speak out of turn. 'I'm sorry. I didn't . . .'

He gave her a tight smile. 'It's my duty. I don't have a say in the matter,' he replied curtly. It was clear he wanted to change the subject and Lilli worried she'd broken the mood.

'Why don't we get some air?' he suggested, rising and holding out his hand to her. 'I don't care to be starred at,' he added, catching an old harridan's glare as she hobbled past.

However, she was not the only one to signal her disapproval of the couple's courtship. General von Urbach had also been watching the pair for a while and didn't like what he saw, either. The mutual attraction between one of his most promising officers and a Jewish dancer was not to his liking. It was time, he thought, to begin flexing his Bavarian talons to nip this mutual attraction in the bud.

'Zeiller seems to be enjoying himself tonight,' he commented to von Stockmar as they watched the pair converse animatedly.

'The Jewish girl?' sneered his nephew, cradling a squat glass of schnapps. 'Yes. Quite nauseating,' he mumbled, allowing his jealousy to show in an unguarded moment.

The general's hawkish eyes narrowed. 'I didn't want her here, but Helene insisted. She gets obsessed by certain people. Perhaps now that the little Jewish bitch seems to have stolen Zeiller's affections from her, my daughter may have regrets.'

Von Stockmar gulped his schnapps. 'Perhaps,' he replied tentatively, although he wasn't entirely sure what to read into the general's comments.

Von Urbach's gaze remained trained on Lilli. 'The wretched Jews are everywhere, like vermin. And now there is one in my castle!' He barked out a false laugh.

'Quite, sir.' Von Stockmar nodded.

'And as for Zeiller . . .' said the general, wistfully. 'He's marked for promotion soon. I would've thought better of him.'

Von Stockmar smirked, realising that merely by showing an interest in a Jewish girl, his rival had put his career in jeopardy.

'Would you like me to have a word, sir?' he asked, suddenly feeling the power shifting into his corner. He fingered the scar on his cheek as he watched Lilli and Marco rise and head towards the terrace.

'I think you better had,' mused von Urbach. A deep furrow appeared on his brow as he observed the impromptu love scene play out before him. 'I would hate to have to lose Zeiller.'

A cold blast hit Lilli and Marco as they left the stuffy, smoke-filled ballroom and ventured outside. The terrace was already covered in a thin veil of snow as they walked out into the night. Lilli, feeling flushed and light-headed, welcomed the fresh air, although she shivered as the cold pricked her naked arms.

'Here. Have this,' said Marco, shedding his tunic. Underneath only a thin, white shirt hugged his broad frame. He draped the jacket around her shoulders. It was warm against her skin and smelled of sandalwood cologne.

They were alone. No one else, it seemed, wanted to brave the snowfall. By now it had dusted the pines in white. Above the silhouettes of the trees a silver moon hung in a deep blue velvet sky embedded with stars.

Marco gestured towards the balustrade and together they walked over to enjoy the view. Away from the music of the orchestra, there was something reassuring to be found in the silence of the mountains – something timeless and unchanging.

It was a relief to leave the stuffy ballroom and finally escape the disapproving glances, the mutterings behind fans and the whispered slurs that had been so obvious to Lilli. She wondered if Marco had been aware of them too.

Taking a breath of fresh mountain air she released it steadily as she gathered her thoughts. 'People are talking. You know that?' she said after a moment.

He turned to her and, without warning, looped a stray strand of hair, displaced by their high jinks on the dance floor, behind her ear. She blushed and lowered her gaze, but he crooked his finger under her chin and gazed into her eyes.

'I do know, but what does it matter?' he said. He spoke with such seeming sincerity that, for a moment, he almost convinced her it didn't matter at all what anyone said; that she could rise above the haters and the nay-sayers. She questioned his wisdom, but admired his courage. 'Whom I choose to spend my time with is no concern of theirs,' he added.

Marco was *choosing* to spend his time with her, despite her background, despite her Jewishness, and the thought made her feel special. *He* made her feel special. In fact, she couldn't remember a time when she'd felt happier, not even when the audience rose to applaud her after *Giselle*. Perhaps it was something to do with the Champagne, but this was a different kind of happy. It was

Giselle and Hanukkah and her birthday all rolled into one. Soft and gentle, and beautiful, but exhilarating at the same time.

'I want to be with you, too,' she told him softly. She knew she was being reckless, but she really didn't care.

Marco put his arm around her as they watched the snow fall and settle on the branches of the trees that surrounded the *schloss*. She wondered if he could feel how fast her heart was beating against his chest. She wondered if this was a dream and if she'd soon wake up. 'It's magical,' she said in a half whisper, to herself as much to Marco, looking out onto the vista.

'It is,' he replied, suddenly turning his head and lowering it. Her heart leapt as, finding her lips, he kissed her gently.

Chapter 12

Lilli awoke the morning after the ball with a searing headache. Her mouth was dry and she had an unquenchable thirst. Leon, getting dressed as she lay squinting against the light from the electric bulb, was unsympathetic. The details of the previous evening seemed oddly out of reach. To her relief, she remembered it was a Sunday, so there were no classes at the academy.

'You drank too much,' her brother told her, buttoning his shirt.

She grunted at first, but when Leon persisted, she denied it, even though she knew he was probably right.

'I only had one glass of champagne,' she protested. She'd had at least two.

Leon's expression grew weary. 'You came home all giddy, mumbling about ballgowns and dancing and some captain.'

'A captain,' she echoed.

Captain Marco Zeiller. A bolt of lightning suddenly sliced through the fog in her brain as she recalled with amazing clarity the handsome officer with whom she'd danced the night away.

'Yes,' she murmured. 'Yes. Captain Zeiller.' She jerked upright as everything came back to her. And that kiss; the kiss that set off a thousand fireworks in her head.

Slumping back down again onto her pillow, she looked up at

the ceiling, recalling the thrill that shot through her entire being when his lips collided with hers. Had he felt the same way? Or had the champagne clouded her judgement and made her behave rashly? But then she remembered that he must've felt something because he wanted to meet her again. Or had she dreamt that part? Mortified, she suddenly realised she had.

Propping herself up on both elbows, she thought for a moment then leapt out of bed. Reality had suddenly dawned and come crashing down on her. Her hands flew up to her mouth.

'What's wrong?' asked Leon, combing his hair.

She began to prowl the room, hugging herself against the cold. She'd made a fool of herself, hadn't she? What could she have been thinking, behaving like that? The captain had been witty and charming and a consummate gentleman and she . . . she had danced and laughed. And then he'd kissed her on the terrace. Or had she kissed him? She blushed as snatches of recollections raced through her brain.

'Oh, Leon!' she cried. 'I've been such a fool!'

It was hard to concentrate on lessons at the academy on the Monday. She kept remembering fragments from the evening of the ball. Mademoiselle Schultz, the pianist with the frizzy orange hair, asked her if she was quite all right and at break, instead of mixing with the other students, Lilli sat alone in the gloom the changing rooms, feeling quite wretched. She had deliberately avoided Helene, too, recalling the disappointment in her hostess's face when she was dragged away from Marco to dance with her elderly godfather. But as she pined in the darkness and the comtesse approached, she knew the moment of reckoning was upon her.

'There you are,' Helene said, her voice flat as she loomed. 'So, you enjoyed yourself at my ball?'

Lilli raised her head to meet her cold stare and forced a smile.

'Very much, thank you. I meant to say . . .' but her voice trailed off half-heartedly.

'And you will see Captain Zeiller again?' Helene was being brusque now.

Lilli's eyes slid away to the floor as she shrugged. 'I don't suppose so,' she replied, trying to sound blasé, but finding it hard to hide the obvious disenchantment in her voice.

'It's probably better if you don't,' replied Helene. 'People will talk.'

Lilli's head shot up. 'What—?' But the comtesse didn't wait to hear the end of the question. Leaving behind her unprovoked barb, she departed. In her wake Lilli felt more wretched than ever.

That evening, as she prepared to leave the academy for home and just when she thought the day could go no worse, Mademoiselle Schultz approached her again as she walked down the corridor.

'Ah Fraulein Sternberg, Madame Eva would like a word with you in her office,' she told her, her lips pursed and her orange head held high.

Lilli's stomach turned a somersault as the 'what ifs' tumbled around in her head. What if word had got back to the academy that she'd been drunk? What if the general had reported her for misconduct?

She stood before Madame Eva's desk quailing at the very thought of being expelled from the academy, but all her principal did was slide over an envelope across the desk, lifting a sly smile as she did so.

'This came for you today, Lilli,' she said, intrigue tinging her voice. 'It is marked *personal*, so I respected your privacy, but I thought it might be from Monsieur Raymond.'

Lilli's stomach flipped again as she reached for the envelope with her name, handwritten, on the front. The principal watched eagerly as she opened the flap with trembling hands to read the contents. Her mouth suddenly went dry, but not because she was being offered a contract with the talent agency, but because Captain Marco Zeiller wanted to see her again.

Lilli refolded the note and replaced it in the envelope. 'It isn't from Monsieur Raymond, Madame,' she said, trying to force down her urge to shout her news from the rooftops. It was, instead, a message from the most wonderful, most charming man in all of Munich.

'Oh?' Madame arched one of her brows.

'It is personal,' replied Lilli. 'From an old acquaintance, who didn't have my home address.' The lie came easily to her.

Madame Eva tented her fingers disapprovingly. 'Perhaps you could ensure that, in future, all your private correspondence is directed correctly, Fraulein Lilli. Any further communications will be disposed of. You understand?'

'Yes, Madame.' Lilli turned to go, then swivelled back to dip a curtsey.

'Thank you, Madame,' she said, and she hurried out of the principal's office with wings on her heels.

Maximillian-ll-Kaserne Barracks,
Munich
Dear Fraulein Sternberg

Forgive me for contacting you via the Académie de Danse, but I could think of no other way of renewing our acquaintance. I very much enjoyed spending the evening of Comtesse von Urbach's ball in your company and hope you didn't think my behaviour too presumptuous. I crave your forgiveness if that is the case and hope you will allow me to explain my actions in person to you.

With that in mind, I wondered if you would do me the honour of meeting me again at a place and time of your choosing.

If you decided that my conduct was unbecoming, then please ignore this letter. If not, I very much look forward to hearing from you at your convenience.

I am, Fraulein Sternberg, your obedient servant

Marco Zeiller
Captain, 21st Infantry (Bavarian) 7th Division, Reichswehr

Lilli re-read Marco's letter for what must have been a tenth time as she waited to meet him a block away from her apartment in Giesing the following Sunday. Ever since she'd first received the note, her anxiety and embarrassment had lifted. She felt different: light-headed, unwilling to eat, unable to concentrate. And yet colours were brighter, smells sweeter. Everything was softer to the touch. Even in winter there was birdsong and there were more smiles on the faces of people she passed in the street. Or was that simply because they were responding to her own smiles that were now bestowed so freely? Her world suddenly seemed a better place. And all because Marco had asked to be in it. A walk to the *Englischer Garten*, the huge park in the centre of the city, was proposed. She hadn't told her parents. Not yet. They thought she was meeting Marsha from the academy.

The day before it had snowed heavily again. Lilli had tugged on thick socks under her boots and borrowed her mother's old fur coat, which was far too big for her around the middle and a little too short to be fashionable, but she hoped it made her look sophisticated. And of course it was much warmer than her thin coat.

As the nearby church clock struck eleven, Captain Marco Zeiller appeared. Away from the heady atmosphere of Helene's ball and in the harsh light of day, she suddenly worried that things might be awkward between them, that the spark might have died, like a candle flame snuffed out by falling snow.

The captain was wearing a greatcoat over his uniform that made his shoulders look even broader. He seemed taller to Lilli, too. It was the first time she'd seen him in the daylight and, as he drew closer, she was struck by his strong jaw and his aquiline nose. Together they made him appear even more Italian.

'Fraulein Sternberg,' he greeted her with a shallow bow. 'I am so honoured that you agreed to meet me.'

Despite the cold, Lilli felt herself flush. 'Captain Zeiller.'

'I was afraid you might think badly of me after . . .' He tilted his head a little as he spoke. 'Well, after . . .'

Lilli frowned. 'But I thought you'd think badly of me. I am the one who must apologise. I am not used to champagne and . . .'

His expression changed. Suddenly he looked very sombre. 'I understand,' he said, his shoulders slumping. 'You made a mistake. I took advantage of you. I am truly sorry. I never . . .'

'No! No Captain Zeiller.' She needed to pull back the moment. 'You don't understand. I am so happy that you contacted me.'

'You are?' His smile returned.

'Yes. Yes, of course I am.'

The air was so cold that when either of them spoke great clouds rose from their mouth like smoke. She saw his relief in a sigh.

'I've been thinking about you a lot this week,' he said. His eyes were shaded by the peak of his cap but he was smiling broadly as he spoke and his words softened any edge of awkwardness there might have been.

Watching his lips, she recalled his kiss – the kiss that exploded inside her. 'I've been thinking about you, too,' she said, feeling the tension released from her chest. 'I was worried that you'd think me just a giddy, foolish girl, who needed – what do they say? – Dutch courage, to help me through the evening.'

He shook his head. 'Not at all,' he said. 'But you *were* very brave. I admired you'

'You did?' Her eyes widened.

'It can't have been easy for you.'

She threw him a wary glance. Was he thinking of the sniggers about her gown, or the whispered rumours behind the fans and the sneers from some of the officers?

'The people, I mean,' he jumped in quickly, fearing he may have offended her. 'Those arrogant generals and their haughty wives.' He pulled a funny face, making Lilli smile. 'You are much better than they are.'

'I am?' She was so glad he felt the same way as she did about the other guests.

'I know you are,' he said, fixing her with a look that set off fireworks in her head once more. She laughed out loud.

'Good, now we are even,' he agreed with a nod. 'So, the park. You lead the way.' He gestured and she thought of the quickest route, down the road that veered left into Untere Grasstrasse, where her father's tailor's shop had stood until quite recently. She hesitated for a moment. Should she show him the blackened ruins? She decided she would.

They were less than a few metres down the street when the dark shell of the burned-out buildings came into view. A cordon had been placed around the charred rubble; the surrounding pavements had been swept clear of glass, but the hideous scar remained as an unwelcome reminder of that terrible night.

Lilli stopped on the other side of the street. The shocking sight was something she wanted to share with Marco, as if by seeing it, he might get to know her better; understand her sorrows as well as her joys.

'That was my father's workshop,' she told him, watching for his reaction.

Marco's eyes widened under his cap then his brows dipped into a frown. 'What happened?'

'The Brownshirts set it alight.'

'Brownshirts,' he repeated slowly, in a knowing sort of way.

'They are no better than thugs,' she muttered, trying to contain her disgust.

'Have they caught the ones who did this?' he asked.

Lilli felt her shoulders jolt as a bitter laugh escaped. 'Of course not. They will never be punished for what they did,' she told him. 'We are the ones who suffer.'

'I'm so sorry, but these people . . .' Marco was shaking his head, a pained expression turning down his mouth at the edges. 'Will your father be able to rebuild?'

Lilli shrugged. 'He says he will. A friend has lent him some-where to work for a short time, but . . .' Her voice dissolved, knowing that, in truth, any hopes of carrying on the business had gone with the fire.

'These vandals should not be allowed to get away with this,' said Marco, still surveying the blackened stumps of wood that stuck out of the debris like rotting teeth. 'We have laws.'

As they turned to continue their journey, Lilli wanted to tell him that laws seemed only to apply to Jews, these days, but she held her tongue. Perhaps it was a mistake to show him so soon the open wound inflicted on her family. Today should not be about her pain. She should put her troubles aside. From now on there would be no sadness when Marco was with her.

It was a long walk to the park, so Lilli set a fast pace, but the pavements were icy and, almost immediately, she found herself slipping. She'd just begun to slide when she instinctively grabbed hold of Marco to steady herself.

'Ah! Ha!' he exclaimed, catching her arm.

'I'm sorry,' she told him, laughing as the soles of her boots slipped from under her again before she could right herself.

'No more apologies,' he replied, putting his arm over hers and holding it there so that, from then on, they walked arm in arm. It felt so natural, yet so thrilling for Lilli to be touching him as they moved along. Her heart swelled with pride to be seen on the arm of such a handsome man – an officer as well – and secretly she hoped one of the rich girls from the academy might spot them and tell everyone that Lilli Sternberg was walking out with a dashing captain in the Reichswehr.

Despite the cold, it was a bright, crisp day with not a cloud in the sky. The park was teeming with families, trussed up in fur coats, hats and boots, all enjoying a Sunday stroll. Children clambered for rides on the carousel, while the older ones built snowmen or staged snowball fights. Away from the clusters of attractions, dogs ran helter-skelter on the great powdery swards of white and the mood was jolly and relaxed.

Lilli and Marco swapped smiles, as if giving one another

71

permission to join in the fun. They gazed up at the famous Chinese Tower and tapped their feet to the Bavarian folk songs belted out by the little oompah band. They lingered to watch skaters glide and prance across one of the ponds and then stopped at the café at the boathouse for hot chocolate.

'That's so good,' Lilli said as they sat on the terrace, sipping the rich liquid from a tall glass cup.

'Wait,' said Marco, holding her gaze and taking off his glove. He reached across the table and traced the top of her lip with his finger. His very touch made her shut her eyes. When she opened them again, she found him chuckling as he held up his finger tip, covered in whipped cream.

'You had a moustache, Fraulein Sternberg!' he teased, his voice deep and comical.

Lilli rose to his bait. Flashing him a scandalised look, she suddenly leaned across and snatched his finger to lick away the cream, before leaning into her seat once more. Marco threw back his head to laugh and Lilli laughed, too.

The surface of the large lake was frozen, and they skimmed pebbles across it, making eerie, hollow sounds as if the surface was a giant drum. A dog suddenly darted from nowhere and ran out into the middle. Its owner screamed after it and for a terrible moment Lilli worried the animal might fall through the ice. But it responded to its master's calls and turned tail to reach safety once more.

'I had two Schnauzers once,' Marco said suddenly, smiling with relief to see dog and owner reunited.

Lilli pictured the breed with their humorous faces and bearded muzzles. No one bad could own a Schnauzer. 'They are so friendly,' she said.

Marco laughed. Lilli loved it when he did. His whole face lit up. 'Hansel and Gretel, they were called. I was only young. My mother loved animals.' As he spoke Lilli noticed a shadow spread suddenly across his face as if the memory of his mother made him sad.

'Does she no longer keep dogs?' she asked.

He turned to give her a tight smile. 'My mother is dead.'

Lilli's face crumpled. 'I'm so sorry. I didn't . . .'

His eyes flickered. 'She died a long time ago.' He lowered his gaze, then switched back to her, the smile returned. 'But I know she would have liked you.'

His words touched her deeply, as if he'd just laid his head gently on her soul, but she didn't know how to reply. Instead she just put her hand in his.

They reached the end of Lilli's street as the winter light began to fade.

'It's been a lovely day,' she said, standing in the lea of a building, sheltering from the chill wind. The cold was nipping her toes and fingers as the temperature started to plummet again.

Marco nodded. 'It has been wonderful.' He leaned forward and kissed her on the lips and the thrill shot through Lilli's body once more. 'Next week?' he asked.

'Next week,' agreed Lilli.

Their meeting couldn't come soon enough for either of them. In fact, they were so focused on each other, that neither of them noticed a lone figure standing in the doorway of one of the apartment blocks opposite. Lilli Sternberg and Marco Zeiller were being watched.

Chapter 13

This time they went sightseeing in the city centre. Arm in arm, Lilli and Marco gazed at the Frauenkirche with its famous domed towers then walked on past the imposing Residenz Museum to the Feldherrnhalle mausoleum, built to honour the Bavarian Army. As they stood admiring the great stone lions, Lilli noticed a dozen red roses, lying like splashes of blood on the cold steps. Marco's eyes followed hers. They both knew they were left as a tribute to Herr Hitler's supporters, killed in a failed coup a few years back, but neither of them chose to remark upon them.

Over the next month they saw each other when they could. For their fifth meeting Lilli suggested they went to see a film, but she was careful to avoid the cinema where she worked. She didn't want the manager, fat, greasy Herr Rubenhold, to spot her. When he wasn't angry with her for being late for a shift, he'd give her one of his leers. She wasn't sure which was worse. She pictured herself in her ridiculous candy-striped usherette's dress, her little pink hat at a jaunty angle, being lectured by him.

'If you are courting a Reichswehr officer, you no longer need your job,' he would growl. Worse still, he might find a way of telling her parents. So she suggested another picture house, far away from Giesing, where they were showing *The Blue Angel*. It starred one of her idols – Marlene Dietrich.

They sat in the back row, alongside all the other young lovers, and Marco bought a big carton of pretzels. Just sitting beside him, brushing against his tunic, gave Lilli goose bumps.

The film was every bit as good as she'd hoped. Dietrich was magnificent as the cabaret performer, Lola Lola.

'I want to be like her someday,' Lilli whispered, staring up at the siren whose presence filled the screen. As soon as she'd spoken, she thought how childish she must sound.

'But you are far more beautiful than Dietrich,' he shot back, offering her a pretzel with a wink.

Biting into the delicious, salty loop of bread she smiled back at him. 'I bet she doesn't eat these,' she said.

Marco leaned over then, wrapped his arm around her shoulder and kissed her. 'Whatever you eat, you are amazing,' he whispered, his mouth brushing her ear.

They strolled back to Giesing, arm in arm. Lilli had told her parents she was going to the cinema with Marsha from the academy. Naturally she felt guilty deceiving them, but she'd wanted to get to know Marco before she introduced him to them. Now, however, it seemed there was no need to hide their feelings for each other. It was time the whole world knew she was in love.

They stopped at the end of her street once more. It was a cold evening and Marco's body felt warm against hers as he leaned in. Lilli closed her eyes, and her mouth yielded to the press of his soft lips as they kissed long and slow. She could swear her soul left her body and soared above the rooftops. And then he whispered it. Marco actually said the words that she'd longed him to say and that she herself had felt for a while.

'I love you,' he whispered on a long breath.

'I love you, too.'

It was painful drawing away from him to leave him that night, but after they'd agreed to meet again the following week, Lilli ambled back to her apartment block, her whole body feeling as though it could float over the city. So this really was love and Marco had felt it, too: a giddy, mad sensation that sent your head spinning and your heart racing. It was amazing, but she was missing him already.

Herr Grunfeld, the janitor, about to lock up for the night, was at the main entrance to the block.

'Fraulein Lilli, there you are,' he said, pointing to the clock on the wall. A big bunch of keys jangled at his waist. 'You girls,' he tutted. Her mother had obviously mentioned she was out with Marsha.

'I'm sorry. I lost track of time,' replied Lilli, even though she wasn't sorry at all. Without bothering to offer any further explanation for her lateness she simply said: 'Goodnight, Herr Grunfeld.'

Yet no sooner had she set foot on the bottom stair than the janitor called her back.

'There's something for you,' he told her, his hand disappearing into one of the wooden pigeonholes behind the front desk.

Lilli turned to see him retrieve an envelope and lay it on the counter. Moving closer, she could see it was a folded piece of paper with her name on it. She reached for it as the janitor's brow creased in puzzlement.

'I didn't see who delivered it,' he told her, scratching his grizzled head.

Lilli opened the note to read the message, written in a neat, educated hand. It took her a moment to take in the meaning of the words. The letters danced in front of her eyes as she re-read them, and a cold shiver crept through her body.

'*You cannot always have your own way, you Jewish whore,*' was all it said.

She tried to still her trembling hands. Herr Grunfeld mustn't know what poison the note contained.

'And you're sure you . . . you saw no one?' she asked, her voice suddenly snagging on her own fear.

'No.' The janitor shook his head and frowned. 'Everything all right, Fraulein Lilli?'

She managed a smile. 'Of course. Why shouldn't it be?' Her answer fired out too quickly to sound true. Only a minute before, she had felt as light as a feather. Now she trudged up the stairs with a new and unwelcome burden on her shoulders. Who could possibly have written such a vile note? Who could be so cruel? Worse still, a thought occurred to her as she opened the door to her apartment: whoever sent the message, must've known she was out. Could that mean someone was watching her?

Chapter 14

Lilli made no mention of the despicable note at their next meeting. Marco was taking her to her first opera. He wanted to share his love for it. It was going to be a special evening and nothing, and no one, would be allowed to spoil it.

The Bavarian state opera house was every bit as beautiful as the Cuvilliés and filled with the same sort of people who'd watched *Giselle*. The women dazzled in their jewels and expensive gowns, while most of the older men, in white ties and tails, reminded Lilli of penguins, as they waddled about.

She was wearing her one and only evening gown, the one she had worn to Helene's ball – the one she had met Marco in. She'd smuggled it into her bag that morning and changed at the academy. Marco looked distinguished in his dress uniform and she felt so proud that he had chosen her to accompany him.

As they sat in the auditorium, expectation filling the air, he explained the story of *La Bohème* to her.

'It's set in Paris, in the last century and it's about a poor seamstress and her artist friends.'

'A seamstress,' repeated Lilli, thinking of her father's business and excited that she might be able to better understand the heroine's trials and tribulations. But she needn't have worried about feeling distanced from the characters. The whole experience was so intense, so entrancing, that when the diva, Mimi, might have had to surrender herself to a corrupt police chief to save her lover's life, she gripped Marco's arm. Would she sacrifice herself for him? She threw him a loving glance. Of course she would.

The music was sublime and when Mimi died, she could no longer hold back the tears. By the time the curtain fell, Lilli was emotionally exhausted.

'So, you like opera now?' Marco asked playfully as Lilli dabbed her eyes.

She nodded. 'It's almost as wonderful as ballet.'

Marco laughed at her remark. He was relaxed in her company and she in his, but as they ambled out of the auditorium, to return to the foyer, Lilli saw his expression change in an instant. The smile was wiped from his face.

'Marco, what is it? What's wrong?' she asked, scanning the crowd for an answer.

He did not need to reply. Suddenly Kurt von Stockmar was standing directly ahead of them.

'Let's go out another way,' said Marco. But it was too late.

'Well, well, if it isn't Captain Zeiller and the beautiful Giselle,' mocked von Stockmar.

It had been obvious to Lilli at Helene's ball that there was a certain coolness, verging on animosity, between the officers. The two men eyed each other icily.

Marco's face hardened. 'Von Stockmar.'

'Zeiller,' he replied before pointedly skewering Lilli with a glare. As his face turned, the long, silver scar on his left cheek caught the light from the chandelier. 'And the beautiful Miss Sternberg.' He leered at her. 'I believe your father made a suit for me once.'

Lilli looked at him wide-eyed. She opened her mouth to reply that her father was the finest tailor in Giesing, possibly in Munich. She was proud of him, even though, after the arson attack, he would probably never make a suit again. How dare

79

this arrogant Reichswehr officer try to make her feel ashamed of her family? Before she could reply, however, von Stockmar leaned closer to Marco.

'You're playing with fire there,' she heard him growl, before he stepped back and disappeared into the crowd.

'I'm afraid your friend doesn't like me,' Lilli told Marco as he tried to rein in his obvious anger. She saw his fists flex before he took her hand in hers. 'Take no notice of him,' she advised.

Marco shook his head then flashed Lilli a smile. 'You're right,' he replied, tugging at his tunic. 'Let's just say he is a small man.'

On the way back to Giesing in a taxi, Lilli imagined introducing her handsome officer to her parents. The evening had been so magical, and she and Marco were getting on so well that she thought they might put an end to the subterfuge. She resented sneaking around in the shadows, making excuses, when all she really wanted to do was declare her love for Marco to the world. It was time for him to meet Jacob and Golda.

'I have a day's leave next Sunday,' he told her, as the taxi turned into Lilli's street.

It was as if he could read her thoughts. 'Then will you come for a meal?' blurted Lilli. 'I'd like to introduce you to my family.'

For a moment his expression froze. Had she spoken out of turn? Was it too soon? But no. Taking her hand in his, he kissed it gently.

'I'd like that very much, too,' he replied.

The sound of the wireless wafted through the half-open door of Herr Grunfeld's flat as Lilli tiptoed into the reception, keen to avoid attracting the janitor's attention a second time. She was still wearing her evening gown and didn't want her parents to find out where she had been. Once inside the hallway, a sense of dread suddenly knotted her stomach as she remembered the note from the other night. Leaning over the desk, she checked the post. The pigeonhole marked *Sternberg* was empty.

'It's you, Fraulein!'

Lilli's heart leapt into her mouth.

Herr Grunfeld, his keys in his hand, put his head round his door.

'I didn't mean to scare you.' His eyes swept over her gown. 'Been somewhere nice?'

'Just something at the academy,' she replied, brushing his remark aside as she started for the stairs, trying to behave as if she didn't care that he'd caught her out.

'Fraulein Lilli,' Herr Grunfeld whispered hoarsely.

She turned to catch him touching the side of his nose.

'Your secret's safe with me.'

She felt herself redden, like a child whose hand had been caught stealing sweets. Could she trust him? She flashed a guilty smile.

At least, she told herself, as she resumed her climb, she needn't worry about any more spiteful notes. Tonight, at least, she could dream of her beloved Marco.

Chapter 15

Golda Sternberg rose at six o'clock that morning to dust surfaces, beat rugs and sweep floors in preparation for the arrival of a very special guest – a gentile guest. Lilli had announced she'd met an officer at Helene's ball a few weeks back and she'd like to introduce him to them. Golda had reacted with disquiet, as if she had been afraid this might happen. Although she hadn't said so at the time, Lilli was aware her mother always feared she might meet someone who wasn't Jewish. After all, Lilli had been brought up knowing it was unthinkable for her to marry a gentile man. But when she had told her parents about Captain Zeiller, she'd sensed that, despite a certain wariness, they seemed keen enough to meet him.

The previous day Golda had baked her babka cake with chocolate swirls, while *gedempte* chicken with vegetables and spices would be put in the oven soon to make the flesh melt in the mouth by the evening. She had even made Jacob trim his beard and Leon put on clean socks, although Lilli wasn't sure why Marco would be interested in her brother's feet, or her father's beard for that matter.

Ever since the ball Lilli had been dancing on air and her mother had regarded her oddly, suspecting something had happened – that her daughter was carrying a secret around with her. Was it so obvious that she had met someone wonderful? Perhaps. After all, she was in love for the first time. She knew it was love because she'd never felt so alive, so happy, so full of longing to see Marco again. Instead of concentrating on her chores, her mind was in another place and her appetite had all but disappeared. She'd even refused one of her mother's special knotted pastries last Sabbath. Now Lilli had been honest with them, her parents wanted to see her handsome young Reichswehr officer themselves, no doubt to gauge if they thought him a suitable match.

Lilli, on the other hand, was dreading having Marco to dine. He already knew that she lived in a poor area, but now he would see for himself the mould on the apartment ceiling, the threadbare rugs and the peeling paint. Away from her shabby apartment, she could be anyone she wanted to be. But here, within these four damp walls, there was no hiding the truth. Her family was poor and, because of the arson attack, growing poorer by the day. As for her parents, she feared they would embarrass her by asking Marco awkward questions. No doubt Mutti would want to know about his family, but it had become clear to her that he really didn't like to talk about it. His mother was dead, he had no siblings and he never spoke of his father.

When the evening finally arrived, the *kachelofen* was blazing, making the room comfortably warm for the first time in many months. Golda had insisted on the best dinner plates and the napkins bought for Leon's bar mitzvah were freshly laundered. No effort had been spared to make the apartment appear at its best and Lilli was excited.

Captain Marco Zeiller arrived exactly on time and gallantly presented Golda with a bouquet of hot-house roses. Her mother appeared both delighted and flustered in turn. Lilli wasn't sure if that was the effect of the flowers or of Marco in his uniform. Leon was tasked with taking the officer's cap while Lilli showed him into the main room where Jacob was waiting to welcome him, his kippa nestling in a forest of wiry grey hair. The two men shook hands formally, but Lilli saw her father's lips twitch in a tentative smile at Marco and that made her smile, too.

'Please, sit,' said Jacob, gesturing to the settee, lined with newly plumped cushions.

Golda seemed to take this as a signal to move into the kitchen, dragging a nervous Lilli with her. Her mother would leave her father to begin the interrogation of their guest alone. But while Golda busied herself stirring the stew, Lilli watched the proceedings through a chink in the door, willing them to go smoothly.

'You have come far?' asked Jacob.

'No, my barracks are in the north of the city,' replied Marco, adding: 'I'm in the Reichswehr's Seventh Division.'

From the look on Jacob's face, this fact was of no interest. He disregarded it and ploughed on. 'So your family—'

'My father was in the Seventh Division before me,' Marco jumped in.

Jacob nodded. 'And where are your parents now?'

From the doorway Lilli cringed. Why was Vati probing Marco like this before he'd barely sat down? She knew Marco didn't get along with his father. She gauged from the momentary flinch of his face that the question was difficult for him to tackle.

'My father is in Stuttgart, but my mother is no longer with us.'

Lilli suddenly regretted not telling her parents about Marco's loss. She knew it saddened him to think of her.

The clink of lids and the clatter of spoons came from behind.

'We are ready,' Golda suddenly announced, surveying an array of dishes and two baskets of bread lined up on the kitchen table. 'You can help me carry everything through.'

Leon was summoned to help them in the kitchen and the three of them proceeded to the table laden with steaming bowls of vegetables, little loaves and a large pot of stew. Marco was directed to sit opposite Lilli, while Leon, sullen as ever, sat next to his sister, making it clear he'd rather be reading in his room. Her parents were at either end of the table.

Once seated, Jacob ordered everyone to lower their heads.

'We must bless the Lord for giving us our food,' he explained.

Lilli swapped an apologetic glance with Marco, but he willingly obeyed as Jacob proceeded to bless not just the Lord, but also give thanks for both his children, his wife, and, out of politeness, their guest.

As Golda ladled out the stew, Lilli was aware the atmosphere was as stiff as the napkins her mother had starched specially. She hoped the wine her father was pouring might make her parents more relaxed, but when she looked at the full plate of food in front of her, she knew it would be a struggle to eat any of it, let alone finish it.

Marco did his best to make the conversation flow. 'This buckwheat is very good. So tasty,' he remarked cheerfully, lifting a second forkful of *kasha*.

Golda straightened her back and smiled. 'It is an old recipe from the Ukraine,' she replied.

'Is that where you are from originally?' asked Marco politely.

Lilli's head shot up. *Why did Mutti have to mention Ukraine?* she thought to herself, glancing first at Golda and then at her father, fearing what was to come. It was too late.

'My wife's family was driven out of the Ukraine during one of the pogroms,' Jacob said gravely.

Marco glanced at Lilli, whose face was blanching with embarrassment, but, instead of brushing over the remark, the captain acknowledged it.

'Your family must have suffered terribly over the years,' he said. 'You are the victims of grave injustices.'

For a moment the table fell silent as everyone digested the unexpected remark. A moment later, however, Leon, who had remained quiet throughout the meal, suddenly stirred and threw a grenade.

Lifting his gaze, he skewered Marco directly in the eye. 'What does a Reichswehr officer know about justice?' he asked in a hiss.

'Leon!' cried Golda.

Jacob, equally shocked, jerked out his arm and cuffed the side of his son's head.

'Manners!' he boomed, then, as if surprised by his own anger, he added in a more measured way: 'The captain is our guest. Now go to your room.'

Lilli wanted to leave the table as well – to join Leon and hide her face in the clouds of her own pillows. The meeting was an unmitigated disaster. It couldn't be salvaged. Hopes that her parents would agree to her seeing Marco again lay in ruins, like the charred remnants of her father's shop.

Jacob's jaw jutted out, something that Lilli knew only happened when he was riled. Pinning his outspoken son with a glare he explained: 'You must forgive my son, Captain Zeiller. He speaks his mind. He wants to be a lawyer someday.'

Marco, however, remained calm. He flapped a hand. 'I am sure he will make very good one,' he replied graciously. 'A lawyer must stand his corner, so please, Herr Sternberg, don't banish him on my account.'

Leon, halfway across the floor, stopped in his tracks to allow his father time to think twice about his punishment.

'You are very understanding,' Jacob told Marco, before directing his son back towards the table with a jerk of his head. 'Thank you.'

Marco acknowledged the thanks with a smile then slid his gaze towards Lilli, her face now a study in admiration. He had rescued the explosive situation. He had diffused the bomb and now she wanted to leap across the table and cover him in kisses. In the meantime, Leon returned to his seat and, without prompting, offered a half apology.

'I acted rashly,' he said, picking up his discarded knife and fork.

'You reacted like a lawyer,' replied Marco evenly, as if drawing a line under the matter. After a moment's pause, in which everyone settled down to eat once more, he asked Golda: 'So, I am sure you saw your daughter perform as Giselle.'

His words were balm on the uncomfortable sore. It was if all those around the table breathed a sigh of relief and could begin again on a subject upon which everyone could agree: Lilli's talent.

Golda beamed at her daughter then turned to Marco. 'The Lord in his wisdom has given her a real gift,' she said, before pointing to the dish of buckwheat. 'More *kasha*?' she offered. The evening had been clawed back from the brink of disaster from that point on. Thanks to Marco's diplomacy, Lilli could relax again. She even ate a little. Marco complimented Golda on her babka cake and asked for a second slice and even managed to engage Leon in conversation about his dreams of studying law. There was talk of rebuilding Jacob's tailor's shop, too, although the plans were still not finalised.

Lilli learned other things about her suitor, as well: that he was born in Stuttgart, where he went to school, that his mother was Venetian and that his brother died at just five years of age.

When the wine bottles were emptied, the dishes cleared and the coffee drunk, Marco thanked his hosts for their generous hospitality.

'I have had a very enjoyable evening,' he told Golda with a bow.

'So have we,' she said, almost girlishly, Lilli noted.

Even Leon managed to smile.

'Goodnight,' said Jacob, extending his hand. Marco took it and any reserve that there had been on the first shake seemed to have dissipated, like smoke, into the air.

'I'll see you out,' said Lilli, eager to snatch a few minutes alone with Marco.

They walked side by side along the narrow corridor to the front door, their arms brushing against each other. She handed him his cap from the nearby hook and felt her pulse race as they came face to face.

'They like you,' she said softly, lifting her gaze to meet his.

'I hope so,' he replied, gently stroking her cheek. 'You think they will let you come out with me officially now?'

She nodded and smiled. 'I am sure of it.'

He leaned in, poised on the brink of a kiss, when footsteps could be heard on the landing outside. Before they knew it, the door handle had turned and a Brownshirt was standing on the threshold.

'Herr Backe!' cried Lilli, taken off guard.

Dressed in his uniform with his swastika armband proudly displayed, the lodger returned a grunted greeting, before switching to Marco, his eyes popping when he saw his rank insignia. Clicking his heels and standing to attention, he flung out his arm in a Nazi salute.

'*Sieg Heil!*' he barked.

Backe's actions were clearly designed to impress the officer, but he did not anticipate Marco's response. The captain simply shot him a reproachful look and, turning his back on the thug, proceeded to ignore him.

'Goodnight, Fraulein Sternberg,' he told Lilli, as a stunned Backe remained standing to attention. 'Until next time.'

Lilli watched Marco start to descend the flight of stairs, with Herr Backe still at her side, as if dazed by what had just happened. An officer of the Reichswehr in a Jewish family's apartment: from the look on his bullish face, the very idea was outrageous. Lilli threw him a victorious look, as she watched him retreat into his room, shaking his head and mumbling to himself. It was a small triumph for decency, but she claimed it, nonetheless. Returning to the kitchen, Lilli found her parents standing by the sink. She was happy. After a rocky start, the dinner had gone well, hadn't it?

'Isn't he wonderful?' she gushed over Marco, thinking Golda and Jacob would readily agree. She was so proud of the way her captain had handled the evening, she couldn't stop beaming. It was only when her parents didn't reply, she knew something was wrong. Their silence spoke volumes.

In those few short moments since she'd bid Marco goodnight and returned, their mood seemed to have changed.

'What is it, Mutti? Is something wrong?' Lilli asked as Golda filled the washing bowl with water at the sink.

Her mother's shoulders heaved in a sigh before she turned to face her, drying her hands on a towel.

'Oh, Lilli' she replied. 'We can see you have lost your heart to this young man already. He is handsome and charming.'

Lilli could sense there was a 'but' about to be tacked on to the compliments. She was right.

'But he is not our kind.'

She felt her chest gently compress and her breath caught in her throat. She was shocked. Everything had gone so well in the end. Everything was perfect after Leon's outburst. The conversation, stilted before, had become free and easy. Or so she'd thought. But Marco was not their 'kind.' He was witty and funny and polite. He had a prestigious job, a steady income and was highly regarded in society, but he was not a Jew.

Now Jacob, standing by the draining board, chimed in. 'Lilli,' he said, shaking his head. 'He does not understand our ways, our culture. He is half-Italian. A Roman Catholic. Catholics hate us because they say we killed their Christ.'

Lilli switched back to her mother and searched her lined face. Her mouth was pursed and her look sour. There was sorrow behind her eyes, but something else as well: disapproval.

'Not all gentiles hate us,' Lilli pleaded. 'Marco is good and kind and . . .'

'It's not enough,' Golda snapped, throwing the tea towel down on the draining board. 'We should never have agreed to let him dine here. Whoever you marry, he must be a Jew. You will marry a Jew, Lilli, and there's an end to it.' And with that she pushed past her daughter and out of the kitchen.

Jacob's mouth drooped and his eyes filled with sadness. 'Oh Lilli. Your mother doesn't want to see you hurt. Nor do I.' He opened wide his arms to enfold his daughter, but Lilli didn't rush forward to rest her head on his shoulder like she usually did.

Instead she stepped back. 'You know we have your best interests at heart. Just go carefully, *mein Liebling*. For all our sakes,' he told her.

Lilli starred at her father in disbelief. Had he been in the same room as her just a few minutes before? Had he seen the laughter in Marco's face; had he heard his kind words? His compliments? Had the captain not lowered his head at the blessing of the food and expressed outrage on behalf of persecuted Jews? What more could he have given? All these questions she wanted to ask, but her throat was so tight that her words could not escape. She did not understand. There was no reasoning behind their reaction, only entrenched traditions and values that brooked no argument because Captain Marco Zeiller wasn't a Jew. She shook her head as a great wave of sorrow threatened to engulf her.

Suddenly, without warning, her parents had become strangers.

Chapter 16

Lilli woke the morning after the dinner and wanted to die. Through the blur of sleep, she saw the damp patch in the corner of her room and the faded poster of Greta Garbo. She heard Leon looking for something in his drawer and, through the half-open door, her mother berating her father for dropping a slice of toast. There were footsteps on the stairs, doors banging, Frau Reuter's children squealing. She could hear them all; the music of the everyday and she knew there was no way she could ever live without Marco.

A few moments later Golda came into the bedroom. 'Get up Lilli. You'll be late for class.'

She turned over in bed, drawing up her limbs, hugging her knees to her chest. 'I'm not going.'

Her mother strode towards the bed and leaned over her.

'You have been crying.'

Of course I've been crying, thought Lilli. *You have forbidden me to see the person who gave me a reason to live.*

Unfurling her body, she sat up in bed. Her eyes were red and sticky. In the night, Leon had complained her sobs were keeping him awake, so she'd done her best to cry into her pillow. It may have deadened the noise, but not her pain.

Golda eased herself onto the edge of the bed and Lilli had to resist the urge to push her away. But her mother reached out her hand and laid it on her daughter's shoulder. Lilli shrugged it off, her eyes were downcast, as if she could not bear to look at her.

A moment passed, but the gap between mother and daughter only grew. Seeing her presence was inflaming Lilli's mood, Golda heaved herself up again. Any softness in her tone now hardened.

'You must write to this captain. You must tell him you have changed your mind; that you no longer wish to see him again.' It was her mother's voice all right, but Lilli did not recognise her heartlessness. 'You understand?'

Lilli brushed the hair away from her face and pushed back the covers.

'Yes, Mutti,' she replied sullenly. Of course she understood what was demanded of her, but she had no intention of obeying. Now she knew how her parents looked on Marco, she could no longer be happy sharing her feelings for him. 'I will write to him,' she told Golda, standing defiantly by her bed.

So that is what Lilli did. The tiles from the *kachelofen* were cold to the touch that evening. Less than twenty-four hours before the stove had blazed furiously, and the room had been filled with warmth and light. Now it was chill and silent as she sat in fingerless gloves to write her letter to Marco.

Over in the corner, Golda was sewing by candlelight. Now and again she would glance towards at her daughter, peering over the rims of her spectacles, to register if any progress was being made. Jacob had taken to bed, complaining of chest pains, and Leon was reading in the bedroom.

Lilli had, in fact, written the letter to Marco earlier in the day – the one she planned to show to Golda, that was, the one in which she finished her relationship with him.

The one that she really wanted to write, however, the one that came from her heart, was much easier. The words pressed on her chest so hard that she knew she needed to spill them onto the page. When she picked up her pen and the nib touched the virgin paper, they started to fall like rain.

My dearest Marco

As I write this letter to you, my heart is breaking. You will have received two letters from me: one contains the news that my parents want you to hear, but this one is how I really feel.

After you left, they told me I was not to see you again, that you were not of our kind. So now I may as well be locked in a cell. When I imagine your face it is on the other side of an iron grille. I can reach out to touch you, but the cold bars will always be in my way. If I can't be with you, I can never be truly free.

My parents say they are acting in my best interests, but what do they know? They have no idea about our special bond; I love you and that is all that matters.

She looked up from the letter. It was strange to see those words committed to paper, as if by writing down her feelings for him made them even stronger. She remembered the way he looked at her, the way his eyes lit up when she smiled at him, the way he would brush away her wayward curls so tenderly.

'You have finished the letter?' asked Golda.

'Almost,' she replied, making sure the decoy letter was to hand to show her mother.

Golda's head bowed once more and she resumed.

So, I plan to disobey my parents. It is not my wish, but the thought of never seeing you again is too hard to bear. We must continue to meet in secret.

Please come to the Académie de Danse after classes on Thursday. I can't wait to see you again, my love.

Yours, forever,

Lilli.

Chapter 17

Now that Lilli had a secret – a real secret; the sort of secret that makes young women jealous and old ones frown and tut – she was not sure how she felt about it. Marco had replied to her letter, declaring his love for her and wanting to carry on seeing her. One minute she was positively bursting with excitement at the prospect of meeting him after lessons at the academy, and the next her stomach was knotted with anxiety in case her parents found out that they were still together.

There had been no more vicious notes, so she hoped it was the first and the last. Someone was obviously jealous of the love she and Marco shared. But what if they discovered they were still together and informed her parents? She'd told Golda that Madame Eva was planning a new ballet and had asked her to help with the choreography. In reality, however, there were no rehearsals after class. Marco would come to the back door of the academy once a week and they would go for a hot chocolate, or stroll in the *Englischer Garten*. On cold nights they would go to the cinema. Last week they'd seen Fanny Brice in *My Man*. She'd loved the song called *Second Hand Rose*, about a poor girl longing for stardom. It kept her dream alive, although, in her heart of hearts, she didn't want anything to take her away from Marco.

'What's the matter with you?' Jens shouted at Lilli in front of Madame Eva the following week. 'Ever since *Giselle*, you've been sloppy.' He turned his back on her and flounced over to the barre.

It was proving another trying day at the academy. Madame Eva had asked Lilli to go through some new steps with Jens in the studio. But she'd be the first to admit that ever since she'd met Marco she was finding it hard to concentrate. Sequences seemed to be more complicated. Steps more elaborate. She'd just mistimed a plié and trodden on Jens' foot. Now he was making an unearthly fuss about it.

Madame Eva intervened. To Lilli's surprise, she seemed to take her side, admonishing the youth. 'Jens. There is no need to be so angry. Control yourself.'

The trouble was Lilli knew her dance partner was right. She was losing her edge. She needed to pull herself together. Marco occupied her waking thoughts and filled her dreams. There was no room for anything else in her life and, as a result, her dancing was suffering.

'Lilli.' Madame Eva beckoned her protégé at the end of the rehearsal. 'I'm not sure what is going on, but I suggest you give your future some serious thought.'

The words wounded her. The past three months had passed like a whirlwind and her ballet had been a casualty of a maelstrom with her passion for Marco at its centre.

'Yes, Madame,' she replied, a part of her dying inside at the thought that her standards had slipped so much.

A single light bulb burned dimly in the centre of the changing room, casting a dim glow on the space, leaving the corners in shadow. Lilli didn't notice Helene at first, slipping on her skirt in the corner. Ever since the ball, Helene's behaviour towards Lilli had changed. She no longer hung around hoping to talk with her. She ignored her in class. In fact, it seemed to Lilli that the comtesse went out of her way to avoid being alone with her.

Both of them stood awkwardly in the silence. At first Lilli said nothing and simply began towelling herself down, and as Helene came closer, she seemed to pretend to be unaware of Lilli's presence. Without a word, she reached for her coat from a peg, but knocked down Lilli's bag in the process. They both bent low to pick it up and caught each other's looks as they rose.

'Helene, I . . .' Lilli began, although she wasn't quite sure how to finish what she'd started to say. She guessed her hostess must still be smarting from losing her chance to spend the evening with Marco at the ball. But Lilli couldn't help falling in love, practically at first sight. Nor did she deserve to be cold-shouldered, because Marco had fallen for her, too. There would be no apology.

'It's all right,' snapped Helene, tugging on her coat and moving away.

'Wait!' called Lilli. 'I wanted to tell you about Marco. We . . .'

When Helene turned back, her expression had changed, her features contorted into a scowl. 'Once he met you, I didn't stand a chance,' she growled.

A twinge of guilt pinched Lilli as hard as Madame Eva's fingers.

'I didn't know,' she protested, even though she had seen the light in Helene's eyes when she'd looked at Marco that night at the ball.

But Helene persisted, her face growing darker as she spoke. 'I expect you've had fun, laughing at me behind my back.'

Lilli shook her head. She tried to make Helene listen. 'No. It wasn't like that at all. I never meant—'

But Helene had stormed out of the changing rooms, shouting as she went: 'We are through, Lilli Sternberg. I no longer count you as my friend.'

That evening when Lilli arrived home, Helene's words still roaring in her ears, Herr Grunfeld was there behind the desk to hand her another note in person.

'This came for you,' he told her. 'A courier brought it.'

Lilli's whole body began to tremble as she opened the envelope with her name on it. Inside the note read: *I hope you are enjoying yourself with him, you slut. I go to sleep every night thinking of you in stockings and suspenders, you dirty Jewish whore.'*

A wave of nausea suddenly rose up inside her. Someone was watching her when she went out with Marco. Up until now she suspected Helene could have been the note's author. Judging by her reaction in the changing rooms today, she'd certainly had the motive. But this had to be the work of a man – a vile, twisted man.

'Everything all right, Fraulein Lilli?' asked Herr Grunfeld, his wireless blaring out a German folk tune through the open door of his apartment.

Lilli felt unsteady on her feet. Someone hated her enough to do this. 'Yes, thank you,' she replied. 'Everything is fine.'

Chapter 18

At the end of March, winter turned suddenly to spring, just as quickly as if someone had flicked a switch in the heavens. The dirty piles of snow that had lingered for so many weeks on street corners and in parks suddenly disappeared. Pink and white blossom emerged from black branches and Marco announced he had a day's leave. He suggested they drive out to one of the lakes just over an hour from the city. The sun was growing stronger every day and there was a green haze on trees and bushes. He would bring a picnic.

Lilli waited at a road junction not far from her block. She'd told her parents she was going to a friend's, although she wasn't sure her mother believed her. Nevertheless, among the horse carts, the lorries and the occasional automobile that drove up and down the main road, Lilli's eye was caught by a green sports car powering towards her. But it wasn't until it slowed down right by her that she realised Marco was behind the wheel. He was wearing civilian clothes and sunglasses.

'Jump in,' he told her.

She squealed with girlish delight as she slid into the front seat next to him.

'This is wonderful!' she cried above the roar of the engine. 'Is it yours?'

'Just for the day,' he said with a smile as they sped along the highway. 'I borrowed it from a friend, but it means we can be free!' They drove out to one of the lakes south-west of the city and parked the car by a pebbled beach, fringed with silver reeds. Little white clouds stitched the blue sky and the birds in the surrounding woods were in full voice. Lilli spread a plaid rug out on the ground. The officers' mess kitchen had made up a wicker hamper and Marco produced a bottle of red wine and two glasses.

As they sat side by side, overlooking the blue-green lake where herons fished, Lilli watched Marco open the Pinot Noir. He'd rolled up his short sleeves to expose his forearms. She could see his tendons flex as he pulled at the cork.

'You look different out of uniform,' she remarked, her attention now focused on his face.

He smiled. 'In what way?'

'More Italian.' She was thinking aloud.

'Is that a good thing?' he asked.

Lilli nodded. 'Yes, because when you are dressed like this, I forget that one day you might go to war.'

He threw his head back to laugh. 'You don't think we'll ever go to battle again, surely? After the Great War only a madman would want to fire a machine gun in anger!'

The cork made a satisfying pop when Marco freed it and the wine glugged into the glasses.

'To Giselle,' he toasted, as he handed Lilli one.

'To Duke Albrecht,' she replied softly.

They sipped their wine and watched the warm breeze ruffle the surface of the lake. A strand of Lilli's hair broke loose from her ponytail and whipped across her face. Marco reached towards her and tamed it with gentle fingers. They kissed once more and she tasted the sweetness of the wine on his lips.

Lilli wanted the moment to last forever, but suddenly Marco broke away and jumped up, laughing. Without warning he began to take off his shoes and socks then his shirt.

'What are you doing?' she shrieked.

'I'm going for a dip, of course,' he told her, stepping out of his trousers and striding naked into the lake, except for his shorts. Before she knew it, his broad shoulders had disappeared under the glassy surface and he was swimming.

She sat up and shook her head. 'You'll freeze!' she called out, a laugh following on behind. Then, on a whim, she decided to join him. Turning her back to the lake, trying to preserve some vestige of modesty, she quickly unfastened her woollen stockings from their suspenders, rolled them down and kicked off her shoes. Lilli knew she would retreat if she thought about it twice, so she bundled up her skirt and ran, full speed, into the lake.

The icy water took her breath away. She squealed as the cold crept up her legs and sent her feet numb, but then the warmth rushed in. The laughing began again – and the splashing. Marco started splashing her, too. It didn't matter that he soaked her clothes. Nothing mattered, other than the fact that they were together, and they were in love.

Afterwards Marco found a towel in the back of the car and insisted on drying Lilli's legs and feet. As they lay on the rug, he ran the towel down her smooth shins and stopped at her ankles. Taking her right foot in his hand, he studied it.

'How can something so beautiful contain so much power?' he asked, before lowering his mouth and kissing her toes.

She closed her eyes as she felt his hot breath on her skin and a thrill ran through her entire body. His lips travelled upwards until they finally met Lilli's and they kissed again, his body warming hers as they lay next to each other, drying in the spring sunshine. After a while, Marco slipped back into his trousers and shirt. She watched him as he dressed and noticed he wore a silver chain with a small medal on it around his neck. She supposed it was his army tag.

For lunch they ate hunks of bread and slices of cheese. Marco also sliced bratwurst and offered her some unthinkingly. He saw her hesitate.

'I'm sorry. I . . .' He withdrew the plate, but Lilli stopped him.

'I will try some,' she said. She had never eaten pork before. It was strictly forbidden by her religion – her parents' religion – but she was tired of abiding by pointless laws made up by old men with long beards. 'I shall eat what I like.'

Admittedly the moment she swallowed the spicy sausage she was half expecting to be struck by lightning. Or the heavens to open or the nearby trees to crash down upon her. But they didn't.

'You see. The world didn't end,' teased Marco.

She nodded, still chewing slowly, finding she rather enjoyed the taste of the bratwurst. 'Not bad,' she conceded.

She helped tidy away the picnic basket and they lay side by side on the rug, looking up at the sky, watching the clouds scudding along, being blown by the gentle breeze.

'What pictures can you make from the clouds?' Lilli asked.

'Pictures?' Marco repeated, his hands clasped behind his head. 'When I was younger, I thought I could make out my mother's face.'

Lilli turn towards him and eased herself up on her elbow so she could look down on him. 'You must miss her.'

'Of course, but I hadn't seen her for a while before she died.'

Lilli was puzzled. 'What do you mean?'

He let out a bitter laugh. 'My father divorced her and took me with him.'

Lilli sat up. 'That must've been so hard.'

He closed his eyes and winced, as if she had just touched a raw nerve.

'It was hard for me, but even harder for my mother, not being allowed to see her only remaining son.' Lilli saw his chest heave then a shadow scud across his face at some painful memory. 'So she jumped off a bridge.'

Lilli's hands flew up to her mouth. 'Oh Marco!' she gasped, horrified. She pictured a desperate woman flinging herself into an abyss. Suddenly she wanted to hold him to her and never let him go.

Now he sat up, resting his weight on both elbows and forcing a wan smile. Lilli laid her head on his shoulder and wrapped an arm around his waist. 'It was ten years ago. My father raised me, sent me away to military school. I joined the Reichswehr and here I am. Life goes on.'

Lilli leaned back to look at him. She could tell he was masking his pain, just as she had forced herself to do in the dance. She felt his body turn towards her and their eyes met as he gently pushed her down on the rug once more. He leaned over her, so his face blocked out the sun and lowered his body onto hers. His entire weight pressed against her. The sensation made her want to dissolve into him and she circled her arms around him, holding him tight. He nuzzled his face into her neck, brushing it with his mouth before he began to kiss her lips urgently. His touch stirred something deep inside her that she'd never felt before, like a butterfly emerging into the light after being dormant for so long.

'I love you, Lilli Sternberg,' Marco whispered breathlessly, his fingers working frantically at the buttons on her blouse.

'I love you, too. So very much,' she replied, feeling as though she was burning up with a fever. As his kisses rained on her, she thought she might burst into flame. 'I'm yours, my love,' she gasped, tearing at her top.

For a moment she closed her eyes, anticipating what was to come. She'd heard some girls talking about it at the academy. *This is what it means to love a man so much that you give yourself to him completely, body and soul.* They would be as one. She held her breath, the pounding of her heart and Marco's sharp gasps filling her ears. She waited and she waited, expecting . . . she wasn't quite sure, but his kisses stopped abruptly, so that when she opened her eyes once more, she found Marco simply staring at her, his eyes glassy.

'What's wrong, Marco?' she asked urgently.

'Oh, Lilli, my love, I want you, too,' he said. 'But not like this.'

He eased himself off her and, free from his weight, she filled her lungs once more.

'What is it, Marco? What's wrong with me?' she asked, scrambling upright, grasping at her blouse buttons.

He shook his head. 'There's nothing wrong with you, Lilli. You are perfect, but this is your first time and when you give yourself to me . . .' He stopped. 'When we give ourselves to each other, it should be in a bed strewn with rose petals and silk sheets.'

Tears suddenly sprang from her eyes. 'But I don't understand. I've never—'

He lifted his forefinger to her lips. 'You are better than this. Our love is better than this,' he told her. He cupped her face in his hand and wiped away a tear with his thumb. 'Let us wait until the time is right. Not here. Not now.'

'But you still love me?' She needed reassurance.

He nodded. 'It is because I love you so much that I think we should wait. Here,' he said suddenly, reaching for his neck, and looping the chain over his head. 'You see this? This was my mother's. A Saint Christopher.' He put it over her head and laid it on her chest. 'I want you to wear it, as a symbol of our love.'

Lilli looked at it and saw, for the first time, an image of a man with a staff and a small child on his back. 'What . . .?'

'Saint Christopher is the patron saint of travellers,' he explained.

'But Jews don't have saints,' she protested.

'You have good men and women to inspire you. There is no difference.' He kissed the medal. 'It will mean wherever we travel, we will still be together.'

At these words, she kissed the silver medal, too, and he helped her put it on. It lay flat against her chest, just above the cushion of her breasts.

'I will wear it always,' she told him. But deep inside her a seed of dread was planted. Marco was talking about travelling, about leaving her. Did it mean they might soon be parted?

Chapter 19

After that day on the shore Lilli yearned for Marco even more. They saw each other as often as they could. Marco continued to come to the back door of the academy after classes and walked her home when his schedule allowed. They'd been to the cinema again, too, but meeting remained difficult. Kisses were snatched, moments of intimacy stolen. The lies she told her parents continued, but she knew she had to be careful. There were signs that they were beginning to suspect. They were asking more questions about which girlfriends she had seen and where. Then, one night, Leon confirmed what she feared.

The two of them were in their bedroom. Leon sat cross-legged on his bed, reading as Lilli brushed her long, dark hair.

'You're still seeing him, aren't you?' said her brother, looking up from his book to watch her face in the mirror.

Lilli froze for a moment, staring back as she clocked Leon's reflected expression. She turned, narrowing her eyes. 'You've been spying on us,' she growled, pointing her hairbrush at him.

'Not on you,' he replied, unfazed. 'On Mutti and the Ram.'

Lilli thought of Frau Grundig and her scolding tongue that loved nothing better than a good gossip.

'She says she saw you the other night at the cinema with a soldier.'

Lilli felt her stomach roil. 'What did Mutti say?'

'She swore she must be mistaken: that you wouldn't dream of seeing anyone without her permission.'

A shiver pimpled Lilli's skin. Perhaps her luck was running out.

When they couldn't see each other, Lilli and Marco would write. Lilli told Herr Grunfeld that Fraulein Giselle Albrecht was a close friend, who was studying at the academy, but had nowhere permanent to stay during her studies. Any communications for her must therefore be given to Lilli, who would pass them on. Marco's letters were loving and tender. He'd often illustrate them with little sketches or cartoons. Sometimes he'd quote the translated lyrics of an aria. Sometimes there were funny snatches from his days: how his valet had mixed up his uniform in the laundry, or how his commanding officer's horse had reared when a mouse ran onto the parade ground. And always he would tell her how much he loved her. They only made her long for him more.

Lilli's replies were usually accounts of her time at the academy or of her father's health, which seemed to be growing worse. They were so dull compared with Marco's anecdotes. She had decided not to mention the other letters she was receiving, too. Four so far. Unwelcome, vicious ones, full of scorn and vitriol that she'd received over the past two months. She'd even asked Anna Kepler, the annoying girl with the braces, to keep an eye out for the person who delivered them. From her usual vantage point on the stairs, she was well placed to spot the perpetrator. But whoever the author was, they weren't brave enough to drop off their sickening messages in person. An errand boy was always the courier.

Then, one morning, in early summer, just six months after their first meeting, Marco wrote to tell Lilli they had to meet.

'St Peter's Church,' she read aloud. 'Old Peter' everyone called it. She knew the building well, even though she'd never been inside it. Its high tower rose from the centre of the city, like a grand old man amid a sprawling family of shops and houses. It was somewhere far away from Giesing's prying eyes and gossiping tongues. He had something important to tell her, he said. Subconsciously she fingered the Saint Christopher medal she wore hidden under her blouse. The seed of dread that had been sown on the lakeshore a few weeks back stirred once more.

The day had been dull and cloudy, and the night was close. Marco was waiting for her by the main church portico, bathed in a pool of light from a nearby lamp post. Lilli flew into his arms and held him for a moment before stepping back.

'What is it, Marco?' she asked, worried that someone – maybe the author of the sick notes – had reported him to his commanding officer on some false charge. Or, worse still, that he was going away.

Marco gestured to the door, but Lilli hesitated. She had never been into a Christian church before.

'We shall go up the tower,' he explained, taking her hand and leading her to a narrow staircase. She looked at the steps.

'There are only 306,' he said with a wry smile.

Up they climbed, past the historic bells, to the viewpoint. She'd heard that on a fair day you could see the peaks of the Alps from where she stood, but tonight all that was visible were the pinpricks of light that dotted the houses and buildings and their reflections in the River Isar.

'Worth the climb?' he asked her, enfolding her in his arms, as together they looked over the city.

'Yes,' she said, even though she wondered why he hadn't brought her all the way up here during the day. 'But . . .' She turned to face him with questioning eyes.

'They're posting me, Lilli.'

His words slammed into the night air and reverberated.

It was what she'd been dreading most. Even though she knew the day had to come the news felled her as surely as if someone had kicked her hard in the stomach.

106

'Posting you?'

'Yes. To Leipzig.'

Instantly she clamped her arms around his neck and laid her head on his shoulder. 'You can't go. I won't let them take you!'

He prised her arms away from him. 'You know I have to do my duty.'

'Duty.' She spat the word as if it was burning her mouth. In his world, the ugly world of marching and weapons and war, she knew that duty trumped love every time. 'But what shall I do without you?'

His face was solemn and earnest. 'You will write to me every day and I to you. And I will come back on leave. Once or twice a year for a whole two weeks at a stretch,' he told her, but his words were wasted on the air.

It was if the breath had been sucked from her lungs, the blood from her heart, the feeling from her soul. She was empty inside. Until she was with her beloved Marco again, her life would not be worth living. She hid her face in his shoulder and cried. Then came the anger.

'Why did you bring me here, to such a beautiful place, to tell me something so horrible?' she protested. Her fists were balled and suddenly she was pounding his chest.

Marco grabbed her by the wrists. 'I brought you here to tell you something much more important than news of my posting.'

She looked up and frowned. 'What?'

Taking her by the shoulders, he gently turned her around.

'Before I go, I want us to make a promise to each other.'

'A promise?' Her tears had left her confused.

Marco lifted her face to his and clasped her hands to his heart. 'Will you marry me, Lilli Sternberg?'

His words took a moment to register, but as soon as they did her face broke into a smile and, once again, she wrapped her arms around him. 'Yes! Yes! A thousand times yes!' she cried.

Taking both her arms from round his neck, Marco kissed

her tenderly before pulling back. His eyes were now filled with tears, too.

'I don't have a ring right now, but we have the stars. That's why I brought you up here.' He tilted his gaze towards the sky that was a dark, murky grey.

'But there are no stars tonight,' Lilli said, her eyes following his.

He switched back. 'Oh, but there are,' he told her softly. 'There are always stars. It's just that sometimes we can't see them.'

She laid her head on his chest. The coming months carried with them dread and loneliness, but Marco had asked her to be his wife – to stay by his side forever – and that thought, in the days and weeks ahead, she knew, would comfort her through the longest and coldest nights.

Chapter 20

True to his word, Marco wrote every day from Leipzig, telling her about his new barracks, his duties, even what he ate for dinner. His letters went some way to lessen the pain of their separation, but nothing could soothe the dull ache in Lilli's heart. Then, one day, six weeks later, it shattered.

The telegram bearing the crest of the Reichswehr was waiting for her on the sideboard when Lilli arrived home from the academy. Lilli's eye locked onto it. Golda was wringing her hands. Her father looked sombre. They were fearful.

Seizing the telegram, she flew into her bedroom to open it, her body shaking uncontrollably as she tore open the envelope. Marco was wounded, or dead. *No. Please God. No!*

The truth was even harder to bear. In Marco Zeiller, Lilli believed she had found true love – a soul mate. For a few, short magical months after they met at Helene's ball, the lights of Hollywood dimmed by comparison to her dashing young officer. Their love for each other shone so much brighter. She'd even pledged her future to him, been prepared to forsake any dreams of a career for him. She would have given him everything, including her body, in return for his promise of undying love. She was his 'Giselle' and he her 'Duke Albrecht.' That was before he'd been posted to barracks in the east. She'd pined for him. She'd lost her appetite. She could not wait for them to be reunited. She lived for his tender letters which she would pore over for hours on end in secret. So, when this telegram arrived, it came as a bolt from the heavens.

This time Marco's words were ice cold. *I must put my duty to my country before any feelings I may have for you. I wish you happiness, but it must be without me.*

With those few short, bitter words, her world collapsed around her.. The lights went out. The birds stopped singing. Her tears flowed as they'd never flowed before. This was how Giselle suffered when she'd been betrayed by Duke Albrecht. Left alone in her room, her pillows bore the brunt of her punches and she took off her shoes and threw them against the wall in anger. She railed into the air and cursed her own stupidity for believing in Marco. She would never trust a man again. Like Giselle, she would die of a broken heart.

That evening, in her bedroom, Lilli lay on her bed and studied a photograph of Marco she'd taken with his camera shortly after they'd first met. They'd been walking along the river at the *Englischer Garten*. He'd posed for the shot by a bridge. It was so hard to believe that behind that wide smile and those gentle, eyes, so full of light and laughter, lay a heart of a stone. In reality, Captain Marco Zeiller was cold, calculating and callous.

Leon, unable to sleep for her sniffing, came to sit on her bed. Tentatively, he reached out and laid a comforting hand on her arm. After she'd confided in him, he'd often covered for her when she'd been with Marco. He knew just how much the captain meant to her and now he suggested a reason for his apparent cruelty.

'His commanding officer will have ordered him to do it,' he told her, patting her arm as he spoke. 'You're a Jew.'

She lifted her gaze to his. For a moment his words stemmed her tears. She thought of von Stockmar's insults, of the hateful notes, possibly even penned by him, and realised her brother was probably right. Marco had declared his undying love for her in his previous letter. And he'd proposed marriage on the top of St Peter's tower!

'You're right,' she replied, sitting up. 'For him to have changed so much, there must have been someone putting pressure on him.'

Leon nodded. 'It could be.'

Lilli scowled. 'But a telegram. Not even a letter!' She threw her hands up in despair. The way Marco had broken off their affair was cowardly, even if he had been instructed to end it by his superiors. 'I will write to him,' she announced after a moment.

'You're not going to beg him to take you back?' Leon's voice was scratchy.

She shook her head. 'No. I will write to him to satisfy myself that this is what he truly wants.'

If it was, then she would show him. She would show everyone that she was stronger and better and braver than any cowardly man.

Choking back the tears that threatened once more, Lilli lifted her gaze to the poster of Greta Garbo above her bed. Her screen idol was her own woman: enigmatic, alluring and aloof. Garbo didn't need a man in her life and nor did she. If Marco had forsaken her, she could still reprise her dreams of Hollywood. Lilli Sternberg was going to be a star, and she would make it on her own.

Chapter 21

I must put my duty to my country before any feelings I may have for you. The words of Marco's telegram played themselves over and over in her head and bounced around her brain. Almost three weeks had passed since she'd written to him in Leipzig, asking if he really meant what was said in the telegram. There was still no reply.

The candle of hope that Leon handed her – that Marco's commanding officer must've forbidden any liaisons with Jews – was now snuffed out. Reality was dawning. Her brother's suggestion had only made her chase rainbows. Marco Zeiller's charm had masked his true self. He was heartless and brutal and he'd stop at nothing to rise through the ranks in his division. The way he'd broken off their affair made him a coward, too. His was not the behaviour of an officer, but a deserter.

The week had passed in a blur but somehow she'd managed to claw her way through lessons at the academy. After classes, on that particular afternoon, Lilli returned to the changing rooms to find Helene loitering in the shadows. Was she waiting for her? The pair hadn't spoken since the comtesse had ended their friendship a few weeks before.

For a moment their eyes locked, but neither said a word as

Lilli proceeded to change her clothes. But seeing Helene brought back memories of the ball and of Marco. Try as she did to hold them back, the floodgates opened. Helene watched her erstwhile friend's shoulders heave in a sob before approaching her.

'What is it?' she asked softly.

Lilli, sitting on the bench, looked straight ahead, choking back her tears. 'Nothing. It's nothing,' she snarled, tearing out her clips so that her long hair hung loosely over her shoulders.

Helene paused, then returned to her own locker and resumed changing out of her leotard.

'I'm sorry,' Lilli called over after a moment. She stood to slip into her skirt. 'I shouldn't have snapped at you like that. It's, well . . .'

'It's Captain Zeiller, isn't it?' Helene's voice was measured as she approached once more.

Lilli, her cheeks wet with tears, squinted at her as she moved out of the shadows. 'How do you know? Did your father tell you?'

Helene gave a little shrug, but remained impassive. 'It's probably for the best,' she said, turning away.

If her words were designed to anger, they succeeded. Reaching out, Lilli grabbed hold of her shoulder and pulled her round hard, so they now faced each other. 'For the best? Whose best?' she roared. 'Not for mine and that's for sure.'

In a rage she flung open her locker door, threw down her outdoor shoes and stamped them on. 'Why must everyone interfere? Just keep out of my affairs, will you?' she shouted at Helene, as she grabbed her bag. Then, wrestling with her jacket, she stalked out into the darkness and slammed the door behind her.

Lilli couldn't see him at first. Perhaps it was her fury that still blinded her as she barged out of the studio's back door. She was angry with Marco and with Helene, but above all with herself for being played for a fool.

The night was cold and the chill caught the back of her throat as she took her first breath. Just as she did, she heard a noise.

A rat, perhaps? She stopped in her tracks. Footsteps? There was someone in the shadows.

'Who's there?' she called, her heart drumming in her chest. 'Anyone?' she asked.

Smoothing her jacket, she took a few paces down the side steps. A gust of wind suddenly seized hold of a discarded beer bottle, sending it clinking along the cobbles to land nearby in the pool of dim light from an overhead lamp. Her unease remained.

'Who's there?' she called again.

This time, from out of the shadows, stepped a figure – a figure in uniform. Her heart missed a beat.

'Marco? Marco, is that you?'

He hadn't sent that telegram after all. He'd been made to do it. He'd come to explain; to sweep her off her feet and take her away from all this. He loved her with all his might. She stepped forward cautiously, readying herself to dive into his arms. But instead of Marco's soft, lyrical voice, she heard another.

'Lilli Sternberg.' No, it wasn't Marcò, yet the tone was vaguely familiar.

As the figure emerged into the dim light of the alley, she could make out the small, broad frame of a man dressed in uniform with a long scar on his face. Suddenly she realised it was Kurt von Stockmar.

'I thought this was where I might find you,' he told her, coming closer, but still in silhouette.

The tide of disappointment that had rushed over her, was suddenly replaced by an incoming fear.

'Captain von Stockmar,' she said nervously. 'What are you doing here?'

'I imagined you might need comforting.' He emerged from the gloom, but his eyes remained in shadow under the peak of his cap.

'Comforting?' Lilli's brows knotted. 'I don't understand.'

She saw his lips tighten into a smirk. The light caught the scar on his cheek, turning it into a slash of silver. He started to circle her.

'I heard that you've been discarded.'

'Discarded? What do you mean?' The thought of Marco's telegram reared itself and the bile rose in her stomach. She turned to follow his gaze, as if dancing a dangerous pas de deux.

He moved closer again, so that now he was entirely drenched in the light from the lamp above the door. 'I heard,' he said, in a half whisper, 'that he's got rid of you.'

'Rid of me?' she repeated. The phrase was harsh, pitiless.

'Yes, rid of you,' he repeated, adding, 'like the piece of Jewish trash you are.'

Suddenly Lilli knew for certain what she'd suspected before. 'Those letters!' she cried. 'You—' But before she could say anything else von Stockmar lunged towards her. Any fear that she felt a moment ago quickly turned to fury. Her arm shot up to strike, knocking off his cap. He reacted quickly, grabbing her wrist in mid-air and twisting it behind her back. When he thrust his sneering face close to hers, she could see fire in his eyes.

'Don't play with me!' he growled. Clamping her chin in the vice of his hand, his fingers worked to open her lips. She tried to bite him but failed. She could barely breathe, let alone cry out for him to stop. Shaking her head from side to side, she pummelled his back with her free fist. It was no use. He seemed possessed.

Her hair fell over her face, blinding her for a moment, as he began grabbing at her jacket buttons. A moment later he was clawing at her skirt, trying to thrust his free hand between her thighs. The other hand he clamped over her mouth, pressing her skull against the brick wall.

'I'll teach you a lesson,' he hissed. As he moved closer, she saw the pulse at the base of his throat, throbbing fast.

Lilli's eyes filled with hot tears. She knew what he wanted to do, but she wouldn't give in. Swallowing down the red rage that threatened to overwhelm her, she started kicking. She kicked his shins as hard as she could and he cried out, releasing his hand from her face. As he leapt back, he sent a dustbin flying down the alley.

The clatter raised the alarm. From by the studio door a startled scream split the night air, then a voice. 'Who's there?' Someone was calling out in the darkness.

Von Stockmar froze then panicked. 'You stupid whore!' he yelled, striking Lilli hard across the face.

'Who's there?' came the voice again, only nearer.

Von Stockmar bent down to pick up his cap, then turned and broke into a run down the alley.

Exhausted, Lilli slid down the wall, clutching her face as it pulsed with pain. Something was trickling down over her lips. She put her hand to her mouth and saw a ribbon of blood on her fingers.

A second later she heard another cry, followed by footsteps echoing along the alley.

'Lilli!' It was Helene, crouching down at her side. She gasped in horror.

'Oh my God! Did he . . .?'

Through the tears and the blood Lilli managed a few words. 'No. No, he did not.'

'Let's get you inside,' Helene coaxed, looping her arm under Lilli's to help her up.

Lilli said nothing about her attacker's identity. No one could know. Her parents could never find out the reason for the assault. But as Helene helped her clean up her wounds that night – all trace of acrimony seemingly gone – Lilli knew that although von Stockmar may not have violated her literally, his attack made her feel valueless and humiliated. It stripped her of any vestige of dignity or self-esteem that remained to her after Marco had so cruelly broken off their romance. Her life was no longer worth living. Not in Germany, at any rate. Here, she was just a poor Jew, someone to be despised and shunned.

Suddenly she was reminded of the conversation she'd had with

Marco on that day by the lake that she'd never wanted to end. After she'd eaten the pork bratwurst, forbidden by her religion, she'd opened up about being Jewish in Germany. 'It's like I was born with a label round my neck that says *JUDEN* in big letters,' she'd told him.

In the still blackness of the dirty alley that night, von Stockmar had made her realise she couldn't rely on anyone else to help her break the chains that shackled her to this dismal existence. She, and she alone, had the power to change her life for ever. And that was precisely what she vowed she would do.

Chapter 22

Lilli stood on the side of the lake in the *Englischer Garten*. It was a warm afternoon in late September and half a dozen young boys, watched by their mothers, were making the most of the summer's last hoorah, paddling in the shallow water. One of them had made a little boat from folded newspaper. When he launched it, it floated for a few seconds, then another child made a well-targeted splash and it keeled over. The little boy cried.

Life can be so cruel, Lilli thought. She recalled the carefree times she'd spent in the park with Marco: listening to the band, taking photographs of each other, how he'd gently wiped the whipped cream from under her nose. How could he have ended it all so brutally?

After the night of von Stockmar's attack, Lilli felt she had no reason to stay in Munich and every reason to leave. In vain she'd waited for Marco to reply to her letter asking if he was breaking their affair of his own free will. But he never did. He had betrayed her love, so she erected a fence, protecting herself from any friendships that might distract her from her goal. She ignored other pupils at the academy, including Helene, and barely communicated with her worried parents and Leon. Despite Golda's best efforts, she would not open up to her mother, focusing all her energy instead on her dance – her passport to freedom.

When, less than four weeks later, Monsieur Raymond, the talent scout from the American agency, who'd seen her in *Giselle*, came to watch her perform at the academy's summer show, he'd offered her a contract in Vaudeville. There'd been no hesitation. It didn't matter that she would be on the stage and not on the screen. It would be in America.

Standing by the lake, she held the Saint Christopher medal and began turning it over in her palm. It was the last vestige of Marco that she had. She'd burned all his letters and cried over the telegram so many times that the paper had disintegrated. Taking a deep breath, she gave the medal a final glance before slanting it and flinging it, like a skimming stone, like the pebbles she and Marco had thrown together, out into the deeper water. It plashed twice on the surface then sank, sending out ripples across the water for a few seconds. Then calm.

The little boy with the sunken paper boat was being comforted by his mother, but Lilli was sure the best way to heal her own broken heart was to escape. She needed to free herself from her family's suffocating love, get away from the prejudice she'd encountered for being a Jew, and, above all, achieve her dreams as a star. There was only one thing for it. She would leave Germany and head for the bright lights of the United States.

On a cold day in November, under a leaden sky, she said her farewells at Munich railway station.

'We will miss you, *Liebling*,' sobbed Golda, hugging her daughter one more lingering time.

Her mother had baked her some *lebkuchen* for the journey and Frau Kepler had knitted a pair of socks because, she warned, in some parts of America it could get colder than the Alps. Jacob had recited a blessing upon her before they left the apartment but Leon, as always, had dropped back from the flurry.

As they all stood on the platform, waiting for Lilli to board, Golda's loose tears kept escaping and Jacob shook his head in quiet disbelief. Seeing her parents so sorrowful made Lilli unhappy, but she knew if she said what she felt, her own heart would break in two and the train would leave without her. For the past few months she'd managed to put a distance between herself and her family, thinking only of the hurt her parents had caused her over Marco. She could no longer allow herself to be sucked in by the over-protective love that couldn't see beyond its own prejudice. She found it difficult to forgive them for the way they'd treated Marco and her unwillingness to do so made it easier for her to leave. Now, more than ever, she had to be strong for herself. She hardened her heart.

'Goodbye,' was all she said as she climbed aboard. Leon went ahead of her, carrying her battered suitcase. They both squeezed their way along the narrow corridor into the designated carriage and Leon heaved her luggage onto the overhead rack. Turning to face his sister, his brown eyes suddenly widened as he grabbed hold of both Lilli's hands.

'I wish I could come with you,' he told her. It was the first time he had expressed his own feelings about her departure. Lilli was momentarily stunned.

'One day,' she told him, floundering for a reply. 'When I have found my feet, you'll join me,' she heard herself say, even though she wasn't sure if she could deliver on such a promise. 'Look after yourself, Leon,' she added, her voice beginning to crack.

'I will,' he replied, squeezing her hand tightly just as the guard blew the whistle. It was the signal the train was about to depart and Leon turned to leave the carriage.

Lilli watched him go, the weight of her guilt pulling her down. She was doing the right thing, wasn't she? She was young. She needed to live. Brushing away a wayward tear, she checked her ticket. The reservation put her between a middle-aged woman in sensible shoes, who was reading a novel, and an elderly man with a songbird in a crate on his knee.

When, a moment later, she stood to look out of the window to see her family clustered below, she felt the train jolt. A cloud of steam suddenly enveloped the platform, dissolving the outlines of her parents, making them disappear. Leon, however, broke free and started to run alongside the carriage as it pulled away, his long arms failing like windmills, battling against the steam. For a moment she even thought he might catch up and jump aboard. He seemed to be gathering speed. She laid her palm flat on the carriage window and held her breath. But soon the platform petered out and with it, the sight of her brother. Slowly exhaling, she settled herself down in a seat that she had chosen carefully. It was facing forward, not backward. Her new life was about to begin.

Chapter 23

New York, America

1933

It was a languid late afternoon and Lilli had just taken a shower in the bathroom of her rented Manhattan apartment when her cream-coloured Bakelite phone rang. Securing her wet hair, now dyed blonde, under a turban and wearing nothing but a towel, she went to the bedroom to answer it.

Over the past two years her memories of Giesing had started to fade. But in quieter moments, away from the grease paint and the glaring footlights, Lilli's thoughts of home and for what might have been with Marco still lingered. The guilt, too. Every time she received a letter from Golda or heard a German accent or even ate a bagel, she felt homesick. But the feeling never lasted long.

She sat down on the king-size bed and glanced at the framed photograph of her in the arms of the fabulous Fred Astaire. It was a still from the show they'd just done together in London and on Broadway, *The Band Wagon*. She lifted the receiver to her ear to hear a familiar voice on the other end of the line.

'Lillian darling, it's Jessica.'

'Hello Jessica.' She crossed her legs, still damp from the shower, knowing this could be a long conversation.

'I've just had this fabulous idea, which I simply had to share.'

Lilli smiled as she took off the turban and shook down her hair, letting it fall over the top her shoulders. She had grown fond of Jessica's unfettered exuberance. 'Then please do,' she said, intrigued.

'You know how I love you and Fred.' Jessica paused to await a reaction.

'Yes,' Lilli obliged.

'And you know I think you're the best dancers ever.'

'Yes.' Her friend was always so – what was it the Americans said? – *over the top*. Lilli continued to towel her hair.

'So, I thought you're already a great team on Broadway, why not Hollywood?'

Lilli shifted the telephone receiver from one ear to the other. This was getting interesting. 'Well, I . . .'

But Jessica was in a hurry. There was no time for false modesty in her world.

'So, I've invited some big Hollywood producers over for a drink at our place next month to introduce them to you and Fred.'

Dancing with Fred Astaire was like nothing Lilli had ever experienced before, like stepping out with Peter Pan. He was light and graceful, and a perfectionist, too. His sister and former partner, Adele, had been a hard act to follow, but once they'd ironed out a few teething problems, she and Fred were dancing together like they were joined at the hip. When he'd been contacted by Hollywood for a movie called *The Princess and the Porter*, he'd recommended her for the part of the princess in the classic uptown girl meets downtown boy story. But there was still all to play for.

'You have?!' said Lilli.

'Everyone knows that your two-bit agent has more interest in a client by the name of Jack Daniels than in you,' retorted Jessica.

Victor Selig was the name of Lilli's agent. Big and brash as a neon sign on Broadway, he smoked Cuban cigars like they were cigarettes and wore plaid suits so garish they made you feel queasy. Teaming her up with another dancer straight off the boat from Germany had been his idea. Tap and singing lessons seemed to do the trick and the double act – *Lulu and Lilli, the Dancing Lovelies*, toured the Vaudeville circuit for six months. Forced to settle for third place billing behind an axe thrower called Chief Redskin and an Al Jolson impersonator, she and her partner Lulu played five matinees a week for six dollars a time. Reviews, when they came, appeared in second-rate newspapers that few read. They were often mixed, but Lilli was always singled out as 'the classy one.' That's how, thanks to Victor, she'd signed a lucrative contract to appear in a lavish Broadway musical. Since then, she'd coloured her hair blonde, taken up smoking Turkish cigarettes – 'They make your voice sound so sexy,' advised Victor – and ditched her real name. 'Sternberg's too Jewish' he'd declared. So although it had been a while coming, 'the fabulous dancer *extraordinaire*', as *Variety* magazine called her, Miss Lillian Stern, had become a star on Broadway.

What Jessica said was true. Victor set her on the right road at the start of her career on Broadway, but her success seemed to have gone to his head, along with the liquor he drank. There was no harm in Jessica moving things on a little with her famous powers of persuasion.

'That sounds good. No,' Lilli corrected herself. 'Amazing. Thank you, Jessica,' she said.

'I'll drop you a line with all the details,' Jessica had said and so that is how, two weeks later, Lilli found herself with Fred Astaire at her side on her way to the Van Haselts' bash in their honour on Long Island.

Long Island lay stretched out before them like a lazy cat basking in the sunshine. Behind them Manhattan's dark towers and spires shimmered in the heat, but a cool breeze from the river fanned Lilli's face. A long silk scarf kept her hair – now worn in soft waves – in place as she sat in the passenger seat of the red roadster. Fred, at the wheel, was wearing shades, so Lilli found it hard to read his mood, but she could tell the news that Adele had lost her first child had hit him hard.

Lilli owed a lot to Adele, or Dellie, as her friends called her. Everyone loved her outrageous and flirtatious nature. Until her marriage she'd been one of the biggest stars in the Broadway firmament. She'd even taught the Prince of Wales to tap dance.

They were driving across Queensboro Bridge, heading for Jessica Van Haselt's luxurious mansion, shared with her industrialist husband Vincent, in Southampton Village. Lilli had met the eccentric millionairess, or rather been engulfed by her when Adele married an English aristocrat by the name of Lord Charles Cavendish at a ceremony at a magnificent stately home called Chatsworth House.

Jessica was a ferociously dynamic woman. Lilli recalled their introduction. 'Is that a *Ger*-man accent, I detect?' she'd asked loudly.

Lilli had nodded. She'd been working hard trying to lose it and suddenly felt like some exotic novelty.

Nevertheless, Jessica Van Haselt had simply flapped a bejewelled hand in the air. 'Well, well! My husband is Dutch, so we're virtually related!' she'd remarked, before adding cheerfully: 'And the British royal family is practically German, as I'm sure you know!'

The Van Haselts' 'little get-together for our dear friends,' to most everyone else, translated as a lavish casting party. The couple were great patrons of Broadway and on first-name terms with every theatre producer, not to mention godparents to several of their offspring.

The whole event was carefully choreographed. Jessica had even suggested Lilli wear an emerald-green ensemble and loaned her a pair of diamond and emerald earrings 'to make your eyes look even bigger,' she'd said.

Lilli and Fred's arrival had been planned for maximum impact, too. Some of the guests had bagged prime positions on the first-floor balcony at the front of the mansion, awaiting their entrance. The Washington Masons, the Trumpshaws from Santa Fe and the Krugers were there. They'd all seen Fred and Lilli on Broadway and had travelled specially for the party.

A cheer went up as the roadster turned through the gates and crunched to a halt on the gravel drive. Dozens of pairs of eyes were trained on the star arrivals from above. Lilli lifted her gaze to the balcony and waved.

'They're treating us like royalty,' she mumbled to Fred through clenched teeth as he helped her out of the sports car.

'Crazy, huh?' he said, flashing one of his debonair smiles before pivoting to salute the waiting guests. Another cheer rose into the sultry air.

Jessica suddenly appeared at the front entrance to greet them both, looking resplendent in a yellow chiffon creation.

'Welcome, dear friends,' she cried with outstretched arms. 'Everyone is just dying to meet you.'

Lilli and Fred were led through to the terrace at the back of the house, where the party appeared to be in full swing. A waiter handed them glasses of champagne.

'Love your moves, Mr Astaire,' called out one guest.

'Such a superb dancer,' commented his wife to Lilli as she passed by.

'The Connecticut Wilsons,' explained Jessica, as if that should mean something to her.

'Miss Stern!' Someone else shouted her name and Lilli looked up, only to be snapped by a photographer. 'And another, if you please.'

Both she and Fred smiled and nodded graciously. Fred played his part well, despite not really being in the mood to deal with banalities, while Lilli, assisted by the champagne, managed to keep up appearances. She even signed her autograph for eager fans.

'You're my wife's favourite,' said a man, whose buttonhole carnation was drooping in the heat, as he thrust out a card for her to sign.

'I'm so glad,' replied Lilli, forcing a smile, aware of Jessica hovering behind. It was evident that Jessica was keen for her star couple to 'meet the men that matter,' as she put it.

Servants with silver platters of canapés wove in and out of little knots of people. The women wore flimsy floral frocks, while the men were in lounge suits or blazers. Lilli noted that the older men all seemed to be accompanied by women half their age and at a quarter their waist size.

The sun was beating down on the lawn and large parasols had been strategically placed over the tables and chairs that dotted the grass. Under a gazebo a four-piece band was playing a medley of show tunes from Broadway musicals. Several guests had sought the shade and women were fanning themselves with napkins, while some men had even abandoned their jackets.

Lilli noticed that one of them, smouldering in his striped boating blazer with ivory slacks, looked familiar. He looked every inch an Englishman. She thought she might have met him at Adele's wedding last year and leaned over to Jessica.

'Is that . . .?'

Lilli's hostess's face lit up as the slender gentleman approached, looking slightly lost, and with his fair fringe flopping over his left eye.

'Ah, the Honourable James Marchington,' she replied, a little too quickly to convince Lilli that she had not engineered a meeting. 'Did I not mention he'd be here?' she asked disingenuously, pressing her heavily jewelled hand to her breast.

'No,' replied Lilli, remembering his disastrous attempt at conversation. They'd drunk champagne on the terrace at Chatsworth House and talked about the topiary. He didn't look at ease in this sort of social setting. More like a rabbi at a rodeo, mused Lilli. 'No, you did not,' she said.

They'd been introduced to each other by Gwendoline, Adele's good friend and James's sister. Tall and thin, with hair just a shade darker than Lilli's bottled blonde, James's fringe kept flopping over his narrow face and he kept pushing it back with an immaculate hand.

Jessica's carmined lips twitched. 'You two really are star-crossed lovers, you know,' she said with a wink. Then before Lilli could protest that they really weren't, she heard her hostess hailing her handsome guest.

'James, darling, over here!' she cried, beckoning him with a wide, circular movement of her arm.

There was no escaping. Jessica Van Haselt's voice carried over the hum of conversation and even the quartet's rendition of a Cole Porter number. James Marchington's attention was caught and he self-consciously obeyed his hostess's command.

'Here he is,' announced Jessica, putting a maternal arm around James as he stopped beside her.

Lilli could see he was rather embarrassed at their hostess's gushing familiarity. Although she had grown used to the exuberance of the theatrical community, even she could see that some people might find Jessica a little overpowering.

'He's here on an art-buying trip, aren't you, darling?' she continued, clutching the young man to her large breast.

James nodded unsmilingly, while at the same time managing to extricate himself from Jessica's grasp.

Lilli came to his rescue. 'So, you are an art dealer, Mr Marchington.'

'Yes,' replied James, taciturnly.

'He sees art in everything, don't you darling?' commented Jessica.

James shrugged. 'I suppose it's true. I do.'

'And what do you see in Lillian?' asked Jessica, playfully.

Turning to Lilli, James held her gaze.

'Degas,' he replied after a moment's thought. 'I see a Degas ballerina.'

'Ah, how romantic,' commented an enraptured Jessica, clasping her hands together across her camisole top. 'What did I tell you, Lillian? Star-crossed lovers you surely are.'

Before the situation could become any more embarrassing for Lilli, however, a man with a shoe-lace necktie, caught Jessica's eye. He was signalling to her from the other side of the lawn.

'I'm so sorry, I'm going to have to break-up this romantic reunion,' she said, taking Lilli by the arm. 'You and Fred are needed, my dear,' she explained.

'Another time,' said James with a shallow bow. Lilli couldn't help but notice he looked slightly relieved at the prospect of being left alone. She was rather wishing she could be, too.

'Yes. Goodbye Mr Marchington,' she said, as she was led off towards a secluded corner of the garden.

Fred was already there, seated at a large, shaded table, screened by a high box-hedge. Victor Selig, Lilli's agent, had insisted on an invitation. He spilled over the sides of a chair, his big cigar clamped between his jaws. He sat alongside three other men. Lilli recognised one of them as Fred's agent, Leland Hayward, but the other two were unfamiliar. They all rose when she and Jessica arrived.

'Gentlemen, this is the lovely Miss Lillian Stern,' Victor introduced her.

Lilli nodded and smiled, but inside, nerves fluttered in her stomach.

'And these gentlemen here,' he continued, 'are Mr Chas Borowitz and Mr Bertram B. Lewis from KLO Studios in Hollywood.' Lilli felt her pulse race at the very mention of the place of her dreams. Could this really be happening? 'They've seen you and Fred on Broadway and they'd like to sign you up for a film.'

Lilli had had rave reviews on Broadway, of course, but with half a million dollars riding on the project, the studio would still be taking a big box-office risk. She really couldn't remember much that was said around the table from then on. That same feeling she'd experienced on the stage at the Cuvilliés returned. She had risen from out of her body and was looking at things from above. Words like 'contract' and 'money' and 'release' swirled around but they meant nothing to her. This was the moment she'd longed for all of her life. She wanted to capture it like a photograph and keep it forever. And, as if on cue, just then the man with the camera seemed to appear from nowhere.

'Let's record this for posterity, shall we?' suggested Victor, when hands had been shaken and the deal agreed, in principal at least.

So they bunched together in that shaded nook. Lilli Sternberg was at the centre, next to Fred. Both were flanked by producers and agents. The photographer, his camera on a tripod this time, asked them all to smile. They were all so busy posing, basking in the moment, that no one noticed behind the box hedge, James Marchington was watching the proceedings. Just like the photograph being taken for the record, in his mind an idea was developing.

Chapter 24

Côte d'Azur, France

1934

As well as a home on Long Island, the Van Haselts also had a villa in the south of France. Lilli was sitting on a bench in its grounds, serenaded by cicadas and swathed in an emerald silk evening gown. Jessica had first raised the prospect of a French *séjour* while Lilli had been working twenty hours a day on *The Princess and the Porter*. Now was her chance to recover from the gruelling film schedule that had just wrapped up in Hollywood. Off set, she also thought more about her family.

She read Leon's letter again. It had arrived just before she'd set sail for Europe and it troubled her. Her brother communicated very infrequently and had long ago given up begging to join her. But while her mother's letters often focused on life's domestic hardships – on repairing garments to make ends meet, on Frau Weber's arthritis or the mice in the skirting boards – his words were always more serious and often about politics. One paragraph in particular shocked Lilli.

Our lives, dear sister, are growing harder by the day. Jewish doctors, editors, civil servants and barristers are being barred from practising their professions. I fear my studies are in doubt.

'Lillian!' a loud voice broke through Lilli's thoughts. Quickly she folded Leon's letter and returned it to her evening purse. It was going to have to be one of those things she would continue thinking about, but later. Right now, Herr Hitler's Germany was a world away. Tonight she would do her best to enjoy the luxury she'd come to relish over the past few years.

Lilli rose and smiled.

'So, are we ready?' asked Jessica Van Haselt, a blue silk evening gown draping her bulky body. She glanced over at the Rolls Royce parked in the drive. 'Can't keep His Royal Highness waiting, can we?' she added in a feigned English accent.

'No, we can't,' Lilli replied walking slowly to the waiting limousine. Since she'd finished filming with Fred her foot had caused her much concern. Each time she put weight on it, a pain shot up her leg.

'Still sore?' asked Jessica, noting her guest's slow progress.

'It'll be fine with a little rest. It's nothing' she replied, even though she knew it wasn't nothing. By any stretch of the imagination.

Fred was a perfectionist. She'd done her best to match him, but an old injury had reoccurred and she'd ruptured a ligament in her foot. Lilli's consultant advised rest for at least three weeks, so while the film was in the editing suite for the next two months, a short vacation in the south of France couldn't have been timed better.

Forced to swap her usual high heels for blocky pumps, Lilli hoped her full-length gown would cloak the fashion faux pas. It hurt her to walk but, as ever, she remembered *to dance through the pain.*

It was the first time Lilli had returned to the Continent since she'd set sail for New York with her suitcase full of dreams three years before. En-route, she'd stopped off in London to do an interview for *Tatler* magazine and dined with Adele and her husband Charles at the Ritz. Munich now seemed a lifetime away. Naturally she missed her parents and wrote to them regularly, sending them money. Leon, too; the image of him running along the train platform, yearning to escape with her, would stay with her forever. She'd promised to visit them several months ago. For the first two years she hadn't been able to afford the fare home, but now that she did have the money, she had no excuse. After France, the next stop would be Munich. It would be a surprise visit. That way she would spare her mother all the inevitable cooking and cleaning. She would also be able to see for herself how her parents and Leon were faring and what was really going on with the new government.

It seemed that all wealthy English and Americans took villas in the south of France in August: the Washington Trumpshaws, the Virginian Johnsons and, new on the scene the Baltimore Simpsons, Ernest and Wallis, who appeared to be particular friends with the Prince of Wales. And, of course, there was James Marchington, the art dealer and the second son of the Earl of Lindsey who, it seemed, had an invitation to every society occasion.

Lilli could see why Jessica had a particularly soft spot for him. She had to admit that she, too, found him attractive with his fine, aristocratic nose and his soft blue eyes fringed by long lashes. He was clearly in demand in upper crust social circles, although she'd never heard his name linked romantically to any of the society beauties so often pictured with him in the press.

Villa Mauresque was the retreat of the English writer William Somerset Maugham. Lilli considered it an impressive building, yet not so grand as to prevent an old mongrel sleeping fitfully on the front step. On arrival she and Jessica – whose husband was away on business in Milan – were greeted by a butler. Green shutters and purple bougainvillea garlanded terracotta walls that glowed in the setting sun. They were led onto a terrace surrounded by tuberoses and oleanders. The strains of '*Ain't Misbehavin*'' wafted up from a gramophone, as stewards offered round white lady cocktails in long-stemmed glasses and tiny canapés of smoked salmon and caviar.

'Jessica, darling, welcome to the Villa Mauresque,' came a voice from behind them. Lilli turned to see an older man with a wrinkled face. His hooded lids made him appear to be continually squinting at the sun. It was Willie Maugham. 'I'm so delighted you were able to c . . . c . . . come,' he stammered, kissing her on both cheeks. His wife, Syrie, was fussing over foie gras nearby.

'Willie, darling, it's so wonderful to see you again,' Jessica replied, offering her hand for him to kiss. 'And this is Miss Lillian Stern,' she told him.

'Ah, yes. The fabulous dancer,' he exclaimed, taking Lilli's hand. 'Oh, m . . . my dear I heard about your film,' he told her. 'How exciting.'

Before she could respond to this introduction, the butler reappeared and announced the rest of the guests. James Marchington arrived with Gwendoline on his arm. Like her brother, she was slender but with wiry, copper-coloured hair and freckled skin. A few paces behind them followed another couple; a military man by his posture, with a pencil moustache and a stick-thin woman. The woman's dark brown braids were coiled just above enormous gold earrings that accentuated her determined jaw. For an instant Lilli was reminded of the Ram, back in Munich.

Jessica's lips lifted in a wicked smile. 'Wallis Simpson,' she muttered mischievously to Lilli, her eyes darting from her fellow American to the Prince of Wales.

Lilli studied the woman intently. So this was the famous socialite, the latest married woman who'd reportedly caught the future king of England's interest. There'd been speculation in the American press about their relationship and here, right in front of her, thought Lilli, was fuel to stoke the flames of scandal.

'Come, let's say hello to David before *she* gets her claws into him for the evening,' said Jessica. David was how close friends addressed the heir apparent. Suddenly Lilli was being taken by the arm and shepherded towards the prince who was looking every bit as debonair as he always did in the newspapers. Slicing her way into the conversation with the practised precision of a surgeon, Jessica waited until the prince had drawn polite laughter from the couple he was regaling then spoke. 'David, how wonderful to see you and how well you look,' she greeted him.

The prince, his skin a dusky bronze against the white of his stiff evening shirt, smiled broadly. 'The climate agrees with me, dear Jessica,' he replied, kissing his friend on both cheeks. 'And of course the Riviera beats bloody Balmoral any day!' His audience chorused its approval, as his eyes settled on Lilli.

'This is Lillian Stern. She's Fred Astaire's dance partner,' said Jessica gleefully.

'How do you do, Miss Stern?' greeted the prince, quick to take Lilli's hand to kiss. 'Stern – that's German for star, which you most surely are,' he said with a disarming smile. 'I saw you on stage.'

Jessica rolled her heavily mascaraed eyes. 'Oh, David, you really are such a terrible flirt.'

Lilli gave him a smouldering smile; one she had perfected during hours spent in front of the camera.

'Adele was very hard act to follow, sir,' she replied, trotting out a regular phrase.

The prince's gaze remained on her. 'Indeed, Miss Stern' he agreed. 'But you brought something fresh and exciting to the role.' His lips twitched. 'And I very much look forward to seeing your film. I'm sure it'll be a tremendous success.'

Lilli was about to reply when the prince broke off suddenly. 'Now if you'll excuse me . . .' She did not need to turn to see who had won in the war for his attention.

'What did I tell you?' murmured Jessica from the corner of her mouth. Together they watched as the heir to the British throne hurried over to greet Wallis Simpson. As his eyes lingered on her face, it was clear for all to see he was besotted. Jessica nodded. 'Hook, line and sinker!'

They dined outside as a small jazz band played. The scent of lavender hung in the air. Lilli was seated next to James, whether by accident or design she wasn't sure. He had sought her out just as dinner was announced and she'd found they were next to each other on the seating plan.

'So you've just finished your first picture with Fred, I believe, Miss Stern,' he said, unfurling his napkin and laying it on his knee. 'I keep up to date with all the Hollywood gossip. A lot of my clients are in film, you see,' he explained with a wry smile.

'I see,' replied Lilli, already distracted. True, James was easy on the eye, but she found the interplay between Wallis Simpson and the Prince of Wales on the opposite side of the dining table far more interesting.

During the meal the wine flowed freely and the atmosphere was very convivial until, that is, just before dessert when the conversation turned to Germany. Without warning, the prince called Lilli out across the dinner table.

'You are German, Miss Stern,' he remarked suddenly and in such a loud voice that the rest of the guests stopped talking immediately. 'You must have an opinion of Herr Hitler?' he asked. 'Or should I call him the Führer?' A polite titter rippled around the table

All eyes were upon Lilli, as if she had suddenly become a curiosity. She paused for a moment. German domestic politics were a matter she preferred not to think about; it was the sort of thing she'd spent most of her younger years trying to escape. But now it was becoming harder, especially since Herr Hitler and his National Socialist Party had come to power the previous year and after Leon's most recent letter. Before she'd often dismissed his rants, given that her bookish brother had always fought against authority of any kind. Her opinions were certainly shifting, but now, she told herself, was not the time to enter into a serious discussion. Instead she decided to make light of the question.

'I hear the fairer sex finds him most attractive,' she replied in her husky voice. Her response prompted more laughter.

'My dear Miss Stern,' the prince told her with a smile, dropping his napkin on the table as he spoke, 'sometimes one needs to think of the greater good. I believe, for example, that unemployment is down in Germany and that there is better housing for the poor.'

'All those military rallies and salutes sound a bit much to me, old chap,' ventured Ernest Simpson, aping an English upper-class accent. 'No one wants another war.'

'War?' repeated the prince indignantly, tugging at his bow tie. 'Who's talking about war? Herr Hitler is a peace-loving man.'

The conversation suddenly became slightly heated.

'But the National Socialists' laws against Jews are surely far too repressive?' After barely saying a word all evening, James Marchington suddenly weighed into the fray.

Lilli had noticed that as soon as Hitler's name was mentioned, his expression had darkened. 'And I fear that so far, the Reich Chancellor has demonstrated a complete disrespect for democracy,' he added.

The prince arched a brow and, sensing the political temperature was rising, Syrie, ever the perfect hostess, suggested the ladies withdraw from the table. They would leave the men with their port and cigars while they adjourned inside to the drawing room.

'Time to retreat, ladies,' she ordered.

Chapter 25

The drawing room at the Villa Mauresque was large and airy with Impressionist paintings hanging on white walls. An interior designer by profession – that was how she'd met Wallis Simpson while styling her London apartment – Syrie's taste was quite impeccable. Lilli noted there were books in every recess and above the stone fireplace sat a gilt-carved wooden eagle that reminded her, ironically, of the symbol of the Nazi Party.

Lilli seated herself next to Gwendoline on one side and Jessica on the other. On the opposite sofa sat Mrs Trumpshaw and Mrs Johnson, while Syrie and Wallis opted for a high-backed chairs nearby.

The stewards poured coffee and offered round chocolate mints, but Lilli detected a distinct sense of unease among her fellow guests. It was something she'd felt before in an all-female environment without the diluting, or perhaps dominating, effect of men. Or maybe it was that everyone's real attention was on the royal affair that was being conducted so openly in their midst. Either way, the tension became too much to bear for Jessica. She was the first to break ranks. Taking a delicate sip of coffee from her demi-tasse, she asked Mrs Simpson pointedly: 'You must be flattered to be the latest object of His Royal Highness's affections.' She emphasised 'latest' because there had been a long line of mistresses.

Syrie, mid-sip, almost sprayed out her coffee, but she quickly managed to recover her composure.

Wallis's brow shot up. She was a rattlesnake, thought Lilli. It would only take her a moment to size up her prey and attack. As predicted, the American came right back. 'I wouldn't be too interested in His Royal Highness's private affairs if I were you, Mrs Van Haselt,' she said coolly. 'After all, he could make life very trying for you, if he chose.'

Jessica turned a fetching shade of pink. 'Are you threatening me, Mrs Simpson?'

It was the first time Lilli had seen Jessica riled. She decided she really ought to intervene before the situation span out of control.

'I'm sure Mrs Simpson would never do such a thing, Jessica,' she said calmly. 'No one would dare deprive you of shopping in Aspreys or Harrods or Fortnum & Mason in the future.'

Some of the other women laughed politely and for a moment it seemed all-out war had been avoided, but the truce was short-lived.

Wallis, unbowed, rallied. 'My dear Mrs Van Haselt, all I am saying is, you might not be welcome in England for a while.' And with that veiled threat, she rose quickly to her feet. 'I need some air,' she announced. 'I'm going onto the terrace. It's a little stifling in here,' and with a toss of her head she disappeared through the French windows.

A stunned silence filled the room on Wallis's dramatic exit.

'Really Jessica, you went too far this time,' Gwendoline remarked waspishly.

Syrie winced. 'I must go with her,' she bemoaned, then wagging a finger at Jessica, she added, 'You are too, too naughty!'

Jessica pretended to be outraged at Syrie's accusation, palming her décolletage and looking around the room at the other women as if butter wouldn't melt in her mouth.

'I only told the truth,' she declared with a shrug before asking Lilli for a cigarette from her case. 'Just a little harmless fun.' She drew in her lower lip and giggled. 'I don't see what the big deal is. Kings and princes have always had mistresses,' she said, as Lilli lit a Sobranie for her.

Gwendoline shook her head. '"The big deal" as you call it, Jessica,' she pointed out, 'is that she is married. And has been before, to boot.' Ernest Simpson was Wallis's second husband.

From the opposite sofa, Mrs Johnson, the reserved Virginian, spoke. 'This one's different,' she chimed in, her voice high-pitched and girlish. She hadn't said a word for the entire evening, yet now she leapt to Wallis's defence. 'I know Wallis. She doesn't want to be a concubine. She wants to be a wife.'

Jessica, leaning forward, was intrigued. 'My dear, what can you mean?'

Mrs Johnson, uncomfortable with all the sudden attention, looked about her, then said, as if the answer was perfectly obvious to anyone with half a brain: 'I mean she wants to be Queen of England.'

A stunned silence suddenly enveloped the room, as if the very notion of a twice-divorced American holding such a title was utterly unthinkable.

Gwendoline parried the suggestion with a flap of her hand. 'But that's ridiculous,' she said after a moment's consideration. 'How can she possibly be that?'

'Simple. She'll divorce Ernest on the grounds of adultery, marry David and be crowned,' said Mrs Johnson, as if she were giving instructions for a cake recipe.

Gwendoline closed her eyes in exasperation. 'I'm afraid you don't understand the way the British Establishment works,' she replied patronisingly. 'You see, our king can never marry a divorcee.'

Jessica was clearly relishing the conversation. 'He could if he abdicated,' she suggested, as if it were the most normal thing in the world for a monarch to do.

'What?!' snapped a scandalised Gwendoline.

Jessica's gleeful gaze settled on Lilli. 'Your Kaiser W
didn't he?'

Lilli, who had deliberately decided to retreat after h
outing into the ring, now tilted her head, thinking of
maniac who took Germany to hell and left it there. 'Yes,
she reflected.

Gwendoline crossed her arms in front of her. 'But that wa
he lost the Great War and God knows we don't want anothe
of those! Besides,' she huffed, 'as if David would ever abdic

Just then the double doors into the drawing room swung o
and the excited voices of men made loud by alcohol could
heard, like so many braying donkeys.

'Here comes the cavalry!' exclaimed Jessica.

Lilli looked up. 'Don't flatter them,' she mumbled as the male
guests, all trussed up in their dinner jackets, filed in.

Willie Maugham, standing at the threshold addressed them.
'Ladies, dear ladies, I trust you are being well looked after.'

'Yes, thank you, Willie darling.' Jessica was on her feet and
clasping his hand to her cheek affectionately.

James, who'd entered the room behind his host, walked over
to Gwendoline. His sister glanced up unsmiling. Even though
the future king of England had just entered, no one stood on
ceremony. In private company the prince was no lover of protocol,
so no one paid any particular attention to him until he scanned
the room, frowning.

'Where's Wallis?' he asked anxiously, tugging at his shirt cuffs.

Ernest Simpson looked around blankly from where he'd just
assumed a pose by the fireplace. His colour rose slightly at the
prince's question. Since no one else answered, Lilli decided to
step in. 'Mrs Simpson went out onto the terrace for some fresh
air, I believe,' she informed him.

The prince nodded his thanks. 'I'd better see if she's all right,'
he replied awkwardly before making a hurried exit through the

French doors. Lilli saw the broken look on Ernest's face. It was clear to her that he knew he had already lost his wife.

The prince's departure was the signal for the other men to be seated. Mr Johnson remained by the patio doors talking to the male half of the Washington Trumpshaws who was, apparently, a real estate developer. Gwendoline and Jessica sat side by side, their earlier differences reconciled, on the surface at least. Syrie made sure the liqueurs flowed, allowing the prince and Mrs Simpson to remain uninterrupted in the garden. James Marchington seized his chance.

'May I?' He was motioning to the seat by Lilli and his blond fringe flopped forward, causing him to rake it back in a slightly exaggerated gesture.

Lilli looked up at him. He really was quite beautiful, she thought. 'And if I said no?' She took a laconic drag on her cigarette holder.

'I'd be the saddest man in the south of France,' he replied, tugging at the creases of his trousers to sit. 'So what next for the dazzling Lillian Stern?' he asked.

Lilli shook her head. 'You will have to see,' she teased. Her contract with the studio meant she was tied to KLO for the foreseeable future, but she was not sure herself what the future held. 'First my leg must mend.' She shot a disdainful glance at her own bandaged foot.

James looked deep into his brandy glass. 'I'm sure everything will work out for you.'

'Thank you,' she said, finding to her surprise that her smile had broadened.

After a short pause, he fixed her with a frown. 'Do you really not care about what is happening to your country?'

His questioning made her feel uncomfortable, but she didn't show it. 'What *is* happening?' she asked disingenuously.

'Hitler and the Third Reich.'

'What of them?' She gave a little shrug.

James sighed. 'You know he's passing anti-Jewish laws?'

Lilli looked at him quizzically. She couldn't be sure of this Englishman's motives. Had he guessed she was Jewish? She'd changed her hair colour along with her name, yet could it be he'd uncovered her secret? She turned away.

'I am aware, yes. But what has that to do with me?' She took a self-conscious drag of her cigarette, as if she could blow away the problem with the smoke.

James made an odd noise that passed for a chuckle and inclined towards her.

'Do you know that Herr Hitler is a real film buff? He loves Mickey Mouse.' She didn't.

Lilli's lips puffed a little at the information. She'd no idea if he was joking. 'How fascinating,' she replied, trying to sound disinterested. She took another drag of her cigarette, wondering if he was giving her an opportunity to tell him about her background and the secret of her heritage. She didn't take it.

James looked away. 'Hitler's re-arming at a shocking rate, too,' he told her, almost casually.

'Re-arming?' repeated Lilli. She really wasn't sure where this conversation was leading. James Marchington seemed intent on goading her into saying something about her own politics. The truth was, in Hollywood she'd lived in a bubble for the past year. Apart from Leon's letters, she had very little knowledge of what was going on in Germany and even less about this weedy man with a laughable moustache called Adolf Hitler.

James switched back and nodded. 'He's dangerous. Anyone can see that,' he said, playing with his manicured fingernails. 'Will you return? To Germany? To visit, I mean?'

Lilli was taken off-guard by the question. It wrong-footed her, as if she'd suddenly been lassoed by a cowboy in one of the new Westerns the studios were making. An image of her aging parents comforting each other after the shop had been burned down suddenly flashed through her mind. They were so very vulnerable. She was glad that she'd already made up her mind.

'I don't see that it's really any of your business, Mr Marchington,' she replied coolly, not wanting to play into his hands. Even though she had to return to America in a few days, Leon's troubling letters had already persuaded her to fit in a visit to Munich as well.

He looked her in the eye. 'Forgive me. I've overstepped the mark,' he said enigmatically. He took another gulp of his brandy and, glancing up, saw Willie Maugham hovering by the French doors, talking to a tanned young cocktail waiter with a slick of black hair. Lilli saw their host glance towards James and the two men's eyes met before Maugham disappeared out onto the terrace.

'Anyway,' he said, his gaze suddenly switching to the open doors, 'I feel the need for a breather. Excuse me, will you?' He rose and taking her hand, kissed the back of it lightly. But the damage was done. His mention of Hitler and his regime had unsettled her. It was yet another thing she would have to push back to the dark recesses of her mind.

Lilli watched James vanish into the Mediterranean night just as Jessica returned from an excursion to the cloakroom where she had clearly reapplied another layer of lipstick in anticipation of yet more socialising. Gwendoline had long since taken Ernest Simpson into her care and Syrie, chatting with the Washington Trumpshaws, was having her coffee cup filled by a steward. No one seemed to care about the absence of Wallis and the prince, nor indeed of their host and James.

Jessica sidled up. 'Lost your Prince Charming?' she asked, her breath smelling of crème de menthe.

Lilli shook her head. 'He's not my Prince Charming.'

Jessica smiled, grabbing another liqueur from a passing waiter. 'He wants to be, my dear,' she said, patting her friend on the arm. 'He's clearly in love with you.'

144

Chapter 26

Munich, Germany

The landscape changed imperceptibly at first; steeper hills, more pines, perhaps; cooler, too. Lilli even reached for her shawl from her holdall under the seat as the train chugged through Alsace-Lorraine. The journey would take thirty hours, but she was heading home and that gave her some comfort. Her conversation with James Marchington had played on the anxiety Leon's last letter had aroused in her. She'd planned to rest on the Riviera for the next few days and spend just one night in Munich at the end of her trip. Now there seemed to be an urgency behind her visit. She had taken the overnight train from Cannes to arrive later that day.

Lilli was relieved to see that her home city didn't seem to have changed much during her three years away. Her taxi ride from the main railway station back to Giesing, assured her that although the buildings were perhaps a little drabber, the people, too, life went on.

Summer was turning into autumn and the trees in the *Englischer Garten* were starting to glow gold as they always did, and the fountain was playing as it always had. In the evening sun, mothers pushed perambulators and lovers sat on the park benches, just as she and Marco used to do. A little stab of pain pricked her heart at the thought of how things once were between them. She wondered how he was, what he was doing; how many other young women he had used and abused in the meantime and if he had declared undying love to them just as he had to her.

Normal life in Munich went on, despite what James Marchington would have her believe. So when her taxi pulled up outside her old apartment in Giesing, she was excited to see her family and friends once more. She really needn't have worried.

'Fraulein Sternberg!' Herr Grunfeld cried in surprise as soon as he saw Lilli enter the apartment block. As the taxi driver deposited two large suitcases behind her on the tiled floor, the janitor sashayed out from behind his desk counter to shake her hand warmly. His hair was streaked with a few more grey hairs, and his moustache was a little straggly, but otherwise he looked exactly the same.

'Elspethe! Elspethe!' he called. In Lilli's absence, he'd found himself a pretty young wife. Golda had mentioned the wedding in one of her letters. The wife appeared at the door of their apartment, swiftly followed by Felix, the cat.

'Oh, but you must be Fraulein Lilli!' she exclaimed, wiping her hands on her apron. 'Axel has spoken of you a great deal. Welcome back!' She was marvelling at Lilli's well-cut suit and her fashionable straw hat. 'But you are so elegant!'

'And you made it to Hollywood!' Herr Grunfeld's eyes were alight. 'Your mother shows us the newspapers.' Lilli sometimes sent magazine cuttings to Golda. 'America agrees with you. The films, the stars . . .' The janitor waved her hand in a big, circular sweep at the sky, as if Hollywood was to be found in heaven.

Lilli smiled and lifted her gaze up the stairs. 'They are in?'

The mood suddenly changed. Herr Grunfeld and his wife looked at each other.

'Yes. Yes,' said the janitor.

'Good.' Lilli was relieved to hear it.

'But they didn't say you were coming.'

Lilli beamed. 'It's a surprise.'

'Ah!' His eyes widened then he winked.

'How are they?'

The janitor's moustache drooped and he gave a shallow shrug. 'Your father . . . well, his heart isn't too good these days,' he said touching his chest.

Lilli nodded. She'd suspected as much, even though Golda hadn't mentioned her father's ill health directly. 'I had better go to them,' she said.

As soon as she began to walk to towards the stairs, Herr Grunfeld grabbed her bags. 'I will bring these,' he told her. It was then that he noticed Lilli's bandaged foot.

'You can manage?' he asked, staring at it and frowning.

'Thank you. Yes. From dancing,' she explained. 'It just needs rest.'

Slowly Lilli made her way up the stairs. Despite each step proving quite painful, it felt strangely comforting to tread the same steps from her past, like re-reading a familiar story. She was half expecting to be heckled by Anna Kepler with her braces. But the little girl was no longer there, nor was there any sound coming from the Reuter children – there were five of them now apparently – as she passed the door to their apartment.

As soon as she reached the fourth floor – her family's floor – she stopped outside to compose herself. Her stomach pitched at the thought of what she might find behind the door. She took a deep breath and knocked. A moment later she heard shuffling footsteps.

'Who is it?' came Golda's voice. She sounded nervous. The key stayed silent in the lock.

This wasn't how Lilli had pictured her homecoming. When her mother heard the knock, she'd fling open the door and Lilli would shout 'Surprise!' There would be squeals of joy and laughter as they embraced each other. But it wasn't to be.

'Hello Mutti,' she called through the door.

From the other side she could hear a sharp intake of breath. 'Oi vey! Lilli? Is that you?'

'It is, Mutti. Let me in.'

An unfamiliar sound – a chain – was lifted from its hook and the door opened a crack, as if her mother just wanted to reassure herself that it really was her long-gone daughter who'd come to call. A beady eye appeared.

'Lilli!' came the cry, then, satisfied, Golda threw the door wide open. 'Lilli. Oh Lilli!' she cried again, this time flinging her arms round her daughter and bursting into tears.

'Don't cry, Mutti. Don't cry,' Lilli comforted, as her mother dabbed her eyes with her apron.

She could see she had lost weight. That sturdy, well-upholstered frame was diminished and when she looked at her face, as well as the usual resignation, Lilli saw something else that she couldn't quite place. Anxiety, perhaps? Or fear?

'Jacob! Leon!' Golda called down the hall, shuffling towards the main room.

Suddenly Leon appeared at the doorway and when he saw his sister he hurried down the hall to meet her. For a moment he stood awkwardly in front of her, as if preparing to embrace her, but Lilli beat him to it, lurching forward and enfolding him in her arms.

'What a fine young man you are!' she cried, hugging his bony body. She'd left him a spindly fifteen-year-old, serious and angry, trying to find his place in the world. Now he was taller and broader, although still very slim, and had just embarked on a law degree at Munich University. Still that serious, steely expression remained, only now it had been joined by a look of – what was that, Lilli asked herself – resentment?

'Where is Vati?' she cried.

'I'm here,' came a croaky voice.

Lilli found her father trying to get up out of his chair, but the effort was too much, and she saw him slump back down.

148

'*Mein Liebling!*' he said, breathlessly. 'What a surprise. A wonderful surprise.'

'You should have told us!' Golda said, plumping a cushion as she spoke. 'I could have baked babka and . . .'

'Mutti, that is exactly why I didn't tell you. I didn't want you to go to any trouble,' she said, smiling.

Lilli was pawed and hugged and fussed over. Golda was horrified to see her daughter's injured foot but reassured that it would soon be mended. She insisted Lilli sit on the settee with her leg resting on a stool. Her daughter was not to move a muscle.

Black tea was served in Lilli's favourite cup and lebkuchen passed to her on a plate. Later a glass of Riesling accompanied the stew that arrived on a tray on her lap.

Her family's questions came thick and fast. What was Fred Astaire really like? Which other stars had she met? Who was her favourite? What was her own apartment like? Was she eating property? (That from Golda.) As the bombardment continued Lilli tried to answer their queries as best she could. But the real questions, the burning questions, were the ones she wanted to ask them, and Leon in particular.

Apparently, Herr Backe was still in residence, but away for a few days, so Golda instructed Leon to vacate his bedroom and sleep in the lodger's room so that Lilli could have some privacy. Greta Garbo's image had been taken down and in its place, Leon had hung a poster proclaiming '*Freedom for the Jews.*' Lilli thought it was a risky move if Herr Backe was still a zealous Brownshirt and happened to see her brother's small act of defiance, but then that was typical of Leon – always ready to pick a fight. So as Leon gathered his things, Lilli took the opportunity to speak with him alone.

She reached for her clutch purse. 'I have something for you,' she told him, as he searched for his pyjamas in a drawer. He turned to face her. Before she'd left for Europe, she'd spent a couple of days shopping in New York and had paid a visit to Bloomingdale's.

'Here,' she said, handing him a thin rectangular box, wrapped in tissue paper.

With a wary look Leon took it from her and tore away the paper. When he opened the box it revealed a silver pen.

'It's engraved with your name,' she told him, pointing to the shaft. 'Lawyers need the finest quality pens.'

Leon, however, simply looked at her, almost despairingly, she thought, working his jaw. He didn't even bother to take the pen from the box.

'What is it? Don't you like it?'

Her brother shook his dark head. 'It's not that,' he replied. 'It's a fine pen, but I fear I won't have use for it.' He set it down on the bed by her side.

'What do you mean? Your studies . . .' Lilli couldn't understand.

Leon shrugged. 'There are new laws. Jewish students are being banned from some universities,' he told her. There was a flash of anger behind his eyes as he spoke.

'But they can't do that!' she exclaimed, her face crumpled in a frown.

He lifted his gaze to hers and stuck out his jaw. 'We're already restricted in certain professions,' he replied with a sneer. 'I told you in my letter, we can no longer get qualified in many fields. I'm not sure how long I will be able to keep on with my studies.'

For a moment Lilli was horrified. 'What?'

'They are gradually denying all our rights, Lilli.'

Searching his pinched face, the gravity of the current circumstances began to dawn on her. Wrapped up in her own cocoon of endless hours of rehearsals and filming, she'd lost sight of what was happening in the world outside. In the German newspaper she'd read on the train she'd been horrified to learn about the public burning of books by Jews and how Jewish shops were being boycotted, but she'd found it hard to believe the situation had grown so much worse since her time in America. Of course she remembered how her father's shop had been deliberately torched, but that was an act of vandalism, not something condoned by the government. But this – the systematic stripping of Jews' rights – was worse than she could have imagined. Before, she'd not really grasped the gravity of the situation. Now it struck her like a blow to the face.

'Oh Leon,' she said, suddenly reaching out and hugging him. 'What will you do?'

At that moment Golda appeared in the room and smiled when she saw her children embracing each other. Lilli did not want to change her mother's mood. She would not be staying for long and she wanted the memory of her visit to be a happy one for her parents. She decided to say nothing of politics, unless they raised the matter themselves.

After dinner, they talked over coffee for a while until Lilli could talk no more. She'd slept fitfully on the couchette on her journey from France the night before and was grateful to climb into her old bed, even if the mattress was nothing like as comfortable as the one she'd grown accustomed to in Hollywood.

Though she felt exhausted, sleep eluded her. Leon's news had disturbed her. She wondered what else was happening to her homeland that wasn't widely known elsewhere. What other injustices were being inflicted? What other scandalous acts were going unreported in the international press? Part of the answer came from an unexpected source.

The bell in the nearby church had just struck ten when there was a knock on the apartment front door. Lilli heard it open and her mother's voice. Two sets of footsteps walked into the main room.

'What troubles you?' her mother asked.

The half-whispered reply came from a woman. Frau Grundig. Lilli would know her rasping voice anywhere. Why on earth would she be calling so late if there wasn't a problem?

When she'd asked her mother how the Ram was keeping, Golda's response had been muted. It transpired that her nosey

151

neighbour had joined the National Socialist German Workers' Party after a revelatory encounter with Herr Hitler himself. She had been meeting an old friend from Munich Station when none other than the great man himself, accompanied by his large entourage, had stepped out of one of the special carriages. Frau Grundig had been so in awe of him that she was rooted to the spot, unable to move as he headed straight towards her. In the next moment their eyes met.

'He reached into my very soul,' she'd told Golda.

From that moment on, she knew Adolf Hitler was Germany's Messiah, so she'd started spreading the Party's word, calling on her fellow Germans to join the ranks of the righteous. Then, just recently, she'd been honoured to be appointed a teller on the voting committee of the referendum to give the government far greater powers than the constitution currently allowed.

This much Lilli already knew, so, slipping out of bed, she put her ear to the paper-thin wall to hear what was being said. And what she heard that night, on the other side of partition, she found not only unsettling but terrifying, too.

'I know it's late, but I really had to share my worries with you, Golda,' Frau Grundig began. 'As a Jew, you may not support our glorious leader, but I wanted to tell you what is being done in his name.'

'Of course, Klara,' Golda replied, as if her friend had just asked for a bagel recipe. 'A drink?' she added, ever the hostess.

'If you have a schnapps . . .' Frau Grundig seldom drank. Lilli listened harder. 'As you know I was proud to be a teller in the recent vote.'

'Indeed,' said Golda, as Lilli heard liquid being poured.

'We officials were made to sign a document before the count to ensure complete secrecy.'

'Yes.' Lilli imagined her mother nodding, as she handed her friend a glass of schnapps. 'But then when the polling booth closed that evening and we all gathered together to begin the count . . .'

Frau Grundig broke off and Lilli heard her sniff. Was she crying? 'The chairman read out a document. It said . . . it said that we were to announce a voting figure of 98.5 per cent in favour of the Party.' Another sniff. 'None of the voting papers were counted at all.'

'Oh, I see,' was all Golda could say. Lilli felt that her mother, more than anyone, seemed to be accepting what was going on around her with a quiet resignation. After all, who was she to interfere with the ways of powerful men?

'I'm sure the Führer would be horrified by what is being done in his name. What should I do?' came Frau Grundig's plaintiff plea. 'I cannot tell anyone in the head office because they would think me disloyal. Who can I turn to?'

Golda paused before she replied. 'You must say nothing, dear Klara. You must keep quiet, or you may get into terrible trouble.'

Lilli pictured her mother looking grave and shaking her head at her friend. Now even she, a woman usually only ever concerned with feeding her family and darning her husband's socks, was living in fear.

Chapter 27

London, England

All the way from Munich, on the train and on the ferry from Calais to Dover, Lilli had been rehearsing what she was going to say. She'd even written her own script, as if she was about to go onto a film set and act out a role. Only this was no make-believe. The situation was real and it was frightening. Over the past four days she'd spent with her family she'd come to realise how grave the situation in her homeland was becoming. Where there had been friendship, there was now division. Where there had been a mutual respect between cultures, there was enmity. Her family needed to leave Germany, to escape with her to America, but when she'd mentioned the idea just before leaving, Golda had made her feelings clear. 'This is our home,' she'd said firmly. 'We are staying put.'

Lilli needed to talk to someone and the only person she knew who would listen, who would take her fears seriously, was James Marchington.

When, from out of the carriage window, she saw the mountains of Bavaria turn to gentler hills of France, she couldn't believe that everything looked the same as it did a few days ago. The horses were still working the fields, the pickers were in the vineyards and the cut corn was standing in stooks. Everything was changed and yet everything was just how it was before. Just how it should be.

As the train rumbled at high speed towards Paris, a guard passed along the corridor. For a fleeting moment, seeing the uniform reminded her of Marco. By now her handsome officer would have travelled up the ranks. He would have put his precious duty before his conscience and at the very least would be wearing the oak leaves of a major on his tunic. Did he condone the behaviour of Herr Hitler and his henchmen, she wondered? She was only thankful that she would never have to see him again.

Lilli arrived in London burdened with a new and disturbing knowledge that weighed her down and made her heart feel heavy. England's capital was looking dreary under a blanket of low cloud and drizzle. The weather reflected her mood. It was so very different from the sunlit vibrancy of the Mediterranean just a week before when she'd last seen James. She'd sent a telegram ahead, just to make sure that he would be at his Mayfair Gallery when she arrived.

Afterwards she planned to see a consultant in Harley Street. Her foot was still extremely painful. It was throbbing continuously, and she was concerned that she might not be ready in time to start rehearsing for her second film in November, let alone the premiere of *The Princess and the Porter* in December. So much was riding on the need for her to be in perfect physical condition over the next few months.

She took a taxi to New Bond Street in Mayfair. The gallery was one of several in an understatedly elegant thoroughfare. In its large plate glass window, taking pride of place, hung a large canvas. Lilli stopped to study it. It was very bright and colourful, but rather abstract and not at all to her taste. She guessed it was probably by Picasso.

A bell tinkled over the door as Lilli stepped inside. The gallery was long and narrow, with a plain wooden floor and a dozen or so paintings of various sizes hung on white walls. James was seated at a desk at the far end, deep in conversation on the telephone. At the sound of the bell, he looked up and raised his arm to acknowledge her as he dealt quickly with the person on the other end of the line.

'Lilli!' he called, striding to greet her, even pecking her on the cheek. His spontaneous gesture seemed to surprise them both. 'Is everything all right?' he asked.

Her telegram had been completely unexpected and admittedly rather cryptic. James, she knew, would only have been back in England for a couple of days after the trip to the Côte d'Azur when she sent her communication from Munich. '*Need to talk urgently. Returning to London September 2. Will come to gallery.*'

'I'm so glad we could meet,' Lilli said. 'I need to tell someone what is happening in Germany.'

James walked to the window and glanced up and down the street. Lilli wasn't sure why, but then he flipped the sign on the gallery door from *Open* to *Closed*. She felt relieved that he would take her seriously.

'Let's go through, shall we?' he said, leading the way.

Lilli followed him into a neat office at the back of the gallery. The cold made her shiver and she decided to keep her coat on. A fashionable young woman wearing a thin blouse, who obviously wasn't bothered by the temperature, stood by a cabinet, filing.

'Tea, please, Miss Braham,' James instructed. The young woman looked up, lifted her pouty red lips into a smile and teetered out of the room on stiletto heels.

'Your telegram,' he began, lifting one of his brows. 'Most intriguing.' He seated himself behind his desk. His expression was grave to match his visitor's.

Lilli sat opposite him and tugged at the fingers of her gloves. In the next room Miss Braham could be heard arranging china on a tray. Laying her gloves on the desk she reached for a silver case from her purse and tried to steady her trembling hands as she placed a Sobranie in a holder. James reached for a lighter from his drawer and lit the tip for her, watching her intently as he did so. The cigarette flared into life and Lilli took a long, hard drag.

'As you know, I've just returned from Germany,' she said, breathing out a lungful of smoke and wafting it away from her. 'I saw for myself what is happening there.'

'Ah!' James sat back in his chair, remembering their conversation at Willie Maugham's villa.

'You were right,' she told him, crossing her legs. As much as it pained her to say it, everything he had told her about Hitler's regime was true. And worse. So much worse.

Taking a deep breath, she tried to remember the lines she'd rehearsed on the train, about Leon's plight, about the suffering and the discrimination against the Jews, but her mind was too cluttered to be coherent. There was so much to tell and all the feelings of fear and helplessness that she'd pent up since Munich suddenly came tumbling out.

'It's true what you said. This man Hitler is very dangerous.' The articles she'd read in one of Leon's underground pamphlets spoke of a coup recently staged. 'Politicians who oppose the government have been sent to prison. Some even murdered. And I think you are right when you say that he wants war.'

James's brows knitted. He nodded and looked at her intently as she drew breath. 'Hitler plans to pass even more devastating laws against Jews, too.'

Lilli frowned, uncrossed her legs and leaned forward. 'How do you . . .?' She thought for a moment, fixing him with a piercing look. She remembered how passionately he had argued against Hitler at the villa; almost as if he was in possession of knowledge that no one else round the table had. 'How much more do you know that you're not telling me?'

James side-stepped her question. Was he just being difficult, or did he have something to hide? Even after their first meeting his aloofness had led Lili to think that, like her, he regarded himself as an outsider. He was the quiet child at the party who refused to join in the games. She could never be sure why that might be, and the observation intrigued her.

'Start at the beginning, Lillian,' he instructed her gently. He picked up a pen and took a notepad from his desk drawer.

Her mouth was suddenly dry. 'You will tell someone?'

He nodded. 'Someone sympathetic.'

She swallowed and thought of her family, vulnerable in Munich. 'No one must know you heard this from me.'

'You have my word.'

Just as Lilli was about to start, Miss Braham reappeared with a tray.

As soon as he saw her, James laughed rather too loudly than was natural. He then smiled at the young woman and thanked her for the tea.

'I'll take care of it,' he told her.

Waiting until she'd left again, James lifted the pot. 'Milk? Sugar?'

'Black, please,' replied Lilli. 'No sugar.'

'So,' he said, handing her a cup and saucer over the desk. 'Take your time.'

Lilli reflected on her meeting with James in the cab as she travelled to her appointment in Harley Street. He'd been so understanding, but not at all surprised at what she told him about Leon's university or about Frau Grundig and the election fraud. And when she'd asked him, rather foolishly looking back on it, if he was a spy, he hadn't replied. Did that mean he thought her question was laughable, or accurate? And when, at the end of their meeting, she asked him what he was going to do with the information she'd just divulged, he'd told her he had 'friends' who would see that her report would go to the right places.

Her *report*. It made her sound as though she was an agent, feeding information to the British government, not merely a troubled young woman who'd heard, second hand, what Herr

Hitler and his cronies were doing to her homeland and its people. For a brief moment she'd worried she was taking things out of context. After all, Leon was always trying to find some corner to fight and her parents were continually gloomy. But only for a moment. Her brother's ambitions might be dashed and her mother was losing weight through constant worry. If the world knew about what was intended, how Hitler planned to officially demonise the Jewish race, someone would put a stop to it, wouldn't they? The rest of Europe couldn't just stand by and watch, could they?

Leaving James, Lilli felt both relieved and concerned. It was good to unburden herself to someone she thought she could trust. But just how he would use the information she'd supplied was still unclear. Had she done the right thing? Or had she just exposed herself – and more importantly – her family, to danger?

Chapter 28

Lilli's podiatrist in Hollywood had given her the name of the London consultant she was about to see. Mr Eli Cohen specialised in her particular condition. Yet although she had every faith in his professionalism, she was dreading her appointment. A bad prognosis was too terrible to contemplate. Her ankle was still so very painful, but she dared not think too deeply about the consequences if it didn't heal before rehearsals started with Fred. She could hear Madame Eva now. *Dance through the pain.* So Lilli had, but now she feared she might have to pay the price.

The consulting rooms were housed in a perfectly ordinary block that, from the outside, looked to Lilli as though it was still residential. Carbolic soap with undertones of pine wafted through the air as she thumbed through glossy magazines in the small waiting room. Its red plush chairs and a large vase of gladioli were obviously designed to make patients feel at ease, but it was going to take more than a few casually arranged flowers to quell her anxiety.

'Mr Cohen will see you now,' the prim receptionist told her.

Lilli was shown into a room lined on two sides with books. There were charts on the remaining walls; large diagrams of feet, drawn from every angle. A leather armchair was placed in front of a mahogany desk behind which sat a balding man with a thick neck.

'So, Miss Stern.' Mr Cohen hooked his wire-framed spectacles onto his large nose and glanced down at various papers in front of him that Lilli's Hollywood consultant must have sent him. 'A dancer, eh?' The word dripped from his mouth. He did not bother to hide the contempt in his voice. 'Musicals. I'm a ballet man myself.'

'Ballet or ballroom, we all suffer,' said Lilli bluntly as she seated herself in the armchair. She was in no mood for English arrogance.

'Quite,' he replied. 'So, let's take a look, shall we?'

Lilli was directed behind a screen where she removed her shoes and stockings and put on a gown. She then perched on a high couch while the specialist examined her feet and legs. His hands were cold and she winced at his touch, but he carried on prodding and poking with various instruments. He worked silently, referring to the notes on his desk now and again and ghostly X-rays of her feet and ankles illuminated on a light box. She couldn't read anything in his face that told her whether her injury was healing well or not. After a few minutes he invited her to slip into her stockings and shoes once more. He made Lilli nervous.

Perhaps that's why when he did sit down back at his desk to deliver his prognosis, the fear that she'd tried to suppress for so long suddenly grabbed hold of her entire being. Just as Samson's power lay in his hair, hers lay in her dancing feet. Without them, she had nothing. Her whole career, her whole life depended on the verdict that this man was about to deliver. She felt her body start to shake as Mr Cohen studied his papers, then whipped off his spectacles.

'What did you find, sir?' she jumped in, no longer able to wait.

The podiatrist looked up and frowned at her, as if she had spoken out of turn. When he did finally speak, he did not mince his words. There was no attempt to couch his findings in platitudes or soften them in caveats.

161

'I found, Miss Stern, that the damage you've sustained to your foot over the years is considerable.'

'Considerable,' she repeated. 'What does that mean?' Her panic was rising.

'It means that I'm afraid there's nothing else for it,' he replied.

Lilli felt her throat constrict. What was this man talking about? Nothing else for what? The sword of Damocles was poised over her head and all he could do was play games. 'I'm afraid I don't understand,' she told him, the dread making her feel light-headed. Was he really about to tell her what she feared most?

The specialist leaned forward and clasped his hands together, like a judge, to deliver his final verdict. Lilli held her breath as he pronounced sentence.

'It means your dancing days, I fear, Miss Stern, are well and truly over.'

Chapter 29

Lilli tried her upmost to hold back her tears in the rear of the taxi. But it was useless. Tomorrow she was due to board the liner at Southampton that would return her to America and what then? Her career was surely now over, her three-film contract as good as shredded. She felt like a bird whose wings had been clipped. No longer being able to dance would mean she could no longer fly. She'd been so intent on being a star that she'd even sacrificed her own body for it. Now her dreams lay shattered all around her.

As soon as she told the driver her destination, the dam burst. She sobbed the entire journey but managed to compose herself before she paid her fare and passed through the revolving doors of the hotel. Catching sight of herself in the foyer mirror, she straightened her hat and adjusted her collar before hobbling to collect her key at the reception.

'Room 309, if you please,' she asked the man in a morning coat with long sideburns behind the desk.

'Ah!' he said suddenly, holding a finger in the air as if the mention of the room number had reminded him of something. He turned, went to a pigeonhole behind his desk and pushed an envelope towards her. The handwriting was unfamiliar.

As she took the lift, Lilli had to purse her lips to keep them from trembling until she flipped over the envelope and saw the sender's name and address on the back. Once in her room, she sat down on the bed, more than a little intrigued to see the letter was from Wallis Simpson.

> *Dear Miss Stern*
>
> *I am just dropping you a note to thank you so much for standing up for me at the Maugham's dinner party. By now I am growing quite used to slanderous taunts that certain members of the royal circle, in particular, are keen to hurl at me, but your intervention was most welcome.*
>
> *As a German I'm sure you'll agree there is a certain empathy between us. We are both surely treated as outsiders by the English and therefore it would make perfect sense if we banded together in sisterhood.*
>
> *I do so hope that we can renew our acquaintance in the not-too-distant future. Both our schedules are undoubtedly hectic, but one must always make space for friendship, don't you agree? Next time you are in London, I do so hope we can meet up for tea. We surely have so much in common. I know we will get on splendidly.*
>
> *I wish you a very successful premiere of your new film. I know the Prince of Wales is most excited to see it, as am I. I have watched you on stage myself and know you have an amazing talent. We are very much looking forward to seeing you and Mr Astaire on the big screen.*
>
> *Sincerely yours,*
>
> *Wallis Simpson (Mrs)*

Lilli found the letter slightly puzzling. She pictured its author: her boyish figure, her face angular and almost manly in its confidence. In her experience, women like Wallis Simpson only made friends when it suited them. Lilli wondered for a moment what the Prince of Wales's mistress – the fact that she used the word 'we' was surely proof of an affair – might want from her. Presumably an introduction into the glitz and glamour of Hollywood. Invitations to premieres, weekends at Martha's Vineyard and yacht parties with Errol Flynn and Barbra Stanwyck undoubtedly held more appeal for Wallis than stuffy house parties at Balmoral.

Lilli stifled a sob as it juddered in her chest and stretched her aching leg. She wondered if Wallis would still hold out the hand of friendship once she knew that her days of dancing with Fred Astaire were over.

Chapter 30

Hollywood, America

Lilli was sitting in the dark. The only light came from a beam high up in the wall behind her. In front of her stood a large blank screen and her stomach felt as if it was clamped in a vice. This is how it must feel to be in prison, she thought.

'Relax,' Victor told her, sensing her discomfort. The pain in her foot and leg was relentless and she'd taken to wearing trousers in public to hide the thick strapping she was forced to wear. She caught a whiff of whiskey on his breath, even though it was still only ten in the morning.

They were at the showing of the first cut of *The Princess and the Porter* in the studio's private viewing room. Her agent's bulky body impinged on her seat as well as his own. His cigar smoke curled in the shaft of light from the projector and made her feel sick.

'Hey, lil lady, it's only natural to be nervous seeing yourself up there, warts an' all. You know what I mean. It gets better,' Victor told her. His words were meant to be of some comfort, but they only made things worse. Not only was this going to be her first time on the big screen, but in all probability her last – as a dancer – as well.

After her return from England, she'd decided to seek a second opinion about her condition. She still clung to a shred of hope that the English specialist was wrong, but his counterpart in Los Angeles confirmed the diagnosis. She'd agonised over what to do, but in the end, she'd had no choice. The news was broken to Victor in his office three days ago. He'd immediately reached for the Jack Daniels.

'So here's the deal,' he'd told her on his third glass. 'We say nothing. Stay *schtum*.' He put a finger up to his flaccid lips. 'Not until we've got the premiere out of the way.'

'But . . .' she'd protested. She didn't want to mislead the studio bosses. She'd signed a three-film contract. They would expect her to deliver. Besides, the thought of limping along the red carpet would do nothing for her reputation or the studio's. He'd flashed up his palm. 'If the movie-goers love you after the premiere – and they will – it'll put you in a stronger position.'

'A stronger position for what?' She didn't understand what he was driving at.

His eyes had slid away from her at that point. 'For auditions for speaking parts.'

'Speaking parts,' she'd echoed. 'But I'm not a serious actress. I'm a dancer. If I can't dance, I'm worthless.'

And that was where the conversation was left: dangling in mid-air, just like Lilli's future.

There were others in the private theatre that day, too: a couple of editors, the screenwriter and director, the head of publicity and his secretary and, of course, Fred. He'd come over to say hello and was his usual, charming self.

'How's the foot?' he asked.

Lilli laughed. 'Oh, much better now, thank you,' she lied. She was grateful he couldn't see her cheeks colour in the dark.

'That's good. You wouldn't want to go back into rehearsals not fully recovered,' he said, shaking his head.

Did he suspect? The nausea suddenly rose once more in her

stomach. Next month they were due to start schedules for their second film together. It wasn't going to happen. A sharp pain suddenly shot into her ankle and she had to stifle a scream. She needed another painkiller. The LA consultant had prescribed her a month's worth and they definitely deadened the pain.

'I'm just going to powder my nose,' she told Victor, easing herself out of her seat. She tried to hobble to the ladies' cloakroom without being noticed. A runner with a clipboard hurried by. Lilli stopped, pretending to adjust the cuff on her blouse then carried on. She was in luck. The room was empty.

Limping to the mirror over the hand basin she looked at her reflection. She'd had to rely on heavy make-up to mask the dark circles under her eyes. The pain had been keeping her awake at night and the strain had begun to show in her face.

Dance through the pain, she mumbled to herself.

Taking a small bottle from her purse, she put a pill on her tongue and scooped some water from the running tap to swallow it. The tablets were a help, but they only dulled her agony. They couldn't cure the cause of it.

Just then, another woman entered. Lilli recognised her as the studio boss's secretary. A halo of tight brunette curls hugged her head, and she began fussing with them in front of the mirror. She'd begun to tug at a stray lock, when the secretary suddenly saw Lilli's reflection and realised who she was.

'Oh, hey, but you're Lillian Stern, ain't ya?' she said wide-eyed. 'You're a great dancer. I've seen the rushes. You and Mr Astaire look just swell together.'

Lilli smiled as the girl turned quickly, forcing her to step back a little, but as she did her ankle gave way. She let out a yelp and felt her legs crumple beneath her. Staggering back, she tried to clutch at the dressing table behind her, but it was no use. She sank to the floor.

The secretary gasped in shock and dived down to help her. 'I'm so sorry!' she cried, flapping frantically as Lilli's face contorted in agony. 'I didn't mean . . .' It was then the young woman saw the strapping around Lilli's ankle. 'Oh, but you're hurt,' she blurted, both her hands cradling her face in alarm.

'Please. It wasn't your fault,' Lilli assured her, trying to right herself and wincing with the effort. She held out her hand and the young woman took it, helping her to her feet.

'Shall I get a nurse?' she asked, settling Lilli on the low stool nearby.

'No!' Lilli snapped quickly. Then, more calmly she said: 'No thank you. I'll be fine.'

'Let me help you back to your seat,' the secretary persisted.

'No, really,' repeated Lilli. She knew, only too well, that if she was spotted limping again, the Hollywood rumour-mill would gear into action. 'I'll be fine if I take it slow,' she said.

'You okay?' asked Victor as she lowered herself back into her seat.

Once again, she lied. 'I'm fine.'

Just then the studio boss, Bertram T Lewis, entered the screening room. He was a man who worked hard and played hard. Even his cigars were twice the size of Victor's. Little wonder, thought Lilli, he was said to rely on pills to get him through the day.

On his way to his own – specially upholstered and very spacious – seat, he nodded at Lilli. She forced a smile in return. She was nervous enough awaiting his verdict on the film, but she was absolutely terrified of his reaction when he discovered that she couldn't fulfil her contract. It turned out he was nervous, too. She saw him pop a pill – *for my blood pressure*, he'd disclosed just before the reel started to roll.

The theme music played in and for the next ninety-five minutes no one moved. The small audience was so utterly spellbound that to shuffle or whisper would have been a crime. Lilli was a perfect match for Fred. Together they were a dream team. The dance routines he'd choreographed were imaginative and flawless and the set design and costumes exuded glamour and elegance.

Lilli held her breath when 'The End' flashed up on screen. A split second later, as the lights came up, rapturous applause resounded around the room. It was then that relief flooded her body and for a few brief moments she forgot about her throbbing leg and the undoubted turmoil that lay ahead.

'You were swell, lil lady!' said the director, shaking her hand.

'Congratulations,' said Fred with a wink. 'You made it, Lillian.'

Victor squeezed her arm. 'You nailed it, lil lady. I'm proud of you.' He raised his eyes towards the imposing figure of Bertram T Lewis as he approached. 'Now let's see what the boss has to say.'

As Lewis loomed over her, his face remained inscrutable. What if he thought she didn't match up to Fred? What if he decided the whole film was a disaster? She needn't have worried. Nor did Bertram T Lewis. His blood pressure was just fine and he broke into an enormous smile as he held out his equally enormous hand.

'Ladies and gentlemen,' he boomed, turning to the rest of the exclusive gathering, 'a star is born.'

Lilli wasn't sure whether to laugh or cry. Her star, she thought, may be dazzling now, but as she lifted her lips in a wide smile and bobbed her head, acknowledging the applause, she couldn't help thinking it would surely be fading all too soon.

Chapter 31

Henley-on-Thames, England

1935

James Marchington sat in a winged chair in the study at Hartwood Hall, a Georgian mansion that lay solidly on the banks of the Thames, near Henley. It was the country seat of his father, the Earl of Lindsey. With its heavy, dark drapes, its thick rugs, and roaring fires, it always provided a welcome refuge from London life, especially in winter.

It was a bitter day in January. Christmas had come and gone leaving in its wake a trail of leftover food and unwanted presents. The wind whistled round the mansion's tall chimneys and snow threatened to fall from the leaden sky.

In the study grate a fire blazed, fending off the draughts that blew in from under every door and through each loose window-pane. With the willow trees now naked, the window offered James a view of the Thames below the lawn. Yet neither the weather nor the view bothered him, particularly. He had just taken delivery of the latest copy of the American edition of *Vogue* magazine and he knew he was in for a treat. He always loved the chemical smell of the printer's ink and the feel of its glossy pages, not to mention its ravishing photographs. This issue, however, was to be prized above all others. Its cover was graced by none other than Miss Lilian Stern. Furthermore, inside a whole eight pages were devoted to full colour images of her.

Lilli's large eyes, made even larger by – according to the inside credits, Max Factor mascara – stared out from beneath a black velvet toque hat. Her chin was propped on her gloved hands and her coat was cherry-red, edged in mink. He brushed her glossy cheek with his fingers and traced her full red lips with his finger. She encompassed elegance, mystery and sophistication – all the qualities that had made James Marchington fall in love with her at first sight when they'd met at Adele Astaire's wedding.

Next he turned to the inside spread. Lilli was pictured in sumptuous settings, with backgrounds of tapestries and marble pillars. These were followed by shots of her in evening gowns that clung to her breasts and the curve of her hips and made her appear like some Greek goddess. In some scenes her hair was plaited with silver or gold and tiny jewels. In others she wore it wavy and loose and golden. Whatever she was wearing and whichever way she posed, Lillian Stern, he thought, was incomparable.

He was thumbing through the magazine pages for the third, or perhaps the fourth time when he heard the telephone ring in the hall. Reith, the butler, answered it and, a moment later, appeared at the study doorway.

'Sir, Lady Cavendish is on the line for you.'

The news came as a surprise. Adele's calls were infrequent since her marriage and when she did communicate, it was usually with Gwendoline. For a moment he wondered whether she was calling about Lilli's splendid photographic spread in *Vogue*. Setting down the magazine on the desk, he strode through to the hall, where the telephone was out of its cradle on the console table.

'Adele, to what do I owe the pleasure?'

'James, darling. Thank goodness I've got you.' Her American accent had all but disappeared.

'What's the matter?'

'It's Lillian.'

His glance slipped through the open study door towards the magazine on the desk and he frowned. 'You've seen American *Vogue*? Isn't she stupendous?'

There was a worrying pause on the line before Adele tutted and said: 'No, James. Not *Vogue*. I can't reach her and I'm worried she could be really in rather a state.'

James perched himself on the corner of the console table. 'State?' he repeated. 'What on earth do you mean?'

The spread in *Vogue* gave Lilli wonderful exposure. And there'd been more. Just before Christmas he'd seen a report in one of the American newspapers that the premiere of *The Princess and the Porter* had been a glittering affair. There was an accompanying photograph of her looking fabulous next to Astaire. The critics loved the film and they loved Lillian. One had even hailed her as 'the Marlene Dietrich of the dance.'

James had joined in, sending her a bouquet and a congratulatory note, which she'd acknowledged. She was rising high, on the crest of a wave. So how could she be in a 'state'?

Adele sighed heavily down the line. 'They've just published a beastly article about her in *The Hollywood Examiner*. It says she was found in agony in a rest room at the studios and that her foot and leg are so badly damaged that she's going to have to give up dancing.'

Immediately his mind flashed to the way she walked into his gallery the last time he saw her. He remembered he saw her wince as she sat down.

'Oh dear,' he replied, knowing only too well that it could, and in all probability would be, the end of the line for Miss Lillian Stern.

'They've all piled in like vultures, James,' Adele told him angrily. 'Louella Parsons and the other gossips are having a field day!

Fred's in touch with her, of course, but won't say a word. Have you heard anything? Is it true? Tell me, James.'

James thought of the Hollywood birds of prey, circling over their wounded carrion. 'I fear it might be,' he told her.

A gasp came down the line as Adele digested the news.

James knew Lilli was pretty much friendless in Los Angeles. Mostly everyone was, it seemed. Out there, under the blazing Californian sun, it really was 'dog eat dog,' 'every man for themselves,' 'survival of the fittest.' Ultimately and ironically, he told himself, the attitude in the celluloid world was *Mein Kampf* but with champagne and caviar thrown in for good measure.

'Don't worry, my dear,' he told Adele, trying to calm her down. 'Leave it with me.'

A deep sigh of relief blew down the line. 'I knew I could rely on you,' said Adele.

James had always been the dependable, sensible one of their little social set. Carefully, he replaced the receiver on the handset and thought what to do next. Without her dancing, Lillian Stern's Hollywood days were behind her. That meant she needed rescuing. With her screen career over, she may well be more amenable to looking for an alternative one. And he knew just the vocation to offer her.

Chapter 32

Hollywood, America

Bertram T Lewis was getting nervous again and, as everyone in Hollywood knew, when Bertram T Lewis got nervous he took pills – lots of them. He possessed a bottle of purple tablets, a bottle of red ones and a box of blue and yellow and at times of stress – there were many in his hectic and important life – he didn't hesitate to swallow quite a few.

On the morning she was hauled in to see Mr Lewis, Lilli noted he'd laid out a range of receptacles in front of him on his big-as-a-pool-table desk in readiness for a threatened crisis.

As usual Victor was late for the meeting.

'Jeez! Where is that goddamn Selig?' Lewis cried reaching for his purple pills.

In front of him was the article in the *Hollywood Examiner* and next to that, more worryingly, Lilli thought, a copy of her contract.

'I can explain, Mr Lewis,' Lilli began. There was no point waiting for Victor. This was her battle, and she would fight it alone. Fred had been his usual, gallant self, sending her flowers. There'd been a letter from James Marchington, too, inviting her to spend a few weeks resting in England. But the Hollywood press had declared open season on her and everyone was piling in to take pot shots.

Lilli explained that she'd sought – and found – a second opinion on her injured foot when she'd returned from Europe and that she was about to tell him that she wouldn't be able to fulfil her contract, but then there was the premiere and . . .

'Well look who's here,' Lewis stopped Lilli mid-flow as Victor Selig suddenly joined them.

'Is this a private party or can anyone join in?' cried the agent, rolling into the office twenty minutes late and stinking of alcohol.

Lewis's face turned a deep shade of red. He looked as if he might explode at any moment and Lilli knew that her fate was sealed.

'Hey, why the frown, sweetheart?' Victor asked Lilli. 'I just got you an audition for a speaking part in the next Rita Hayworth movie!' he announced, settling himself next to her opposite Lewis. 'Ain't that swell?'

Lewis reached for a bottle of pills and swallowed two. Lilli was left speechless as he turned to her. 'So that means you definitely won't be available for *Follow the Fleet* with Fred, then,' he hissed through clenched teeth, trying to keep a lid on his obvious anger.

Embarrassed, Lilli closed her eyes in the hope that all this was a nightmare and she'd wake up soon. But it wasn't and she didn't and all she could say when she opened them was: 'I'm sorry, Mr Lewis. I didn't—'

Lewis slapped the desk. 'I've heard enough.' His head switched towards the door. 'Carol!' he shouted through to his secretary.

The girl with the halo of tight brunette curls appeared, notepad in hand. She avoided eye contact with Lilli.

'Get me Ginger Rogers's agent on the phone, will you?' boomed Lewis.

'Yes, sir. Right away.' The brunette scuttled off.

Lewis turned back to Lilli. 'This role will go to someone who can handle it,' he told her pointedly. And with that he picked up her contract lying before him on the desk and, with his enormous hands, he began to tear it to shreds.

'There's really only room for one Marlene Dietrich in Hollywood,' he scowled. 'If I were you, I'd get back to Germany, 'cos, after this, Miss Stern, you'll never work in Hollywood again.'

That was when Lilli realised there was no use staying in America. Her dream had come crashing down round her ears. She'd outstayed her welcome in Tinsel Town. Suddenly James Marchington's invitation to return to England sounded not just tempting, it was the only real option open to her.

Chapter 33

Henley-on-Thames, England

The pavilion was a small but ornate wooden structure overlooking the Thames in the grounds of Hartwood Hall. Lilli sat inside, thankful for the warmth of her mink coat against the biting wind that snarled down the river valley. Her right leg, still swathed in strapping, rested on a footstool. She'd arrived back in England only two days before. James's letter had been her lifeline. In it he'd offered her a place to '*rest and recoup.*' Now that her dancing days were most assuredly behind her, she certainly needed to do both those things.

At Lilli's side in the pavilion was a small butler's table covered in letters. She'd brought her writing case with her and, away from the noise and bustle of the grand house, she'd hoped to tackle her correspondence. Leon's latest letter loomed large in front of her, and with it came thoughts of home. It had arrived the week before she'd sailed from New York.

It seemed the situation in Germany had deteriorated even further since she saw him last in September. There were even more draconian laws targeting Jews, like excluding men from military service and students from qualifying examinations in medicine and law, which, of course meant Leon. But in this message what

Lilli found particularly worrying was his plea, not for himself, but for Golda and Jacob.

'*I think it is time Mutti and Vati left Germany before it is too late,*' he wrote. '*I must remain to carry on the fight on behalf of all Jews, but our parents are old and Vati's heart grows weaker. I am therefore asking you, dear sister, to make the necessary arrangements for them so that they can travel to America to live out the rest of their days with you in peace. I look forward to hearing from you as soon as possible. I fear the situation for us Jews grows worse by the day.*'

Lilli had read the letter twice, but she'd been so mired in her own problems that she had not yet managed to pen a reply. How could she tell her family and everyone back home about her fall from such a dizzying height? Leon, she accepted, always thought the worst, but she had also seen articles in the American press raising concerns about Hitler for the first time. Some politicians in England were warning about the Führer's jealous eye being cast into his neighbours' gardens. She also understood James's anxieties about Germany's re-armament. Her family was asking for help, but she wasn't in a position to give it without first telling them the truth. Mutti and Vati couldn't make a new life in America because Lilli didn't live there anymore. She was effectively homeless. Her own bad news about her ruined dancing career needed to be delivered to her parents in person, but she wasn't ready to do that. Not yet. Instead, deciding to play for time, she wrote:

> *Dear Leon,*
> *I understand your worry. I have been very busy lately but hope to come to Munich in the next few weeks. When I first suggested they leave for America, Mutti refused. Their home is in Germany, she said. Have they changed their minds? If so, we can talk over plans for them on my next visit.*
>
> *All love,*
>
> *Lilli.*

She moved on to the next and wholly unexpected letter from Wallis Simpson. It had been posted directly to Hartwood Hall. James had apparently let it be known in his social circles that Lillian Stern was 'resting' at his family country seat and, hey presto, a missive was delivered. It was inviting her to tea at Wallis's London home, Bryanston Court.

Lilli was in two minds whether to accept the invitation. She was musing on the prospect of scones and jam with the mistress of the heir apparent to the English throne when James suddenly appeared. He was looking very boyish in a sports jacket and muffler. When he opened the pavilion door, a blast of cold air made her shiver.

'In like a lion, out like a lamb,' he remarked.

Lilli didn't understand. Was James making a veiled reference to her failed career? Her forehead crumpled into a frown.

'It's a saying we English have,' he explained, seeing her puzzlement. 'It's about the month of March. It starts off cold and windy, like this, but by the end of it spring will be here.' He smiled at her reassuringly, at the same time rubbing his hands together to revive his circulation.

'Let us hope so,' she replied with a weak smile.

'May I join you?' he asked, pointing to the Lloyd Loom chair beside her.

'Of course.'

'I've asked Reith to bring us down some coffee.' He looked at the table beside her. 'News from home?'

'Yes,' she said, returning Leon's letter to its envelope.

'It's not good, is it?'

Lilli felt the breath leave her lungs. She knew she could talk to James. Perhaps it was time she did again. She needed a new purpose in her life; something positive and meaningful that would fill the gaping hole left by the absence of her dancing, even though she had no idea what that might be – yet.

Recalling their meeting at the gallery, her eyes latched onto his. 'Did you pass on what I told you about the election in Germany?'

180

James nodded seriously. 'I took your concerns to the appropriate channels.'

A dry laugh escaped from her glossy lips. 'You talk like a politician,' she teased him. 'Or a spy!' She'd always found his shy, schoolboy charm endearing, but his silence and the way he looked at her prompted her to go further. She'd wondered for a while, but now she came right out and said it. 'You *are* a spy.'

His eyes suddenly unlocked themselves from her gaze. He didn't need to say anything else. He didn't confirm or deny the accusation. But in that moment Lilli knew that what she had suspected ever since their conversation on the Côte d'Azur was true.

James thrust his hands into his pockets and seemed to make his neck withdraw into his muffler as he looked straight ahead. All he would say was: 'I care, as I know you do, otherwise you wouldn't have reported what happened at the election count in Munich.'

Lilli lifted up her gaze towards the river that ran grey and cold before them. She shook her head. 'Remember I was an actress, James, and I put on a show for those around me as well as on film. But there are things . . .' she began, but her words were suddenly lost on a sigh. It was then that she turned to him. 'I lie awake sometimes, thinking of my family in Germany and what will become of them. But what can I do, James?' She slumped back in her chair. 'There's a song that Irving Berlin wrote for the movie I was supposed to star in.' She gave a bitter shrug. 'The lyrics say something about even if trouble is ahead, while we still have wonderful things like moonlight and love and romance, we should – what is it? – face the music and dance.'

James's lips flattened and he shook his head. 'You're not in Hollywood anymore, Lillian. You're in the real world now,' he told her softly. 'People don't live happily ever after in this one: they struggle, they fight and, sometimes, they die.' He paused then tilted up his head. 'And I, for one, am not prepared to just pay for my ticket to watch Europe fall prey to a monster. I think you might feel the same about what's happening in Germany.'

Their eyes met as he spoke these last words and a new understanding seemed to dawn between them.

'That's what I've been trying to tell you, James,' Lilli replied. 'If I can no longer dance, then maybe it's time for me to *face the music*.' She reached for his hand and he gave it freely. 'I want to help, if I can.'

James allowed a smile to flit across his lips as he studied their clasped hands, then lifting his face he told her: 'I knew it was a mask. I knew you were Jewish.'

A knot tightened inside her. She suddenly felt vulnerable and withdrew her hand. He was putting that label around her neck once more; the label she'd fought so hard to take off.

'So my hair colour didn't fool you?' she asked lightly, fighting off her desire to snap at him.

James smiled. 'You can dye your hair, but not your eyes. I only had to look into them when the prince mentioned Hitler that night at dinner. I saw how much you care for your loved ones in Germany.'

She was silent for a moment, knowing that she'd only been fooling herself when she'd kept her fears for her family and her country locked away, deep inside her. 'Yes, I cared,' she replied softly. 'So much more than I ever showed.'

Suddenly her dark eyes clamped onto his as she leaned over. An impulsive charge arced between them. James reached towards her and, closing in, he found her mouth and his kiss unfurled into something long and delicious.

When she finally broke away from him and allowed herself a deep breath, she saw James's serious expression dissolve into a smile.

'I care, too,' he whispered, just as Reith arrived with the coffee.

Chapter 34

London, England

Number Five Bryanston Court was to be found in an elegant part of London, just north of Marble Arch. The apartment, in a smart, discreet Art Deco mansion block, was the English home of Mr and Mrs Ernest Simpson.

It didn't take much persuading from James for Lilli to accept Mrs Simpson's invitation. He'd told her about the rumours concerning the American's right-wing political leanings and asked her to find out if they were true. 'I have it on good authority that the prince and Mrs Simpson are very sympathetic towards the Fascist regime,' he'd said, adding pointedly: 'But we need proof.'

'Proof?' she'd repeated.

'Meetings, letters, anything that pins down their allegiance to the Nazis,' he'd told her gravely.

During the course of the journey from Henley to London, Lilli mulled over what she'd learned from James about the married American who'd stolen the Prince of Wales's heart. While she'd been away in Hollywood, rumours of the royal affair had spread like wildfire. The scandal was gripping the Court. What Lilli had regarded as a secret known only to a few elite the previous year in France, was now common knowledge. The storm was gathering.

On her arrival at the grand block Lilli was greeted at the door by a maid and shown through a spacious hall into the drawing room. It was light and airy – the very opposite of Hartwood Hall – and Wallis Simpson sat, rather regally, Lilli thought, in a high-backed chair, a small terrier on her lap. She rose to receive her guest, tucking the small dog under her left arm.

'How lovely to see you again, Miss Stern,' she said, holding out a formal hand.

'And you, Mrs Simpson.'

'Wallis, please.'

Lilli moved towards her, trying to hide the sharp pain that was shooting up her leg as she walked.

Wallis handed over the dog to the maid before gesturing to the sofa. Lilli noticed the magnificent sapphire on her left hand. 'I was so devastated to hear about your accident,' she said, her eyes straying to her guest's flat, unfashionable shoes. 'Such a devastating blow to your career. You must be beside yourself.'

Lilli hid her discomfort with a smile. 'I am disappointed,' she replied, surprising even herself by her understatement.

Just why she'd been invited to tea, Lilli was yet to discover. It was obvious that Wallis Simpson had no intention of being a real friend from the way she instantly tried to put her down. She could only guess that she had a hidden agenda and was intrigued to see what that might be. Over cucumber sandwiches and cups of Darjeeling, it became clear that her suspicions were right.

'I'm sure you know, Lillian – I may call you Lillian, yes? – that it's not easy being a foreigner in a strange country, especially a foreign woman.' Wallis took a sip of tea from her Crown Derby cup.

Lillian nodded her agreement. She'd spent almost four years flitting around the United States and latterly England and had always felt regarded as a sort of curiosity wherever she went. 'I understand what you mean,' she replied.

'It was so naughty of David to put you on the spot like that at Willie Maugham's,' she said. Lilli was quite surprised that she openly referred to the Prince of Wales as 'David'.

Lilli gave a tight shrug and smiled. 'I am used to being, as you say, put on the spot.'

Wallis's large mouth, set in flawless skin, widened into a smile. 'I'm sure you are, my dear,' she said nodding, then added: 'And as for Jessica Van Haselt . . .' Her smile switched to a disdainful smirk. 'I can handle her sort.' A little laugh tripped through her lips. 'We must stick together, yes? Especially now.' Her gaze moved pointedly to Lilli's ankle once more.

Lilli crossed her legs self-consciously. So this was Wallis Simpson's war strategy. She was amassing her troops around her before she went on the offensive. The society hostess Emerald Cunard was apparently her latest chief of staff. Her fellow American was hosting so many *quiet suppers* for her and the prince that the famous Noel Coward, Lilli heard, had declared himself *sick* of them. He flatly refused to go to any more.

'I'm assuming you don't have to dash off to Hollywood again so soon,' she said. Lilli had not made it publicly known that her days on the screen were over. For the time being she wanted to keep it that way. 'I know the Prince of Wales is very taken with you, so I thought I could have a little dinner party. You'd bring a guest, of course. I know you're staying with the Marchingtons at Hartwood and that divine James.' She laughed out loud and looked heavenward. The gold bangles on her wrists clattered as she clasped her hands together. 'He's like a love-struck puppy around you. It's so plain for all to see.'

Slowly Lilli laid down her plate and wiped her fingers on the dainty linen napkin, playing for time. So this was the posting that Wallis Simpson was offering her in her own personal army: heading up the advance party. She saw Lilli as a society ally without any loyalties to the Establishment. Someone who could feed her morsels of gossip. Her go-between.

In Hollywood Lilli had been content to keep her distance from these people but now, back in England, she found herself being drawn further into their treacherous alliances. Wallis was playing a dangerous game when she drew up battle lines. On one side were the old guard: the king, the queen and indeed the Archbishop of Canterbury, who was being so critical of the prince's relationship with a divorcee. And on the other, were those who saw themselves as the progressives: press barons, industrialists and a few City bankers. That was what this invitation to tea with Wallis had been about. Lilli was being sounded out on her views about joining the ranks of Mrs Simpson's army. The question was, should she accept a commission?

Lilli and Wallis parted on friendly terms with a dinner date suggested, but not confirmed. Since she'd been inside the apartment, a fog had descended on the city. Lilli knew it must be one of the famous poisonous London fogs called pea-soupers. They were as thick as, well, pea soup, and inhaling the fumes could be deadly. The fog forced her taxi to crawl along at less than ten miles an hour. Car headlights were dimmed and sounds muffled. The windows misted up and the cab driver kept swearing under his breath, swerving now and again to avoid pedestrians and parked vehicles that suddenly appeared from nowhere.

Finally when the taxi did arrive at Paddington, Lilli had to be led by the blurred glare of lights into the station entrance. She held a scarf over her mouth so the toxic fog didn't creep into her lungs. From somewhere nearby she heard a newspaper boy shouting at the top of his voice. He spoke in a strange, harsh dialect that she couldn't understand, but, turning to her right, she saw him standing underneath a lamp post. Moving closer she noticed that hooked over his shoulders was a large sandwich board and on it a headline. As soon as she read it Lilli stopped dead.

HITLER RE-ARMS GERMANY!

All the noises that surrounded her; the engines, the shouts, the car horns were drowned out by the drumming of the blood in her ears. James's horrifying prophecy made at the villa in France was confirmed. Adolf Hitler had officially announced he would re-arm Germany. He'd just torn up the Treaty of Versailles.

Chapter 35

Henley-on-Thames, England

Lilli arrived back from London too late for formal dinner at the hall with Lord and Lady Marchington. Instead, James joined her for a tray of cold cuts in the dimly lit study. As soon as they were alone, he put his arms around her, and she laid her head on his chest. It had been a very long time since she'd been held by a man. She allowed herself to dissolve into James's warmth and security.

'You must tell me all about your visit,' he said eagerly, breaking away. He took out glasses from the nearby drinks cabinet and poured two sherries. Handing Lilli one as she sat behind the desk, he settled in the winged chair next to her. She stared down at her plate, on which lay an unappetising array of pressed tongue and tomatoes.

'I can't eat,' she said after a moment, pushing the food away.

James gulped a mouthful of sherry. 'You've seen the headlines in the evening paper?'

'Yes.'

'Did Mrs Simpson mention anything?'

'About Germany? No.'

Lilli paused for a moment, as if wrestling with her thoughts. 'She wants us to dine with her and the prince.'

Both James's brows flew up at the same time. 'Really?'

'She's giving a small dinner party.'

'Interesting,' he said, adding: 'You've done well.'

His unexpected praise brought her up sharply. His behaviour towards her seemed slightly odd, as if he was teaching a dog some new tricks.

'I've done well,' she repeated. 'You make it sound as if I was running an errand for you.'

James frowned, put down his glass and went to her side. 'I'm sorry. I didn't . . .' He took her hand and searched her face. 'I don't want to pressure you into anything that makes you feel uncomfortable.'

She stuck out her jaw. 'I will do everything in my own time, James, and it is a big step to go from being a dancer to a . . .' She stopped short of saying the word, but they both knew it was 'spy.'

James patted her hand. 'Of course. I was asking too much of you to . . .' He scrabbled around to find the right word. 'Help,' he said euphemistically. They both knew what he really wanted Lilli to do was spy on the Windsors for the British intelligence agency. He fingered his collar. 'You need time to consider. I will leave it up to you to make the next move.'

Lilli nodded. She was glad to establish the parameters of this new relationship. She would not take orders from James, nor was she ready to be a spy. Not yet. She would simply assist him where she could, gathering information from time to time, but nothing more formal than that. Their partnership, if there was to be one, would be on equal terms.

'She mentioned something about a fort,' Lilli continued after a moment. She sipped her sherry recalling snatches of the idle chit-chat she'd had with Mrs Simpson.

James perked up again and nodded. 'Fort Belvedere, in Windsor Great Park. It's where she and the prince spend as much time together as they can. She's splashed thousands of pounds on the place over the last few months,' he told her. 'Apparently it's a veritable love nest,' he added disdainfully. He drained his glass.

Lilli took another sip of her sherry. 'She wanted us to meet another couple, too. She said she was sure the man would love to talk politics with me.'

James arched a brow. 'Any names?' He asked, helping himself to another glass.

'Moses?' she asked tentatively.

He almost choked on his sherry. 'Good God,' he spluttered. A look of unease clouded his face. 'Not Oswald Mosley?'

'Yes, that's the name. Oswald Mosley. Who is he?' Lilli asked.

James turned to her, his eyes wide. 'He's only the leader of the British Union of Fascists, my darling.'

'I see,' replied Lilli, the relaxing effect of the sherry suddenly wearing off.

'He's a great friend of both Mussolini and Hitler,' he added. 'A nasty piece of work if ever there was one.'

Lilli nodded reluctantly. At the mention of Hitler, her thoughts returned to Leon's last letter. Her reply may have sounded far too dismissive. Somehow, she must arrange for her family to leave Germany before it was too late. Draining the dregs of her glass, she said: 'Then I suppose we'd better accept.'

Chapter 36

Fort Belvedere, Windsor Great Park

Fort Belvedere's turrets rose from the trees as the Jaguar drove Lilli and James through the Great Park, near Windsor. It was early summer, and the rhododendron and azalea bushes were in full bloom, providing a riot of reds, purple and pale pink to line their route. A huge lake glowed gold in the setting sunlight, while the eccentric building itself reminded Lilli of Rapunzel's tower in the Grimms' fairy tale; more like a child's idea of a fort than a real one.

The whole, picturesque setting was so at odds with what she and James both knew they would face that evening. Only four weeks ago Mosley had come out publicly challenging what he called 'the Jewish interests' in Britain.

'He's modelling himself on Hitler,' James told her as they were driven through the wrought-iron gates. 'He's saying all Jews are dangerous.'

Lilli knew it would be hard for her to hold her tongue if provoked. No doubt Mosley would be spouting his poison round the dinner table. His blatant anti-Semitism would surely rear its ugly head during the course of the meal and would probably garner ringing endorsements from the prince and Mrs Simpson. But she and James would be forced to remain silent. Certainly James could no longer afford himself the luxury of speaking his mind as he had at the Villa Mauresque if he intended to ingratiate himself into this circle. He could easily attract unwanted attention and suspicion. And as for Lilli? Well, it was agreed she would do what she always did best. She would put on a mask. Play a part. Hide her anger and her pain.

'Have I told you how beautiful you look this evening?' asked James as they slowed down in front of the fort. Lilli's gown of shimmering amber silk made her eyes sparkle even more than usual.

She smiled graciously. That first kiss had been quite different from any other kiss she'd ever had. It was tender, rather than passionate. It made her feel warm inside, rather than lusted over and, more importantly, it left her wanting more. James had persuaded her to stay at Hartwood Hall for a few more days, but after that, Lady Marchington, perhaps suspecting romance was in the air and generally disapproving of anything German, made it very obvious that her welcome was not indefinite. Lilli had moved out.

For the past few weeks she'd been renting a passable flat in Bayswater. James had been a regular visitor, although not once had he asked to stay the night. Lilli had never been involved with an Englishman before. James's manners were like his dress sense, impeccable. Perhaps he was just very *gentlemanly*.

The prince and Wallis greeted them in the grand drawing room. It was elegant, yet homely. Lilli admired Mrs Simpson's good taste, even if she did feel there were far too many cushions on display.

'Welcome to Fort Belvedere, Lillian,' Wallis cried, embracing her guest rather dramatically in the French fashion. 'And the dashing Honourable Mr Marchington,' she purred, holding out her hand for James to kiss. 'We're so glad you both could come, aren't we David?' She turned to the prince, standing next to her.

'Yes, quite,' he agreed. 'Especially Miss Stern,' he told Lilli with a good-natured wink.

Loud voices were suddenly heard in the hall and Wallis's attention was immediately distracted as Sir Oswald Mosley and his mistress Diana Guinness, entered. Mosley was suave and elegant and as soon as he walked in the room, Lilli found him strikingly handsome. She could easily see how his sharp style and good looks made him charismatic to many female followers. If he hadn't been a politician, he could have made it in Hollywood, she told herself. His mistress was equally beautiful. The ravishing Diana was one of the scandalous Mitford sisters, and famed for her bohemian lifestyle.

Wallis dived straight in as soon as introductions were done.

'Have you seen Miss Stern's fabulous film?' she asked Mosley as the Champagne was dispensed. 'Everyone's talking about it.'

'I have,' Diana butted in. She fixed Lilli with a look of barely disguised envy. 'How lucky you were to dance with the divine Astaire.'

Lilli forced a smile. James had told her all about this woman who had been having an affair with Mosley even before the death of his young wife.

'Yes. Very,' she replied, taking a sip of champagne to fill an awkward silence.

'Do you plan to work with him again?' continued Diana, but Wallis jumped in before Lilli could explain.

'Miss Stern has sustained an injury,' Wallis blurted. 'She has left Hollywood for the time being and so we are to have the pleasure of her company for the foreseeable future.' She threw Lilli a loaded smile. 'I'm sure she will put her considerable talents to good use.'

Lilli returned the smile, even though she was unsure what Wallis meant. The image of her at the head of an army flashed into her mind once more. It was certainly clear that Mrs Simpson was counting on her support.

Wallis and the prince were seated at either end of the table, while Oswald Mosley was on Lilli's left. James sat opposite her. The conversation centred on the season so far, on polo and horse racing at Royal Ascot. Chilled Vichyssoise soup was served for the first course, followed by turbot, but it was when the entrée appeared that the conversation took a darker turn.

When the servant deftly served the meat on the plate in front of her, Lilli let down her guard for a moment. It was pork. Three oval slices of hot pig flesh. She had eaten pork before, of course, even though it was forbidden by Jewish law, but tonight, in such company, the thought of consuming it suddenly troubled her, as if the meat had become almost symbolic. Her concern must have registered in her face because Oswald Mosley picked up on it immediately.

'Something wrong with the pork, Miss Stern?' he asked, leaning slightly towards her plate to inspect it.

Lilli felt the colour rise in her cheeks. 'Whatever can you mean, Sir Oswald?' she replied, slightly tetchily. 'Nothing is wrong. Nothing at all.'

He barked out a laugh. 'For a horrible moment,' he said, looking around the rest of the table, 'I thought you were going to tell us you were Jewish.'

The prince, helping himself to gravy from a silver boat, joined in the laughter and Mrs Simpson tittered. 'Oh Oswald,' she chided. 'You really are too bad.'

Clearly Mosley took her reaction as a sign of encouragement. 'You can't be too careful these days,' he carried on, arming himself with his knife and fork. 'The Yids are everywhere. Running the whole bally show!'

From the other side of the table Diana joined in. 'I expect there are lots of Jews in Hollywood, Miss Stern.'

Lilli wanted to catch James's eye, but she was aware that if she did, she would give herself away. She dared not look at him. This was what they had both anticipated.

'Quite a few,' she replied, picking up her own knife and fork and slicing into the meat. She wanted to avoid eye contact at all costs.

'Quite a few is still too many,' barked Mosley. He lifted his wine glass and took a sip to allow the ripple of laughter from Diana and Wallis to die down. James even managed to raise a false smile.

Lilli saw the prince nod in agreement and suddenly she found herself unable to swallow. *Dance through the pain*, she told herself. The situation was becoming unbearably difficult.

It was Diana who piled on the pressure. Stroking the stem of her wine glass, she asked cattily: 'So if you are not returning to Hollywood, what will you do with your time, Miss Stern?'

Before Lilli could muster a reply, Wallis leapt in. Fixing Lilli with an intriguing smile, she announced: 'We have something that might interest you, don't we David?' She looked at the prince who suddenly dabbed the glistening gravy from his chin with his napkin.

'Yes, indeed. It's a project very close to my own heart,' he replied.

'The AGF?' asked Mosley, setting down his knife and fork.

'Indeed, dear fellow,' replied the prince, lightly slapping the table.

James had been rather reserved for most of the evening, speaking only when spoken to. He'd left Lilli feeling rather isolated, but now he stepped up and made the running.

'The Anglo-German Fellowship group,' he volunteered.

'That's right,' the prince said cheerfully. 'We need to offer the hand of friendship to our German cousins. They've had a tough time of it since the war. We need to build bridges, not fences.'

'It's your pet, isn't it, David?' said Wallis patronisingly. She spoke directly to the others as if the prince were not at the table. 'He's got great plans: banquets, receptions at the German Embassy. Even the kaiser's daughter has agreed to be a guest of honour.'

Lilli saw James suddenly come to life. 'What a splendid idea!'

'Isn't it just?' the prince smiled smugly.

'And what about you?' Wallis asked Lilli pointedly. 'What do you think of the idea, Lillian?'

Lilli swallowed down a forkful of potato dauphinoise. 'It

sounds interesting,' she managed, hoping she hadn't sounded too cool as soon as she'd replied.

James added his approval. 'Very. Tell us more,' he urged, shooting a glance at Lilli.

The prince nodded. 'It was all inspired by that "hand of friend-ship" speech I gave recently.'

'The one at the Royal Albert Hall,' interjected James. He'd read a transcript of the speech. On the surface it had seemed harm-less enough, reaching out to former enemies and all that, but he knew a deeper purpose lay behind it.

'That's the one,' replied the prince, leaning forward. 'Got a lot of interest and now top people want to be involved; bankers, army men, the odd newspaper tycoon: none of your riff-raff, of course.' He chuckled as he flapped a hand.

Wallis, however, didn't laugh, although she was smiling rather enigmatically at Lilli. Her hostess's penetrating gaze made Lilli feel a little uncomfortable, as if it foreshadowed something. She soon discovered her intuition was correct.

'And that's where we thought you might like to come in, Lillian,' Wallis ventured. Her eyes clamped onto her guest.

'Me?' Lilli's hand flew up to her breast.

'We thought you'd be an excellent ambassador for us,' said the prince.

Lilli felt her stomach suddenly clench. She'd known all along that this evening wasn't a merely social occasion; it was a care-fully engineered ambush. Mosley and Diana Guinness had been recruited as reinforcements. They might have been fully informed of the plans – probably even shaped them.

The pork that she'd just managed to swallow suddenly threat-ened to show itself involuntarily once more. Nevertheless, she managed to suppress the distaste she felt at the mere suggestion she should join these people in some sort of organisation. Her eyes slid to James. The enormity of what had just been said was almost too much for her to take in. She found herself floundering.

James was forced to jump in. 'What an excellent idea,' he said, nodding vigorously. It wasn't the reaction she'd hoped for from him. 'You'd do a splendid job, Lillian, I'm sure.'

She could hardly believe he was volunteering her for something so totally abhorrent. But her fears were confirmed when she felt his foot nudge hers under the table.

'I'm flattered,' she replied.

Encouraged by her reaction, Wallis went on: 'You'd have a small team to work for you, of course.'

'Of course,' reiterated the prince.

Mosley wiped his chin with his napkin and turned towards her. 'And there'd be quite a bit of fund-raising, schmoozing the donors, that sort of thing,' he continued, adding with a leer: 'But I imagine you're rather good at that sort of thing.' Suddenly she felt his hand squeeze her thigh under the table.

A chill ran through her whole body. It took all her resolve to remain seated. She wanted to escape. James had warned her it might be like this. He'd told her there would be snobbery and prejudice, bigotry and racial slurs, but she hadn't been prepared for how uncomfortable it would make her feel; how hard it was to hide her anger. She was having to draw upon all her reserves as an actress to veil the contempt she felt for these people. *This is a film set*, she kept telling herself, *and I must act out my role.*

Lilli was silent at first in the car on the way back. She was numb. It was as if she had been assaulted so badly that she'd lost all feeling. Her thoughts flicked to her frail parents and to Leon; how they were forced to endure persecution one hundred times worse than this every day while the world turned its back. They were being mocked and vilified for no other reason than their birth, and she could not stand idly by and watch while that happened.

It fell upon James to bring her round. He took her ice-cold hand in his.

'I'm so sorry you had to go through that,' he told her. He

brought her fingers up to his mouth and kissed them gently. She felt the warmth of his lips. 'I'll write to them to say your parents are ill and that you need to nurse them in Germany, or something. You certainly can't do what they've asked of you.' He sighed deeply and looked out of the car window. 'I should never have let you come.' He shook his head. 'I encouraged them and it was wrong of me.' He switched his head round to look at her once more. 'Will you ever forgive me for getting you into this mess, Lilli, darling?'

He looked at her profile silhouetted in the darkness. The lights of a car travelling in the opposite direction suddenly threw its beams onto her face and he could see her cheeks were wet with silent tears.

Once more he clasped her hand. 'Oh Lilli, talk to me. Say something, please.'

She remained silent for a little while longer then turned towards him.

'I will do it, James,' she said slowly and calmly.

'What?' James held his breath. 'What do you mean?'

She switched back, her unseeing eyes fixed straight ahead. 'James,' she whispered into the darkness.

'Yes, dear Lilli.'

'Tell me how I can join your British secret service? I want to become an agent.'

Chapter 37

London, England

From the outside, the bookshop at No 205 Charing Cross Road looked just like every other bookshop along the thoroughfare. The paintwork was flaking, just as it was on most of the front-ages, and like almost all of them it gave off an air of genteel and erudite decay.

The large, plate glass window offered passers-by a glimpse of the wares inside. Books. Hundreds of them. Large, medium, small, leather-bound, case-bound and cardboard-covered: they lined the shelves inside like troops on parade.

Lilli studied the piece of paper in her hand. This was the correct address. Her own misgivings whispered inside her head as she held the door handle firm. But she turned it and ventured inside, setting off the bell. She walked into a sort of cave made entirely of dusty volumes that stretched from floor to ceiling. There appeared to be several rooms leading off from the main shop, all crammed with specialist books, stored under strange headings, such as *anthropology* or *ecclesiology*. She'd no idea what the words meant. It certainly was a warren of knowledge.

The smell of leather mingled with dust and damp and caught

the back of her throat. She meandered through a labyrinth of shelves until, after a moment, she became aware she was being watched by a plump, elderly man behind the counter.

She cleared her throat. 'Good morning,' she greeted him cautiously.

He threw her a suspicious look and tugged at his woollen cardigan which had ridden up over his large belly.

'Yes,' he replied warily.

Not to be put off, she glanced at the piece of paper once more then summoned her courage and announced: 'I'm looking for a copy of *The Conquest of the Troublesome Mind* by JB Baltimore.' The statement was made with great conviction and met with the required response.

'Are you, indeed?' said the man, his eyes disappearing to slits. The title clearly registered with him. 'Then you'd better follow me,' he beckoned.

He shepherded her into yet another room and through a hidden faux door that was cut into the bookshelves. Lilli felt like Alice, being led by a portly white rabbit into a strange Wonderland. Inside there was another small office, where a young woman sat. Her hair was tucked under a knitted scarf that was swathed around her head. She looked up.

'She wants Baltimore,' the man relayed.

The young woman switched her gaze to Lilli and gave her a peremptory look. She said nothing but went to a large, black safe in the corner. After turning the dial four times it gave a satisfying click and she reached inside to retrieve the elusive copy.

'Guard this with your life,' she warned Lilli. She handed over the volume with a calm efficiency then reached for a dowdy mackintosh hanging on a peg.

'This way,' she said, unlocking the back door and opening it wide. And Lilli stepped out onto a gated courtyard to begin her journey through the unknown back streets of central London.

One lane seemed to join with another; a hidden back entrance opened onto a second and a third. There were archways and alleys, gates and gratings. The route was tortuous and clearly designed to confuse so that Lilli would never be able to remember the way there, or indeed, find her way back. After about twenty minutes, the young woman, who'd remained silent throughout the journey, turned to her charge outside a black, studded door underneath a brick arch. Her eyes slid towards a buzzer at the side.

'Cheerio and good luck,' she said, as if Lilli were about to go over the top of a Flanders trench. She disappeared the way they had come, leaving the new recruit alone on the front step.

Lilli's finger hovered over the buzzer. Once she had pushed it there would be no turning back. She thought of her parents and of Leon. She pressed hard.

The building seemed to be a residential block. A washing line was strung from one window across the alley. After a moment she heard footsteps on the stairs and an older woman in serviceable tweeds answered.

'You have something for me?' she asked.

Lilli nervously handed over the volume, which seemed to pass muster, and followed her up a rickety staircase to the fifth floor of the building.

Miss Tweed went ahead through another door and a man's voice was heard shortly after.

'Come!' he barked.

Lilli was ushered into a room where a uniformed officer stood to greet her. British Army, she guessed. He had a peninsula of sandy hair on his head and a neat moustache.

'Plimpton,' he told her, reaching a hand over his desk. His shake was firm and precise. 'Colonel Plimpton. Have a seat, Miss Sternberg.'

Lilli was slightly unnerved. This man knew her name. Her real name. He knew her secret. He held a file in his hand. It must contain information about her; the information that James had compiled, she thought. She took a seat, trying to stop herself from shaking.

Plimpton tapped the file. 'You come highly recommended. Bilingual. Good connections. Just the sort we need,' he said, pulling out his chair and sitting down. He spoke in an odd, clipped accent which Lilli found a little hard to follow.

James had asked her all sorts of questions about her childhood, schooling and her family and written a testimonial for her. Now the colonel had the report in front of him, she found herself feeling like a student again, back at the *Académie de Danse*, hoping for praise and dreading censure.

'Thank you, sir,' she replied.

'And, what's more you're Jewish.' He skewed her with a dour look. 'Axe to grind, I dare say.'

Lilli felt suddenly vulnerable, as if this man had just taken off her clothes. She had to show him she was strong; she was aware of the threat posed by the Hitler's government. 'I know that the Fascists are persecuting German Jews, sir. My brother writes to me about the situation. I am helping my parents leave the country.' In her last letter home, Lilli told Leon to begin the process of documentation. She'd promised the necessary funds.

'Very wise,' he agreed.

'The Nazis are dangerous, not just for Germany but for Europe, too,' she added, surprising even herself with the conviction in her voice.'

Colonel Plimpton nodded. 'Quite so. Munich, eh? In the thick of it.'

He scanned the file in front of him once more. 'But you'll know that what interests us particularly, Miss Sternberg, is your connection with . . .' He broke off and cleared his throat, as if he could not bring himself to speak the Prince of Wales's name. As if to do so would be tantamount to treason.

Since the dinner at Fort Belvedere, Lilli had met with Mrs Simpson and the prince twice to discuss the promotion of the Anglo-German Fellowship group. They'd supplied her with a list of names and contact details. Her first task was to organise a fundraising event at the Ritz to be held in the autumn, the details of which James had written in his report.

'I believe they consider me an ally,' she ventured. 'I am working for them in an unofficial capacity.'

'But they're not aware that you're Jewish?'

'No.' She suddenly shuddered at the recollection of the incident with Oswald Mosley and the pork at Fort Belvedere.

The colonel studied her for a moment. His eyes played on her hair and her face as if she were an insect on a laboratory slide. 'Can I ask you why you have deliberately hidden your heritage?'

The question shocked her. She paused to frame her reply, but when it came it was delivered with conviction. 'I don't wish to go through life with a label that was given me at birth. I want to make my own decisions, my own way in the world. Is that so wrong?'

Colonel Plimpton stroked his neat moustache, his mouth drooping beneath it and his head nodding. He seemed impressed by her reply.

'So you are not afraid of it?'

It was another question that surprised her. 'I changed my hair colour for professional reasons, Colonel. My name, too.'

He glanced down at the file. 'Ah, yes. Lillian Stern.'

'But acting as a gentile has been, how you say, a real eye-opener.'

'Oh?' He frowned. 'In what way?'

'It means I can mix in circles, powerful circles, where true feelings about us Jews are freely discussed.'

Plimpton understood what she was driving at. Fascists weren't just ruling Germany. They were poised for power in Britain, too.

'Then you'd better sign this, Miss Sternberg,' he told her, slipping a piece of paper across the desk. Lilli read the heading in large letters. *Official Secrets Act.* 'You'll need to pass a couple of tests: psychological stuff and all that malarkey.'

'Excuse me?'

Plimpton was talking in riddles, using unfamiliar words.

'Forgive me. All that *business*,' he said. 'But I'm sure you'll do well. Then we could start you off working for British Intelligence in an "unofficial" capacity,' he added with a smirk. 'Given your specific area of expertise—'

'Specific?' Lilli cut in.

'Normally we'd require you to go through the hoops, days of training and what-not, but because we have a particular target in mind, that won't be necessary.'

'You mean Mrs Simpson?'

The colonel scowled, as if Lilli had spoken out of turn. 'You are here, Miss Stern, because of your relationship with a certain person in royal circles. Therefore, your task is plain and simple. You must inform us about every contact she makes, every intention she has, every meeting she holds and every thought she confides in you. Understood?'

'Understood,' Lilli repeated, before scribbling her signature on the bottom of the paper.

'Just a word of warning, Miss Sternberg,' said Plimpton, as Lilli handed back the paper. 'I don't have to tell you this is dangerous work. You may be called upon to take risks in providing information about the enemy. You understand?'

Lilli wasn't sure if Colonel Plimpton was being overly dramatic or deadly serious. Was he referring to Wallis Simpson as 'the enemy'?

'I understand,' she replied.

'You'll get a thorough briefing in the next few days, but until then . . .' He stood to shake her hand. 'You must say nothing of this. Only Marchington can know. *Capeesh?*'

Lilli smiled at the colonel's Italian. 'I do,' she replied, taking his hand once more.

She expected to be shown the door, but instead Plimpton beckoned her to the window that looked out onto a relatively busy street. Motor cars were driving by and pedestrians were going about their business. Lilli saw nothing unusual until the colonel pointed to the corner below them. A man in a trilby hat was lounging against a wall, smoking a cigarette.

'Been there all morning,' he told her. 'Leave by the back door, will you?'

Lilli looked at Plimpton. 'You mean he's . . .?'

'Hitler's agents are everywhere. London's crawling with them. Just be careful,' he told her.

And with those words Lilli was dismissed into the outside world, knowing that her life was now split in two and one must know nothing of the other. She had just become an agent for the British secret service.

Chapter 38

James suggested they dine at a little French bistro he knew just off Carnaby Street. The woodwork was very dark and prints by Renoir and Cezanne hung on panels on the walls. Although there were glass chandeliers and crisp, white linen cloths, it was much more intimate than anywhere they'd dined before. He was waiting when Lilli arrived, a candle already lit on the table and a bottle of Krug in an ice bucket on the side. He rose as soon as he saw her and the moustachioed waiter took her fur stole, while another poured the champagne.

'So, the deed is done? The die is cast?' James whispered after the waiter retreated.

'It is,' she replied.

He smiled and lifted his glass to chink it with hers. 'To us.'

'To us and to what we must do.'

They gazed at each other, Lilli's diamond earrings glinting in the candlelight. There was a newfound intimacy between them, a new bond that tied them inextricably together.

'I think you're terribly brave,' he told her. 'You're standing up to protect your people. You don't have to. You could so easily ignore everything that's going on, but you chose not to.'

She shrugged, partly to hide the shiver that had just run

down her spine and partly to cover her guilt. When she'd left for the States, she'd put her own dreams before her family and given them little thought when she was in Hollywood. Informing on the political activities of the British elite who were colluding with and threatening those she loved, was her small way of making amends.

'I'm doing no more than you, James. We're both standing up for what we believe is right, that's all.'

As he sipped his champagne the waiter arrived balancing a large plate of fat oysters on a silver tray. He laid them down on the table.

'I took the liberty,' James said, tucking a large, white napkin under his chin. 'The food of love.'

They talked without pausing. Lilli told him more about her life in Munich and he went on to explain the intricacies of the English primogeniture laws, unsuccessfully as it happened. But his wit and knowledge only attracted her to him even more.

'So as the second son of an earl, I get nothing when my father dies, although luckily my grandmother left me a tidy sum. Gwen won't get anything, either, but she'll marry someone frightfully rich anyway, so it doesn't matter.'

Lilli's lips curled at the edges. 'You English with your titles and estates,' she said, smiling. 'It's money that makes the world go round.'

Her words stopped James in his tracks, and he arched a brow in thought. 'I suppose, in the scheme of things, it is.'

'Money gives you more freedom to choose. To think and say what you believe. To love who you want to,' she suggested.

James had moved much closer to her during the course of the dinner. The sleeve of his dinner jacket was now brushing her naked arm.

'You really are truly remarkable, Miss Stern,' he said, looking deep into her eyes. 'Not like any other woman I've ever met.' He held her gaze for a moment then reached into his pocket. 'That's why I simply have to ask you something.' He brought out a small red box and opened it in front of her.

Lilli let out a muted gasp. Sitting on a red velvet cushion was a large emerald, surrounded by diamonds and mounted on a gold band.

'Will you marry me, Lilli Sternberg?'

Chapter 39

Kensington and Chelsea Register Office was not the fairy-tale *schloss* where Lilli had dreamed of getting married since childhood, but the wedding was a happy, if quiet, affair. Golda and Jacob were absent, of course. So was Leon. Even if her parents had been comfortable with her marrying a gentile, Jacob wasn't fit enough to travel and, besides, Golda wouldn't leave him. Moreover, despite her brother's repeated efforts, they'd all been denied the appropriate exit documents on some flimsy excuse. The chances of them being allowed to leave Germany, let alone come to England, were fast receding.

James's relations didn't seem enthused by the union, either. Only Gwendoline attended from the groom's family and her sour expression was mirrored in the acidic yellow of her suit. They'd invited the prince and Mrs Simpson out of courtesy, but were very relieved when they both declined, citing the fact that their presence would probably attract more pressmen and photographers than guests. While many of Lilli's erstwhile Hollywood friends sent their congratulations, in the end Jessica Van Haselt and Adele and Charles were the only other guests who attended to throw confetti, quaff champagne and wish the happy couple well.

Even though she no longer needed to pretend to be someone

she was not in front of James, it had still taken Lilli two months to give her answer to his proposal. The Honourable James Arthur Montague Marchington was one of the few people who knew what she was really carrying round with her, deep inside: the baggage of a past that dragged her down so heavily in the present. Yet James had been very persistent, sending her flowers, love poems and even a brooch that had once belonged to his grandmother until Lilli had finally agreed to marriage. Not that she'd been free of her own misgivings. James was no Marco. He was a completely different type of man. But he was serious, sensitive and financially secure – surely qualities that most sensible women look for in a spouse? She liked the fact that he had never been anything other than a perfect gentleman, too. He'd put no pressure on her to become his lover. That was another of the reasons why she'd finally succumbed to his charms. With hindsight, she should have realised.

At first Lilli attributed James's awkward fumbling between the sheets to wedding-night nerves. He had, after all, confessed that he was a virgin. She coaxed and cajoled, but even her Parisian lingerie, it seemed, was not enough to excite him sufficiently. The build-up to the wedding had been rather stressful, especially when Gwendoline initially refused to attend, although she later relented. It was clear to Lilli that her sister-in-law regarded her as nothing but a proverbial gold digger. She supposed Gwendoline's cold shoulder had upset her new husband.

It would be different on the Côte d'Azur, Lilli told herself. Willie Maugham had suggested the newly-weds honeymoon in a delightful little hideaway just along the coast from the Villa Mauresque. A cook, a steward and a concierge would be at their disposal. The villa even had its own swimming pool.

Lilli was certainly enchanted by its setting. The evening of their arrival, they drank cocktails on a terrace looking out over the Mediterranean. A Bloody Mary for her, a Martini for him. Lilli thought there was something vaguely familiar about the young man who served them.

To their left lay Italy, shimmering and magical in the heat; to their right St Tropez, whose bright colours were smudged by an opaque blue mist. The air was heavy with the smell of rosemary and lavender and an orchestra of unseen crickets played the soundtrack. Together they watched the sun sink low in the sky.

Over dinner, as Lilli admired James expertly tackle a lobster claw, her new husband delivered some news.

'Syrie telephoned earlier,' he told her.

'Yes.'

'She said she simply has to take you shopping in Antibes tomorrow.'

They were seated at a table under a vine-clad pergola. Little boats fished by oil lamps and pinpricks of light dotted the coastline like glow worms. James's announcement broke Lilli's mood.

'Oh,' was all she could manage at first, arching her brow. She was a little disappointed. 'I'd rather hoped we could spend tomorrow together,' she told him, playing with the stem of her wineglass. 'The pool looks—'

James cut her off. 'She really was most insistent, darling,' he said with one of his disarming smiles. The candlelight made him look even more attractive to her. 'I'd love you to stay, too, but her car's due here at eleven.' He returned to his lobster, teasing out the flesh with silver pincers. 'She wants you to spend the whole day together. Something about a market then lunch at a seafood bistro.'

Lilli did not argue, but leaned forward, flaunting her cleavage to allow her new husband to light her cigarette for her. 'I shall miss you,' she purred, as obligingly he took out his lighter and stole a peek down her neckline. For an instant she thought he might react. She even toyed with the idea of taking his hand and placing it on her breast, but when he'd extinguished the flame, he leaned back once more and resumed his tussle with the lobster. Quietly admitting defeat, Lilli also retreated into her chair, throwing back her head and blowing smoke into the warm air as she looked up at the stars. Her new husband's seduction would take a little more work.

They'd spent another awkward night together. There had been more gauche pawings from James. A wet kiss had shown promise, but it was not followed with anything of real note. This time his excuse was that it was 'jolly hot.' He had simply pecked her on the forehead and turned over to sleep.

The following day Syrie duly arrived and whisked Lilli off into Antibes. The market hall was bursting with fruit and vegetables of all kinds and colours, its stalls a dazzling array of red tomatoes, dark black cherries and lemons. Bunches of herbs, of thyme and sage, perfumed the air and fat cloves of garlic packed a punch. Clusters of sausages festooned the cross beams, hanging above hocks of smoked ham and large loaves dusted with flour vied against blocks of sweet, white nougat.

'*Vous voulez, Madame?*' A market woman thrust a thin slice of tarte au citron in front of Lilli and, after a little encouragement from Syrie, she took it, a sharp lusciousness exploding on her tongue.

They moved outside where, among the plane trees, the bric-a-brac stalls nestled in the shade. There were great bundles of bedlinen and embroidered tea cloths, shawls and nightgowns. Syrie picked one up and held it to her own body. It reached up to her chin and down beyond her knees.

'A passion-killer,' she said with a laugh. 'Although I daresay it won't be needed.'

Lilli, not quite understanding what Syrie meant, nevertheless dismissed the remark with a coy smile.

There were brass candlesticks, mirrors, iron bedsteads, trunks and paintings – so many paintings – but Lilli's fancy was taken by some silk handkerchiefs. She bought one for James and then decided a few little cloth bags of lavender would be perfect to scent her armoire. Syrie bought a lace shawl then announced it was time for lunch.

'I know this divine little place,' she said before they ventured into the back streets to find the bistro, tucked away between a printer's and what appeared to be a brothel. They ate Coquilles St Jacques and salad. The restaurant was very authentic and very enjoyable, but the wine and the heat, took their toll. They proved an almost unbearable combination. By two o'clock Lilli could no longer cope with the searing pain in her temples.

Fanning her face with her menu, Lilli told Syrie: 'I'm so sorry, but I have a terrible headache. I need to lie down.'

'Too bad, darling,' Syrie commiserated. 'Another time.'

The chauffeur dropped Lilli back at the villa. James had told her he would take the opportunity to catch up on some gallery paperwork while she was away, so she was slightly surprised to see his bathing robe draped over a sun lounger by the pool. Wet footprints leading inside told her he'd been for a swim. In fact, there seemed to be rather a lot of prints on the slabs. Had someone dropped by unannounced? she wondered. The French doors were open. It took a moment for her eyes to adjust from the outside glare, but there was no sign of her husband in his study, either. The kitchen was silent, too, and then she remembered James had given both the cook and the concierge the afternoon off. The whole place was eerily quiet.

Setting down her packages on the hall console table, she started to climb the stone staircase. Her head was still throbbing and she hoped she'd remembered to pack some aspirin in her vanity case.

'James,' she called softly from the landing. 'James, darling, are you there?' From the bedroom she heard a faint thud, then a creak of bedsprings. She supposed she must've woken him from a siesta. She imagined herself slipping naked between the cool sheets, even though her headache meant that she was now the one in no mood to consummate their marriage.

'James, darling,' she muttered again, pushing against the door. The next sound she heard was a little disembodied scream escaping from her own mouth, followed by one from her husband.

'God, no!' James shrieked, pulling the sheets over his groin.

Lilli remained rooted to the spot as her wide eyes switched from her husband to the person rising unashamedly from the dishevelled bed. As James floundered, grappling with sheets, his lover, a bronze-bodied Adonis glistening with sweat, appeared to pose naked before her wearing nothing but a smirk.

'Darling, I can . . . I can . . .' James blurted.

Yet his jumble of words fell on deaf ears. Lilli's attention was fully occupied by the young man, who now slid unhurriedly into his white boxer shorts. He was the waiter from the previous evening; the one she'd thought she recognised from somewhere else. As he calmly reached for his discarded trousers, her mind flew back to the drawing room in the Villa Mauresque.

'Lilli, please.' James was panicking as he swaddled himself in his dressing robe, but she paid him no attention. It was his lover who drew her gaze, the tanned skin and the slicked hair. To her horror she remembered he was the young cocktail waiter she'd seen talking to Willie Maugham by the French windows that night she first laid eyes on Wallis Simpson.

Chapter 40

London, England

Lilli's return to London, and to the new marital home in Kensington Square, was obviously not as she'd planned. In the past two weeks she'd discovered that the Honourable James Arthur Montague Marchington was not what he seemed. He was handsome, yes, debonair, yes, rich, witty and cultured – all those things, too. Indeed, he was everything a woman could want in a man, apart from a lover.

Lilli had fallen for him and now found herself trapped. The same sense of betrayal that had engulfed her after Marco ended their affair, threatened to overwhelm her yet again. The rest of the honeymoon had obviously been spent in separate rooms. She had cried herself to sleep that first night. She was not only angry with James but with herself, too. She'd gone for what she thought was the sensible option and it turned out to be anything but. This time, however, she vowed she'd be stronger. No one need ever know about her humiliation. And by the end of their two-week honeymoon she had a plan.

For all intents and purposes, she and James could be a perfectly normal married couple, in name at least. After all she wasn't the first woman to marry a homosexual man and she wouldn't be the last. Syrie Maugham must certainly be aware of her own husband's antics. Her remark about the nightgown at the market now made perfect sense. She knew James was a homosexual and probably thought that Lilli did, too.

Several times James had apologised for misleading her, claiming that he loved her but couldn't help himself with other men. Still, it took Lilli a few more days after returning to the marital home in an affluent residential area, just off Kensington High Street, before she felt strong enough to address the issue.

In the meantime, she had work to do. Important work. During her time in France, a detailed briefing had arrived from the Prince of Wales. Throwing herself into working for the Anglo-German Fellowship would make a welcome diversion from dealing with her own domestic crisis. Soon she discovered that supporters willing to part with their money in order to dine at the Ritz or the Savoy, or dance till dawn at the Café de Paris with people of a similar ilk, were easy to find. The likes of newspaper editors, admirals and even Prince von Bismarck flocked to the Prince of Wales's coterie, partying in public, but making political plans behind the scenes.

Now, as Christmas approached, and the personal invitations to soirées and dinners piled up on her Kensington mantelshelf, Lilli thought it time she and James had a serious discussion about the public front they should display. In the four-storey house they shared, she tended to avoid him. It was hard to be in the same room, let alone sleep in the same bed or eat at the same table. On this occasion, however, she'd proposed that they sit down together over a civilised drink or two. She'd given Madame Dupont, their French housekeeper, the evening off.

Lilli sat on the sofa to the left of the fireplace; James, looking nervous, sat on the chair opposite. Battle lines were drawn, only from the look of resignation on her husband's face, she detected he'd already conceded that the victory was hers for the taking. On her lap sat a notepad on which she'd written down her demands before any sort of truce could be called.

'It's been hard for me, James,' she began.

He doubled over so that his elbows rested on his knees.

'You know I'm so terribly sorry, but I still love you, Lilli. If I'd told you the truth, you'd have run a mile.' His fringe had flopped forward and his beautiful face was contorted with despair.

Lilli's back stiffened. She hated to see him grovel like this. She thought of an English expression she'd recently heard. *To have your cake and eat it*; when someone wanted the benefit of two things when it was only reasonable to have one.

'Any woman with self-respect would have run a mile, as you put it, James. Luckily for you, while I do have respect for myself, I am also, *was ist dar Wort*, pragmatic.'

James perked up. He lifted his head to reveal an intrigued look on his face. 'What do you mean?'

Her manner was brisk, forthright. 'I've drawn up a set of rules that we should both observe so that we can continue to live together.'

James sat up straight and nodded. 'Fire away,' he said.

So Lilli reeled off the conditions under which she was still prepared to live under the same roof as her legal husband.

'I have, of course, considered an annulment on the grounds of non-consummation, but,' she picked up a silver cigarette case from the coffee table, 'I've decided if I did that it would only destroy the network I've built up for the intelligence service.' She selected a cigarette, and tapped the tip on the case's closed lid. She needed the valuable social contacts her marriage legitimised, the powerful network of influential donors to the prince's new group who accepted her as one of their own.

James reached for the nearby lighter and obligingly clicked it. She dipped her face towards the flame and dragged the cigarette into life.

'As your wife I still intend to be presented at Court in the season and to enjoy all the privileges my status offers.' She did not look at him as she spoke, her words rolling out on the tobacco smoke that she kept wafting away. She talked as if she was reeling off some imaginary shopping list. In short, she wanted all the doors that her aristocratic union with James presented to be opened for her.

'Is that understood?' she said firmly, flicking ash into a Lalique ashtray.

James clearly had little say in the matter. 'Understood,' he replied, sounding like a small boy in trouble at school.

'But it also means we need to trust each other, James,' she added. 'We are in this together,' she pointed out, as if her husband needed reminding of his obligations to British intelligence. 'Although,' she added with her brow arched: 'affairs are permitted, as long as they are discreet.'

Lilli had decided that in return for his social kudos, James would be left to follow his own sexual appetites without arousing general suspicion.

She stubbed out her cigarette slowly and deliberately in the ashtray and leaned back on the sofa. 'So, now that we are, how you say, singing from the same song sheet, we need to host our own get-together,' she told him.

James, who had really said very little over the past hour, lifted his brows. 'Our own?' he repeated.

Lilli's laugh was deliberately caustic. While she was past exacting revenge for her husband's betrayal, she still felt hurt. 'We're happily married and huge supporters of the great Fascist movement, remember, James? Why wouldn't we welcome all our rich and powerful friends into our happy home this festive season?'

James digested her proposition. 'Good thinking,' he replied with a nod. 'Straight from the horse's mouth and all that.'

Lilli was unfamiliar with the idiom, but she got the gist of it. 'Yes, James. We don't have a moment to lose.'

* * *

There had been what the caterer had described as 'a spot of bother with the smoked salmon', but apart from that, and the fact that there seemed to be a shortage of ice in Kensington, all the preparations for the cocktail party went relatively smoothly.

Thirty invitations had been issued and twenty-four acceptances received. Only the Hallam-Boyces and the Monteiths had prior engagements and Sir Oswald Mosley was in the Midlands organising more marches. Lilli was not too sad that he couldn't make the party. More important were those who could, like the head of the new organisation for Germans living abroad, Ernst Wilhelm Bohlen. According to British intelligence, he was born in Britain. James had said he would be happy to tackle him over a vol-au-vent or two.

Lilli had supervised the florist's decoration of the apartment on a silver theme with the Christmas tree as the centrepiece. It reached to the drawing-room ceiling and shimmered with little silver candlesticks and trumpeting angels. It reminded Lilli of the tree at Helene's ball.

'We have so much for which to thank the Germans,' remarked Sir Hubert Fry, appreciating the tree as he sipped Bollinger.

'Prince Albert, I believe,' agreed his wife, whose diamond teardrop earrings rivalled the candles flames in their capacity to dazzle.

'Yes,' said Lilli. 'I think he introduced gingerbread at Christmas time, too.'

'Ah, *lebkuchen*. My favourite!' boomed the voice of another guest, Lord Maldon, a close friend of Sir Oswald Mosley. He sidled up to the little group and Lilli could tell from his ruddy complexion he'd already had too much to drink. In one hand he held a glass of Scotch and with the other he endeavoured to feel Lilli's buttocks. She side-stepped him and laughed lightly, just as a very special guest walked into the room.

'You must excuse me, please,' she said, weaving her way towards a striking woman in a cream cocktail dress that showed off a fabulous emerald necklace to full advantage.

'Wallis, I'm so glad you could come!' Lilli greeted Mrs Simpson enthusiastically. She had pulled off a great coup. She had no doubt that Wallis's cocktail party conversation would be interesting to say the least.

'So am I, my dear,' she replied, looking a little pale.

'Champagne,' called Lilli to a passing maid. But Wallis shook her head.

'I'm in no mood for it. A sherry, perhaps,' she replied.

Seeing Wallis was obviously out of sorts, Lilli ushered her away from the large drawing room to the more intimate dining room. There were two or three other couples who seemed quite content to ignore the Prince of Wales's mistress, either inadvertently or on purpose.

'What's wrong, Wallis?' Lilli asked, sitting the American on the window seat. She sat by her side.

'It's the king,' she said. 'You know his sister . . .'

Lilli was aware that Princess Victoria had just passed away and that King George, the Prince of Wales's ailing father, was deeply upset.

'Herr Hitler sent him his condolences, which was so sweet,' Wallis continued. Lilli had never heard the Führer described as 'sweet' before. 'But he still seems to be sinking rapidly.' As long as old King George remained on the throne, most politicians dared hope that Britain would remain out of the clutches of right-wing extremists. But the monarch's health, it seemed, was fading fast.

'And the prince? How is he?' asked Lilli, as the maid proffered a glass of Tio Pepe to Wallis on a silver salver.

Wallis sipped her sherry. 'You mustn't say anything.' She looked around conspiratorially.

'Of course not,' Lilli played affronted at the notion.

Wallis came closer, fingering her magnificent necklace. 'He and I are flying to Paris this week to talk with the French Prime Minister about how we can smooth things over with Mussolini.'

Lilli drew a deep breath. '*Mein Gott*, Wallis. Does anyone else know?'

This was, indeed, a revelation which would astound the British secret service: a member of the royal family and his mistress in secret talks with a foreign power about appeasing a likely enemy.

The American nodded. 'Some politician will be joining us out there to try and do a sort of land swap between Ethiopia and the Italians. Hopefully, that'll please Mussolini.'

Wallis made the secret negotiations sound as if they were children's games in a school playground: like swapping marbles or cigarette cards. But Lilli knew that this information was explosive. That the Prince of Wales and his mistress were conducting their own foreign policy, without the knowledge and against the wishes of His Majesty's government, was dynamite.

'What strain you must be under,' said Lilli, feigning sympathy.

'Oh, my dear. All this intrigue is really getting me down,' Wallis replied, taking another sip of sherry. 'It's so good to know I can talk to you.'

Chapter 41

1936

The shrill ring of the telephone cut through Lilli's brain like cheese wire. It jolted her awake so violently that she knocked over a glass of water as she scrambled to pick up the receiver. It was Wallis.

'What is it? What's happened?'

Lilli sat up in bed, clutching the telephone receiver in one hand, while reaching for the table lamp with the other. She rubbed her eyes. The clock on her bedside console said a quarter to one.

'He's dead. The king is dead.'

The Prince of Wales had been summoned to Sandringham, one of the king's estates, three days previously. Suspecting matters were serious, he'd flown up in his private plane. His father passed away shortly before midnight.

'David is now king. He is king!' There was a note of hysteria in Wallis's voice. 'God help him, Lilli. He is so very weak. I don't know what to do.'

Lilli was surprised by Wallis's reaction. Rumours about the royal couple's wild sex life abounded. The prince's affairs with mature, married women were notorious, and Wallis's prowess in that department was already the subject of much gossip, but

Lilli had often thought their relationship was more like a mother and son. The prince was the naughty boy and Wallis wielded the stick, both metaphorically and literally from what she'd heard.

At the Villa Mauresque, before she'd known and understood all the intricacies of English society, Lilli had naively thought that once the prince became King Edward VIII, he could marry whoever he chose. Now she knew how wrong she had been.

'All you can do is support him in his hour of need,' she replied.

Lilli realised, however, as soon as the words had left her mouth, that support was not something that this American woman did well. She needed to be in control, the captain of the ship. In the coming weeks and months, Lilli knew it was Wallis Simpson who would be at the helm. She only hoped the new king's mistress would not steer too close to the rocks.

Although the arrangement that Lilli had agreed with her husband seemed to be working well for both of them, in the autumn, towards the end of the first year of the ascension of King Edward VIII, James arrived back at the house in a particularly bad mood.

The new king remained besotted with Mrs Simpson and her divorce from Ernest was proceeding. That summer the couple had even spent a highly publicised few days cruising around the Mediterranean on a luxury yacht. Lilli was occupied gathering names and details of supporters of the new right-wing party that was forming, while James, still working at his gallery, was also passing on useful information to the British secret service. What he told Lilli that evening, however, was deeply troubling.

Over a brandy he spilled the metaphorical beans. 'There's every reason to believe that Mrs Simpson, and, indeed, the king himself are being . . .' He licked his lips. 'How can I put it? They are being careless in voicing their opinions to people who wish us ill.'

Lilli raised one of her pencilled brows. 'What have you discovered?'

James looked grave. 'It appears they could be sharing secret documents.'

'Secret documents?' The words tumbled involuntarily from her mouth.

'I have it on good authority that the king leaves state papers lying around Fort Belvedere and that Mrs Simpson may be divulging their contents to the new German ambassador.'

Lilli's lips parted. 'Von Ribbentrop?'

'Yes, Lilli. Von Ribbentrop. It's serious.'

Suddenly remembering Leon's letter that had arrived that morning, Lilli fetched an envelope from the writing desk and handed it over.

'You need to read this,' she said.

James scanned the tightly written sheet. In it, Leon spoke of the crippling effect the latest laws were having on the every-day lives of Jews.

'You read it,' he told her brusquely, handing it back to her. So she did.

'*With the Olympic Games in Berlin, Hitler wanted the world to think that his treatment of us is not as bad as critics abroad make out.*' Lilli paused to take a breath. '*In reality our situation grows worse by the day. The new laws mean Jews are no longer allowed to marry non-Jews and our citizenship has been taken from us.*'

James looked up and raked back his hair in acknowledgement. 'The Nuremberg Laws.'

'So the intelligence service knows this is happening?' Lilli asked; a note of desperation in her voice.

'Of course we know,' he told her dismissively, before realising he needed to soften his tone. 'Good God, darling, how much more evidence do the king and his kind need before they begin to mistrust these Nazis?' He waved the paper in front of her then flicked it with his fingers. 'Your brother is right to be fearful.' He shook his head. 'Word is that hundreds of "undesirable" prisoners, including Jews, are being rounded up and sent to enforced labour camps.

'Labour camps?' Lilli repeated in horror.

James nodded and his voice suddenly thickened. 'I've seen the evidence. Communists, Socialists, Roma.' He paused for a moment then looked up and said: 'Homosexuals, too. I have a friend . . .'

Seeing his distress, Lilli stood up and walked over to him, to sit at his side. It was strange to put her arm around him and feel the warmth of his body and his breath on her cheek after all these months of trying to avoid him.

'We must do what we can,' she told him softly. 'Hitler must not be allowed to win.'

Chapter 42

The newspapers were full of it. The headline in *The Guardian* newspaper proclaimed: *Mrs Wallis Simpson free*, although as Lilli tried to fight her way through the posse of pressmen waiting outside Cumberland Terrace, it seemed that the king's mistress was anything but free. The Regent's Park apartment, Lilli thought, had become her new prison since her much-publicised divorce from Ernest.

Lilli's visit was in response to a letter she'd received from the beleaguered divorcee. In it she complained she was: '*so frightfully unhappy. I am being treated as a scarlet woman, receiving the most terrible poison pen letters daily. I really am in fear of my life. Do come and visit as soon as you can. I miss you awfully.*'

Bulbs flashed and shouts almost deafened her as Lilli ran the gamut of waiting photographers and journalists on the pavement. Inside, the atmosphere was only a little less menacing. As she followed the butler into the drawing room Lilli happened to glance through the open door into the dining room where two glaziers were at work replacing a pane.

'My dear Lillian,' came Wallis's drawl across the hallway. In her arms she held Mr Loo, the terrier. 'I am so glad to see you.'

'What's happened?' Lilli asked, stopping to stare at the broken window.

Wallis closed her eyes in exasperation. 'My dear, you would not believe the horrors I'm having to endure.' She gestured towards the drawing room and put down the dog which scampered off. 'Let's talk over tea.'

Wallis was looking quite strained. She was immaculate, of course, with not a hair out of place. A fabulous flamingo brooch dazzled on her breast. In the three months since Lilli had last seen her, however, she'd aged several years. If she didn't pay so much attention to her appearance she might actually verge on the ugly, Lilli thought.

'You can't imagine what it's like to be the object of such hatred. I'm a whore, a gold digger . . .' Wallis waved her hand heavenwards, an enormous sapphire on her finger. She narrowed her eyes and leaned forward conspiratorially. 'There's even talk that I'm a German spy.'

Lilli remained poker-faced, allowing Wallis to show her hand first.

The American leaned back and laughed heartily. 'As if the Germans are our enemies!' She shook her immaculately coiffured head. 'I'd sooner they were in charge of this country than stuffed shirts like Prime Minister Baldwin and his bombastic cronies. Besides,' she added, her eyes sliding to an enormous vase full of red blooms: 'they are so much more romantic!'

Lilli studied the flowers. 'Carnations,' she remarked, as if Wallis needed help identifying them.

'Yes. Seventeen of them every day. From Count von Ribbentrop,' she replied with a wry smile, adding wistfully: 'One for each time.'

Lilli returned the smile over her tea cup. So the rumours about Wallis and the new German ambassador Joachim von Ribbentrop were true – seventeen times over. She decided her best reaction was to pick up the previous thread of conversation. 'It must be hard for you,' she continued, feigning concern. 'And what does the king say about it all?'

Wallis shrugged and snorted a little, as if he couldn't possibly

227

understand her torments. 'Naturally the little man tries to be sympathetic to my plight,' she said, then gave an odd little laugh. 'He wants me made his queen once we are married. He even says he will abdicate if he doesn't get his way.'

Lilli stared at her. She'd heard the word bandied about – even mentioned it herself once in France – but she never thought it would come from Wallis's own lips. 'Abdicate,' she repeated. 'That is a big step.'

'The biggest,' agreed Wallis, lifting her cup to her lips. 'David really is like a spoilt child. I've told him not to talk such nonsense, but I know if he can't make me Her Royal Highness, he would rather throw away the crown.' She lifted a plate of glossy pink squares displayed on a linen doily and proffered it to Lilli. 'A French fancy?' she said.

Lilli politely declined, wondering how, at times like these, Wallis could be occupied with such fripperies. The world was going mad around her, but she was so enveloped by her own problems that she really didn't seem to care about the bigger picture. It was as if Wallis saw herself as taking the starring role as the hard-done-by heroine in a Hollywood movie. But would she get her happy ever after? Lilli looked at the plate of pink fancies. Sometimes such distractions were helpful when the enormity of reality threatened to overwhelm.

Chapter 43

1937

Lilli was one of the privileged few to attend the much-vaunted wedding of the decade. King Edward VIII had abdicated from the throne in December the previous year. There had been an outcry in some quarters. Oswald Mosley even tried to rally a working-class uprising to support the wayward royal. But it all came to nothing and the king's brother, Bertie, known as King George VI, duly acceded to the throne.

That meant that the newly titled Duke of Windsor – as the former king was now known – could marry Wallis Simpson. The ceremony was conducted in a chateau in France in June and Wallis became his duchess.

Naturally the royal family all stayed away. The new Duke and Duchess of Windsor were virtually *personae non gratae* as far as King George and his queen, Elizabeth, were concerned. But Lilli's presence seemed to be greatly appreciated and the twenty or so guests rallied round as best they could.

Wallis, dressed in a tight, pale-blue crepe gown and halo-style hat, posed for photographs with her new husband. A few hours later, however, as the duke dressed for dinner, he received the news he'd been fearing. Wallis would not be given the title 'Her Royal Highness'. Yet another shadow was cast over the proceedings.

Secretly Lilli hoped the ducal couple's plans now meant that they would take a back seat away from their political activities. Their star was surely waning in Europe. They would no longer be of any value to Hitler and his Fascists, would they? That's why, barely a month later, when Lilli was back at home in London, she was puzzled to receive a letter from Wallis. Sitting in the conservatory of her Kensington house, she examined the postmark. It was sent from Austria and its contents surprised her.

> *My dearest Lillian*
>
> *It seems an age since the wedding and the duke and I* (Lilli noted the use of her husband's official title as opposed to the usual David) *have been enjoying ourselves enormously here at Schloss Wasserleonburg. We even have a new addition to our family. Her name is Pookie and like poor Mr Loo, she is a cairn terrier. But although we are having a marvellous time, the duke is growing restless, as I feared he might. He's asked Charles (Bedaux) (whom you met him at the wedding), to arrange a little tour. On our agenda is a trip to Germany to inspect some factories and also to meet the Führer.*
>
> *While making the arrangements the duke met with one of Herr Doktor Goebbels's aides in the Ritz in Paris, an apparently charming officer by the name of Major Marco Zeiller. I believe he knows you from way back. He enquired after you and told the duke he is a big admirer of yours, as are Goebbels and Hitler himself. They would all love to meet you – and indeed have a proposal to put to you – so I'm writing to ask you if you will join us on our excursion?*

Lilli suddenly felt the room spin. 'Marco,' she gasped. 'Marco Zeiller.' It was a name she'd thought would never pass her lips again, even though his image had flashed before her eyes on some many occasions over the last few years. A volcano of rage and hurt began to bubble up inside her as her heart thundered furiously in her chest. Might they really meet again? How could she react with anything but animosity towards him? She loathed him not just on a personal level, but what he and his regime represented, too. The prospect of seeing him again filled her with absolute dread.

The rest of the letter updated Lilli about the couple's recent stay at a hunting lodge in Hungary and was peppered with trifling details, but the postscript was also of interest.

My dear, I trust you will say nothing about this proposed visit to Germany. I know the prince is keen to show me what a State visit would be like, had I ever been queen, and the snobs at Buckingham Palace will find their noses out of joint when news gets out.'

Over dinner that night, Lilli broke news of the invitation to James. He almost choked on his cream of tomato soup.

'My God, Lilli! Germany! Hitler!' He put down the spoon to study the letter she'd just handed him. 'This is big! This is very big.'

'I know,' said Lilli. She had been unable to eat properly since she'd received the letter.

'This could be very useful to us. Give us a unique insight,' James, told her. 'Will you go?'

By 'us' she knew he meant the British secret service. She'd already informed Colonel Plimpton. He had reacted with unbridled enthusiasm for the trip. It was a unique opportunity to gain insight into the Nazi *modus operandi* and perhaps into both Hitler and Goebbels. As much as the thought of coming face to face with pure evil sickened her, there was no question. Of course she would go.

Chapter 44

Munich, Germany

The train journey from Paris to Munich took Lilli back to her past. Away from her hectic life, organising meetings and social events for Wallis in London, she had used the time to reflect: on her years at the *Académie de Danse* and, of course, on her first love affair with Marco. Wallis said he was a great admirer of hers. Was he a liar as well as a coward? From somewhere inside her hurt re-emerged.

As they approached the main *bahnhof* at Munich Lilli stared out of the window. Memories resurfaced as fast as the rain that fell. For a moment she even fooled herself into thinking she'd caught sight of Marco scanning the carriages on the platform. She'd told herself her imagination was playing tricks on her. After all, one uniformed Nazi looked very much like the other.

When the train juddered to a halt Lilli stood up and smoothed her skirt. A tall man in a black fedora offered her assistance as soon as she reached up for her small suitcase on the rack. She accepted. The rest of her bags were in the luggage carriage.

The Duke and Duchess of Windsor were staying with Hitler's head of the air force, Hermann Goering, and his wife Emmy at their country estate, but Lilli had declined an invitation to join them and decided instead to remain in the city where she would be closer to her family home. She intended to spend at least part of a day with them in Giesing before heading out to the countryside.

She edged her way out of the compartment and through the narrow train corridor to the carriage door. The platform was busy, but from out of the corner of her eye she saw the crowd parting to allow someone to pass. Turning, she saw it was a Nazi officer, accompanied by two soldiers. They were ploughing their way through the clusters of passengers. As soon as he came level with her carriage door and saw her, the officer, to her horror, raised his arm in a salute and called 'Heil Hitler!'

For a moment she simply stared at him as a cold fear crept over her skin. Could it really be Marco? Below her, on the platform, stood the man she had once loved with all her heart and soul. Now, with his Nazi insignia on his uniform, he was a stranger to decency and to his former self. Lilli didn't know how to react. She was looking at the ghost of the man she used to imagine spending her life with. But there was nothing left of their shared past. It was like trying to retrace a footprint left behind on wet ground. Words failed her. She remained silent.

'Fraulein Stern,' Marco said after a moment. He, too, seemed uncertain at first, gazing on her with a fierce intensity that frightened her.

'Major Zeiller.' She forced his name from her mouth.

He held out his hand to help her down from the carriage. She hesitated before taking it, but had to concede. He gripped it tightly until she alighted and seemed almost reluctant to let it go.

The major's driver, Linz, who'd been with him for years, picked up her bags from the platform with one hand, while juggling an umbrella, which he somehow managed to hold above her head, with the other.

'My car is waiting,' said the major.

From out of nowhere, a group of shouting men jostled in front of her on the platform. A burst of light caught Lilli unawares. The bright flash of cameras made her blink, as bulbs smashed and popped around her. A dozen photographers vied for position to take their shots.

'I hope you don't mind,' said Marco, suddenly finding his tongue. 'Reich Minister Goebbels . . .' His voice petered out apologetically.

Lilli shot him a horrified look. Once upon a time she had been used to photographers scrambling to take her picture. When *The Princess and the Pauper* was released in Europe, she had enjoyed the limelight. Now, however, she'd been out of the papers for some time. She certainly hadn't asked or expected to be treated like a celebrity in Germany, but now she realised why. The primary purpose of her visit, she'd thought, would be to accompany the Windsors. Wallis had mentioned Hitler and Goebbels were fans of hers, but never once had she thought they'd use her as a pawn to win over hearts and minds.

'A famous daughter of the Reich returns home!' exclaimed a reporter.

Instead of the wide-eyed grins they wanted, Lilli looked downcast and bewildered. This was not the homecoming she'd pictured. She darted an angry look at Marco. She was being used by the Nazi propaganda machine.

'Smile!' another shouted. 'Smile, Miss Stern!'

So, reluctantly, she did. She put on her mask once more and flashed her dazzling white teeth as the major led the way through the concourse to a waiting automobile parked outside the station. Thankfully the rain had stopped. She noted the swastika flag on its bonnet as she climbed in. Marco sat beside her, although a respectful distance away.

'I trust you had a pleasant journey, Fräulein Stern,' he enquired as the car's engine started. He was still being very formal – a model officer of the Reich.

'Yes, thank you,' she replied. Her eyes settled on the glass screen between them and the driver which remained open. Why wasn't it closed so they could talk in private? Or had Marco Zeiller really deserted all his principles and sold his soul to the devil named Hitler? She couldn't be sure if he'd surrendered his integrity entirely to the Reich, or if there was some vestige of the old Marco left – the Marco who knew right from wrong. Lilli found it impossible to read his actions. Until she did, her guard must remain up.

'You will notice many changes,' said Marco, registering the bemused expression on Lilli's face as they drove through the city. They were passing a building site where a large new apartment block was rising from the rubble of a derelict tenement. As she watched men crawl up scaffolding like ants, their automobile came to a halt. Looking around Lilli realised that this was the junction where she used to stop and stare at the film posters. The gigantic advertising awning was still there, the one that had once loomed so large in her dreams, but instead of her own face publicising her film as she had once imagined, an image of Adolf Hitler glowered down on the passers-by; his arm held out straight in a salute.

'Yes, many changes,' she replied with a nod, thinking to herself: *And not all of them good.* Marco had clearly allowed himself to be brainwashed. She mustn't show her hand in this dangerous game of chance.

Since her last visit many of the flaking facades had been restored and the shop windows were no longer bare: strings of wurst, boxes of apples and pears, slabs of cheese and great flitches of bacon were all on show.

A little further up along the road they drove past the alley where she remembered whores used to peddle their wares. It was deserted. Beggars no longer congregated on the steps of Stefan Kirsch. Could Germany now be so prosperous that women didn't have to sell themselves to feed their children and limbless old men weren't forced to beg, she wondered.

The silence that hung between them remained awkward, although the major did attempt to make polite conversation.

'I have seen your films, you know, Fraulein Stern.'

She turned her head to face him. 'So I believe. The Duchess of Windsor told me.'

'Ah, the duchess,' he closed his eyes for a split second. 'Everyone is talking about her. They say she would have made a good Queen of England.'

Lilli shrugged. 'That we'll never know,' she replied absent-mindedly, looking out of the window once more.

They drove on and soon came to the *Feldherrnhalle*, the great mausoleum that Lilli used to pass daily on her way to the *Académie de Danse* and the place where she and Marco had walked arm and arm and deliberately ignored the tribute to Hitler's fallen comrades less than six years before. The steps were almost deserted, apart from a number of guards stationed on them. She found it strange that so few people were around.

Marco saw her expression and knew what she was thinking.

'*Druckerbergergasse*,' he said.

Lilli switched round. 'What?'

'Slacker's Alley,' he replied. 'People are required to give the Nazi salute when they pass the *Feldherrnhalle*, so instead some choose to take a diversion, down the alley.'

'And if they do?' Lilli was shocked.

'They are punished, of course,' he told her.

Just then Lilli saw Linz, the driver, glance in his rear-view mirror. Was that a smirk on his face?

'The hotel, *mein Oberstabsarzt*. Which entrance, *bitte*?' he called out.

Lilli had been booked into a suite at the *Bayerischer Hof* on *Promenadeplatz*. When she was a child she had never imagined that she would one day stay here as a guest, let alone of the German government.

'The main, Linz,' Marco replied.

As the automobile drew up outside a huddle of young women surged forward. When the liveried porter opened the limousine door for Lilli, they started calling her name and thrust autograph books in front of her.

'Fraulein Stern! Bitte!' they shouted.

'Not now!' exclaimed Marco, trying to brush the fans aside, but Lilli slid him a sideways look to signify her displeasure.

'It's quite all right, Major,' she told him and took an outstretched pen from one of the girls, flourishing her signature on a blank page. This she did two or three times before freeing herself to accompany the waiting major. He whipped off his cap as he escorted her inside the hotel's magnificent reception. Linz followed on with her two large suitcases.

The manager, wearing a formal morning coat and an obsequious expression, was there to welcome Lilli personally, along with two maids and a porter. He assured her that she was in excellent hands and that his staff were there to cater for her every whim. He would even escort her to her suite himself and called to reception for her room key.

Marco, remaining close, began to take his leave.

'I very much hope you will enjoy your stay here, Fraulein Stern,' Marco told her formally, giving a shallow bow.

At least the monster still doesn't click his heels like the rest of them, she thought.

'A car will call for you tomorrow for your meeting with Reich Minister Goebbels at his Munich office. Until then my driver is at your disposal.'

His words reminded her of her true purpose in Germany, the real reason for her visit: 'the proposal', as Wallis, or should she now say 'Her Grace' had dubbed it. Joseph Goebbels – one of her ardent fans – had devised a plan. All she knew at the moment, however, was that it might well involve a film role. If that were to prove the case, Colonel Plimpton had encouraged her to accept it. What she discovered, he'd pressed upon her, could prove *awfully useful to our chaps.* Any previous hope that Marco might not be completely sympathetic to the Nazi cause had bitten the dust. He was as fanatical as the rest of them. Now, however she feared she may have walked into a trap. What's more, it appeared she was on her own. Her heart sank as he turned to go, but just as he did, she saw him drop the cap he'd tucked under his arm. Deliberately, she wondered?

Bending low beside her, he whispered: 'Tonight. I'll come to your room.'

The shock of his words made her heart lurch. She felt her lips part but had to bite her tongue. She tried to search his eyes, but he rose too quickly for her to see what lay behind them. Beneath the Nazi uniform was it possible a vestige of the old Marco still existed? Could she count this as a small, reassuring step in the right direction? Yet he was still the man who betrayed her. If he could be so cruel towards her once, then, if he knew she was a spy, he could easily betray her to Hitler's regime. She still needed to be on her guard. Major Marco Zeiller could not be trusted.

Chapter 45

The hotel manager, whom Lilli learned from his badge was called Herr Blum, maintained a continuous smile on his chubby face. He accompanied her in the lift up to her suite, talking all the while.

'I hope you will be comfortable, here. We are most honoured by your presence,' he gushed over and over until the lift deposited them on the second floor and Lilli was led to her suite.

'*Et voila!*' announced Herr Blum with a flourish as he opened the door. Lilli could barely believe her eyes when she saw what awaited her inside. The rooms were filled with flowers. There were vases of roses on the walnut coffee table in the grand drawing room and on the ormolu chest of drawers. As she walked into her bedroom, she saw bouquets here too, on the dressing table and at the side of the magnificent bed, draped in purple and gold. She'd never seen so many red roses, not even at a film premiere. She recalled the bouquet in Wallis's London apartment. *The Nazis certainly love their flowers.* She was vaguely unnerved by the gesture, assuming that either Goebbels, or even perhaps the Führer himself, was trying to impress her prior to their meeting.

The manager's grin had widened even further. 'If there's anything else, Fraulein . . .' he began.

'No,' Lilli snapped, still in shock. 'No thank you,' she reiterated. Herr Blum retreated, bowing as he went.

On a silver salver on the coffee table lay an envelope. She moved closer. It bore her room number on it. Curious, she opened it, but as soon as she read the first line, she felt her nerves knot.

Dear Miss Sternberg. Lilli swallowed hard. *Sternberg.* The flowers were sent by someone from her past – her Jewish past. She read on.

> *Welcome back to Munich. You may remember we parted on less-than-favourable terms. Nevertheless, I have followed your career with interest ever since. I trust I am forgiven for my past indiscretion and hope you will do me the honour of dining with me during your stay.*
>
> *I remain your obedient servant,*
>
> *Karl von Stockmar.*

A shiver ran down Lilli's spine. The card in her hand suddenly repulsed her. She threw it down as if it were infected. Of course she recalled him. How could she forget his attack on her? Why on earth did he want to ingratiate himself with her now, with this letter, these flowers? There could only be one reason: blackmail. He would try and force himself on her, just has he'd tried to before and if she refused he'd threaten to expose her Jewishness. A wave of fear swept over her, but she could not let it drown her. She would ask Herr Blum to have the flowers removed; tell him she had an allergy to roses. The note would be ignored. She tore the card in two and threw it away. After all, she was the guest of Reich Minister Goebbels and the Führer himself. If von Stockmar were to hurt her, then it would reflect badly on her Nazi hosts. Besides, her family was awaiting her arrival. She must wash and change. The driver, Linz, would be taking her to Giesing, back to her old home, very shortly. Back to the people she loved.

Chapter 46

Could Linz, the driver, be trusted? Would he suspect she was Jewish? It was a risk she would have to take. Giesing was a mixed area of the city, where Jews and gentiles lived side by side, so Lilli pushed the fear to the back of her mind when she asked him to drop her at her parents' home. Several neighbours in the block had gathered to greet her in the downstairs hall. There was even a large publicity photograph of her in Fred Astaire's arms as the princess in *The Princess and the Porter*. Herr Grunfeld had placed it on his desk by the pigeonholes.

'Lilli! Lilli, *mein Liebling!*' Golda flung her arms around her daughter, tears streaming down her face before she pushed her away to look at her. 'But you are so glamourous, and too thin. You haven't been eating. I can tell. I hope that new husband of yours is not making you starve.' Golda pulled a stern face.

'He treats me very well and is sorry he couldn't come to meet you this time, Mutti,' Lilli told her, summoning all her acting skills. Although her parents had sent their congratulations, her marriage to a gentile remained a disappointment to them – as it did to her for obvious reasons.

Golda broke into another smile and reached out to her daughter once more. There were tears in Lilli's eyes now, too, as she hugged her mother again. The old woman felt even less solid than she did on her last visit; her firm upholstery had sagged like an old sofa.

Lilli looked round at the smiling faces she knew so well. Leon stood awkwardly in the shadows, leaner and more gangling than she remembered. His black hair was slicked back off his pale face and his deep, dark eyes gave him a haunted look. Frau Grunfeld, the janitor's wife, joined them. Lilli noticed she was heavily pregnant. Her pretty face was filled out and radiant. Frau Grundig, the Ram, still wearing her hair in braids, was close by while the old matchmaker, Frau Weber, leaning over the bannisters, waved to her from the top floor. Herr and Frau Kepler were there with their daughter, Anna, too who, now in her teens, also stood on the stairs, smiling and showing off her perfect teeth.

There were some neighbours, however, who didn't want to share in the joy of the homecoming. According to one of Leon's letters, the Reuters' two eldest sons were now enthusiastic members of the Hitler Youth, while their ten-year-old, Heidi, had just joined the League of Young Girls. They would not turn out to welcome home a Jew. And as for Herr Backe? He remained a fully-fledged member of the Nazi party and no one missed him at the gathering. Yet a word to the authorities from any one of them about her Jewishness could put her whole plan in jeopardy. She had no choice but to take the risk.

So many people from her past had come to greet Lilli and yet . . . 'Vati! Where is Vati?' she asked, twirling round in a panic, suddenly realising her father was absent.

'He is in the apartment, *mein Schatz*. His heart,' said Golda, making a fist with her hand and hitting her chest. 'He can't manage the stairs. Come, we must eat!'

Golda led the way. The apartment remained as dark and as heavy as Lilli remembered it. Little had changed, except that the carpet was even more threadbare and the plaster even more dilapidated. Jacob sat in his armchair by the window, covered in a blanket. His face was waxen and thin, but it broke into a broad smile when he saw Lilli. He held out both his arms to embrace his daughter, but the effort made him cough.

'My dear child,' he greeted warmly. He always made her feel like a little girl. It used to irritate her, now she loved him for it. She bent low and took his cold, blue hands in hers, holding one of them to her cheek.

'Oh Vati, you are not well,' she murmured.

'I feel better now you are here,' he wheezed, managing a smile.

She stood up straight again and tugged at her green peplum jacket that she'd bought from a chic London boutique.

'It is well cut,' remarked her father, feeling the fabric with his sinewy hands.

'Yes,' she agreed, although in the shabby apartment with black mould creeping in the corners, she felt uncomfortably conspicuous. She'd even struggled to climb the steep stairs in her pencil skirt.

The table was groaning with food. A large platter of *gefelte* fish was decorated with capers and gherkins and tomatoes cut in the shape of flowers. There were plates of sauerkraut and boiled eggs, too.

'Come, let us eat!' Golda exclaimed.

Her exhortation was the signal to allow the neighbours to enter the apartment. Jacob managed to struggle to the head of the table and called for silence to say a prayer. Lilli bent her head. In all the years she had been away from her family she had never once said the blessing over food. They were so grateful for what little they had compared with the lavish parties she'd attended in America. A trace of shame suddenly nudged her conscience.

Her mother cut the fish ceremoniously and everyone helped themselves to boiled potatoes and sauerkraut. There weren't enough chairs to go round, so the Keplers brought some of their own. Leon offered a large flagon of sweet white wine to the women and beer to the men. Lilli had forgotten how good her mother's cooking tasted after all these years. She even allowed herself the indulgence of mopping up the caper sauce with a large hunk of freshly baked bread.

Of course everyone wanted to know about her glamorous life in Hollywood and she kept them spellbound with stories about filming with the great Astaire and her meetings with Charlie Chaplin, the young clown who'd stolen everyone's heart. She talked of parties with Mary Pickford and Ronald Coleman and of her trip to the Riviera. She made a brief mention of James and her other aristocratic English friends. And, of course, she talked about the Windsors.

'The King of England!' Golda clasped her hands with glee and Lilli did not like to correct her mother and point out that he was no longer the king because he'd given up his crown. 'To think of it! My daughter with the King of England and his new American wife.'

Lilli watched her mother turn to all those clustered around her, basking in the reflected glow from her famous daughter's light. Golda was so immensely proud of her, of what she had achieved. News of her injury had, inevitably, reached one or two German newspapers, but she had assured her mother they were vastly exaggerated. How could she possibly tell her family that her Hollywood dream had turned to dust, that she would never dance again? Lilli had rehearsed her speech, as often as she'd rehearsed her part in *The Princes and the Porter*. But now, faced with her mother and her excitable audience, she found she had stage fright. It was not the time to break the bad news.

The women indulged Golda's pride with little gasps of delight at Lilli's royal friends.

'The duchess always looks so elegant,' ventured Frau Grunfeld.

'And the jewellery she wears!' remarked Frau Weber, who'd made an extra effort to struggle downstairs on her arthritic legs.

The men, it seemed, were less impressed. 'A gold digger,' mumbled Herr Grundig to Herr Kepler. Leon, observing the proceedings with a dispassionate distance, remained silent. Nor was Jacob seduced by such trivial talk, nevertheless he was clearly proud of his daughter. Looking at her now, as she regaled these impressionable women and girls, Lilli could tell he was praying that underneath that expensive suit of hers, a Jewish heart still beat.

After the food was cleared away, Leon filled the glasses again and Lilli decided it was time to bring out the surprise she'd brought from London. Linz had carried the large box up the stairs for her, but everyone seemed to have forgotten about it in the mêlée.

'I have a surprise!' she cried. They all gathered round as Golda was given the honour of opening the large cardboard box that sat on the coffee table. 'Here, let me help,' said Lilli as she delved inside and brought out a hinged wooden cabinet. She opened the lid.

'It's a portable gramophone player,' she announced. 'And here are some recordings of Fred Astaire's songs.' She held up two seventy-eights, still in their sleeves. She waited for the gasps, the expressions of delight. But instead of the excitement she'd hoped the gift would bring, the squeals of joy and the anticipation of singing and dancing, an embarrassed silence fell on the party.

Lilli looked at Golda's face, then at Leon's. 'What it is? What's wrong? It's a record player. Look,' she told them eagerly as she proceeded to show everyone the stylus. 'It works like this,' she said, pulling one of the shellac seventy-eights from its sleeve. She couldn't understand why no was sharing her enthusiasm.

Finally Leon stepped forward, his eyes dipping and darting at the other guests. 'We know how it works, Lilli,' he told his sister. 'But it is forbidden.' His nostrils flared in suppressed anger.

'Forbidden?' repeated Lilli. 'But it's a record player. For music.' Why was everyone behaving so oddly, as if a spaceship had landed from Mars.

Golda shook her head. 'Lilli, your brother is right. Jews are not allowed such a machine. The new laws forbid us.'

'Bicycles and typewriters, too,' chimed in Klara Grundig, almost gleefully.

Lilli, bent double over the table before, now straightened herself and looked at the expressions on her neighbours' faces. The elected government had openly banned a large proportion of its people from owning small luxuries and no one raised a dissenting voice. Some of the neighbours were feeling awkward. There was no doubt. But their silence was deafening. Their silence, thought Lilli, was their tacit acceptance. She remained stunned as not a word of condemnation of the new laws passed anyone's lips until Herr Grunfeld chirped up.

'I'll go and fetch my accordion,' he said cheerfully, as if nothing had just happened.

The announcement lifted the awkward impasse and was met with expressions of approval. As soon as the janitor re-emerged from downstairs with his accordion, he asked for requests. Frau Weber's young granddaughter, Monika, who was staying with the old woman, wanted a polka and danced with Anna Kepler when it was played. There were some lively renditions of popular songs and later came old German folk tunes. With their vocal cords loosened by wine and beer, everyone sang along. Even Jacob hummed a few bars of an old lullaby.

When she finally managed to grab a moment alone with Leon in the kitchen, Lilli enquired about their father's health.

'Is Vati . . .?' She could barely bring herself to ask Leon as he stacked dirty plates at the sink.

She saw his shoulders slump. 'He has not long,' he told her matter-of-factly.

Lilli nodded. He was only confirming what was evident to her. She watched him load the cutlery in a separate bowl.

'And you? What do you do now?'

Again a shake of his head. 'I am no longer allowed at the university, but some of us still continue to fight for our rights.'

Lilli looked at him sternly. 'Don't do anything stupid, Leon. For their sakes.' Her eyes shot towards her parents in the main room.

Since her last visit all Jewish students had been banned from universities, as Leon had predicted. His childhood dreams of being a lawyer and standing up for the rights of Jews in the courts, were shattered.

'Oh Leon,' she said, suddenly reaching out and hugging him. 'Why don't you come back to England with me?'

Leon snorted out a laugh and shook his head. 'Vati is too weak to travel and I am not allowed. They will not give me documents. We are trapped in this hell with no way out.'

'Lilli! Lilli!' Her mother's shrill call pierced through the sombre mood in the kitchen.

'Coming, Mutti!' Lilli cried. She grasped hold of Leon's hands. There was so much she needed to know from him. 'How can I help?' she asked.

'Tell your English and American friends,' he replied. 'We are being erased from public life and pushed into the shadows. They want all us Jews dead.'

'No, Leon,' she said. Now she felt he was going too far. 'That's not true. It can't be true.'

Her brother fixed her with an intense glare that found its way deep inside her. His dark eyes suddenly caught light. 'I fear it is, Lilli. Already there are labour camps in the east and Himmler talks of mass extermination.'

Lilli knew about the labour camps, but mass extermination? Such scenarios were impossible for her to believe. Not even James would give the idea credence. Yet there was so much that she needed to know, so much that she suspected neither the British nor the Americans were aware of, things that went on in secret, away from the world's glare. But even if other governments were told, she had the distinct impression that they might turn a collective blind eye. Hitler and his cronies were certainly seducing the Windsors with their flattery and fawning, but could they dupe everyone else?

'Trust me, Leon,' she told him, tightening her grasp. 'You are not alone.'

Lilli re-joined the party as Herr Grunfeld played out the final notes of an old favourite about a hunter from the Rhine. Monika and Anna were pink and excited from dancing and everyone clapped.

'Do you know "*Hop Mayne Hamentashen*"?' asked Jacob.

Axel Grunfeld smiled: 'Ah, the song about the cookies and the scolding woman! It's one of my favourites,' he replied, fanning his fingers and looking for the right cords to play.

'Why don't you sing it for us Lilli?' suggested Frau Kepler.

Lilli smiled. 'I don't think—'

'Yes. Sing it for us, Lilli, please,' urged Golda.

'Very well,' she agreed, rising and making her way over to Herr Grunfeld.

It seemed, however, that not everyone was excited by the prospect of such a performance. Over in the corner, Lilli noticed the Ram's expression suddenly change. Her features hardened and her lips pursed as if she had just tasted something sour. '*Hop Mayne Hamentashen*,' she mused. 'Isn't that a Yiddish song?'

Her husband, a wiry little man, sitting next to her and lighting a cigarette, shrugged his indifference. He was enjoying himself. 'Perhaps,' he replied.

Frau Grundig's neck reddened and she rose suddenly. 'I think it is time we went, Gunther,' she declared, looking pointedly at her husband. 'Thank you for your hospitality, Golda, Jacob,' she said unsmilingly. 'Good to see you Lilli,' she managed, nodding her head.

'But Klara . . .' protested her hapless husband.

'Come Gunther,' she ordered and swept out of the room, Herr Grundig managing to throw an apologetic glance behind him.

For a moment everyone in the room went quiet, unsure as to

what just happened, as if a balloon had burst. Then a voice from the kitchen doorway broke the awkward silence.

'Does anyone else mind if we sing a Jewish song in our own home?'

It was Leon's. His eyes were bloodshot with drink and the smoke from Herr Kepler's pipe. 'We are Jewish, you see. And you are all guests here.'

'Leon!' Jacob's voice sounded stern despite his frailty.

Leon simply stared at his father, then at the assembled neighbours, his face simmering with an unspoken rage. Suddenly he stormed forward, grabbed his coat and headed for the door.

'Leon, where are you going?' asked Golda anxiously.

'Out!' he cried. 'I cannot stand to be around watching you all fiddle while Rome burns.' He slammed the door behind him, leaving the room stunned into another difficult silence.

It was Lilli who spoke first, glancing at Herr Grunfeld, his accordion still strapped to his torso. She took a deep, steadying breath. She needed to show resolve. 'I will sing in C,' she told him. He nodded graciously, found the cords and began to play.

It was towards ten o'clock when the proceedings finally drew to a close. Jacob was tiring and besides, Lilli had already ordered her car for that time. Saying goodbye would be hard, she accepted, especially to her father. Gazing into his tired, rheumy eyes, that had seen so much sorrow and pain, part of her felt she was deserting him. He had sacrificed so much for her education; invested so much in her life and she'd repaid him by her absence. Guilt tugged at her heart, but she could see his poor health gave him no choice. There was no escape.

'I love you,' she whispered as she embraced him. She knew it would be for the last time.

Golda tried to be brave. 'We are so proud of you,' she told Lilli on the front steps of the apartment block.

'Thank you, Mutti. Take good care of yourself,' Lilli replied, her voice trembling. But at least knowing her parents were proud of her was some recompense.

249

'Don't forget to write!' called her mother as Linz opened the back door for his important passenger.

Once inside the limousine, Lilli wound down the window. 'Tell Leon I won't forget what he said,' she called to her mother, as the engine started up. 'Tell him it'll be all right.'

Chapter 47

As Lilli's limousine approached the hotel, she took her powder compact from her handbag and inspected her face in its mirror. Her mascara had smudged, as she feared it might. She'd cried silently for much of the way back. She'd cried for her father, whom she knew she'd never see again, and for her mother and Leon and the uncertain future they faced. But a few firm strokes from her handkerchief erased the black streaks and a reapplication of red lipstick worked wonders. By the time the hotel porter opened the limousine door, she was looking her glamorous self once more; prepared for anything, or anyone.

Taking the lift up to her suite on the second floor, she opened the door to be immediately struck by the perfume from the dozens of red roses. Herr Blum had instructed his staff to remove them from the suite, but their scent still lingered. Away from the hotel, she'd managed to put the unwelcome delivery and the note to the back of her mind. Now she was suddenly reminded of von Stockmar. As she found herself dwelling on him, a knock at her door made her jump. Her whole body tensed.

She padded over to the door. 'Who is it?' she said softly.

'Major Zeiller,' came the reply.

Taking a deep breath, she opened the door a crack. Marco

stood on her threshold, still in his uniform, still in his cap. Bowing formally, his expression remained serious.

'May I come in, Fraulein Stern?' He glanced behind him, into the corridor.

She opened the door wide. 'Please.' She gestured inside.

As Marco strode into the room he filled it with his presence. In his immaculately cut uniform and his high boots, he looked every inch the Nazi: authoritative, arrogant and superior with a hint of menace. The knot of apprehension in Lilli's stomach tightened. It had been more than six years since the end of their affair. So much had changed in that time. Once she thought she might be able forgive him for what he did to her. They were both young, after all, but seeing him now only reopened the wound. Her anger remained, raw and painful.

Marco took off his cap and surveyed the room, as if he was trying to frame his thoughts away from her gaze. He switched back and looked at her in silence, then shook his head. Lilli found it hard to read his mood. The anticipation was almost too much for her to bear.

'Oh Lilli,' he said finally. 'It is so good to see you.' His voice was soft and she thought she saw tears as he moved towards her, or was it just the way the light caught his eyes?

She gathered her strength. 'What do you think you're doing?' she asked. 'Don't you dare pretend that nothing happened between us.'

He shook his head and frowned. 'You're angry. I don't under-stand.'

He moved closer again, the edges of his lips now lifted in a smile. Not the broad, joyous smile she remembered from her youth, but a smile, nonetheless. Another shake of his head. 'I don't understand why you are so angry,' he repeated. 'After all, you were the one who ended our relationship.'

Lilli frowned and spat out her words. 'What are you talking about? You betrayed me because of your precious career then didn't even have the guts to finish with me to my face.' She turned her back on him and marched to the window. Below the lights of Munich burned brightly.

Marco lifted up both hands and shrugged. 'What do you mean?'

She puffed out a laugh. 'I'm not a fool, Marco. You sent me a telegram, remember?' She turned to face him and quoted it back at him in a pompous voice: '*I must put my duty to my country before any feelings I may have for you.*'

His back stiffened. 'What telegram? I never sent you a telegram!'

Lilli's anger was turning to confusion. 'Don't play games with me again,' she warned. She'd been wounded and she thought it only right that he knew about her hurt. 'I read it so often; I cried over it so much that the paper fell apart.'

'No.' He was shaking his head. 'You have to believe me. I never sent you a telegram. I always thought it was you who finished with me.'

Her shoulders sagged. 'So you didn't get my letter, either?' She'd followed up Marco's telegram, asking him if he truly meant that he wanted to break up with her.

'What? I wrote to you three or four times, but my letters were always returned.'

'Wait! You're saying someone else must've sent the telegram?' Her dark eyes latched onto his. 'And you never received the letter I sent to your barracks.'

Marco's expression suddenly changed as he thought of a possible explanation and the culprit's image came into his vision. 'Von Stockmar!' He spat out the name as if it were poison on his tongue.

Lilli froze, recalling the note and the flowers she'd found in her room. Von Stockmar was evil and twisted and he knew she was back in Munich.

Marco did not notice her reaction. He was too preoccupied reliving old wrongs. 'He was always jealous of me. He was passed over for promotion shortly after the ball. And, of course, he wanted you.' She remained silent, feeling sick with fear. Of course Marco had no idea that von Stockmar had attacked her. 'For a while every time I saw him, he mentioned your name. Said vile things about you.'

Lilli wrapped her arms around herself, pretending to feel cold, but really trying to stop her body from shaking.

Marco drew closer. 'I swear it is true. Seeing you today . . . it brought back so many memories.' He hooked his gaze under hers and stared into her eyes. He could see them glistening.

'Oh Marco!' she cried, her head cracking up towards the ceiling as she wheeled away from him. Her anger had given way to confusion and Marco took it as a sign that he was forgiven. He moved forward to hold her, his arms outstretched, but she pushed him back. 'No,' she said, shaking her head, flattening her palms against his grey tunic. 'No. I can't do this. Not with you in this uniform.'

'Ah!' He stopped still and lowered his arms. 'I am a Nazi now. That's it, isn't it?'

She nodded and took a deep breath. 'How can you support a monster?' She thrust out her jaw in defiance as she made her accusation. It was a challenge. For a moment she stood still, waiting for his reaction. He could arrest her; throw her into prison. Instead his features softened.

'Oh Lilli,' he told her. 'There are some good people left in Germany. Remember the ones who go down Slacker's Alley rather than make the Nazi salute?'

'Yes,' she nodded.

'It is their small show of resistance, but they are all so afraid.'

It was the moment she'd be waiting for. 'Oh Marco!' His name left her mouth in a long sigh. She reached out towards him, knowing that he wanted no part in the hatred and evil that his uniform represented.

He put his arms around her and held her tight, speaking in a whisper. 'You need to know, Lilli, that some of us officers are working behind the scenes. There is more than one plot

254

to overthrow the Führer. I cannot say more.' He pulled back and regarded her with his large, brown eyes. 'You see these,' he said, pointing to them. 'Remember, my mother was Italian. I am Catholic. Your people are not the only ones suffering. Hitler is now sending priests to prison camps, too.'

All her doubts faded. His gaze was direct and intense, and she suddenly became that eighteen-year-old girl who had wanted to give herself to him on the shore of a lake so long ago. Her heart swelled with joy as their lips drew close and he began to kiss her passionately. It had returned; the magic was still there, but after a moment she withdrew. She'd told herself she mustn't give in so easily this time. She lifted her hand and fanned out her fingers to show him her wedding ring.

'But I am married now,' she said.

'I know,' Marco replied. 'But you do not love him.'

'How . . .?' She wondered if he could still read her mind as he used to, like the pages of a book.

'I was briefed,' he told her.

Lilli flashed him a look of disquiet. It was unnerving that the German secret service had such information on file, but perhaps not surprising. Nor did she contradict what he said. So, taking her softly by the wrist, Marco began caressing her hand, kissing it tenderly before slowly easing off the gold band to leave her finger naked.

'Tonight,' he whispered as he set the ring down on the nearby table, 'we will love each other.'

Chapter 48

Lilli lay in his arms for a long time afterwards, thinking of that day on the lakeshore, when she'd offered herself to him. It seemed like a lifetime ago. She was little more than a girl. She'd been nervous, but desperate for him. He'd called her his 'Giselle'. He was her 'Albrecht.' He had been gentle, self-assured and oh, so, sensible, telling her they must wait. This time they'd both been wild, outrageous, if as expending all the pent-up energy of the last six years. Despite lovers in between, the special bond Lilli felt with Marco was still there.

Eventually Marco stirred and lit a cigarette. He inhaled then handed it to her. She took it from him, her head on the pillow, lying on her back; her blonde hair splayed out around her face.

He turned to gaze at her and his playful smile returned. 'So, are you satisfied you have proof now, Giselle?'

She smiled and dragged on the cigarette. 'Yes,' she said, then turned her head so their eyes met. 'You haven't changed.'

Reaching out, she stroked the nape of his neck. She'd been wrong to doubt him, but now they were reunited in their struggle.

As if remembering they had a common enemy, she asked suddenly: 'Does Goebbels know?'

He raised both brows. 'That you are Jewish?' He shook his

head. 'Even if he does, you are still Lillian Stern, the famous German film star who made it big in Hollywood. You are worth more to him if you are a gentile. He won't want it broadcast that you are Jewish.'

'What do you mean?' Panic rose in her voice.

'He doesn't tell me everything, but I know he and the Führer are hatching some big film project.' He pulled a face and announced in an exaggerated American accent: 'Hollywood comes to Hamburg. You know the Führer loves his films. He has plans for you.'

'What plans, Marco?' she asked as he began kissing her neck again. But she pressed her fingers against his lips and he became serious again.

'He has not told me, but you will find out tomorrow, no doubt, at your meeting.'

The thought of coming face to face with Goebbels filled her with dread. Marco felt her whole body tense and stroked her hair. 'He will not hurt you Lilli. You are too valuable to him,' he assured her.

'I hope you are right,' she said, reaching for him and pulling him towards her once more.

They made love again; more slowly this time, admiring each other's bodies, thrilling to each other's fingertips, luxuriating in the sensation of skin on skin.

'All those wasted years,' Marco said softly afterwards, studying her mouth as she shaped it round another cigarette and blew out a ring of smoke. As soon as he'd uttered them he could tell his words brought back painful memories.

She was looking blankly at the ceiling when she asked suddenly: 'Where is he now?'

'Who?' She had broken their peace.

'Von Stockmar.'

Marco scowled. 'Let's not even think about him.'

'I need to know,' insisted Lilli, turning towards him.

Marco let out a long sigh. 'He transferred to another regiment, which means I no longer have any contact with him. Thank God. He was posted up north, but he is back here, in Munich now, although you mustn't worry,' he told her. 'He wouldn't dare do anything while I am near you.' But his words did not have the desired effect. He could see fear remained in her eyes. 'What is it?' he persisted. 'There's something else.'

She could not look at him. 'He sent me roses. Dozens of them. And a card.'

'Von Stockmar?' Marco's expression hardened. 'What did he want?'

She shrugged. 'To see me.' She looked up at his face. It was set in a scowl and growing angrier by the second. It was not what she wished for. Von Stockmar was coming between them yet again. She clasped her hand in Marco's. 'Don't let him spoil tonight.' She tried to pull him closer to kiss him, but he resisted.

'I have to go,' he told her. 'I am on duty early tomorrow.' He eased himself off the bed, stood up and reached for the trousers he'd abandoned on the floor.

'But Marco, we need to talk more. When will see I you again?' Her arm was stretched out towards him. He frowned then took her hand to kiss it.

'Soon,' he told her, suddenly tender again. 'I don't intend to let you go so easily this time, with or without this on your finger.' He held up the ring on the bedside table and gently slipped it back on her hand. 'I have a confession to make,' he added, pulling on his shirt and jacket.

'A confession?' repeated Lilli nervously as she watched him check himself in the mirror. The words felt like a knife. His uniform made him every inch the Nazi officer once more. Had he deceived her again?

Marco nodded and drew a deep breath. 'When I heard you were accompanying the duke and duchess, I couldn't quite believe it at first. Of course I knew that your dreams had come true, that you'd made it in America, but I never thought I'd see you again.

Then when I got the chance, I volunteered to be the officer to wine and dine you. I told them about us. My orders were to seduce you, to get information about the Windsors.'

She raised a brow. 'You certainly seduced me,' she told him. 'And now what will you report back? That I'm a fantastic lover?'

She'd always found it hard to accept that Marco was one of those goose-stepping flunkies who were following their ruthless leader blindly on the road to war. And now she knew they were on the same side, even though he didn't know she was a British agent. But she still felt she needed to keep some secrets from him.

'The best,' he said, leaning over and kissing her tenderly. 'I love you,' he whispered as he stroked her hair on the pillow and laid a gentle hand on her stomach before covering her with a blanket. 'You must sleep now, my darling,' he told her. 'You have a big day tomorrow.' He turned out the bedside lamp, leaving only the glow from the streetlights to cast the room in soft shadow.

'Yes,' she said. With her head on the pillow, she watched him stride out of the door and listened to his footsteps disappear down the corridor. She found her body longing for him already and reached for the pillow where his head had rested. Putting her arm around it, she held it to her breasts. It smelled of him and she started to drift off to sleep imagining he was still there beside her.

That was why when, a few moments later, she felt a hand slide down along her back and up between her legs, she hoped Marco had returned. Through the fog of sleep, she let out a little moan of pleasure, yearning for him to come inside her again until there was a sudden stab of pain.

'Marco?'

In the darkness she turned to reach out to him, but instead of his naked flesh she felt the bristle of coarse material and cold buttons.

'No, not your precious Marco,' came a voice from the darkness. 'No!' she cried as she felt herself being grabbed from behind and flung onto her back. A hand was suddenly clamped over her mouth.

'Not so loud, you beautiful whore!' hissed the man who sat astride her, two scars on his left cheek.

Karl von Stockmar was leaning forward, pressing on her chest and robbing her of her breath. She felt him fumbling with his belt buckle. It was sharp against her thighs, cutting into her flesh as she struggled to break free. The weight of his body was squeezing the air out of her lungs. She tried to bite his fingers, but he only pushed harder against her mouth. She kicked out with her feet, but he moved his body downward to pin her legs against the mattress. Yet still there was a fury inside her, boiling and churning and threatening to explode. She felt its energy building as she reached out for the bedside lamp. She grabbed it by the shade, but it slipped out of her hand before she could hit him with it. It fell crashing to the ground, the porcelain base smashing on the marble floor.

As soon as Marco stepped out of the elevator and caught sight of himself in the large gilt mirror in the downstairs foyer, he realised he'd left his cap in Lilli's bedroom. Cursing his own stupidity, he started to retrace his steps. This time he strode up the stairs to the second floor and along the corridor. As he reached the outer door to her suite, he found it open and suddenly heard the sound of smashing glass. Rushing inside, he rattled the bedroom door handle. It wouldn't budge. Inside he could hear grunts and muffled screams.

'Lilli! Lilli!' he cried, banging on the door. He tried it again, this time shouldering it and hurtling into the room to find a man on the bed, sitting astride her, his hands around her throat. Marco dived at him and with a single punch to the jaw, sent him flying off the bed.

'Lilli. *Mein Gott!* Lilli!' He lunged over to her, brushed her tousled hair from her face and saw that she was gasping for breath. She began to cough, and he lifted up her head, cradling her in his arms.

On the other side of the bed, Karl von Stockmar heaved himself up from the floor, snatching at the trousers that clung to his buttocks. Once righted, he wiped his mouth with the back of his hand and, standing in the wedge of light from the other room, he saw blood. Snuffling like a truffle pig, he threw a disdainful look at the bed before staggering towards the open door. Catching sight of him, Marco laid Lilli back down and darted up, barring her attacker's way out. Grabbing him by the tunic, he suddenly found himself face to face with Karl von Stockmar.

'You!' he cried, his eyes wide with rage. His fury spilled over. 'Come near her again and I swear I'll kill you!' he cried, shaking von Stockmar violently. 'You hear me!' he snarled, as he flung him round and booted him in the buttocks, sending him careering face down to the floor.

Von Stockmar pulled himself up and shook his head. Reaching for his cap, he dusted it off on his thigh. The corridor light from the open door illuminated his glistening face. He knew he was beaten.

'You're welcome to your Jewish bitch,' he told Marco, glancing over at Lilli, still gasping for breath on the bed. 'She's not worth my energy,' he growled before skulking out of the room.

Chapter 49

As Lilli sat in the ante-room at the Ministry of Public Enlightenment and Propaganda, she fingered the long scarf around her neck self-consciously. It hid the purple bruises that were blooming after von Stockmar's attack the previous night.

Marco had stayed with her then, comforting her. She'd slept in his arms, waking now and again after a nightmare. 'What if von Stockmar tells Goebbels I'm a Jew?' she'd asked breathlessly after one of her dreams.

'I told you, you are worth something to him. He won't hurt you,' Marco had replied, stroking her hair.

He'd been there to soothe her. For that she was so grateful, but her throat remained sore and her thighs were badly scratched by von Stockmar's belt buckle.

Lilli shuddered as the telephone rang and an adjutant answered.

'The Reich Minister will see you now,' he told her, opening the door to an office.

The short man who limped towards Lilli from behind his imposing desk in an equally imposing office, startled her a little. Joseph Goebbels reminded her of the eponymous character in the film version of *Dracula* she'd seen in Hollywood. His black hair rose steeply from his high forehead before it crested his small skull. His eyes were piercing and his smile beguiling. She'd been warned that he was a lothario, too.

'I have seen your film, Miss Stern. You are an excellent dancer – and actress – of course,' he told her, as he kissed her hand. 'Sit, please.' He pointed to a chair on the other side of his desk, before glancing up at the large portrait of the Führer on the wall, as if to seeking approval for anything he was about to say. There was talk of her journey, the Californian sunshine and a lame joke about English food before he finally cut to the chase.

'So, Miss Stern, you are close friends with the Duke and Duchess of Windsor, I believe.' Goebbels lips tightened and his eyes narrowed in what passed for a smile.

Lilli knew such questions would be inevitable. Her closeness to Wallis gave her a unique insight into the workings of the Windsors' febrile minds. *Were they enjoying their stay? What was the prince's opinion of Germany? What was his opinion of his brother, his own country?* Of course, his questions weren't put so bluntly. They were wrapped up in compliments and beribboned in flattery. Lilli had been warned by Colonel Plimpton to expect such enquiries and she parried them with suitably anodyne answers. They were ten minutes into the meeting before Goebbels produced a rabbit from his hat.

'So,' he said, slapping his palms on his desk. 'I have here a film script.' He picked up a bulky bound document and placed it before Lilli on the desk, so that she could read the title page.

'*Titanic,*' she said aloud. She shot the Reich Minister a puzzled.

'*Titanic,*' he repeated before adding with a nod: 'The *true* story of what happened.'

Lilli remained silent as Goebbels rose and started to pace the floor, both hands clasped behind his back. 'You see Miss Stern, had it not been for the corruption of British officials and engineers, this huge maritime tragedy would never have happened. This film will set the record straight.' He stopped to look out of the window.

'I see,' said Lilli. His motives for the meeting were as she suspected.

'It will allow the Reich to establish a Hollywood on the Rhine.' He switched his gaze to Hitler's portrait as he spoke. 'It'll have a cast of hundreds and a budget of four thousand Reichsmarks. What do you say to that?' He pivoted suddenly to fix her with an unsettling wide-eyed glare.

Now it was clear to Lilli. Goebbels wanted to offer her a role in this extraordinary vanity propaganda project of his. He walked back towards her to stand so close that he was almost brushing her sleeve with his hand. He may as well have been crushing her, the pressure she felt was so immense.

She inhaled deeply, trying to restore some order to her thoughts. 'Herr Doktor, I am flattered,' she said after a moment. 'I really am.' Another deep breath. Colonel Plimpton's words echoed in her brain. Her collaboration would be *awfully useful*. Yet still she simply couldn't bring herself to work with such monsters. There had to be another way. 'But I fear cannot accept the role.' Every muscle in her body clenched.

Goebbels studied her resolute expression for a moment; her jaw firm, her eyes unblinking then he barked out a laugh. 'What?' He started to circle her. 'You jest, yes?'

She could hear her own heart pumping faster. 'No, Herr Doktor.'

Another moment that seemed like an age to her passed.

'Why might that be?' His voice was disturbingly even.

Lilli swallowed hard. 'I have many commitments, Herr Goebbels.' She dared not say that the idea filled her with revulsion and loathing. Playing the lead would make her nothing more than a Nazi puppet. First and foremost, she needed to keep close to the Windsors. Filming would take her away from them for long periods. It would also make her more vulnerable to the demands of the Nazis. It was foolish and risky.

Goebbels snorted out another laugh. 'That is not what I heard,' he shot back. 'You would refuse an offer from the Reich?' His back was to her now, but it almost seemed that he was playing games with her – *Who's afraid of the big, bad wolf?* Suddenly he wheeled round sharply. 'I hardly think you are in a position to turn down a role, and such a prestigious one at that.'

Lilli's stomach roiled as Goebbels reached for his telephone. What could he mean? *Hardly in a position to refuse.* He couldn't possibly know that she was Jewish, let alone an informant. Could he?

His eyes were clamped on hers as he barked down the line. 'Bring him in.' Lilli felt the nausea well up inside her and she twisted round on her chair to watch as the Reich Minister rose and marched towards the double doors just as they opened. There, flanked by armed guards, was a young man, his body so limp, he had to be dragged in and held up. She almost didn't recognise him at first. But when she did . . .

'Leon, no!' she cried, leaping up and rushing towards her brother.

Leon lifted his gaze. The socket of his left eye was purple and his jaw badly bruised. There was dried blood on his lip. Despite his obvious pain, he managed to grunt at her. She reached out a hand to touch him but one of the guards shoved her away.

'What have you done to him?' she screamed at Goebbels.

In reply, he simply smirked. 'This is what happens when you disobey the Reich. Your brother attended a student resistance meeting last night at the university.'

'Lilli . . .' Leon began. She switched back only to see him be struck in the face by a guard before he could say any more.

'Let him go!' she screamed, lunging at one of the guards and pummelling with her fists. 'He's done nothing wrong.'

Goebbels held up his hand to signify the guard to restrain her. He remained coldly detached. 'I'm afraid he has. He's contravened an Enabling Law. Technically he is a traitor, Miss Stern. Or should I say Miss Sternberg? I could have him guillotined like that.' He drew his fingers across his throat then grinned. 'But I shall show mercy, if you agree to be in our film.'

Lilli shook her head in disbelief. If this monster knew she was a Jew, why did he want her in the leading role of his film? 'I don't understand,' she said. 'Why me? There must be plenty of other actresses who would be happy to star in your film.'

Goebbels let out a muted laugh. 'Of course,' he replied. 'With much bigger names, too. But none of them are on such intimate terms with the Duke and Duchess of Windsor – our friends and potential allies.'

Suddenly he moved closer, so that she could feel his breath on her cheek. Her body started to stiffen. 'And if I agree you will let my brother free?' Her eyes scooted towards Leon, still hanging between the guards.

'Naturally,' said Goebbels with a smile. 'As soon as the film is finished. You have forty-eight hours to give me your answer, Miss Sternberg.'

She felt like a mouse being taunted by a cat. Goebbels nodded at the guards and they began to haul Leon away.

'Leon!' cried Lilli once more, as her brother disappeared, and the double doors slammed shut. She rushed towards them, but found they'd been locked. In a panic, she turned to face Goebbels.

'You really have little choice, Miss Sternberg.' He walked towards her once more and cupped her chin in his hand to spit the words in her face. 'You're a dirty, Jewish whore and if you want to see your brother alive again, you'll do exactly as I say.'

He dropped his hand and stood back from her to straighten his jacket. 'You are an impostor and the only reason I will let you walk out of here free is because of the Windsors. You understand?'

Everything in the room seemed to tumble around her. The floor swallowed the desk. Hitler's portrait flew off the wall. Books and papers collided in mid-air. So this was how von Stockmar had wreaked his revenge for her continued rejection. He'd reported her for being a Jew.

'You understand?' Goebbels barked at her, barring his pointed teeth.

'*Ja*,' she replied. 'I understand.' She hated every fibre of his being.

'Good,' he countered, sitting himself back down in his chair, like a headmaster who'd just delivered a school report. 'You may go now.'

Lilli's head was swimming. Rising slowly, she steadied herself on the desk before she turned. She swallowed back her tears. She would not give Goebbels the pleasure of seeing her cry. In her throat she felt a scream simmering. But a scream would not wound. Her parting shot needed to be precise and devastating.

'The Jewish race is bigger than the Nazi Party,' she told him, her voice unwavering. 'You will not get away with this, Herr Goebbels.'

He jerked up his head, his eyes wild with rage, but his face remained a mask. Nor did he shout at her. Flinging his arm towards the door, he simply hissed through his pointed teeth. 'Get out. Get out of here before I also have you arrested for treason.'

Chapter 50

The Berghof, Austria

The towering peaks of the Alps made a welcome change from the oppressive buildings of Munich as the official Mercedes, its swastika pennant fluttering, drove them out to Adolf Hitler's mountain retreat. The Duke and Duchess of Windsor sat on the back seat, while Lilli perched opposite them. She kept a scarf tied tightly round her neck to cover the bruising from von Stockmar's attack. Worse still, her head throbbed, and her stomach remained in a vice after her meeting with Goebbels.

Leon's bruised and bloodied face kept looming into her vision. Her brother's fate was in her hands. From now on she would worry that every knock on the door might be an SS man dumping his dead body on her doorstep. James's words filled her head. 'Thousands of political prisoners are being sent to concentration camps,' he'd warned. Now her brother might be one of them.

Twenty minutes into the journey Lilli could see Wallis start to fidget. Evidently bored by the mountain scenery, she took out her powder compact and began inspecting her make-up in its small, round mirror. Lilli noted she was wearing less rouge than usual, and her lipstick was a muted shade. She wondered if Wallis knew just how evil the Third Reich was and, if so, if she even cared.

'I thought I'd wear something practical,' Wallis told Lilli, gesturing to her tweed coat. Her felt hat was also uncharacteristically ordinary. Lilli merely smiled politely. She supposed Wallis's dress was chosen to please the Führer's tastes. He was known to regard glamour as 'un-Aryan'.

The glass shutter of the limousine was drawn to keep their conversation private from the driver. 'So you must tell me how your meeting with Herr Goebbels went, my dear,' said Wallis gleefully. 'I expect he was charming.'

Lilli had rehearsed her reply. 'Yes,' she began, mustering as much enthusiasm as she could, although it was hard knowing she was about to enter the lion's den. Hitler must surely have been informed about Leon's arrest and about her meeting with Herr Doktor Goebbels. 'Charming.'

Wallis nodded. 'We have found the Germans to be so courteous. I've even been called Your Royal Highness on occasions.' She let out a little laugh and looked at her new husband. 'If only your brother and sister-in-law could have heard that!' she sniped. 'Yes,' she went on, straightening her back, 'in Germany we have been accorded the respect we deserve, but are not shown in Britain. In fact, we were just saying, weren't we David, that if war were . . .'

The duke had been listening to his wife, while looking out of the limousine window. He turned his head swiftly to deliver a disapproving look.

'I'm sure Lillian is not in the least interested in silly speculations, Wallis dear,' he told her sharply.

As the road rose higher, winding in on itself like a corkscrew, Lilli was relieved when Wallis shifted the conversation to German fashion and how it erred on the dull side. She let her drone on, smiling politely, while all the time plotting how she might excuse herself from being in the Führer's presence.

Hitler's famous mountain headquarters soon came into view, perched high above them. The sprawling edifice was more like a fortress than a retreat. 'No wonder it's called the Eagle's Nest,' Wallis remarked.

They halted at a checkpoint just a few meters away from large, guarded gates. When the driver stated his business, the sentry bent low to inspect the passengers. He recognised the duke and duchess immediately. Their photographs were in all the German newspapers. Standing back from the limousine, he gave the Nazi salute. '*Sieg heil!*' he shouted, prompting the other three guards to follow suit. The automobile passed on its way and through sturdy gates unimpeded.

It was to be an informal visit, but it also had a serious purpose. There was to be a luncheon and time for socialising on the terrace, but there would be work, too. Although the duke spoke fluent German, he was keen for Lilli to attend some of the discussions with Herr Hitler so that she could keep an unofficial record of what was said for his own papers.

Lilli shivered as a familiar figure stood on the steps to greet them. The mere sight of the Führer made her want to retch. She had seen him spout hatred so many times before on a ten-foot high Pathé screen in London. Surrounded by thousands of adoring Germans, he'd had them eating out from the palm of his hand. In grainy black and white celluloid he'd seemed almost superhuman. Now, in the flesh, he looked unsettlingly normal; his skin the colour of pale pastry, his hair so oiled it looked like treacle, yet now she knew, first hand, that he was evil incarnate.

There were handshakes and smiles as he was introduced to the duke and duchess. '*Willkommen, willkommen,*' he told them in his metallic voice, so recognisable to Lilli.

'And, of course, Miss Stern needs no introduction,' the duke said gallantly as he touched Lilli lightly on the back, pushing her forward. She tensed as she held out a hand to shake Hitler's, just as Wallis had done. Underneath her kid leather gloves she knew her palms were sweating. This time, however, she saw the Führer's smile suddenly dissolve. Her heart stopped. For a fraction of a second, Hitler skewered her with a calculated and surgical regard. It was not the sort of look noticed by anyone else except the intended recipient. A slight bow swiftly followed, as if, thought Lilli, he didn't want to sully his hands by touching Jewish flesh. As he stood upright again, she caught a lingering whiff of his stinking breath. *He knows*, she told herself, as their eyes met. *But he will not say anything – for now.*

To her surprise and – if she were truthful – relief, Lilli was separated from the Windsors and their domineering host. She was directed to wait in another room, although she had no idea for whom or what she was waiting. She supposed it formed part of her punishment for being Jewish – part of the game she was being forced to play but couldn't possibly win. With each passing second she grew more anxious. Might she be the first Jew ever to stay in the Berghof? The Jewish God, the one she was taught was the true God who had chosen Abraham to father his chosen people, meant nothing to her by the time she'd reached the age of sixteen. Now she didn't believe in him at all, even though she still felt guilty for eating pork. *The blood of Abraham and David and Moses flows through your veins*, her mother had lectured her once. *They would have to bleed you dry before you can rid yourself of it.* Perhaps her mother was right, after all.

An armed guard stood by the door, presumably to see that she did not stray. His presence made her feel very uneasy. She stood by the small window to take in the view of the snow-capped summits. She could also see most of the large terrace with its chairs set out in regimented rows. Below she spotted the Führer and the duke, already deep in conversation. They were looking out over the mountains as they spoke, as if seeking to gain some kind of inspiration from nature. She noticed that Hitler had the annoying habit of pressing his little moustache every so often, as if it was glued on to his upper lip. A short, bald man, notebook in hand, was in tow. Snatches of bland talk drifted up to her: comments on the German factory system and of living conditions for workers were what seemed to interest the duke most. Herr Hitler's agenda, she suspected, was less altruistic.

Lilli knew she should be down there. The duke had asked her if he might make notes of their conversations, too, but until she was summoned, she would keep out of Hitler's sight.

She had just sat down when she heard light footsteps outside the door and a thin young woman in a traditional dirndl and braided hair walked in. For a moment Lilli thought she must be a secretary, come to escort her, but when the guard suddenly clicked his heels and saluted, Lilli thought again.

'*Guten Tag*,' the heavily made-up woman greeted cheerfully. 'You are Fraulein Stern. Fraulein Lillian Stern, *ja*?'

Lilli rose. She recognised her visitor from photographs James had shown her.

'How do you do, Miss Braun?' she said.

The young woman looked at her with wide eyes and a guileful expression. 'You know who I am?'

Lilli nodded. 'Of course. You are the Führer's . . .' She stopped herself. She could not use the word mistress, so she opted instead for something more neutral.

'Friend,' she said.

'Friend,' repeated Eva, somewhat disappointedly, thought Lilli. The problem was that the Führer was, as everyone knew, wedded to Germany. Her red lips lifted into a polite smile. 'I am sent to entertain you. Shall we drink coffee on the terrace?' she asked, taking Lilli completely off-guard. She'd assumed Hitler's concubine would be entertaining Wallis.

'Thank you,' Lilli replied, as Eva motioned to a door. 'You are not with the duchess?' she added unthinkingly as she followed her hostess.

'I'm not allowed.'

'Oh.' Lilli suddenly became aware that she was feeling her way across a minefield.

They walked side by side along a corridor. 'Besides, she speaks no German and I no English. Magda Goebbels is hosting her and the Führer's deputy, Herr Hess.'

Lilli was led through another door that opened out onto a small, private terrace that faced west, away from the main area. They sat at a bistro table and Eva ordered two coffees.

'Do you have a cigarette?' she asked, as a maid set down two espressos in front of them.

Lilli opened her handbag and offered her one from her silver case.

As Eva reached for it, Lilli noticed her polished nails. 'The Führer doesn't like anyone smoking, but if it's outside with a guest, well . . .' She threw out a mischievous look as she puffed the Sobranie into life, courtesy of Lilli's lighter. Inhaling deeply, as if she'd been craving a smoke all day, she said: 'I saw your film. You are a good dancer.'

'Thank you,' replied Lilli, unsure if the compliment was genuine, or if Eva was just being polite.

'So what's it like in Hollywood? Is it as glamorous as it looks?'

Lilli felt flattered that Eva should have followed her career. She also took out a cigarette, and dispensing with her customary holder, cupped her hand over the tip and lit it and as she did so a faint feeling of her own vanity fizzed into life. 'It was.' Tinseltown seemed a long way in her past now. It had been two years since she was last in Hollywood.

'Was?' Eva picked up on the past tense.

'I injured my foot,' explained Lilli. 'I can no longer dance. I made just the one film but . . .' Her voice dissipated with her exhaled smoke.

'I think I read something about that, but I didn't realise . . .' replied Eva, narrowing her eyes as she dragged on her cigarette. 'I'm sorry to hear it. You must miss your life there.'

273

Lilli paused to frame her answer. Of course she missed her dancing, more than anything else, but did she miss Hollywood? If she was being honest, she would say no. She remembered the long hours, the agonies she suffered in rehearsals, the acting both on and off screen.

'Of course I miss it,' she replied. 'There were parties and premieres and gowns.' She refrained from mentioning the endless days, the directors who shouted at you one minute, then wanted to bed you the next and the stress of learning songs and lines. Somehow she thought it was wrong – like telling a three year-old child that Santa Claus didn't exist.

At the mention of parties Eva's eyes lit up excitedly. 'I want to go to Hollywood someday, too,' she said. 'But I'm no actress. I prefer to stay behind the camera, like Leni.'

Lilli smiled and nodded. Leni Riefenstahl, she knew, was Hitler's favourite film maker and Fraulein Braun's close friend.

'Did you see *Triumph of the Will*'? asked Eva, wafting away cigarette smoke with her hand. Lilli had. She'd been impressed – and troubled – in equal measure by the epic scale of the propaganda movie and the thought of it suddenly reminded her that by acting in *Titanic*, she, too, would be forced to participate in an equally unpalatable epic.

'I did,' replied Lilli, sipping her coffee.

Eva looked at her slightly oddly, as if an idea was blooming in her brain. 'The Führer has just given me a new cine camera. It takes moving pictures. How about I do some shooting? Take some photographs of you while you're here?' she asked, leaning forward and touching Lilli's knee like an overgrown schoolgirl. 'We could have fun.'

Lilli thought for a moment before deciding to humour the poor young woman, who seemed so totally forlorn and out of place in this dictator's lair. After all it would be a welcome diversion from her own inner hell.

'All right. After luncheon?' she suggested.

Lunch. With Hitler. Lilli balked at the idea. She didn't even know if she was still permitted to eat with the Führer and the Windsors. It was that look that Hitler had given her, that terrifying glare that had bored into her very soul. He knew about Leon and he knew her secret. One phone call and he could give the order for her brother to be shot. How could she possibly face him over the dining table?

'Though I shan't be going to lunch,' Lilli said abruptly. 'I have a headache.'

Eva paused, but instead of trying to persuade her to attend, she simply nodded her understanding. 'I'm not going either,' she retorted, in such a way that made Lilli believe she understood her reluctance. 'I'm not allowed to mix with guests. As I said, Frau Magda is the hostess today.'

Lilli raised a brow. Why should Magda Goebbels be hosting the Windsors? Could it be that Herr Hitler didn't think his naïve little mistress was sophisticated enough to take on the role? She suspected so. And as for any similarities with Wallis – the two women had about as much in common as sauerkraut and strudel.

Lilli felt she suddenly had an ally. 'Can I get word to the duchess to offer my apologies?'

'Of course.' Eva's eyes widened before she spoke her mind. 'Perhaps we could lunch together in my suite instead?' She paused, as if to give her new friend the benefit of the doubt, adding: 'If your head doesn't hurt too much, of course.'

Lilli actually found herself feeling a little sorry for Eva. She was a lonely young mistress in her gilded cage. No doubt British intelligence would be interested to hear about Eva Braun's disposition, too.

'I'd like that very much,' she replied.

Chapter 51

Eva's suite was not at all like the rest of the Berghof. It was light and feminine and felt almost homely. Almost. Dominating it all was a large, glowering portrait of the Führer, as if he was overseeing all that his mistress was doing, even when he was not there; an ever-present reminder that she never beyond his reach nor his wrath.

'Music! Let's have music!' Eva cried gleefully, rushing over to a gramophone player housed in a large cabinet and plucking a record from a stack of seventy-eights. 'Fred Astaire,' she cried, brandishing the disc in the air. 'Your partner!'

'Yes,' replied Lilli. 'My partner.' It was a sudden reminder that her own family was no longer allowed to enjoy such a simple pleasure as listening to recorded music.

They ate cold chicken and sauerkraut from trays on their laps and drank Riesling as '*Cheek to Cheek*' played on the gramophone. Lilli didn't drink, but by the time Eva was halfway through a bottle of wine, she was becoming quite morose.

'Do you have a lover?' she asked, the whites of her eyes turning pink. She was looking at Lilli's wedding ring as she spoke.

'As you see, I'm married,' she replied, holding up her left hand to show her the ring that masked the lie. For a moment she thought of James and of the secrets they both kept.

'I see that,' Eva said with a nod. 'But does your husband love you?'

'Yes,' replied Lilli, suddenly picturing Marco. 'I am sure he does.'

Eva stared into her glass and Lilli noticed tears welling up.

'Sometimes I think the Führer only loves me when we are in bed,' she said.

There were photographers everywhere to record the meetings between the Windsors and Hitler, both inside the Berghof and outside on the vast terraces. It was a bright autumn day and the sky was clean and cloudless. The mountain peaks seemed to be little higher than eye level. *Where better for a dictator to dream of being master of all he surveys?* thought Lilli as she stepped out into the crisp air.

'Ah, there you are!' Wallis greeted her. She remained seated in her chair on the terrace. 'Feeling better, are we?' she said, shielding her eyes from the bright sun. She didn't wait for a reply. 'We missed you at lunch. Herr Hitler wanted to know all about Hollywood.'

Lilli nodded. 'Yes, it was a pity.' It was also a great relief to her that it sounded as though the Führer hadn't passed on the knowledge he must surely have gleaned from Goebbels.

'But you're better now and that's good news,' said Wallis, 'because I know the duke wants you to help with taking notes very shortly.'

'Ladies!' called one of the snappers as Lilli and Wallis talked. They looked up simultaneously, smiles at the ready as a shutter clicked. They were both seasoned professionals.

'Ah! There you are, Lillian!' It was the duke. 'Headache cleared?' he asked jauntily. Just like his wife, he didn't bother to wait for a reply. 'I'd so appreciate it if you'd take notes,' he told her, flashing a charming smile. 'My meeting with the Führer is scheduled to begin in five minutes,' he added, tapping his watch face.

As if on cue, Hitler strode onto the terrace, his translator straggling behind. 'And so to business,' he said to the duke.

Lilli wanted the paving stones to swallow her up, but it was no use. The Führer had seen her and that same terrible boring sensation pierced her chest as he looked at her once more.

'Miss Stern is much better now,' Wallis ventured with a broad smile.

'So I see,' replied Hitler, his gaze fixed on Lilli. 'But I fear we shall have to talk about her career another time.' His voice was icy. 'The duke and I have much work to do.'

Lilli felt her body slump with relief, as if she had dodged a bullet, for the time being at least. The sigh had barely escaped her lips when, from out of nowhere, came a cry. 'Smile for the camera!' She jerked her head round to see Eva, her Rolleiflex poised. The shutter clicked and she reappeared from behind the lens smiling broadly.

'Eva!' Hitler scolded. 'What do you think you are doing?'

Eva's bottom lip pouted. 'Only having a little fun, *mein Führer*,' she replied, deliberately sounding like a six-year-old.

'You must be Fraulein Braun,' beamed Wallis.

'*Ja*,' Eva replied in German, suddenly emboldened. She stepped forward and to everyone's surprise dipped a curtsey.

The duke raised a brow and swapped a glance with Hitler who seemed equally surprised. Lilli could tell that, for once, the Führer had been wrong-footed. With a nod of his slick, black head he conceded an introduction was in order. 'This is Fraulein Braun,' he told his guest, stating the obvious. Eva curtsied to him, too, but the duke held out his hand.

'*Enchanté*,' he said, fixing her with one of his famous smiles. For a moment, Eva seemed quite charmed by such attention, but then, remembering she held a camera in her hand, she asked: 'Another shot?'

The duke threw his head back and laughed. 'How about one of the ladies with the Führer?' he suggested, stepping to the side.

Now it was Wallis's turn to laugh. 'Delightful,' she said, forgetting that the decision was not hers to make. Hitler, however, did not object. Instead he allowed Wallis to stand close to him. 'Lillian,' she beckoned. 'Lillian, here.'

Lilli swallowed hard and stepped up to stand at the Führer's side, almost touching his sleeve. Wallis smoothed her hair, aware that the photograph was more than a mere snapshot, and Hitler pressed his little moustache. Lilli could feel her shoulders tighten. Eva lifted the camera up to her eye and called for another broad beam from the three of them.

'*Smile, please,*' she called and, with the sun high in the clear blue sky, the Führer, the duchess and the spy duly grinned on demand, as if between them they had not a care in the world.

Lilli spent the afternoon following behind the duke like a lap dog, scribbling down dull talk about the German organisation of labour and factories. Hitler had pointedly ignored her and for that she was truly grateful. As soon as the meeting was over, she was escorted back to the waiting room, but no sooner had she sat down than Eva Braun appeared, clutching a folder to her breast and beaming.

'I have something for you. A souvenir of your visit here,' she told Lilli with obvious delight.

'Oh?' said Lilli.

Eva set down the folder on a nearby table and opened it. 'The photo I took earlier today,' she squealed. 'I developed it.' She leaned over and pointed. 'There you are with the Führer and Her Highness. See how happy you look!' Lilli let out a muted gasp as she saw herself and Wallis posing with Hitler.

'I don't know what to say,' she mumbled, her eyes clamped onto the photograph. 'Thank you,' she managed as the colour drained from her face.

'I knew you'd love it!' said Eva. 'It's a wonderful memento of your visit here, *ja?*'

Lilli peered at the image once more. Hitler's jaw was thrust forward, his eyes glaring, his stance imperious and she . . . well she stood barely half an inch away from one of the most dangerous men in the world and on her face she'd forced a smile. '*Ja*. Wonderful,' she replied.

Chapter 52

For the last night of their tour the Windsors returned to Berlin. Lilli, however, stayed in Munich, as planned. Goebbels was waiting for her answer and Marco was his messenger. Did he know about Leon's arrest and torture? There were still so many things to discuss, so much that needed to be said between them.

At eight o'clock that evening Lilli duly stepped out of the hotel and into a limousine to take her to the *bahnhof* to begin her journey back to London. Linz was at the wheel and stepped out to load her luggage. Marco was waiting in the back seat. The glass shutter was drawn, so their conversation could not be heard. As they moved away from the hotel, Lilli could no longer contain her torment.

'Oh Marco! They have Leon!' she cried in a half-whisper. It took all her strength not to grab hold of him. Her words came out in a flood. 'Goebbels wants me to star in his film. If I don't, they will keep Leon in jail. Or worse. You have to help me!'

Marco looked towards the rear-view mirror. Linz had glanced up, but his eyes switched back down to the road immediately. Horrified, Lilli caught his expression, but reaching out, Marco took her hand in his, to reassure her.

'It's all right. Linz has been with me for years. He is loyal and 'discreet.' His words eased the tension, while reminding her that she needed to compose herself.

'What can I do?' she asked, her voice more measured, as she pulled back, dabbing her eyes.

'You must agree to Goebbels's demands,' he told her calmly.

A pain suddenly shot through her brain and panic rose from somewhere deep inside here.

'What?'

Marco's gaze remained steady and she recognised the look in his eyes. It was familiar and it was chilling. It was betrayal.

'You knew, didn't you? You knew Goebbels had Leon.'

He shook his head. 'I was informed this morning.'

Doubt bubbled through the cracks that had suddenly opened up between them. She'd put her trust in Marco and now, it seemed, he'd betrayed her once again.

Her whole body was suddenly seized by rage. Leaning towards the glass screen, she banged on it. 'Let me out!' she cried to Linz. 'Stop the car.' But Linz just stiffened his neck and checked the rear-view mirror to take his orders from the major. Marco shook his head.

'*Nein*, Lilli! No,' he told her through clenched teeth, pressing her back down on the seat next to him. 'I swear I didn't know before. Don't you think I would have warned you?' He shook his head and bit his lip.

'There's something else, isn't there, Marco? Tell me.' Her voice was quivering with rage.

His chest heaved, as he was preparing to unburden himself. 'Goebbels wants to use you to spy on the duke and duchess as well.'

'What?' There was outrage in her eyes.

Marco could barely look at her. 'You know them intimately. You have access to their private conversations, papers etcetera. You are ideally . . .'

'Enough!' Lilli raised her hand and looked out of the window at the bright lights of the street. 'I know why Hitler allowed me into the Berghof.' She lowered her voice. 'I may be Jewish but I am a very useful Jew.'

Marco nodded gravely. 'Yes, you are and I am to give Goebbels your answer tomorrow morning. If it's a refusal to either, or both demands . . .'

'Then Leon will die.' The words chilled her as she said them.

Again Marco nodded and reached for her hand. 'Say you'll agree, my love. Please.'

For a moment she pictured her frail father, her forlorn mother and Leon, bloody, angry and afraid. She had not been a good daughter, or a good sister. She had been selfish. She'd turned her back on the people she loved in their time of need and now was when they needed her more than ever.

'I have no choice,' she told him. 'If it means my family will be safe, then I will spy on the Windsors for the Reich, as well as act in the film.'

Marco's breath left his mouth in a cloud of relief and he squeezed her hand again.

'I know it's hard, but it is the right decision for you and for me.'

'For you?' She frowned.

'Don't you see, my love? For the moment I need to play the Reich's game.' He glanced up at the glass shutter towards Linz and lowered his voice. 'Hitler is hell-bent on war with Britain. He intends to invade the United Kingdom and when he does, he wants the Duke of Windsor restored to the throne.'

Lilli's eyes were wide. To her it seemed that the duke saw himself as a peacemaker: a figure-head who could unite warring factions. There were rumours. There always were, but not even James had put it so baldly to her. Now Marco was telling her Hitler wanted the duke for his puppet king.

'I see,' was all she could muster at first, unable to digest the enormity of the situation. War clouds were whirling all around her, but she hadn't taken the time to look up at the sky. It was hard to believe this was happening. It was so far from her life in Hollywood – in England even.

Marco shook his head. 'I am not alone in my fears. There are other officers like me. Good men who want no part in Hitler's plans to invade the rest of Europe, but we cannot speak out for fear of the firing squad. We pay lip service, but we are trapped. All we can do is try and get the message out. Tell your British government. Tell the Americans, too. For all our sakes.'

Marco had opened himself up to her completely. He'd echoed Leon's words. Now it was only fair that she should do the same to him.

'You know your secret is safe with me,' she said softly. Marco nodded and, taking her hand in his, he kissed it. For a moment she closed her eyes as she felt a spark charge through her body once more. 'Now I must tell you mine,' she said.

Their eyes locked onto each other's and she wondered if he could still reach into her mind to gage her thoughts as he used to.

'You know I'm working for the British?' As soon as the words left her mouth, she held her breath. She had just gambled with her own life, but her belief in Marco wasn't misplaced.

'I'd hoped you might be,' was all he said, his eyes penetrating deep inside her.

The limousine started to slow down outside the railway station.

'We must trust each other, but no one else. You will do that, Lilli?' he asked, as they slowed to a halt.

'I will,' she told him, the relief flooding through her body. Lifting his hand to her lips she kissed it. She hated herself for ever doubting him.

'I have to trust you for all our sakes,' she said, as Linz opened her door.

Chapter 53

London, England

'I'm pregnant.'

Lilli was quite startled to hear the words she'd been rehearsing for days suddenly spill out of her mouth. It was New Year's Eve and she and James were at a party at the London home of the Washington Trumpshaws. They were surrounded by people wearing ridiculous hats and trumpeting on brightly coloured blowers. The champagne was flowing, but Lilli wasn't drinking. She'd been feeling nauseous since the beginning of December but had only just found out why. Her answer had come in reply to a question from James about her abstinence from alcohol. He was becoming decidedly merry, not even objecting when a drunken woman festooned him in streamers. Lilli, however, remained sober while everyone else partied around her.

She'd agreed to star in *Titanic* to save Leon's life, and to spy on the Duke and Duchess of Windsor. Her brother's bloodied face flashed through her mind. The memory of him made her want to scream. Golda had gone hysterical when Lilli told her he was being held under Goebbels's orders. Her mother knew of too many friends whose sons had disappeared and been found shot in a ditch somewhere. And Leon would join them if Lilli didn't do exactly what her Nazi puppet-masters told her. As with the British secret service, there were strict protocols to follow for the Nazis – certain ways of passing on information; codes to be learned; passwords – all the accoutrements of intrigue that seemed so far removed from reality. Marco had persuaded her to comply. Of course, she had no real choice. As well as putting Leon's life in jeopardy, the Gestapo knew where the rest of her family lived. So, not only did she return home to London from Munich with a film script to learn, but as a fully-fledged Nazi informant, too.

One of the first things Lilli did on her return was tell James, then, of course, Colonel Plimpton about her new 'allegiance'. He'd debriefed her on the trip and declared the Windsors' affinity for Fascism, and for Germany's government 'very troubling'. He told her the information she'd gathered was 'most awfully useful' and said she'd done a 'spiffing' job. She wasn't quite sure what that meant, although from Colonel Plimpton's expression she could tell he was pleased with her work.

Now that the Nazis were on her back, she needed to satisfy their appetite for information about the Windsors, as well. She was walking along a tightrope, and her family was waiting for her at the end. She only hoped that after what she'd endured in Germany, especially at the hands of Goebbels, the intelligence would be useful, that it would go some way to warning Mr Chamberlain about what he was facing when he held talks with Adolf Hitler.

It was a few minutes before midnight. She and James were corralled in a corner in the study. They'd barely spoken all evening and when he'd chided her, she'd just come out with it.

'Pregnant,' he repeated. His flushed face that had been –unusually for him – split by a great grin for the latter part of the evening, suddenly dropped. He took a deep breath as he sidled closer to her. 'Zeiller's, I presume?'

'Yes.' On her return from Germany she had told him how she

and Marco had rekindled their affair. At the time James seemed to think it was a rather good idea. He'd even jokingly called her Mati Hari on a couple of occasions after that. Their marriage was, as she kept reminding him, a purely professional arrangement, allowing them both to enter freely into relationships.

James slugged back the rest of the champagne in his glass. He was clearly drunk and she was aware that he could turn very bitter when he had too much. 'I see,' he replied, not bothering to look at her.

She expected more. 'Is that all you can say?'

'What do you want me to say?' he shot back, picking off the paper streamers lodged on his lapel.

'In Germany we congratulate the mother-to-be.'

He shrugged. 'All right.' He grabbed a half-full glass that had been discarded on a nearby windowsill and raised it together with his voice.

'Congratulations on being about to bring another Nazi bastard into the world.'

'James,' she hissed. The three other couples in the room all glanced over at them. Thankfully the piano music from the hall was quite loud, even so, she couldn't be sure if they'd heard what he'd said. She hoped they were also too drunk to register their conversation.

'Will you tell him?' He sat himself down on a nearby chaise longue and gestured her to join him, patting the upholstery.

'No. Not yet.'

'So you *will* tell him?'

'I will.' The nagging doubts that Lilli felt on her last visit to Munich were now erased. She trusted Marco. She must for her family's sake, for their child's.

James took another gulp of champagne. 'That could be useful,' he muttered.

'Useful?' she repeated. That word again. Everything in England was either useful or useless. She was sitting at his side, but as far away as the width of chaise longue would allow.

He seemed indignant at her question. 'Yes. To us.'

By 'us' she knew he meant British intelligence service. She also knew the way his mind worked. The baby could in some way be used as a bargaining tool in exchange for information from Marco.

She felt herself tense. 'This baby will not be useful to anyone,' she told him. 'He or she will be loved, and of course he or she will be ours, James. Ours. So you'd better start acting like a proud father-to-be.'

From the drawing room they suddenly heard the sound of guests shouting in unison. 'Ten, nine, eight . . .'

One of the men in the study grabbed an opened bottle of champagne from an ice bucket that someone had left on the desk and started refilling glasses.

'Six, five, four . . .'

James held out his glass, but Lilli declined, placing her gloved hand over the rim.

'Three, two, one . . .'

The house fell silent as, on the wireless turned up to full volume, Big Ben could be heard striking midnight. On the twelfth stroke, dozens of voices chorused 'Happy New Year!' and party-streamers cascaded into the air. Someone started playing '*Auld Lang Syne*' on the grand piano in the hall.

'Happy New Year, darling Lillian,' said James softly, his mood suddenly mellowing as he raised his glass to her. 'Your very good health.' His eyes dropped to her torso.

'Thank you, James,' she acknowledged. 'Let's hope 1938 will bring better fortune to all of us.'

Chapter 54

1938

Lilli found the English winter so grey. In Munich it was white, in Hollywood, blue. But in London, in January and February, its colour reminded her of cold porridge; thick and heavy. It lay on her like the weight of being held hostage by the Nazi regime, being forced to star in a propaganda film and to spy on the Windsors in return for her brother's life.

To take her mind away from the seemingly unending trials she was facing, she'd begun making plans for the baby's arrival. The purchase of a cot, a perambulator and the decoration of the nursery suddenly became important. They were small steps towards something positive, even though she realised, to her despair, that a trip to Munich so that her parents and Marco could meet the baby, when it arrived, would put everyone at risk.

It was impossible for Lilli to travel safely until the dates of the filming of *Titanic* were finalised and her business was officially sanctioned by the Reich. She had written to Marco – necessarily in a rather cryptic way – informing him that she was expecting a baby and citing a due date. Counting backwards would alert Marco to the fact that he was the father. She'd had to sign herself by her married name *Lillian Marchington*. If the Reich traced her letter, it might put Marco in danger. Having an intimate relationship with a non-Aryan was now illegal in Germany.

Marco had written back, clearly shocked, but delighted, by the news. He was less cryptic in his reply.

She re-read his letter.

> *My love,*
> *I wish I could be with you at this challenging time, but we must both be strong, for the sake of your family, and now for our child.*

He told her he was doing what he could for Leon, and making enquiries at various concentration camps. Yet without raising suspicion, there was little else to be done. Officially there was still no news of her brother, but for all their sakes, Lilli had to believe he was still alive. Thousands of political prisoners were being held in camps. She prayed her brother was surviving in one of them.

'You must go to Munich,' James told her when he'd found her crying after one of her mother's desperate letters. He'd actually put his arm around her, something he hadn't done since she'd discovered his preference for men. This time, she allowed it to rest there. 'There must be some way to get them out. If they came to England, they could stay with us.'

Lilli dabbed her eyes. 'Oh James, that would be wonderful,' she replied. Even though she feared it was impossible, she was so grateful to her husband for the offer.

Each letter from Golda piled on the hopelessness of their situation. *Your father is very ill. Your poor father grows weaker. Vati has taken to his bed.*

She knew thousands of Jews were already flooding out of Germany but finding it difficult to persuade other countries to accept them. Her parents had never held passports and were surely unlikely to be granted them now, although if she could prove an offer of a home in England, it might hold some sway.

'So you would let my parents live with us?'

He smiled gently and shook his head. 'I'm not a monster, Lilli. I know I've deprived you of the intimacy you wanted, so this is the least I can do.' For the first time, he laid a hand on her belly. 'The child would grow up knowing their German grandparents.'

She kissed him then, on the cheek. 'That means so much to me,' she said, the tears welling in her eyes once more.

The suggestion, however, was met with an emphatic '*nein*' in a subsequent letter. Jacob was not well enough to travel. Golda made it very clear, that their fate was in the Almighty's hands. If they were to die in Germany, so be it. They would die together. Lilli knew then that if her parents were ever to see their first grandchild Lilli would have to take her baby, when it was born, to Munich.

Like the British, the Nazis wanted information from her about the movements and thoughts of the Windsors. The ducal pair had become a commodity to be traded and, unbeknown to them, Lilli was the reluctant broker. After their wedding last year, they'd settled in France, so Wallis's letters had become the only source of information available to her. Should these dry up, then Lilli would become useless to the Third Reich. Every time she received word from the new duchess, she would photograph the letter immediately using the small Minox camera supplied by the British secret service. After that she would fulfil her role for the Nazis by taking the original letter to a locker at one of several designated left luggage offices at various London railway stations. When she'd placed the letter in the locker she would drop the key at a pre-allocated destination: sometimes on a newspaper stand, sometimes in a rubbish bin nearby. The key was retrieved immediately by a Nazi agent and the letter collected a few minutes later.

As Lilli's stomach swelled, so did her anxiety for Leon. Seven months had passed without a word. She needed to know that she wasn't working in vain; that she would be rewarded for this duplicity. News of Hitler's annexation of Austria in March had come as another bitter blow. The German maniac was on the warpath. And so was Lilli.

The next time she received a letter from Wallis she decided not to leave it in the left luggage office. Instead she wrote her own note to her Nazi minder and put it in the locker. It said: '*Meet me at the gentlemen's department in Harrods in half an hour.*'

Pretending to select an appropriate silk tie for James as she perused the racks of various colours and patterns, Lilli's fear grew. She was imagining the tie she held suddenly being looped around her neck and tightened when a man sidled up to her. He was heavy, with a jowly face, and a hat far too large for his head and he mumbled the password she'd been given for such encounters. She regarded him with disdain. She'd seen him once or twice before, loitering near a left luggage office, yet she dared not look him in the eye for fear of unleashing her own fury in public.

Staring straight ahead at a blue and yellow stripped tie, she took a deep breath and said: 'I want proof my brother is still alive.'

The man picked out a blood red cravat. He spoke in German. 'You have the Reich Minister's word. What more do you want?'

She sneered at him. She would no more trust Goebbels than the devil himself. 'I want a photograph of my brother holding a dated newspaper.'

She heard the man snort. 'I will put in the request, but I cannot—'

'Do it,' she hissed, suddenly grabbing the tie and clenching it in her fist. 'Do it or there'll be no more letters and no film.'

Chapter 55

More than a month passed, and Lilli had heard nothing from her Nazi contacts. She was in the upstairs drawing room of the house, rereading Wallis's latest communication that had arrived earlier that day. This time it was a hastily scrawled postcard from Italy. A photograph of the Leaning Tower of Pisa graced the front.

The weight of the baby made her back ache, so she was propped up on cushions on a high chair, stroking the mound of her belly as she read.

> *Having such a fabulous time with the Rogers. Pisa is divine and I felt positively sea-sick looking down from the tower. Ischia was sheer paradise, too. Meeting up with many friends, who are being so supportive. David's American speech went down awfully well. We do not give up hope. Wallis.*

The Duke of Windsor's speech, Lilli was aware, had been recorded by the American broadcaster NBC earlier in the month. In it he pleaded for peace between Germany and the rest of Europe. It had certainly done him some favours, Lilli thought. He'd cast himself in the role of the peacemaker. Nevertheless, she couldn't be entirely sure that he wasn't a wolf in sheep's clothing.

Glancing at the carriage clock on the mantelshelf, she saw it was approaching six o'clock. James would be home soon. It was a pleasant evening and when the weather was good, he enjoyed the fifty-minute walk from the gallery. She eased herself up from her chair to plod over to the French doors that opened onto the balcony. Pulling back the voile curtains, she unlocked the doors and walked out.

The noise of the traffic from Kensington High Street was but a distant drone, like the buzzing of bees. Here it was a quiet oasis of calm. All of the houses faced onto a private square garden, fenced by railings, for the exclusive use of residents. The chestnut trees were decked in their pink and white flower cones, while purple iris and peonies provided more splashes of colour in broad beds, bordered by clipped hedges. Lilli patted her baby's mound and imagined playing with the child on the neatly cut lawns this time next year.

For the past two years London life had paraded outside her window and around the fashionable square. Bankers and civil servants, domestics and tradesmen plied back and forth about their daily business. The trouble was she never knew which, if any of them, might be spies. There was no doubt in her mind that she was being watched by men like the one the colonel had pointed out to her on Caxton Street. As if in response to the frisson of fear she felt, the baby inside her kicked hard.

There were only a few cars parked along the kerb outside the house. An elderly man limped past on a walking stick. A uniformed nanny was pushing a pram. Either one of them could be a spy, she told herself.

Somewhere to her left, she heard an engine start up and, following the noise, she saw a sedan car move off slowly. She thought nothing of it and sliding her eyes to the right, suddenly spotted James come round the corner, briefcase in hand and a rolled umbrella. She recalled, before they were married, he'd told her he always liked to be prepared for all eventualities. Their relationship had certainly improved since she'd been pregnant and she was confident they would both enjoy their new roles as parents. A warm smile lifted her lips as she considered the prospect while watching him walk purposefully along the pavement opposite.

Suddenly, the roar of a car's engine broke the square's tranquillity. Lilli couldn't see anything through the trees, but she could hear the revving come closer until, a second later, the car – the same sedan she'd watched pull away a moment earlier – appeared, heading back around the square. James had just stepped off the pavement as it skirted the corner at speed. It seemed to accelerate even more. He didn't stand a chance. His head turned just before impact, but his feet didn't move. The car hit him with a sickening thud, sending him catapulting into the air like a rag doll.

Lilli screamed. The moment pressed on her as if in slow motion. James's arms flailed, his head jerked and his whole body landed in a crumpled heap in the middle of the tarmac. A young woman, walking nearby, dropped her basket of shopping and rushed to his aid. A policeman was swiftly on the scene. By the time Lilli made it down to the square, a small cluster of people had gathered around James's mangled body. She saw the umbrella cast aside, his briefcase tossed on the pavement and rivulets of blood from his smashed skull trickling along the road. But of the sedan that hit him, there was no sign.

The baby girl was born prematurely in an exclusive London nursing home the day after James's death. Unable to sleep that night, Lilli had been standing at the window, gazing at the spot where her husband had lost his life, when a pulse of unspeakable pain gripped her sides. She knew she was going into labour.

Ten hours later the child arrived. Naturally the tiny girl was the most beautiful baby her mother had ever seen. With brown eyes, a dimpled chin and a mass of dark, curly hair, she was, unmistakably, Marco's.

Lilli felt such an impossible surge of love for her when she held her the first time that she'd cried tears of joy, as well as of sorrow. Of course she was grieving for her dead husband, but mostly she found herself crying for Marco. All the frustration and the longing that she'd managed to keep pent up for so many months now burst through the walls of her dam. She'd smuggled a message to him via the American Embassy the previous month. Naturally there'd been no acknowledgement for fear of arousing suspicion, but the ache that she felt as she held Marco's baby was so deep it was almost unbearable. Had the birth been in Germany, the child would have been illegal under new legislation, as the product of a union between a Jew and a gentile. Both Lilli and Marco could have been arrested because their love was forbidden. Not knowing when or even if, she would see him again was a fear Lilli carried with her always.

James's devastated family – there was no question in his parents' minds that he wasn't the baby's father – all doted on the little girl. She was, in a small way, compensation for the loss of their son. Lady Marchington had balked at Lilli's choice of the name Leeona, after her brother, even though Lilli had proposed using an English spelling on the birth certificate. So a compromise was reached. The little girl was christened Jemima – in honour of James – to the satisfaction of the Marchington family, even though to Lilli she would always be Leeona.

A month later, at Westminster Coroner's Court, a verdict of manslaughter was recorded on the Honourable James Marchington. But Lilli knew it was murder. Premeditated murder. During routine questioning, the police had asked her if anyone might have had a motive to run down James deliberately. The truth – that her husband had been murdered by Nazi agents in response to her uncooperative behaviour – could never come out, of course. So she remained silent. The other two witnesses who'd come forward were of no assistance. There were no leads. No further action could be taken. Lilli had stepped out of line and James had paid the price.

Leeona was her only comfort in those dark times. The destruction of thousands of Jewish shops and businesses on *Kristallnacht*, the Night of Broken Glass, in Germany went largely unremarked elsewhere. Lilli pictured Herr Backe and his thuggish friends smashing windows with relish. The German government looked on, smirking and gloating, while she, and all other Jews, despaired.

Her daughter brought light and hope to Lilli as she struggled to navigate this new world of widowhood and motherhood combined. Then, in the spring of the following year, just when she thought her life could not get much harder, another bombshell hit. Lilli received news that Jacob had suffered a heart attack – his third – and, this time, it had proved fatal. Memories of her father were draped around her like an old, favourite coat. Now, suddenly, she felt cold. She needed to return to Munich to comfort Golda. The trouble was, if she set foot in Germany without official permission, there was no guarantee that she would ever leave. Besides, another even more terrible prospect loomed.

Chapter 56

1939

'*This country is at war with Germany.*' Neville Chamberlain's sombre words broadcast on the wireless echoed around the walls of Lilli's Kensington home. She listened to them as she cradled Leeona on the sofa knowing, at that moment, the world was about to change forever. She glanced over at the chair opposite and the room suddenly felt full of her sighs for his absence. James should've been there.

'How has it come to this?' she asked herself, staring blankly ahead.

A great weight pushed against her chest. She was old enough to remember the last war in which so many millions lost their lives. Although she'd been only a child at the time, she knew fathers and sons who went to the Front but never returned.

The swelling darkness threatened to drown her under a great wave of sorrow. She clasped Leeona's tiny hand. 'We need to be strong, *mein Liebling*,' she said. 'We have right on our side.' An image of Marco flashed into her mind and her heart ached. 'Your papa and I will help make things right, little one.' Lovingly, she stroked her daughter's cheek. 'We have to.'

The Windsors were in France, but now war had been declared, Lilli guessed the couple would want to return to England. They probably felt they needed to at least show solidarity with the nation, even if they weren't inclined to do so. The following day she telephoned the villa at La Croë in the south of France where they were staying. After three attempts she finally got through to Wallis on a crackly line.

'My dear Lillian, how wonderful to hear from you,' she answered, sounding genuinely pleased. 'What a terrible time we're having.'

At first Lilli thought the duchess was referring to the declaration of war, but it soon became clear that Wallis was talking about her own personal plight.

'They've offered David and me a flight back to London. Surely they know I can't abide flying?'

'Surely,' Lilli repeated. She was glad Wallis couldn't see her eyebrow arch as she spoke.

'So, David suggested they send a destroyer for us.'

Lilli bit her tongue. Women and children were dying as Hitler invaded Poland and all Wallis and her husband could think about was their pride.

'We're leaving for England tomorrow,' she continued. 'I hope to see you in the next few days. I'm dying to meet your son.'

'Daughter,' Lilli corrected her. Wallis had even sent Leeona a silver bracelet from France for her christening.

'Of course,' replied Wallis, without a hint of embarrassment. 'I'll be in touch. *A toute à l'heure* as they say over here.' And with that the telephone clicked and went silent.

So, the Duke and Duchess of Windsor were returning to Britain in its hour of need. Whether or not the British people would welcome them back was another question. The secret service would, of course, be aware of the plans, the Reich, however, would not.

Lilli walked to the window and looked out onto the road below. The man with the bowler hat who'd constantly shadowed her since

James's murder, was still there. He served as a perpetual reminder of the evil she faced. She would, of course, have to tell her Nazi minders of the Windsors' return. No doubt Hitler would be most interested to follow their exploits on this side of the Channel.

A week later Wallis stormed into Lilli's apartment like a force eight gale. She practically flung her fox fur at the maid and proceeded to power into the drawing room before Lilli had actually invited her to enter.

'My dear, you would not believe the journey I've had,' she complained, offering her cheek for Lilli to kiss. Of James's untimely death there was no mention.

'Wallis, how frightful,' Lilli said in her best English accent. 'Sit down and I shall ring for tea. Or something stronger?'

'A sherry. I need a sherry!' she said, pulling at the fingers of her glove one by one, as if she were tugging at her enemy's toenails.

Lilli turned to the terrified maid. 'You heard, Clarrie. Sherry for the duchess and tea for me, please.'

'So what happened on your journey?' Lilli began, as her guest made herself comfortable.

'The whole trip was dire,' Wallis replied. 'We arrived at Portsmouth in the blackout and although dear Mr Churchill had organised a band to greet us, they only played six bars of the national anthem. Can you believe it?'

Lilli had no idea why that should matter. 'Six?' she repeated.

'Apparently only the sovereign gets the full version,' she replied ruefully.

'Oh,' said Lilli, hiding a smile.

'Yes. Insufferable, isn't it?' she carried on. 'And to add insult to injury, his brother wouldn't put us up.'

'The king?' asked Lilli.

'Of course it's actually all his dreadful wife's doing.' Lilli knew that Queen Elizabeth was not liked by Wallis's allies. 'She hates David almost as much as she hates me. So we're at friends' for the moment, although I hope we don't have to stay in this dingy little country a moment longer than we have to.'

Lilli needed to probe. 'Really. Why ever not?' she asked innocently.

Wallis lengthened her neck, adopting a regal pose. 'David is in talks. Chamberlain needs him, you see. He will be given an official role.'

Alarm bells rang. 'What might that be?' asked Lilli.

Wallis's lips curled. 'Oh, something ghastly in Wales or a little less ghastly in France.' It was clear she regarded both options as beneath her husband and quickly changed the subject. 'But where is this beautiful daughter you've told me all about? I'm just dying to meet her.'

Just then the maid arrived with the sherry, and Lilli instructed her to ask the nanny to fetch Leeona – officially known as Jemima. It was only then that the duchess remembered that the child had just lost her *de facto* father.

'My dear, but I am so sorry for your loss.' Wallis shaped her face into a grimace that made her look even more unappealing. 'James was such a . . .' She floundered for a word. The dinner party spat about Hitler's motives at the Villa Mauresque had clearly always left a slightly sour taste in her mouth. 'Such a good man.'

'Yes, he was,' Lilli agreed. She'd never doubted that his motives were essentially good, even if she had been the one to fall victim to his deception.

More than a year had passed since his death and yet Lilli still found herself missing James and the support he'd offered. The house remained full of the things left unsaid between them. She was glad that she'd called a truce and that the few months they'd spent to together in Kensington had not been full of bitterness and recrimination.

Leeona, now toddling, was escorted into the drawing room by Greta, the nanny, a Bavarian girl who came highly recommended from the agency.

'How do you do, Jemima?' Wallis greeted the child effusively, holding out her hand. Leeona, however, did not seem impressed and ran to bury her head in her mother's lap. 'Oh, well I don't have a knack with children,' commented the duchess flippantly as Lilli stroked her daughter's mass of untamed dark curls. 'Here. I've brought a little something for her,' she said, handing over a small parcel, delicately wrapped in pink tissue paper and ribbon.

'You really shouldn't have,' Lilli told her, opening the gift to reveal a silver hairbrush and matching comb. 'Oh, they're beautiful. Thank you.'

Wallis smiled. 'She'll need them with all that fabulous hair,' she said, watching the child suck her own fingers. 'And that colouring,' she mused. 'I suppose that's from your side of the family. Those brown eyes, too. Quite beguiling.'

Lilli looked at Wallis. 'Yes, they are,' she replied. The duchess was sharpening her knife. For some time, Lilli had wondered if Wallis knew all along that James was homosexual. Did she suspect that he wasn't the child's father?

She didn't have to wait long for an answer. Wallis was watching Leeona, now inspecting her new brush, with a snide curl on her glossy red lips. 'Funny,' she said, crinkling her nose. 'One would never guess in a million years that she was James's daughter.'

Chapter 57

1940

'Mama, can we go see aminals?'

Every time Leeona spoke, something new, unexpected and delightful would emerge from her Cupid's bow mouth. She sat on Lilli's knee, a cloth book in her plump little hands. Pictures of yellow lions, orange tigers and an elephant in an odd shade of blue decorated the material pages.

Lilli had just read to her daughter a story about an outing to the zoo. With hindsight, she should have anticipated her reaction. All zoos had, of course, been shut since last autumn. She kissed the little girl's head, her curly hair now partly restrained by a pink Alice band.

'Not today, *Liebling*, but soon,' she replied. How soon, she had no idea.

Although Britain and France had declared war on Germany the previous September, not a lot seemed to be happening, in Britain at least. Lilli had received no word from Goebbels about the filming of *Titanic*. She assumed it had been axed. The Reich Minister would have more important things on his evil mind. Everyone was calling it a 'phoney' war because after Hitler's

303

blitzkrieg on Poland, there seemed to be a lull in the action. A week after her first visit to the Kensington house, an irascible Wallis had telephoned to tell Lilli that she and the duke were leaving for France and shaking English soil from their shoes in the process. There was also an open invitation to her and Leeona to stay at their new Paris residence.

When Lilli had informed Colonel Plimpton of the Windsors' move, he saw it as an opportunity. 'You must go with them, Mrs Marchington,' he told her in no uncertain terms. 'By Jove, it's heaven-sent.'

The more Lilli considered Plimpton's words, the more she thought he might be right. Not just on an operational level, but on a personal one, too. With James dead, England no longer held her in its sway. She needed to return to Munich, to comfort Golda and even, perhaps, to persuade her to leave Germany while there was a slight chance she still could. France with the Windsors – and Paris in particular where they were based – would be a good stepping stone for a visit home.

Her plans were just taking shape when she received an unexpected message from her Nazi masters in Munich, deposited in a left luggage locker at Euston Station. It informed her that until filming of *Titanic* started, Lilli would still be expected to report regularly on the Windsors. The communication ended with the chilling line: *Failure to do so could have dire consequences for your brother and your widowed mother.*

So, they knew Jacob was dead, but Leon might yet be alive. James had been killed to keep her co-operative, but filming *Titanic* might still offer her brother a lifeline. It also meant her trip to Munich would have Goebbels's official sanction. If all went according to plan, Leon would be released, and she would see Golda again. More than that, her mother could meet Leeona. Now Lilli knew the Windsors' plans she might be able to use the knowledge to her advantage. But she was also going to need good fortune on her side. Good fortune and Colonel Plimpton.

'Marchington was a capital chap.' Colonel Plimpton was stroking his moustache, gazing into the far-off place where Lilli noted he so often visited when she was in his presence. 'Good agent. Good man.' He turned and slapped the desk. 'You coping all right?' He always asked Lilli the same question every time they met. It had been almost two years since James's murder and, yes, she was coping all right because she had to. She knew the colonel meant well.

'So, all set for France?' Plimpton enquired. 'Springtime in Paris and all that!'

'Yes, Colonel,' Lilli replied.

It had taken longer than anticipated to sort out her affairs, but she was finally moving to France as Wallis's personal assistant for the next few weeks. Filming was due to start in the Baltic port of Hamburg that summer. It was the perfect excuse for her to take Leeona to Munich to meet Golda but she would need more time. To execute her plan she would have to call on Colonel Plimpton's official clout – and forgers. He knew about Leon's imprisonment of course, and the fact that she was being blackmailed by the Nazis into starring in *Titanic*. But what he called 'the powers that be' were putting pressure on him to find out more information about what plans the Windsors were engineering. Lilli's trip to Paris provided the perfect cover.

'So you need the dates altering on your travel documents?' he'd asked, stroking his moustache again.

'I do. I need ten days in Munich, Colonel, before I go to Hamburg to start filming,' she told him, pushing the official travel documents, stamped with the Reich's swastika eagle. She'd collected from the left luggage office at Waterloo. 'These are what they sent me.'

The colonel leafed through them. 'So, these dates.' Her outward bound tickets to Munich were marked June 15th. They would need to be changed to June 7th to enable her to achieve her goal. 'You want them amended?'

She nodded. 'That is all.' Ten days was all time she could give herself before arousing suspicion. The original ticket allowed her just one day to leave Leeona with Golda then travel on to Hamburg. But it would take her and Marco longer to execute her plan. She needed to arrange for her mother's safe passage to neutral Switzerland and to discover Leon's whereabouts.

'Very well,' said Plimpton after a moment. 'Piece of cake,' he told her. 'Better give you a couple of names in Munich, too. American Consulate, that sort of malarkey.'

That word *malarkey* again. This time Lilli knew what it meant. James, she believed, had made good contacts with the US consular in the city.

Plimpton opened a file on his desk and peered at it. 'Calvin J Hooper is the chap's name,' he announced gleefully. He looked up at Lilli. 'Lucky you're an American citizen.' He chuckled to himself. 'Neutral and all that.'

'Yes,' replied Lilli. Applying for US citizenship when she was working in Hollywood was about the only smart piece of advice Victor Selig had ever given her.

'Oh and there's this fellow, too. He's been really rather good.' He wrote down something on a piece of paper and slid it across the desk.

It read: *Major Marco Zeiller*. Below was an address.

Lilli looked up wide-eyed, the colour draining from her face.

'I say, you all right? You look a bit peaky, if you don't mind me saying so,' ventured Plimpton.

It took her a moment to answer, as she composed her thoughts. 'This Major Zeiller,' she began.

'Yes.'

'He is an informant for the British?' Her mouth went dry. She'd kept quiet about Marco, wanting to protect him.

'Yes, and a damn good fist of it he's making too. One of our best. If anyone can help you, Mrs Marchington, it's him.'

Shock waves were still rippling through Lilli's body when she rose to leave the office. She recalled that look Marco had given her in the back of the limousine just before they last parted. It was deep and hard and it was meant to forge their mutual understanding. It was his way of telling her that he, too was an agent, just as she had been telling him. Only now did she realise what it meant and the knowledge of it made her feel safer and so much stronger.

Chapter 58

Paris, France

The spring sunshine streamed in through the long casements of the Windsors' Paris apartment. In the city itself the plane trees lining the wide boulevards released their fluffy white seeds and the sparrows seemed remarkably garrulous. Nature was playing by the rules. Adolf Hitler was not.

The Windsors' departure to France last year had given Lilli the perfect excuse to leave London, taking Leeona with her. The truth was that to Lilli, at least, the war appeared an inconvenience, something that was poised over Europe, at a distance, some drama that was playing out in Poland and Czechoslovakia, whereas her own nightmare was so very real.

For the first few days she had felt safe in the city. Little seemed to have changed. Wallis and the duke regularly moaned about their deplorable treatment at the hands of just about everyone in England, apart from the doorman at the Ritz. Leeona's presence helped lighten their mood on the few occasions the child was allowed to be in the same room with them, but Lilli's stay with the Windsors produced no intelligence of any real note for either the British or the Germans. The only thing of which Lilli could be certain was that there seemed to be no love lost between the duke and the royal family.

Now, however, a long shadow had been cast and soon it threatened to loom over France. Denmark and Norway had fallen in April. People were leaving the city, while many more were arriving. They were mainly Jewish, fleeing Germany, although refugees from northern France, Holland and Belgium were also beginning to flood in after the advance of the Nazi jackboot. For a few souls the spring air was full of promise, but for most, perdition.

With the shooting of *Titanic* in the port of Hamburg scheduled to begin soon, Lilli had given herself ten days to execute her plan. She would go to Munich before filming began to make arrangements for smuggling Golda – and Leon, if possible – out of the country to safety in Switzerland. She would then make her own escape before anyone realised that Lillian Stern was missing.

Marco, in his capacity as one of Goebbels's assistants, had pulled strings. Officially, while Lilli was on set filming in Hamburg, Golda was to care for the child in Munich. Even better, Marco had managed to discover Leon's whereabouts. He was being held in Dachau, the concentration camp only a few miles from the city. He was still alive, but in poor health. She dared to hope she might be given the opportunity to visit him, and perhaps bribe the guards to release him, although she knew that was a very long shot. There was also a chance that Marco might be able to take leave and meet his daughter for the first time.

Lilli presented herself on the threshold of the Windsors' morning room, wearing a hat and light coat. Both the duke and duchess had just finished breakfast. Wallis saw Lilli first as she dabbed her mouth with her napkin.

'Ah, Lillian,' she greeted. 'You must be so excited about the film. I can't tell you how jealous I am of you playing opposite that divine creature. What's his name?'

'Hans Nielsen,' said Lilli, helpfully. She had been informed of two or three of the cast members.

'Max can drop you at the station, if you like,' she volunteered, adding: 'I may come along for the ride, too.'

And there it is again, thought Lilli. *Just when you think Wallis is doing something kind, you realise there's got to be something in it for her.*

The duke looked up from his newspaper. 'Are you sure about that, darling? The station will be full of soldiers. It won't do your new shoes any good if one of the brutes treads on your feet.' He sucked on his pipe.

Wallis, seated opposite him at the breakfast table, seemed riled as if picturing her beautiful new court shoes scuffed. 'You're right,' she agreed. She turned to Lilli, who stood with Leeona, on her hip. 'Perhaps I'd be better off staying here and choosing some new curtain fabric.'

Curtain fabric or French fancies, there was always some distraction to delight Wallis's selfish mind, thought Lilli.

'Perhaps, my dear,' replied the duke, wryly, 'you ought to start packing away your jewellery. Herr Hitler may be charm personified, but I doubt his troops will have many manners.'

Lilli bridled at the duke's complacency. Hitler was threatening to march over all of Europe, but he still believed himself and Wallis immune from the privations of war. She had grown weary of the state of constant denial in which the Windsors languished these days. Just like poor Eva Braun at the Berghof, they were living in their own gilded cage, not seeming to care that millions were displaced and already suffering at Hitler's hands.

The Windsors' driver duly drove Lilli and Leeona to the Gare de l'Est to catch the train. All United States citizens had been advised to leave Paris, but they were heading south or west. Lilli was almost alone in going to Germany. Lillian Stern and her daughter Jemima Marchington were to travel to Munich where the child would stay with her grandmother before Lilli headed north to Hamburg.

The driver took Lilli's two suitcases onto the platform while she carried Leeona through the throng. The station was packed with both civilians and soldiers. The sound of their voices and those of clanking steam trains filled the huge vaulted space above with a cacophony of clatter and reverberation. The child clamped her little palms to her ears.

Ploughing his way through weeping women and desperate men, the driver led them to the correct platform for the next train east. They joined the queue, but Lilli could see the family in front of them was being barred from a train. The father was swearing, the mother wailing and the children – there must have been at least four – were joining in, crying. Suddenly they were surrounded by guards and Lilli began to panic. She held Leeona tight to her chest. Just then an older guard with a walrus moustache approached her. Seeming to ignore the furore that had broken out around him, he took her ticket at the barrier and inspected it. Seeing her destination, his eyes narrowed suspiciously, as if to question her. Why would a mother and her young child be travelling east, when any sane person was travelling west? She held her breath as he returned her ticket.

'*Passez, Madame, s'il vous plaît.*'

Relieved, she smiled.

'*Oh, et Madame.*' He called her back just as she set foot on the platform. If anyone on this side of the border were to find her with Goebbels's letter, let alone the photograph of her with Hitler, she would be immediately detained. She turned.

'*Bon voyage!*'

Lilli was forced to share her stuffy train carriage with four French officers, although she found them quite charming. They even stubbed out their cigarettes when Leeona started to cough. One of them told her in rusty English that he was a father himself and between them they'd managed to keep the child occupied, pulling funny faces and making animal noises.

Strasbourg was the final stop in France before crossing into

Germany. They reached the city around midday. Looking out of the carriage window Lilli saw the station platform was crammed with people, weighed down by their belongings. Some even carried chickens and canaries in cages. She could hear boxes and bags thump and scrape against the carriage as the crowd jostled to board the trains heading south. They were right in the line of the Third Reich's fire and were all trying to leave for the Dordogne or Limoges, or anywhere else where they thought they might be safer, if not entirely safe. Suddenly a woman's anguished face pressed against the window.

'*Aidez-moi!*' Lilli saw her mouth the words in desperation. The sight sent a horrified shiver through her. She shielded Leeona's eyes.

The officers rose to disembark and join the rest of the hundreds of soldiers who were streaming out of the carriages and assembling on the platform. They bid her farewell as they filed through the door.

'*Bon chance,*' said the father who'd been particularly good with Leeona.

The train could not leave the station soon enough for Lilli. At any moment she could be stopped and questioned. The fear that had surfaced at the Gare de l'Est re-emerged. She had to be on constant alert. Each stop on the journey presented a new threat.

'I'm hungry, Mummy,' said Leeona as Lilli stroked her daughter's head, her curly hair turning tousled.

'Here,' she said, pulling out the last hunk of a baguette that the Windsors' chef had given her for the journey. The child took the bread and ate it quickly. Lilli held her close.

The train juddered to a halt at the German border and two soldiers climbed aboard. They stopped outside Lilli's carriage and slid open the door.

'*Guten Nachmittag, frau,*' said the tall, lean one.

'Good evening,' she replied in English.

'*Reichpass, bitte,*' asked the other, his cheeks ruddy and rough.

She tried to keep her hand steady as she held out both their passports. A churning disquiet had re-emerged from somewhere inside.

The soldier with the ruddy cheeks looked up. 'American?'

'German,' she replied, drawing Leeona closer. 'But I used to live in the United States, so I have dual citizenship.'

The tall guard smiled and ruffled the little girl's hair. 'Nice kid!' he said in an exaggerated American accent, but Cheeks was looking at Lilli intently.

'You're not . . .?' he said, suddenly narrowing his eyes.

'Lillian Stern, the film star!' The tall one snatched Lilli's passport and glanced down at it. '*Ja! Ja!* My wife loved your film!' he cried. 'The one with you as the princess!'

His colleague seemed equally impressed. 'Could you sign this for me, Miss Stern?' asked Cheeks, taking out a notebook from his pocket and handing her a pen.

Lilli was happy to oblige – anything that would smooth her journey was welcome. Besides it diverted their attention away from her altered travel dates.

'You go Munich?' asked the tall guard when she had also signed her autograph on a pad for him.

'Yes,' she replied.

'Even film stars need special permission for that,' he said, winking at Leeona as Lilli delved into her handbag. 'But I'm sure if—'

'No one comes here without special papers,' Cheeks made clear. 'Film stars, no exception.'

Lilli felt the breath catch in her chest as she reached for the secret compartment in her handbag where she had hidden the Reich Minister's letter of authorisation. She handed it to Cheeks with a smile. A moment later the two guards leapt to attention, their arms jerked out into salutes.

'Fraulein Stern,' barked Cheeks. Herr Doktor Goebbels had come to her aid. 'We hope you enjoy your time in Munich.'

For the rest of the journey Leeona settled down to nap on her lap. Lilli was grateful, but sleep eluded her. Danger was ever-present. If word reached Goebbels that she was in the country ten days earlier than she should be, it could jeopardise everything. The fact that she was putting her innocent daughter in harm's way as well, made her doubly watchful.

In the early evening, after almost ten hours on the train, they finally reached Munich. The air was much cooler than in Paris and Lilli eased on Leeona's pink coat as the little girl slowly resurfaced from her deep sleep. Shrugging on her own coat, she reached up to the luggage rack for their suitcases.

Suddenly the tall guard who'd been so keen to practise his English entered the carriage. 'Let me help you,' he called. Lilli froze. 'Allow me.' He lugged down the bags and set them on the platform for her.

'Thank you,' she replied in English, as she handed Leeona down to him before she herself alighted. The guard clicked his heels and his arm flew out in a salute once more.

'*Heil Hitler*,' he proclaimed.

Lilli smiled awkwardly in reply.

Munich: the city of her family, the city where she'd grown up. She should have felt that she was coming home, only the place now seemed alien to her. Looking across the station concourse, she could see red-white-and-black swastikas draped from the rafters, on ticket inspectors' armbands and in booths selling cigarettes. Soldiers patrolled the platforms. The signs of war were everywhere. From now on she had to make sure she avoided any trouble. One foot wrong could spell disaster for her plans. The Nazi leviathan was omniscient. She clutched her handbag to her breast. Her letter of immunity meant she and Leeona were safe, as long as she was seen to play by the rules.

Chapter 59

Munich, Germany

Lilli took a taxi to out to Giesing. Leeona sat on her lap. The driver started talking to her about the war, glancing at her at regular intervals through his rear-view mirror, how the Reich army had invaded Norway, Denmark and the Low Countries and had France in its sights. She pretended to ignore him, fussing over Leeona instead. Inside, she was quaking. The Netherlands and Belgium, she'd known, were vulnerable, but now the Nazis had marched into northern France, Paris was threatened. She swallowed down her fear and smiled at the driver's face in the mirror.

Lilli's luggage was deposited inside the hallway and the driver stood, arms crossed, waiting for his fare while she found the money in her purse. It was just as she was handing him a note that she heard a familiar voice behind her.

'Lilli? Lilli Sternberg? Is that you?'

For a second, she froze and her eyes met the driver's. He was not supposed to carry Jewish passengers.

'Lilli? *Ja?*' Herr Grunfeld, had scrambled up from his desk to see who was visiting.

Ignoring the janitor, Lilli shot a forced smile at the driver, who was frowning as he watched Grunfeld approach. 'Thank you. That'll be all,' she said.

Herr Grunfeld, suspecting something was wrong, kept his counsel until the driver was safely back in his cab.

'What a wonderful surprise, Fraulein Lilli!' He could barely contain his happiness at seeing Lilli again. Even Felix, the cat, appeared from nowhere to greet her.

Lilli knew she had to be careful. She wanted no fuss. She glanced up at the staircase that wound round and round like a giant snail shell all the way up to the fifth floor and pictured Anna Kepler crouching between the spindles, lying in wait for her.

'Can we talk in your apartment?' she whispered, lifting up Leeona.

The janitor led her to his front door, just by the pigeonholes, and let her inside. Elspethe Grunfeld was sitting on a rug on the floor, building a tower of red, blue and yellow bricks with a little girl. Lilli remembered that when she had last seen her, she was pregnant.

'Fraulein Sternberg!' she exclaimed. 'What a surprise!' She rose to her feet so suddenly that she knocked over the tower of bricks. The child began to cry.

Her husband put a finger to his lips and shut the door.

'Axel?' said his wife with a frown. 'What's wrong?'

'Please, I can explain,' Lilli began.

Seeing the bricks, Leeona reached out her arm. Lilli set her down and she rushed forward and started to play. At the sight, the other, dark-haired, little girl stopped crying and joined in, building another tower.

Elspethe's face lit up. 'Look at them. Aren't they alike?' she remarked, watching the girls together. 'They could be sisters.'

Lilli agreed, they did look alike, with similar hair colouring and build, but there was no time for small-talk. Her life, and, indeed Leeona's, depended on the Grunfeld's co-operation. She had to place her trust in them.

'I am here to try and persuade my mother to come back to England with me,' she told them. 'I know she is in danger if she stays here.'

The Grunfelds swapped anxious looks. 'You are right,' said Axel with a frown, thoughtfully stroking his moustache. 'It is very hard for Jews here and it is getting worse.'

'Have you word of your brother?' asked Elspethe anxiously.

'I believe he is still alive,' replied Lilli, trying to summon a smile.

Axel shook his head. 'It is a bad business and growing worse, even from when you were last here, Fraulein. But if we say anything . . .' He started to falter.

'I understand,' replied Lilli. She had no wish to watch him, squirm, grappling with his own conscience in front of her. In reality, she found it hard to comprehend how a whole nation could come together on the orders of one man and round on people they'd only recently regarded as friends and colleagues.

Elspethe jumped in to save further embarrassment. 'And you have come just in time,' she said.

'What do you mean?' asked Lilli.

'Your mother took ill last week,' she explained

'Ill?'

Axel nodded. 'She is weak. Some sickness.'

Lilli gasped. 'But Dr Mahler has seen her?'

Axel looked grave. His eyes slid away from hers. 'Dr Mahler is no longer allowed to . . .' He broke off.

'What?'

Elspethe laid her hand gently on Lilli's arm. 'Doctors aren't allowed to treat non-Aryan patients. It's the law.'

Lilli's face registered her horror. 'But she has seen a doctor?' she persisted, her voice rising with anger.

Axel darted a guilty look at his wife. 'Yes, she has. Most Jewish doctors have already left the city, but we found one.'

Lilli sighed with relief. 'Thank you,' she muttered. 'But if she can't manage on her own, who is looking after her?' she asked. As she spoke, she suddenly remembered the lodger. 'What happened to Herr Backe?'

Axel shook his head. 'He joined up to fight, but had his foot blown off. He's on leave, staying with his mother but he comes to collect his post now and again.'

Lilli nodded as the realisation dawned on her. So now Golda had no income at all and no other means of support, other than her own occasional foreign money transfers to her, yet she had been too proud to ask her daughter for help. Guilt, the emotion that so often plague her in the past, suddenly took hold of her again, but this time it weighed her down. She had missed opportunities to rescue her mother from this hell. Now, perhaps, it was too late.

Elspethe tilted her head and tried to explain, but her words came out more as an excuse than an apology. 'We help as much as we can, but if we are caught, it could be difficult for us, you see.'

Her explanation only confused Lilli. 'I'm sorry, I don't see. If you are *caught*. What do you mean?'

Axel Grunfeld's expression became pinched. 'We cannot be seen to help your mother. It is *verboten*, Lilli, because she is a Jew.'

Lilli closed her eyes and pictured all the family's neighbours; the Keplers, the Webers, the Grundigs. They had all joined in the party for her homecoming; all eaten her mother's food. Had none of them come to Golda's aid in her time of need? Had only the Grunfelds seen to it that she was warm and fed and not in too much pain? Had Germany come to this, that they would leave a frail, old widow to suffer rather than risk the wrath of the Reich.

'I must go to her!' cried Lilli, breathlessly flinging open the door. Leaving Leeona still at play, she ran up the stairs to the fourth floor and burst into her apartment.

'Mutti! Mutti!' she called, going first into the sitting room, then to her parents' bedroom. The room smelt of sour urine and a half-eaten plate of stew was attracting flies.

'Mutti!' she cried when she saw Golda lying in bed. She rushed over to her, scooping up the covers that had slipped onto the floor. '*Gott im Himmel!* What has happened?' she said as she began to gather the blankets and lay them on the bed once more.

At first Golda did not recognise her daughter. 'Who . . .? Who is it?' she wheezed. Her white hair was plastered to her head with sweat, yet she was shivering. She'd curled herself into a ball, as if trying to keep warm. Lilli laid her palm on her mother's forehead. She was burning up from fever.

'It's me, Mutti. It's Lilli. I've come to . . .' She was going to say 'Get you out of here,' only now that seemed an impossibility. 'I've come to look after you,' she told her instead.

In the kitchen she filled a glass of water and made Golda take a few sips. Rummaging in her handbag Lilli found some aspirin kept for emergencies and managed to get her mother to swallow two. She found more blankets from a chest at the foot of the bed and laid them on top of the others. She dampened a face flannel and pressed it on her mother's forehead, before clearing away the dirty crockery.

'I'm here now. It's Lilli, Mutti. It's going to be all right,' she told Golda, resting her hand on her shoulder.

It was while she was in the kitchen, fetching more water, that she heard a faint knock at the door. Elspethe Grunfeld stood at the threshold with Leeona in her arms.

'Mama!' cried the little girl, reaching out towards Lilli.

Seeing Leeona held by a gentile woman whose action would be deemed illegal if she were caught, Lilli suddenly felt deeply grateful as she reached for her.

'Thank you,' she said, from the bottom of her heart.

Even though it had been mild outside, the apartment remained cool and fusty. The green glazed tiles of the *kachelofen* were cold to the touch. There was mildew on the walls and the carpets were worn and tattered. A film of dust covered every surface and there were cobwebs in each corner.

'Where are we?' asked Leeona, as Lilli held her tight.

'This is where I grew up, my darling,' she replied. 'I was a little girl just like you, once.'

Taking Leeona by the hand, Lilli entered Golda's bedroom. At the sound of the door creaking open, her mother opened her filmy eyes.

'Mutti, I have someone here to meet you,' she said softly, lifting the little girl onto her mother's bed.

Golda blinked, as if she couldn't quite understand what was going on.

'This is Leeona, your granddaughter.'

A sound escaped from Golda's lips; a sound of joy and surprise melded into one. 'Leeona,' she mumbled, her frail hand moving over the bedcover towards the child. 'Praise be!'

'This is your *Oma*,' Lilli told Leeona.

The little girl looked at her mother, then at the old woman lying in bed and with her pink lips puckered, she delivered a kiss to her cheek.

Another sound escaped Golda's mouth, as if her heart had been touched by an angel – as if, were she to die the next moment, she would be completely fulfilled. At the sight Lilli suddenly felt her hazardous journey, and all the risks she'd run, were all worth it.

Next Lilli carried the child through to the kitchen and sat her on the rug on the floor. She opened a drawer and gave her some spoons and a tin cup to play with. In the cupboard she found a carrot and a potato which she chopped to make broth.

There was very little else to eat in the kitchen: a few tins of peaches and peas, some dried lentils and a jar of honey. Lilli had no idea how she would be able to buy food. Food was rationed for everyone, but even more strictly for Jews. Even if she used her mother's vouchers there'd be barely enough supplies for one, let alone for ten days. What she'd found on her return had unnerved her. There was no question of relying on help from any other neighbours, apart from the Grunfelds. Nor could she contact

Marco through the proper channels because she wasn't supposed to be in Munich. If she, Golda and Leeona weren't going to starve, there was only one place where she could turn for help: the United States Consulate.

Chapter 60

A full day had passed and Golda seemed no better. Lilli spent the night by her bedside, as she tossed feverishly and called out for Leon. Hearing her sick mother invoke her brother's name made Lilli feel all the more wretched. Guilt, again. It reminded her that she hadn't heeded Leon's warnings seriously enough. She'd been too caught up in her own shallow world to take much notice of his dire predictions. Now, in this place she'd always regarded as her childhood prison, her own self-obsession was coming back to haunt her.

'Come, my sweet,' she told Leeona, buttoning up her pink coat. 'We must go shopping.' She did not want to leave Golda on her own but needed to buy food. Clamping her hat down firmly on her head, so that it would be hard to see her face, Lilli left the apartment with an empty shopping bag.

As mother and daughter reached the bottom of the staircase Axel Grunfeld was cleaning the hall floor.

'How is Frau Sternberg?' he asked, leaning on his mop.

Lilli stopped in her tracks then turned to look at him. 'There is no change,' she told him, adding: 'But thank you for asking,' as an afterthought. She'd just started to walk towards the front door when Axel called after her once more.

'Fraulein Lilli!'

She turned.

'Would you let Elspethe care for the little girl while you go out?' His eyes dipped towards Leeona.

'That would be very helpful,' she said, smiling at her daughter. Bending low, she explained it would be fun to play with Angela. 'Mutti will be back very soon with something good to eat.' Then to Herr Grunfeld she said: 'I shan't be long.'

Pulling up the collar of her raincoat, even though it wasn't raining, Lilli hurried to the main street. She had memorised the address of the American consulate. It was the only place she could turn for food.

The United States consular offices were housed in an imposing building near the *Englischer Garten*, where Lilli had spent many happy times with Marco. But seeing the queue snaking outside it came as a shock. The consulate's services were clearly in high demand.

Inside, it was even worse. Dozens of men, women and children were lining the corridors and sitting on their luggage. People spilled out of various rooms as they waited in line to talk to harassed officials behind desks. Now and again there was jostling in the ranks. A baby would start to bawl, setting off others. The constant drone of voices was punctuated by regular outbursts of swearing or pleading when yet another helpless family was robbed of any hope of escape.

Where, among all these desperate souls, might Lilli find Calvin J. Hooper, the official Colonel Plimpton had told her to contact? She looked for someone, anyone who appeared in charge and found a fraught young woman, whose sole job, it seemed, was to turn people away.

'No visas. *Kein Visum!*' she kept repeating over and over in a scratchy voice, as grown men wept before her. 'No visas,' she cried, once more as Lilli approached her.

Lilli shook her head vigorously. 'I don't want a visa,' she insisted in English. 'I need to speak with Mr Hooper.'

'Excuse me?'

'Mr Calvin J. Hooper,' repeated Lilli at the top of her voice. 'My name is Lillian Stern.'

The young woman looked relieved: 'So you're not another Jew,' she said, raising her eyes heavenward in thanksgiving, before adding: 'You wouldn't want to be a Jew in Germany right now.'

The mere mention of her name seemed to open a door to Lilli and after one or two false starts a secretary finally showed her into an upstairs office where a bronzed young man, sporting an enamelled American flag on his suit lapel, sat behind a desk. He rose to greet Lilli.

'Pleased to meet you, Miss Stern.'

'And you, Mr Hooper.' She felt her face lift in a smile for the first time in a while. James had known the official personally. Hooper was, he'd once told her, quite an authority on the work of Gustav Klimt.

'I'm so very sorry about your husband,' Hooper told her as she sat down. 'A tragic accident, I was told.'

'Yes, tragic,' replied Lilli, knowing there was an understanding between them.

'I'm afraid we've got no tea, but I can offer you coffee,' Hooper said as he, too, sat down. 'Or should I say what they call coffee nowadays. It's really chicory and roasted acorns, but hey.'

She smiled. 'I am German as well as American, Mr Hooper. I love coffee, however it comes.'

He nodded. 'Of course, they told me,' he said, touching his temple. 'That you were German, not that you loved coffee.' He motioned to the waiting secretary. 'You heard that, Nora? And one for me, too,' he ordered. 'Anyway, how can I help?'

Lilli explained her situation and was told that the consulate would be able to supply her with a limited amount of provisions for the next few days. The news was a huge relief.

'Now that's sorted, is there anything else I can do for you, Miss Stern?' he asked with a smile. He glanced at the documentation she had just shown him.

Lilli held off with her reply until Nora the secretary had poured out the coffee. 'I take it you know,' she said cryptically.

Hooper nodded. 'I do.' She was relieved that Colonel Plimpton had informed his American contact of what he called Lilli's 'divided loyalties'.

'Then I needn't tell you how important it is that I remain informed of the Duke and Duchess of Windsor's movements to keep the other side happy.'

Another nod from Hooper. 'I'll get our people on the case. I believe they've just left Paris, heading south.'

She stared into her coffee cup, but after the first sip had decided she couldn't stomach it. 'There's someone else I need to contact.'

'Oh?' he asked, clasping his hands in front of him on the desk and watching her delve into her clutch bag.

She slid an envelope across the desk.

'What's this?'

'A message.'

'Intriguing,' he remarked, looking at the name.

Lilli nodded. 'I believe you have secure ways of delivering the communication.'

It was addressed to Major Marco Zeiller. Lilli knew he was based at the Ministry of Public Enlightenment and Propaganda in Berlin but that it would be suicide to send an unencrypted message to him there. She'd done as much as she could alone, now she was putting the fate of her loved-ones in Marco's hands.

Chapter 61

The days passed slowly, as days of sickness do. But Lilli knew the clock was ticking. Golda's coughing was worst at night and the sound of rattling and wheezing kept her awake. One day turned into three, then to five until finally, on the seventh morning Golda said she felt she might sit up in bed. She was suddenly brighter and more lucid. The pain in her chest had dulled to a tightness, she said. For the first time since Lilli had arrived, a little hope returned to the household.

The news from the west, however, had been bad and was getting worse each day. As Golda's health seemed to strengthen, so the reports of German advances in northern France worsened until on June 15th Lilli read the unthinkable. Her mother had been forced to hand over her wireless last year, but Axel Grunfeld slipped a newspaper under the door when he could. At first Lilli could not believe her eyes. It was the news she'd most dreaded. The headline of the *Munchner Mercur* declared: *Paris falls to the Reich.*

Her fear must've been palpable because Leeona, playing nearby, noticed her reaction. 'Mummy, what's wrong?' she asked. 'Why are you sad?'

Like a flimsy house of cards, the rest of France would surely follow within the next few days, Lilli told herself. Her lifeline had been destroyed. There was no way out for Golda and for the thousands of other Jews like her. Germany was now their prison, unless, of course she could get her to the safety of somewhere neutral.

Lilli, the newspaper still in her trembling hands, looked up and hurried over to her daughter. Scooping her up in her arms, she kissed her on the head. 'Nothing's wrong, my sweet,' she told her. 'Everything's going to be just fine,' she said, even though she feared it was a lie.

So far, there had been two trips to the American Consulate to collect food: a little meat, some pâté, some bread, fruit jellies, a cabbage and ginger *lebkuchen* that Leeona loved. They could get by but that wasn't good enough. They needed to escape.

There was another reason for her visits to the consulate, too. Calvin J Hooper kept her updated. From him she'd learned that the Windsors were heading south to Biarritz. She hoped that would be sufficient to satisfy both the Nazis and the British for the time being. There were plenty of other associates happy to keep British intelligence informed in the meantime, especially as Wallis was apparently, according to Hooper, feeding von Ribbentrop details of their whereabouts.

Little Leeona spent much of her time playing with Angela downstairs. The Grunfelds were decent people, Lilli knew that, but they were not living in decent times. It was hard for them, too. The other neighbours avoided her and Leeona all together: the Reuters, the Keplers and the Grundigs. The Ram, once again, proudly sported a Nazi lapel badge. If they saw Lilli on the stairs, they would look the other way; if they passed her in the reception lobby, they pretended not to know her. There seemed to be a tacit understanding between them that she did not exist; like a ghost or a spirit that passed through walls, her presence might be felt in a change of temperature or a brush on the skin, but could be dismissed as a figment of the imagination. Lilli did not mind. It suited her that way, knowing that if she were to be reported for helping her mother, she could be arrested at any moment and deported or worse. But she also knew time was running out. Goebbels was expecting her in Hamburg to start filming in three days' time. When she did not turn up there would be hell to pay. She would be a wanted woman.

Lilli kept telling her mother that all would be well, but of course it wouldn't be, unless they were able to escape. And still there was no word from Marco and she had to leave for Hamburg in two days. Madame Eva's mantra popped into her head once more. '*Dance through the pain*,' she told herself. But it was growing harder by the day.

That evening, while Golda and Leeona slept, Lilli was tidying away a few playthings – an old tin car and a fluffy rabbit that she'd loved as a child. The blackout meant she had to work by candlelight. It was while the drawer of the old sideboard was open that she spotted the case she'd given to Leon on her penultimate visit home. She opened it to see the silver pen untouched and she recalled her brother's anger at being excluded from his studies at university.

'Why didn't I do something?' she asked herself. 'I should've helped you,' she mumbled, choking back guilty tears.

A wave of regret washed over her, and her body suddenly went into spasm. Her mouth opened and she had to clamp her hands over it to stop the terrible sound that was bubbling in her throat from escaping. Falling to her knees she felt her tears brim over and she started to sob uncontrollably. Her own despair melded with fears for the future and engulfed her as she crumbled, weeping on the floor.

Just how long she was held in the grip of her remorse, she could not say, but it was only the sight, a while later, of a pair of high leather boots on the hearth rug that stemmed the flow of Lilli's tears. She hadn't heard anyone enter the apartment, but now someone was here, standing before her. Terrified, she feared the moment of judgement was upon her.

Chapter 62

Fear had grabbed hold of her sob and stopped it in her chest as Lilli followed the army boots upwards to their wearer. But it was not a Nazi soldier who stood before her, waiting to make an arrest, but Major Marco Zeiller. As soon as he caught sight of her tear-stained faced he, too, fell to his knees and put his arms around her.

'Marco. Oh! Marco!' she cried, and her tears began again.

'It's all right. I'm here now,' he told her, cradling her head and kissing it. He rocked her like a baby for a moment then guided her towards the sofa.

'I was afraid . . . I thought . . .'

He put his finger to her lips. 'I know. I know. It's been hard. But I'm here now and we don't have much time, so you must listen carefully.'

Her head jerked up from his shoulder. 'What do you mean?'

Lilli saw his expression switch and felt his arms encircle her once more. Trying to squirm out of his embrace, she faced him, knowing he was holding something back.

'What's happened?'

The answer was delivered silently in his expression at first then confirmed in words. 'There is no need for you to go to Hamburg. Leon is—'

'No!' she redoubled her efforts to break free. 'No, it can't be true.' The embers inside her suddenly died. Even though she'd kept a flame of hope burning for the first few months since his capture, she'd feared for some time that Leon had been unable to withstand the cruelty of imprisonment. The chance of his release was one of the main reasons for her return to Munich and now that had been snatched away, the ground was collapsing beneath her.

Despite her struggling, Marco tightened his hold. 'You must listen to me, my love,' he said, putting his hand gently over her mouth as she frantically shook her head. 'And listen carefully.'

Her look latched onto his and slowly he loosened his grip to wipe away her tears.

'I'm so sorry about your brother, but there is nothing I could've done. They are dropping like flies in those camps. I know it's hard, but we must concentrate on you and your mother.'

'And our child,' said Lilli through her sobs.

Marco suddenly looked at her, wide-eyed. 'She is here? You brought Leeona here? I thought you would leave her in London.'

'I brought her with me to see her grandmother and you.' In London and in Paris, she'd often spoke about 'Papa' to Leeona, but she'd been careful not to say too much in case anyone realised she was, in fact, not referring to James.

Taking him by the hand, she led him through the darkness to her old room where Leeona was tucked into the large blanket chest at the foot of the bed. Marco smiled in wonderment as the candlelight picked out the tousled mop of her hair and the curve of her cheek in the diffused glow.

'She is perfect,' he whispered, the light playing on the little fingers curled at the ends of her plump hands.

'Yes, she is,' Lilli agreed.

Just then, the little girl stirred, rolling over onto her back. Her long eye lashes started to flicker, sensing she was being watched.

Marco gasped, as if marvelling at some miracle about to unfold in front of him. A small hand reached up and rubbed her right eye then her little lips formed themselves into a round and she yawned.

Marco looked at Lilli, as if seeking her permission to touch his daughter. Equally enchanted, she nodded and he reached down and lightly brushed her hand. Leeona's grasp immediately closed around her father's finger like a clam shell.

Lilli thought her heart would break with happiness. 'It's your papa, my darling,' she whispered.

'Papa,' echoed the little girl through a haze of sleep.

Hearing his daughter call him 'Papa' for the first time brought tears to Marco's eyes, too.

'Your papa loves you very much,' he said, his finger still in Leeona's grasp.

'Papa,' she whispered again, as she turned over and closed her eyes once more.

Leaning over the bed, Marco kissed her curls and made the sign of the cross.

'May the Holy Mother protect you, my little one,' he told her, turning back to Lilli, his eyes blazing. 'I can get papers,' he told her with a renewed energy, as if seeing Leeona had spurred him into action. Nothing and no one would harm his child. 'She can go to Switzerland with your mother. They'll both be safe there.'

They walked back into the main room and Marco held her to him again on the sofa, stroking her head. As they sat in each other's arms, Lilli told him that she knew he was a British agent. She glanced up to gauge his reaction.

'Ah!' He raised both brows. 'You have caught me out!'

'How long?'

He shrugged. 'For a while now.'

'What are you planning?' she asked.

His expression reminded her of the look Leeona sometimes gave her if she was caught in the act of doing something mischievous.

'Remember I told you that not all Germans are bad, just afraid,' was his reply.

'I know that, Marco.' Her face was still white with shock. A thousand questions swirled around in her head, but there was only one that really mattered then, and Marco answered it without being asked.

'I intend to do everything I can to help defeat Hitler. Trust me, I beg of you, but I need your help.'

'My help?'

'Don't you see, Lilli? I am playing Goebbels's game. After Hitler invades Britain, he wants the duke restored to the throne. If he refuses, he is even prepared to force him.'

Lilli's eyes were wide. It was hard to believe what Marco was saying, even though she'd suspected he had some sort of plan.

He continued: 'All we can do is try and defeat him from within.'

'From within?' repeated Lilli.

'Yes, my love,' he told her. 'I've volunteered to be part of the operation.'

'Operation?'

'A military operation, codenamed Willi.'

'Willi? But that's . . .' She thought of the vengeful spirits in Giselle.

'I suggested the name.' He allowed his lips to twitch a smile before he resumed. 'The plot has been designed by one of Hitler's leading generals, Walter von Schellenberg.'

'Von Schellenberg,' repeated Lilli. 'Didn't he . . .?' Golda had mentioned something about General von Urbach's daughter, Helene, marrying a von Schellenberg.

'Yes. The very same.'

'And he has cooked up some plot? What are you up to?' she asked warily.

Marco drew a breath. 'Von Schellenberg has been authorised to offer the duke up to fifty million Swiss francs to betray Britain and either live in a neutral country or become Hitler's puppet king.'

She was silent for a moment then remembered the latest intelligence from the American Embassy. 'The duke and duchess broke their journey in Spain, but they've just left for Lisbon.' Lisbon, she knew, was a neutral port in Portugal where ships and planes were still operating, helping thousands to flee Europe from its ports and airfields.

Marco nodded, as if he were one step ahead of her. 'The duchess seems to be keeping von Ribbentrop informed of their every move. The Spanish are acting as brokers for the Germans. They may already have turned the duke against the British government.'

Lilli gasped. She could hardly believe what Marco had just told her. 'But he still might refuse to agree to the German demands? What would happen then?'

'Then the orders are to persuade him, working through the duchess.'

Lilli's brows lifted simultaneously. 'I see, and if that fails?'

Marco sighed deeply. 'Then we are ordered to kidnap them.'

'Kidnap them!' As much as it pained her, Lilli knew exactly what she had to do. She needed to get to Lisbon as quickly as possible to see the Windsors did not end up in Hitler's hands. The duke would fall for both flattery and funds if he thought history might regard him as a peacemaker. But he would become Germany's puppet and the tide of the war could turn in the Führer's favour. 'But that cannot happen!' she cried.

Marco nodded emphatically. 'It is up to us to stop it.'

Up until now a fire had burned in Lilli's eyes as details of the plot unfolded. She knew they had to foil it, but then she remembered.

'What is it?' asked Marco, seeing her expression change.

'My mother and Leeona. Our child!' she protested, breaking away from his arms. 'What shall become of them if we go to Lisbon?'

'I told you. I'll make arrangements for them to escape to Switzerland, immediately. They'll be safe.'

Lilli bit her lip. 'And us? When we've completed this mission, what happens then?'

'We leave for America on one of the boats from Lisbon.' He took her by both hands and looked deep into her eyes. 'We can arrange for Golda and Leeona to join us there.'

There was an energy in his voice that she found convincing. She had to trust him.

'When do you leave?' she asked.

'Tomorrow.'

'Then I will follow,' she said. She would see him next in Lisbon, if she made it that far. She swallowed down a sob that threatened to resurface. 'But before we part, please hold me,' she managed to whisper.

He held her gaze and she knew he could sense her fear. There was a chance this could be the last time they ever saw each other. But before he could step forward to enfold her in his arms, Lilli moved towards the gramophone player – the illegal machine – that had lain hidden in the dresser. She remembered the last time she'd wanted to play it, at her homecoming party when all her friends and neighbours had gathered to wish her well. It was the last time she'd seen her dear Vati alive.

That had been the calm before the storm, even though, at the time, she hadn't known it. The dark clouds had been gathering and the thunder rumbling in the distance, but laughter and food and friendship were shared on that special day. Only Leon had seen the approaching turmoil, the impending doom. And she hadn't believed him, couldn't believe him, because his vision of the future was too terrible, too cataclysmic, to imagine. Now that future was here and all the goodness and compassion once found in her neighbourhood, in her homeland, had been forced to retreat; distant echoes of a distant time, leaving only fear and hatred in their stead.

She placed the stylus on the disc on the turntable. Grasping the handle, she cranked it into life and the seventy-eight began to revolve and crackle until the orchestra struck up and finally, a man's voice could be heard; a voice so familiar and comforting that she wanted to lose herself in it; surrender herself to it one last time. It was Fred Astaire's 'Dancing in the Dark.'

She walked back to Marco and draped her left hand on his shoulder, while he slid his arm around her waist and pulled her against him as their free hands closed around each other's.

Looking up at his face, her vision suddenly blurred a little. She didn't want to cry. If this was the last time Marco saw her, she didn't want him to remember her with tears in her eyes, so she forced a smile, even though inside her heart was breaking. 'Let's dance before the storm,' she told him softly.

Chapter 63

Lilli broke the news of Leon's death as gently as she could the next morning. To her surprise, Golda accepted it unquestioningly.

'A mother always knows,' she said quietly, wiping away stray tears. 'I've had a feeling for a while. My poor boy. I knew he was gone.'

True to his word, Marco organised the documents and tickets and made all the other travel arrangements. Golda and Leeona would be given safe passage into neutral Switzerland. Once there, grandmother and granddaughter would be permitted to stay at the house of an old family friend in Zurich. Lilli had slipped out first thing, before Leeona was awake, to collect the papers from the Swiss Consulate. It was when she walked back into the hallway of the apartment block that it happened.

Herr Grunfeld was behind his desk, speaking with a soldier in a Reichswehr uniform, leaning on a crutch. The janitor had just handed over a fistful of post and Lilli wanted to run, but she knew she needed to keep her cool. The soldier had his back to her, but he was a broad and muscular with a bullish neck and Lilli thought there was something familiar about him. Then she noticed at the end of his right trouser leg there was no foot.

The breath left her body as soon as she realised his identity. She scurried past, but not quickly enough to avoid his gaze. His cold eyes followed her as she set foot on the stairs.

'Fraulein!' he called after her, whipping off his peaked cap.

She stopped, her nerves pulled tight. Ignoring him was not an option. She had to turn.

'Yes?' she replied, vainly trying to avoid his direct gaze.

In a split second their eyes met. Lilli held her breath. He recognised her instantly. There was a flash, a charge of hate and fear that arced between them. But then . . .

'*Enschuldegut*,' said the soldier, with a shallow bow. 'I mistook you for someone else.'

The trouble was Lilli knew there was no mistake. She'd realised too late that the soldier collecting his post at the desk was Hans Backe, their former lodger and Jew hater. There was every chance that he would report her presence in the block. All three of them – Golda, Leeona and herself – could easily find themselves detained on trumped-up charges. She hurried up the stairs and arrived back in the apartment breathless and in a panic. Slamming the door, she leaned against it, but not wishing to alarm Golda, she acted positively.

'I've got them,' she called as soon as she'd caught her breath. Holding the papers aloft, she walked triumphantly into the parlour. 'Here they are,' said Lilli. 'You can leave for Switzerland, Mutti. You'll both be safe.'

Yet Golda did not react the way Lilli had imagined she would. Her mother was seated by the cold *kachelofen*. Little Leeona was on her knee, whimpering. Instead of being relieved at the news, she looked up at her daughter as she approached and shook her head. 'We cannot go anywhere, Lilli.' Her eyes slid to Leeona. 'The darling child is sick.'

'What? No!' Rushing forward, Lilli laid the back of her hand on Leeona's forehead. 'She is burning up with the fever.' The little girl's mop of unruly curls was flat with sweat and she was having difficulty breathing. 'My poor darling,' she whispered, kneeling down by her side and stroking her cheek.

'Angela, downstairs, is sick, too,' said Golda, her voice flat. 'Very sick.'

Leeona had been a regular visitor to the Grunfelds' apartment, playing with their daughter most days.

'Do they know what it is?' asked Lilli, noticing her daughter's neck looked swollen.

Golda nodded. 'Yes, Lilli, they do. The doctor says Angela has diphtheria.'

Lilli's face fell. After everything that she'd been through in the past few days, the dangerous trip from Paris, never knowing when she might be arrested, to nursing Golda back and learning of Leon's death, to this. Just when she'd finally seen a way through their problems, a light at the end of the tunnel, darkness had fallen yet again. 'Oh, no. No, Mutti.' Her eyes were glassy with tears. She knew from Herr Grunfeld that all the Jewish doctors had left the city and no others would treat the child.

Lilli thought for a moment. 'Garlic juice. I heard garlic juice is good.' She sprang up and ran into the kitchen, as if her life depended on it. Rifling through the store cupboard, she found a bulb and split it into cloves, crushing them to extract the juice then mixing it with a little water. 'Here,' she said a few minutes later, thrusting a cup up to her daughter's lips. 'Drink this, my darling.'

That night Lilli tended to her child, sponging her hands and forehead with vinegar to bring down her temperature. Leeona, wrapped in blankets in the chest at the end of the bed, wheezed and whimpered her way through to the early hours, when she finally fell asleep. Lilli, too, drifted off, fully clothed, at the edge of the bed. A knock at the door woke her.

Lilli sprang up, blinked and rubbed her eyes. For a moment she'd no idea where she was then she remembered. She glanced at Leeona and felt the pulse in her neck. She was still alive. Another knock. She hurried, blurry eyed, to see who it was. The knock was soft – not a soldier's knock, not Herr Backe's knock – yet still her stomach knotted as she opened the door.

'Herr Grunfeld.' The janitor stood, red-eyed, on the threshold, his cheeks wet and his whole body slouching. 'What is it? What's wrong?' she asked.

Axel Grunfeld bit back the tears as he told her. 'Our little Angela, our little angel,' he began. 'She's gone.'

'Oh, no.'

News of the little girl's death made Lilli weep, too. She reached out and embraced the janitor and he, her. 'I'm so sorry,' she told him, her voice breaking on the words. 'I'm so very sorry.'

After a moment Grunfeld pulled back. He wiped his cheeks with the hand and snorted away his tears. 'I came to tell you because of Lee . . .' Lilli's look made him stop mid-sentence. 'Oh God, no!' he whispered.

'She survived the night.'

Grunfeld swallowed back more tears. 'We will pray for her,' he said before turning to go down the stairs.

As soon as she shut the door, Lilli rushed to check on Leeona. The child still slept and her cheeks remained flushed, but her breathing sounded less erratic. 'Don't die, my love. Please don't die,' Lilli whispered. Nothing else mattered more than Leeona. She glanced at the documents on top of the chest of drawers. They were meaningless, worthless if Leeona died, and yet . . .

Golda shuffled through on her walking stick. 'Did I hear Herr Grunfeld?'

'Oh Mutti. Little Angela is dead,' she said, dabbing her own eyes.

Golda gasped and her hands flew to her mouth before she raised her eyes heavenwards as if to ask God why he had taken the child. After a moment she said: 'But our Leeona?'

'She's sleeping soundly,' replied Lilli.

'What will you do?' she asked, leaning heavily on her stick.

'You know what I should do.'

Golda gazed at her daughter, understanding her loyalties were divided.

'It's in the hands of the Almighty,' she said.

Lilli shook her head. 'No, Mutti. Not this time. This time I can't put my head in the sand. What I do, I do for you and Leeona,' she replied. 'If Hitler wins this war, we'll all be killed anyway.' She looked at Golda with glassy eyes. 'I have to go, Mutti. I am needed,' she told her. 'You and Leeona will be safe in Switzerland.'

A few hours later, Lilli had packed what belongings she could fit into a single suitcase. She needed to travel light. Leeona's fever had mercifully broken and she'd eaten a biscuit. She was out of danger – from diphtheria at least. Now, however, she was sleeping and Lilli didn't want to wake her. Instead, she bent low to kiss her sleeping daughter's forehead. 'Goodbye, my beloved,' she whispered, tears streaming down her face. 'Stay safe until I see you again.'

As Lilli rose from the bed, Golda suddenly grabbed hold of her arm. For a moment she thought her mother was going to plead with her to stay for Leeona's sake. But she did not. Instead Golda, her eyes staring at her daughter from out of her lined face, put her hand on her shoulder and said: 'You must do what is right, my child.'

Chapter 64

Lisbon, Portugal

The short man in the panama hat stood a little away from the press of people streaming off the train. That was how Lilli saw he was holding out a sign with her name on. He was looking in the opposite direction.

'I'm Lillian Stern,' said Lilli, taking the little man by surprise.

'Ah!' He raised his hat. 'Welcome to Lisbon, Miss Stern,' he greeted her, picking up her suitcase.

'David Eccles at your service. We have a car.'

Lilli followed him out of the station.

'Good journey? Bad journey?' he huffed, signalling to the waiting chauffeur.

It had been a terrible journey. Every time they'd stopped in a station, she'd held her breath, fearful that some Nazi flunky would question her papers. Filming of *Titanic* was due to begin that day. When she didn't turn up on set, an order to arrest her on sight would be given. Eva Braun's odious photograph of the Führer standing at her side had been the only shield she could offer if she'd been stopped by Nazi guards as she made her escape south, to Portugal.

With Mr Hooper's help from the US Embassy, she'd managed to track down Wallis and asked her if she could stay for a few days. She told her the filming for *Titanic* had been postponed, and Wallis accepted the lie. But worst of all was the excruciating worry about Leeona and Golda. They needed to leave the apartment as soon as they could, or face the dire consequences. Time was running out. She found herself praying, even though she'd long given up on God. 'Please get them to Zurich safely,' she'd muttered under her breath. 'Please.'

'May we stop off at the telegraph office, Mr Eccles?' Lilli asked as the car zig-zagged its tedious way through the Lisbon streets crammed with vehicles and people.

'Of course,' he replied, dabbing the sweat from his brow. 'Pull over here, will you?' he told the driver.

It was a wasted effort. Golda had promised to let Lilli know the minute they arrived in Zurich. They should be there by now, but there was no message waiting for her.

'Everything tickety?' asked Eccles on her return.

'Tickety?' she repeated.

'Tickety boo,' he said.

'I'm sorry, I . . .' The odd phrase was unfamiliar to her.

'Ah, an English idiom, I fear. It means all right.'

She nodded her understanding. She was still unused to such English eccentricities. 'Yes, thank you,' she replied, even though her nerves had never been so taut. She needed to put on a brave face, when all she really wanted to do was hold Leeona in her arms again. Yet she had work to do. It was her job to persuade the Windsors that the British government was not the enemy, that they must not put their trust in the Fascist Spaniards who were negotiating with the Nazis to hand them over to Hitler. Eccles's assessment only confirmed she had her work cut out for her.

'They're convinced we're after them,' he told her as the car was finally able to get up speed. 'And of course it doesn't help that

Churchill has threatened to court-martial the duke if he doesn't take up this post as Governor of the Bahamas.'

She had walked into a nest of vipers. Of course she'd known that when she agreed to come to Lisbon. It would be up to her to convince Wallis, who would then convince the prince, that he should cease any notion he had of being a peacemaker in Europe. There was no doubt he saw himself as an arbitrator; a go-between, able to span both sides in this unholy mess of a war. If Hitler were to help him regain his throne, then as the newly restored king, he could negotiate a peace settlement between Germany and Britain, if not the rest of Europe.

'And don't believe all the servants tell you,' said Eccles, now fanning himself with his floppy handkerchief. 'They've been bribed.'

'Bribed?'

'By Jerry.'

'Jerry?' asked Lilli.

'No offence,' blurted Eccles, realising his diplomatic blunder. 'I mean the Germans. There've been some funny things going on lately. Stones thrown at windows, a bouquet of flowers for the duchess containing a warning. The staff'll tell you it's the Brits. They're lying, but something's afoot.'

'Afoot?' Lilli wasn't familiar with the expression.

'Awry. Not right. Lisbon is a city of spies, Miss Stern. You can't trust your grandmother here.'

Lilli nodded. 'I see,' was all she said, although, in reality, she knew exactly just what was 'afoot' in Mr Eccles's words. Thanks to Marco she knew Hitler's secret plan and was probably the only person on the British side who did. She didn't dare tell Colonel Plimpton for fear any communication might be intercepted. As they swept through the gates of the magnificent residence where the Windsors were staying, such knowledge made her feel dangerously vulnerable.

Wallis was on the steps of the palatial villa waiting to greet Lilli's automobile. She looked painfully thin.

'Welcome to our prison!' she said. She was laughing as she spoke, although as she held out her long, scrawny arms for an embrace, Lilli knew she meant what she said.

The strain is etched on that flawless skin of hers, she observed. Her cheeks were stretched tight as drums over her bones and grooves had appeared to curve round her mouth.

'Prison? This is paradise,' Lilli quipped. Wallis really didn't know how lucky she was. Eccles had warned her that the duchess's complaints would be as relentless as ack-ack rounds. She began firing even before Lilli was allowed to wash and change after her arduous journey.

'I'm so bored. Thank God you're here. I don't even have my own things around me and they won't allow me to shop. My jewellery, my clothes. What am I supposed to do? I've had to send Madame Moulichon back to Paris to collect some essentials.' Lilli thought of the unfortunate lady's maid. Eccles mentioned she'd been forced to risk arrest by the occupying Nazis to retrieve her mistress's favourite bed sheets. Wallis reminded Lilli of a whining to child when she didn't get her way, but this was only an hors d'oeuvre. The main course, as she was soon to discover, came later as they walked under the shade of a parasol in the villa's grounds.

'There are spies everywhere,' whispered Wallis as they strolled down a path bordered by low box hedges, the gravel crunching beneath their shoes. The prince had gone to play golf at a nearby course as he did every afternoon, leaving his wife to her own devices. 'We must keep away from trees. Near a fountain is best.'

Lilli nodded and let Wallis do the talking. 'Yesterday we were visited by a Spanish emissary. He told us . . .' Her voice started to quaver. 'He told us that the British secret service plans to assassinate us either here or in the Bahamas. He said we must return to Spain for our own safety.'

'What will you do?' Lilli pretended to look shocked.

Wallis shook her head and walked on a little. 'The duke has asked for forty-eight hours to decide.'

Lilli stopped suddenly. 'But returning to Spain would mean deserting his own country.' She hoped her forthrightness might shock the duchess into seeing sense.

Wallis flashed a disdainful look at her and she knew she'd gone too far. 'Surely you, of all people, aren't accusing us of treachery? If I didn't know you better, Lillian, I'd say you were being a hypocrite. When your own country threatens your life, you change sides.'

Lilli's spine stiffened. She could not blow her cover now. 'I am, as you would say, sitting on the fence, but I know that you and the duke cannot.'

Wallis forced a smile. 'Of course, if David had still been king we wouldn't have been in this goddamn mess. We wouldn't be at war. He would have been a force for peace.' It was clear to Lilli she believed what she said.

They began walking again and Wallis looped her bony arm through Lilli's in a gesture of reconciliation. 'Walter Monckton arrives tomorrow,' she said. Lilli had met the large, bespectacled diplomat once at a party with James. 'Apparently he's bringing a letter from Churchill. I doubt it'll be a greetings card.'

A letter of Churchill would surely contain an ultimatum, Lilli guessed. Matters were coming to the boil very quickly. The next few hours would be critical. Perhaps now was the time to lay her cards on the table.

'I have to be frank with you,' she began.

Wallis stopped short and lengthened her neck. 'But I thought you always were, dear Lillian. That's why I count you as such a close friend.'

'I am honoured that you regard me so,' she said. 'So it is my duty to tell you all I know.'

Wallis leaned in closer. 'What do you know?'

'I know that if everything goes to his plan, Hitler will invade Britain and put the duke back on the throne with you as his queen.'

Although both Wallis's pencilled brows shot up at the same

time, she did not seem surprised at all. Instead she smiled. 'Would that be such a bad thing, my dear?'

Lilli pretended to ignore this response. It really only confirmed what she'd feared all along, so she continued. 'Hitler believes this will divide the British people and weaken their resolve to resist. Britain would be ruled by the Reich.'

Lilli saw Wallis's jaw work and her chin jut out. 'And where have you heard this?' she asked. 'Are you a spy, too?' She turned to look at Lilli in the eye. 'Are you another British agent sent to torment us with your outlandish stories of German horrors that lie in store?'

Lilli laughed at her suggestion then shook her head. 'Wallis, I speak as one who is concerned about you and the duke. Please believe me, I have your best interests at heart,' she pleaded.

Wallis moved closer to the trees, the shadow cast by her parasol darkening her face. After a moment she turned to Lilli. 'Up until now I have let it pass unremarked, but you left one of your mother's touching letters in our Paris apartment. I know you are a Jew, Lillian.' She took a deep breath. 'You would do well to remember it.'

Her words struck Lilli dumb for a moment and her blood ran cold. Wallis's mood had turned on a *pfennig*. Her charming mask had slipped without warning.

'Wallis, please. Will you listen? Please,' Lilli begged as the duchess strode back towards the villa. She did not pay any heed.

Chapter 65

When Lilli returned to the villa she went straight to her room. From out of her suitcase she took a framed photograph of Leeona. Looking at it brought tears to her eyes and her insides knotted once more as she wondered where she and Golda were. She gave the picture pride of place on the dressing table, together with Leeona's little silver comb she'd mistakenly brought with her. She'd had both the comb and its matching brush engraved with her daughter's name. Gently she traced the letters with her fingers. But as she did so, she noticed something else. On the dressing table someone had also laid an envelope addressed to her and, beside it, a single red rose. She opened the envelope with trembling hands. The note directed her to be at the casino later that evening. It was signed *Duke Albrecht*. She knew the time to act was growing near.

The duke and duchess would be holding a party in a few hours' time at the Aviz Hotel. 'A great farewell to Europe' was how Wallis described it. Anyone who was anyone was to attend. Lilli had been invited but managed to excuse herself. She was exhausted after her arduous journey, she'd said. Instead she slipped out to the casino at Estoril. She was aware of its bad reputation. If Lisbon was full of spies, the casino was the haunt of Europe's scoundrels, miscreants and chancers – as well as spies. There were officers, too, both Allied and German. Patrons came from every persuasion and in every shape and colour from a dozen or more countries. That was why it made the perfect cover for Major Marco Zeiller.

A wall of smoke hit Lilli as she walked inside the low building. The casino was divided up by gaming tables: roulette, blackjack, poker and baccarat. Men in tuxedos milled around or sat hunched over, in deep concentration, as they placed their bets. The few women seemed to be there for purely decorative purposes, draping themselves around gamblers in the hope that they'd strike it lucky. Financial generosity, thought Lilli, was known to make men very attractive.

She caught sight of Marco sitting on a tall stool at the bar, but she had to look twice. He'd ditched his customary uniform for a suave dinner jacket. They did not acknowledge each other at first. To all the world it had to appear that they were strangers engaged in casual conversation. For that reason, he didn't even turn immediately when she sat down on the bar stool next to him. It took all her strength not to throw herself into his arms and tell him all her woes – how fearful she was for Leeona and Golda; how fearful she was about everything; it was the safety of the Windsors that had to be paramount at the moment.

'Gin and tonic,' she told the barman. It was a drink she'd grown to love in Hollywood. 'A double.' After all that had happened recently, she felt she deserved it.

'Had a bad day, Miss . . .?' remarked Marco.

'Giselle,' she replied.

'Duke Albrecht of Silesia, at your service,' he said, bowing his head.

'A bad day?' she repeated, managing a wry smile. 'You could say that.'

A little further down the bar an old soak was slumped on his stool, his chin propped up on his hand. Marco had been watching him for a while. He could be a genuine drunk or a Nazi plant. One couldn't be too careful in Lisbon at the moment.

The ice in the large glass of gin and tonic tinkled as the barman slid it across the counter. For a while they drank and created idle chatter, fearing that somewhere, someone could be watching them.

'Would you care for a stroll in the grounds?' Marco asked. 'Then you can tell me why your day was so bad.'

The charade reminded her of being on a film set in Hollywood. None of this was real. No one and nothing were what they seemed.

Since late afternoon great, billowing clouds had been rolling in from the Atlantic. Now they threatened a storm. The air was still and hot and thick with the scent of rosemary, nevertheless it made a welcome change from the casino's smoke. Crickets played a noisy soundtrack as they walked side by side along the path that skirted the lawn. Their arms brushed now and again, but they dared not appear intimate, just in case they were being spied on.

'What news from the Windsors?' Marco asked as soon as he was sure they could not be overheard.

'They're in turmoil. The duke's been told he should return to Spain for his own safety. A Spaniard – I don't know his name – has tried to convince him that the British may attempt to kill him and Wallis either here or in the Bahamas.'

'So will he go back to Spain?'

'He'll give his answer tomorrow. But I understand that a diplomat called Sir Walter . . .'

'Monckton? I've heard of him. He gets things done.'

'Yes. He's due to arrive tomorrow, too. He may help to persuade the duke to stick with the British.'

Marco frowned. 'If the duke's final answer is to refuse to side with Germany, von Schellenberg is convinced Hitler won't accept no for an answer. He'll take matters into his own hands.'

'So you really think he'll order the kidnap of the Windsors?'

Marco put his finger to his lips. 'Quiet,' he said, glancing round. 'You need to warn the British and persuade the couple to increase their security.'

'That won't be easy.'

'But I thought you were good friends with Wallis. Has something happened?'

Lilli shrugged. 'I was honest with her. I told her how it would look to the British people if she and the duke were to go to Spain and she . . .'

'Yes?' Marco ducked his head to look into her eyes.

'She knows I'm Jewish. She's as good as told me to keep quiet or she'll expose me. She's no idea I've been exposed already, so it doesn't matter anymore.'

'Ah!' was all he could say at first as he tried to grasp the implications of what she'd just told him.

'There may be a way . . .' she said suddenly, wheeling round to face him.

'Yes.'

'Perhaps I could meet Sir Walter as soon as he flies in and warn him,' she suggested. 'They'd take more notice of him.'

'I think you better had,' agreed Marco.

'Then I shall get back to the villa. I'll need to leave early.' She turned and was about to head down the path when he grabbed her arm and pulled her towards the shadows cast by a clump of tall bushes nearby.

'We can get through this,' he told her, kissing her neck, then seeking her mouth, but she turned her face upward, to search the night sky.

'There are no stars, Marco,' she said, her voice sliding into despair.

She heard his soft sigh before he followed her gaze. 'I see them,' he said. He switched back to look at her once more. 'I see them in your eyes, and in our daughter's. Remember what I told you that night on the church tower? Look hard enough and you will find them, too, my love.'

'Let's hope you're right,' she said, her palms flat against his chest. She wanted to believe him, but hope, she felt, was fast slipping through her fingertips. 'Our lives depend upon it.'

He took a deep breath, composing himself, and tugged at his dinner jacket. 'I love you, Lilli Sternberg,' he said. 'But just in case.' He put his hand in his breast pocket and pulled out an envelope. 'Here. If anything goes wrong, wait for me at the florist's in the Rua das Flores. You understand?'

Lilli took the envelope. She recognised it as the being from the same florist's that delivered the rose to the villa. She put it in her evening purse.

'Be careful, my love,' he told her.

'And you,' she said as they made their farewells near the casino entrance.

All the while neither of them had noticed their entire meeting had been closely watched. A flaxen-haired woman, seated at one of the gaming tables, had suddenly registered Lilli when she walked into the casino and followed her progress to the bar with an exceptionally keen interest. She never forgot a face. Nor a wrongdoing. Her surprise at seeing Major Marco Zeiller could prove equally rewarding, she told herself. Revenge, she knew, was a dish best served cold.

Chapter 66

The villa was in a state of disarray. Wallis had ordered her suitcases to be packed in readiness. Several of them, each with labels detailing their contents, were lined up in the service passage near the kitchens so that when the time came to load them into suitable vehicles, the operation could be conducted in haste. Whatever her husband decided – whether he chose to throw in his lot with Herr Hitler and his Nazis or bite the bullet and accept Churchill's offer of a governorship in the Caribbean – Wallis knew they would not be remaining in the villa for much longer.

The atmosphere on the terrace at breakfast had been as cool as the milk in the jug. Lilli had tried to make polite conversation, but it was clear to her that Wallis had told the duke about her views on their position. Their frosty silence, did, however, make it easier for Lilli to order a car to take her to the port on the pretext that she needed to run some errands in town. Instead she planned to intercept Sir Walter Monckton at the harbour as soon as his flying boat from England touched down.

As Lilli walked towards her waiting taxi, another car pulled up at the villa. It was flying the Spanish pennant. Inside, she knew, was an emissary, whose job had been to persuade the duke that only the Fascists had his best interests at heart. The diplomat had come to hear the duke's final decision. But whether the former king of England was inclined to bind himself over to Spain and therefore to the Nazis, or remain loyal to the British government, Lilli could not wait around to find out.

Sir Walter's flying boat landed only a few minutes later than scheduled. Lilli watched him disembark onto the jetty towards the small customs house on the dockside. Despite the efforts of an over-zealous male aide, she managed to intercept him just as he was about to get into his waiting car.

At first the large, jolly-looking man with spectacles found her hard to place, but Lilli recalled they'd once met at a particularly dull cocktail party in London.

'My husband was the late James Marchington, the art dealer,' she told him helpfully. 'I must speak with you urgently.'

'Mrs Marchington,' he replied looking weighty. 'Awful business, your husband. Please accept my condolences.'

She drew him to one side, out of earshot of the aide. 'What I have to tell you is a matter of the upmost secrecy,' she whispered.

'Oh?' Intrigued, the diplomat regarded her over the rim of his glasses.

Lilli took a deep breath. 'Hitler is planning to kidnap the Duke of Windsor.'

Later that day Brigade Leader Walter von Schellenberg stood in the tower room of the German Embassy in Lisbon watching the port through a pair of high-powered binoculars. Of particular interest was an American Export Lines passenger ship called the *Excalibur*.

'It appears so close I can almost touch it,' he muttered to the major at his side.

'Indeed, sir,' replied Marco.

'They've increased security around the vessel,' von Schellenberg remarked, still peering through the glasses. 'Why do you think that could be, Zeiller?' he asked. He brought down the binoculars to look directly at his aide. There was something in his manner that concerned Marco. 'It was a great pity our generous offer was refused. The Führer will not be happy,' he continued.

'Sir,' came a voice from behind. An adjutant held a telegram in his hand and delivered it to the commanding officer with a salute.

Von Schellenberg read it hastily, his expression growing graver with each word. 'Well, well,' he said finally. 'It seems the Führer has run out of patience.'

'Sir?' asked Marco.

The commanding officer's thin lips twitched into a smile. 'We are to abduct the duke and duchess straight away,' he said. 'Zeiller, you know what to do.'

'Sir!' Marco's arm lashed out into a salute and he clicked his heels. This was the moment he'd dreaded. There had been plans in place for a while. Most immediately he'd been ordered to supervise the sabotage of the Windsor's large amounts of luggage as the entourage transporting it progressed towards the port. Then there were the bomb alerts. An anonymous telephoned warning would be sent to the ship. Even though the vessel had been searched many times over, together with each passenger's hand baggage, a further threat of an explosion on board would help cause another diversion. However, it was the car in which the Windsors were travelling that would be the main target. It was to be ambushed on its way to the port. Yes, he knew what he had to do. And so did Lilli. He was confident she would do everything in her power to stop the kidnapping.

Back at the villa the servants had sprung into action. The dozens of pieces of luggage were being loaded into an assortment of cars and trucks to be taken ahead to the port. The duke and duchess themselves would travel to the ship separately with a police escort, provided by Scotland Yard.

Lilli saw Wallis through the open bedroom door standing forlornly, taking one last look at the view before her departure.

She tapped on the door and approached. 'I know this is hard for you,' she said.

Wallis simply smirked. 'Yes, I suppose you do,' she replied, a steely expression on her face. 'You and I have a lot in common, you know. I suspect that's why I felt comfortable with you at first. We both know what it's like to be poor and we both know what it's like to be shunned by society – you because you're a Jew and me because I'm seen as a twice-divorced, social-climbing gold digger. The difference is that your dreams have long died. Mine have not.' She shook her head and her features hardened. 'I'll never give up believing I should be the Queen of England.'

As if on cue, a voice came from the doorway. 'Your Royal Highness.'

Wallis gave a little toss of her neatly coiffured head. 'You see, Lillian, at least here I'm given the respect I'm due.'

The duchess joined the duke to say goodbye to the servants who were lined up on the front steps. Lilli found Sir Walter looking on, having taken charge of arrangements with Mr Eccles. Loose talk and whispers through keyholes had become occupational hazards. Secrecy was vital. She felt in the pocket of her dress. The envelope that Marco had slipped her last night contained detailed plans of the ambush. It was time to reveal them.

'Sir, a word if I might,' she said to Sir Walter as he powered down the corridor, his aide at his heels.

He peered at her over his spectacles. 'I'm afraid now is not a good time Miss Stern,' he replied, carrying on towards the entrance hall.

Undeterred she followed. 'Sir, please. I have information.'

Sir Walter stopped in his tracks. 'What sort of information?'

Lilli looked at the aide, hovering in the wings. 'Vital information.'

The door of the study was open. 'You'll have to be quick, I'm afraid,' he told her brusquely, leading the way. A raised hand in his aide's face as he closed the door, ensured privacy.

'Well, Miss Stern?'

Lilli took a deep breath. 'What if I were to tell you that this convoy,' she glanced through the window at the waiting limousines, 'will be ambushed. This is how Hitler plans to kidnap the duke and duchess.' Through his thick glasses Lilli could see Sir Walter's eyes widen. He stared at her in disbelief.

'Where have you heard this?'

From her pocket Lilli retrieved the envelope and brought out the piece of paper. Walking over to the desk, she unfolded it and smoothed out the creases. It was a copy of von Schellenberg's annotated map showing exactly how the ambush would be executed.

'Good Lord!' exclaimed Sir Walter.

Lilli's intervention seemed to have the desired effect. Within minutes an alternative itinerary for the Windsors' journey to the port was being finalised.

Meanwhile, back at the German Embassy, Marco was delivering the final briefing to four motorcyclists who were to intercept the ducal limousine and help kidnap its occupants. Without warning the office door opened. It was von Schellenberg himself. Marco looked up, his baton poised over the large map of the Lisbon area. His arm froze in mid-air, as his commanding officer entered the room. Everyone stood to attention.

'Carry on, Major Zeiller,' ordered von Schellenberg.

As it happened Marco had almost finished the briefing, but he continued knowing that his every move was being scrutinised. Von Schellenberg was watching him like a hawk. Did he suspect something? Marco felt sweat prick the skin on the back of his neck.

'Do your duty, men,' he said finally, before dismissing the motorcyclists with a salute. They all filed out past their senior officer.

Left alone in the room with the major, von Schellenberg said nothing at first. Instead he walked over to the map on the board and studied it for a few seconds before turning and moving towards Marco.

'You are a good officer,' he began. 'Efficient, enthusiastic. You volunteered for this mission, I believe.' He'd started to circle. The intimidation tactic was familiar. Marco knew he wasn't about to be promoted.

'Yes, sir.'

Von Schellenberg nodded and picked up Marco's discarded baton from the table. 'I wonder why that might have been?'

'Sir?' Marco frowned. He felt his guts start to tighten.

'There's no need to answer, Major,' said von Schellenberg, cutting him off. By now he was slapping his palm with the baton.

'You see, you may have many qualities, but I know that loyalty to the Reich is not among them.' With these words he jabbed the end of the baton under Marco's chin, jerking his head backwards.

'Guards!'

At the command, two soldiers entered the room.

'Arrest him,' barked von Schellenberg. Marco was grabbed by either arm, but before he was marched off, the commanding officer was able to offer an explanation. 'You see Major, you were observed at the casino with that Jewish spy of yours. My wife, Helene, with whom I believe you were once acquainted, saw you passing information to one Fraulein Lilli Sternberg. If this mission fails it will be because of you. Take him away!'

The cavalcade left the villa a little later than planned. There'd been a hold-up with the luggage that had been sent on ahead, too. Wallis was reportedly even more irritable than usual and the duke was wringing his immaculately manicured hands. Most demeaning of all was that, for some reason, which had not been explained, the couple were forced to travel in a shabby pick-up truck belonging to the villa. Sir Walter had been most apologetic but had assured them it was for their own safety. Unbeknown to the royal couple, Sir Walter had also enlisted the services of an expert military driver. The diplomat's foresight – thanks to Lilli – was soon to pay off.

The two official limousines had gone on ahead and were coming up to the Belem Tower on the outskirts of Lisbon, about four kilometres from the port, when suddenly, from a side road, two motorcycles appeared. They veered sharply in front of the first car, forcing it to break. The second car screamed to a halt, skidding sideways, the stench of rubber on the hot road. Meanwhile, two more motorcycles emerged from nowhere, along with a Mercedes, corralling the limousines from behind. A second later, a black car had sped along beside the two limousines and two officers disembarked, both striding towards one of the cars. At roughly the same time they peered in through the windows to find two bemused Portuguese scullery maids in each car and at roughly the same time, they both realised they'd been duped.

The less-than-salubrious truck that had been following the limousines at a good distance turned off just before the ambush, taking an alternative route to the port. Its originally disgruntled and reluctant passengers expressed relief and gratitude when they learned of the failed ambush. Less than twenty minutes later, the Duke and Duchess of Windsor were walking up the gangplank of the *Excalibur*, much to the excitement of the waiting crowds.

Chapter 67

'Yes!' Lilli snatched at the receiver. She'd been hovering by the telephone for the past half hour, smoking to calm her nerves. In the ashtray beside her, lay the charred remains of Eva Braun's photograph taken at the Berghof that she so reviled: a reminder of a moment that still made the bile rise. Finally, Hitler's image alongside her own, lay in ashes.

Now the news she'd been waiting for – that the duke and duchess had arrived safely on-board ship – made her light-headed. 'Thank you,' she said, replacing the receiver as she let out a breath. She'd been on tenterhooks. The call was her cue to leave. While the Windsors had been expecting her to travel with them, she had other plans.

One of the chauffeurs gave her a lift into the city and dropped her at the telegraph office. There was still no word from Golda. Her head started to pound. Something had gone wrong.

From the centre she knew it would be safer to walk to the little florist's shop in the Rua das Flores. Keeping to the side streets, she moved in shadow where she could. The midday heat shimmered off the old walls. The uneven cobbles made the route hazardous underfoot. Dogs dozed in beaded doorways, old women, dressed in black, sat on steps, their knees splayed under their long skirts.

Everywhere she went, people eyed her suspiciously. She did not belong in their world. She felt alone and afraid.

Finally, as the nearby church bell tolled one, she reached her destination: a narrow, cobbled street, where most of the windows seemed to be shuttered with a permanency that spoke of decay. The florist's shop lay in the middle of the row. There were very few flowers for sale and those that were, were wilting in the heat, their heads bowed. The toothless old woman at the counter was also wilting, fanning herself with a newspaper. Nevertheless, she seemed to be expecting Lilli. For a moment it was clear that she was sizing her up then she jumped in.

'*Deutsch, ja?*'

Lilli nodded. She was not sure if she was being welcomed or condemned until the woman waddled out from behind the counter and showed her through a brightly coloured beaded curtain to the back of the shop. A young man was sitting at a desk, under a large wall clock, writing something laboriously with an ink pen. His tongue lolled out of his mouth like a lazy dog's as he wrote. She guessed he might be making forgeries of documents.

'You wait here,' the old woman instructed her.

So Lilli did, even though she had no idea of how long that would be. Marco would come sooner or later. He just had to. There'd been no time to discuss any of their own plans that night at the casino.

The clock on the wall seemed to tick away the hours so slowly. The clattering of a passing cart marked the end of siesta. Now and again the horn of an automobile sounded. People stirred from their slumber. A cockerel crowed as if it knew when it should wake the neighbourhood. The strains of a nearby guitar drifted through the air thick with dust. It grew dark. At around eight o'clock, just as the young man appeared to be packing away his papers, Lilli heard footsteps on the cobbles outside, then in the shop.

A voice. It was Marco's. She leapt up and ran through the

curtain. He was wearing only a sleeveless vest and his uniform trousers that were torn at the knee. His face was bloodied.

'My God!' she cried and rushed forward, throwing her arms around his waist.

He reached behind for her hands and took them both in his. 'There's no time,' he panted. 'They're after me.'

'Quick,' said the old woman, gesturing them through the curtain once more. She hurried over to a chest of drawers and brought out clean clothes – a pressed shirt, jacket and trousers. There was even a hat. Marco started to dress.

The young man laid a wallet full of documents on the desk. In exchange Lilli saw Marco give him a bundle of bank notes.

'What happened?' she asked, as he heaved on the jacket.

'Von Schellenberg's wife was at the casino. She recognised us.'

'What?!'

'The former Comtesse Helene von Urbach.'

'Helene!' Lilli thought of the general's intense daughter who'd had designs on Marco. As Golda had said, she'd married a high-ranking Reichswehr officer.

'She saw me give you the plans.'

'So they're looking for me, too?' asked Lilli.

He looked at her gravely. 'Yes. They are.'

Helene had managed to wreak her revenge on both of them.

'What shall we do?'

'We'll go to the port. Our friend Chico here,' he nodded to the young man, 'has not only forged me some identification papers. He's bought our tickets, too. We'll be on a ship that leaves in the early hours, bound for New York.'

It was less than three kilometres to the port. They set off along the narrow side streets, avoiding the main thoroughfares. They knew von Schellenberg would have agents out looking for them. They'd only made it as far as the next street when they saw two men coming towards them. Marco grabbed Lilli and shoved her into a doorway, pressing her flat. He could spot the Gestapo a

362

mile away. Neither of them breathed until the men had passed. They carried on, taking cover every time a car drove by until, at last, just before midnight, they reached the port.

The docks were heaving with people, rammed with men, women and children all desperately trying to find passage.

'Keep your head down,' Marco told her, as a guard with a snarling dog passed them.

Thousands of refugees were lining the quayside under the glare of bright lights. It was hard to breathe, let alone move in the mêlée. Lilli was being shoved and pressed from every angle and the noise was buffeting her head like a hurricane. She could see few faces in this tide of humanity; only bodies and hats, but there was one woman nearby she noticed holding her little girl, about the same age as Leeona. The rest of the crowd seemed to fall away, so that all she could see in that moment was the mother with her child and a dagger was suddenly plunged into her heart, as she thought of their daughter. 'God save you, my beloved,' she muttered.

Marco, still by her side, squeezed her hand, locking his fingers through hers. 'Keep hold,' he told her as they ploughed their way through the throng towards a boarding gate. There were uniformed men, Lilli guessed port officials, shouting orders through a loudspeaker. A thousand outstretched arms were pleading to be allowed to board. A thousand desperate voices clamoured to be heard. Papers were being waved. Men were begging. Women were crying. And she was with Marco; just a few more steps to go to freedom.

Forty years later

Chapter 68

Petworth, England

The woman behind the wheel of a German-registered Audi joined the queue of other cars crawling up the long drive leading to an idyllic Tudor manor house. Flicking the automatic into neutral, she looked at herself in the driving mirror. Her eyes were bloodshot and her untameable curls had sprung loose from their clips. She'd been on the road more or less for the past two days, grabbing only a few hours disrupted sleep on the ferry from Dover. But now, braving a chopping Channel and instant coffee in an English roadside café, she'd reached her destination – Gresham Hall, the place that had occupied her thoughts for more than a year.

She was there for what the British tabloid press billed 'the sale of the century'. A firm of international antique dealers was holding an auction at the historic home in Sussex. The fact that it came complete with its very own moat, seemed not to deter the hordes of strangers who'd parked up their vehicles on the surrounding green lawns ready to invade the house.

Everyone was clamouring for the chance to take away an expensive little piece of history. Eager buyers had plenty of opportunities. Up for grabs were Chippendale chairs and tables, Sèvres vases, Meissen ornaments and a Fabergé egg, not to mention a Renoir and a Matisse.

Yet the artworks and the porcelain held no interest for the woman from Munich. She found the two dozen evening gowns, twenty hats and fifty pairs of shoes that were to be sold far more intriguing. She'd read their reclusive former owner had been a minor star in the Hollywood firmament who'd moved to the mansion after the second world war. She went by the name of Lillian Stern.

A collection of black and white photographs, taken in the Thirties, was arousing particular interest among the press, too. Snapshots of glamorous soirées, of men and women in pouting poses, at tennis parties or lounging by swimming pools conjured up a bygone era. What the press particularly loved was the smattering of celebrity shots; the writer W Somerset Maugham was pictured at his French villa, and the Duke and Duchess of Windsor had posed for a souvenir in Paris. But the image that topped them all in the popular imagination seemed to be the one of a hauntingly beautiful woman in an evening dress, in the arms of an equally elegant Fred Astaire in white tie and tails, familiar to millions around the world. Apparently, she'd been a minor starlet in the Hollywood firmament, who went by the name of Lillian Stern.

It was what they called 'viewing day'. The sale for real was the following day, so, for now, potential buyers could just browse at their leisure, window-shop for a tiara or a Baccarat vase before the main event. But the young woman wasn't there to buy costly antiques, or even bag a bargain. The year before she'd had a life-changing shock that had jolted her on this journey. Now, she very much hoped, it was coming to an end.

The woman, her hair now back under control and a coat of lipstick applied, crossed the wooden bridge over the moat to the manor house and went inside. At a table in the entrance hall sat two smartly-dressed young women who seemed to be dealing with enquiries and doling out sale catalogues. She approached one.

'Name, please?' asked the girl in a well-cut blue suit.

'Angela Grunfeld,' said the woman.

'And address.' There was a hesitation. 'For our mailing list,' the girl explained with a smile.

'That won't be necessary,' replied Angela. 'I've come from Germany.' She paused. 'On a personal matter.'

Last year, the man Angela had always considered her father, Axel Grunfeld, had been rushed to hospital in Munich. He wasn't expected to last the night. Elspethe, his wife and her mother, had passed two years before. She'd hurried to his bedside.

When she arrived, a fair-haired doctor told her to prepare herself for the worst. As she leaned over her frail father, his eyes flickered beneath their papery lids, and slowly began to open.

'Vati. Vati, it's me!'

'Angela, *mein Schatz*,' he whispered. 'You must listen to what I have to say and listen carefully. I have something . . .' The effort of speech hurt him and he took a deep, agonising breath. 'I have something to tell you.'

A frown creased Angela's forehead. 'Tell me?' There was something in his tone that made her tense.

'I prayed that God would take me to my grave without warning, so that I could escape this day, but your dear mother made me promise . . .'

Of course Angela had no idea what he was talking about. At first she thought the drugs were making her father delirious, but he seemed lucid enough.

He went on. 'I don't want you to think less of your mother and me after I've told you.' He paused to capture his breath.

'What are you talking about? Don't upset yourself, Vati.' Angela found his obvious agitation worrying. She didn't want it to end this way. He should be at peace.

'It was war and people do strange things,' Axel rasped.

Angela shivered at the mention of war. As in so many German households, the subject of Hitler's tyranny had rarely been

369

discussed. Like an embarrassing illness, the recent past was ever-present, yet seldom acknowledged. As far as she knew, her father played no part in it. He was an innocent janitor who suffered as much as anyone else: the food shortages, the midnight dashes to the air-raid shelters; the burial of loved-ones. What was he saying?

'There was nothing I could do to stop them.' He seemed determined to carry on. 'They just burst in.' Angela's ears started to ring.

Her father's voice began to splinter. 'There were only four other families left in the building. Most of them had left. Fled the city, but some stayed.' He closed his eyes, like a child trying to blink away a nightmare and she knew he was talking about the Jews.

Angela swallowed hard and tried to offer comfort. 'As you said, it was the war, Vati. People were forced to do terrible things. If you didn't obey the laws . . . You had Mutti and me to think of. Don't worry about those things now.'

'But I must . . .' came the breathless reply. 'I must tell you . . .'

He paused then took another shallow breath. 'Our baby,' he whispered. 'Our little girl.' She half expected him to look at her then, as if he was recalling her childhood with a nostalgic fondness. But he didn't. Instead, she saw a tear fall from the corner of his eye and he said: 'She . . . she died. Our Angela died just a few days before.'

For a moment she was shocked then confusion took over. 'You mean I had an older sister?' she said with a frown. 'But why didn't you tell me?'

It was the way he turned his face to look at her that made her freeze. She knew in that split second what he was about to say. It was if everything he had ever told her or done for her was about to be blown apart in an enormous explosion. Her stunned gaze remained on him as the realisation dawned.

'I am not your real daughter.' Somehow the words tumbled from her tongue.

'No.'

Angela let out a gasp. She was stunned. Everything around

her suddenly exploded and for a few seconds her past lay like scattered fragments all around her.

'I see,' was all she could say at first then, seeking reassurance: 'But Mutti was my real mother.'

The silence spoke for him until eventually he admitted it. 'No, Angie. She was not.' His tears were flowing freely now. 'But we both did what any real parents would have done.'

'I don't understand.' The shock had suddenly dried up her tears.

'You were staying with your grandmother, Golda Sternberg, and I took you from her apartment to our own.'

'You took me?'

'Don't you see? I was giving you the chance of life.'

The old man suddenly seemed unstoppable. He had unleashed a genie and they both knew time was running out. 'You were ill. Too weak to cry. That's why the soldiers didn't find you.'

'The soldiers?'

'They came for your mother, but when they didn't find her, they shot your grandmother instead. When they'd gone I collected you and carried you downstairs.'

'You were hiding me?' she asked.

He ploughed on, his eyes suddenly lighting up. 'Mutti said the angels must have sent you, just as they sent us our little Angela. She cradled you in her arms and wrapped you in blankets. She fed you, slept with you, never left your side until you were fit and well again. We knew you could never go back. You were ours. We saved you. We saved your life.'

Suddenly the white dot began to run quicker across the screen.

'We . . . we would have been shot if they'd found us out. Shot as traitors for harbouring a Jew.'

'A Jew!' The word robbed Angela of her breath. 'Are you saying I'm Jewish?'

'Yes, *mein Schatz*. Yes, you are. And your real name is Leeona.'

'Leeona.' She said it slowly at first. It sat strangely on her tongue. Then once again. 'Leeona.'

'Yes.'

'But my real mother! What happened to her?'

He smiled at the thought of the young woman who beguiled everyone who met her. 'Your mother was a beautiful dancer called Lilli Sternberg,' he said wistfully. 'We never found out what became of her.'

Axel Grunfeld died later that night, but not before leaving his adopted daughter a ballet programme with her mother's name on it and a silver hairbrush engraved with the name *Leeona*.

For over a year Angela had been hunting, researching, writing letters and making phone calls in a bid to track down her real mother. The more she thought about it, the more she remembered faint snatches of the distant past: a sensation of being muffled in a blanket; the sound of men shouting. Fear. She'd always suffered from what she regarded as recurring nightmares. After Axel Grunfeld's death she realised they weren't nightmares at all. They were memories.

Only six weeks before, just when she'd managed to fit together all the pieces of the complicated puzzle and discovered her real mother was living somewhere in England, did Angela see the advertisement. It was for an auction at Gresham Hall, the former home of a mysterious German recluse who'd lived there. The press had described her as 'Fred Astaire's former dancing partner' and likened her to Marlene Dietrich. She'd died from cancer the previous year, leaving a large estate. When she'd started on her quest Angela knew, time would be her enemy and time, it turned out, had defeated her. Naturally she was devastated to learn of the passing of the woman she believed to be her mother, Lilli Sternberg. Nevertheless, she decided to persevere with her quest. Leaving her veterinary practice, her husband and two young children in Germany for a few days, she'd realised there was nothing else for it but to travel to England for the auction.

Chapter 69

Armed with a sale catalogue, Angela turned to follow the rest of the viewers as they funnelled away from the entrance and down a dark corridor. Nearby a row of chairs cowered against the oak panelling for the benefit of people who'd already had enough of Limoges and Lalique and needed to take the weight off their feet. A rather large woman in a bright pink dress was occupying two of the seats. Next to her was a boy with a bandaged ankle and next to him an elderly man, with a head of thick white hair, whose hands were cupped over the handle of a walking stick. As Angela passed, she thought he must have been quite striking in his youth. With his large, kind eyes, he seemed intent on scrutinising everyone who walked through the door.

The massive hall with its high, vaulted ceiling was packed with people. Tapestries and hunting trophies were hanging on the walls and even the stags had lot tags draped in an undignified fashion around their antlers. There were portraits, too. She moved closer to one wall. Not that she expected to find blood relatives. She assumed her mother had acquired random ancestors from various art collections and antique shops with the flourish of her signature on a cheque. There were men in Elizabethan ruffles and Victorians looking most austere. There were women too: a

Georgian lady in hunting dress, sitting in the shade of a tree and a beguiling little girl child holding a puppy. Of course, what she was really looking for was a portrait of her mother, and she was disappointed not to find one.

Angela walked to the end of the row of portraits and was about to turn to look at the paintings, mainly still life, on the opposite wall, when, in among the ornate gilt, she spotted a more modern frame. She drew closer. This portrait was much smaller than the rest. The loose brush strokes and impressionistic style gave it away as modern. The sitter was a man in a cravat and cricket sweater, perhaps in his thirties or forties, a leonine mane of hair combed back off his handsome face. His jaw line was strong and his eyes were large and brown. She stopped and stared at him, thinking him vaguely familiar. There was no name on the painting and yet, for some reason, the image captivated her. Her gaze lingered for a moment longer as she wondered.

Making her way out of the hall, Angela returned to the corridor and the row of seats by the main entrance. The woman and the boy had moved on, but the distinguished elderly gentleman was still there. He hadn't budged, both hands resting on the handle of his walking stick. He seemed to be watching the door, just observing everyone coming in and going out. Angela was about to sit down on one of the vacant seats to begin perusing the catalogue, when she happened to glance at him. He'd fixed his gaze on her and when Angela faced him, his eyes suddenly cracked open, as if a thousand volts had just passed through him.

Seeing his reaction to her, she froze and they both looked at each other in silence for a moment. The man's eyes were wide and his mouth was slightly open, almost as if he was experiencing some sort of religious vision.

Angela felt her heart drum in her chest. 'Can I help you?' she asked, trying to suppress her rising excitement. This man could, after all, be a complete stranger. But somehow she knew he was not.

374

'Leeona?' he whispered. 'Leeona, is it you?'

Her heart leapt. The years rolled back. 'Papa?'

In that moment they realised they'd found what they were both seeking. Marco lost his grip on his stick as his arms reached up and Angela dropped the catalogue to return his embrace. Time stood still as they hugged each other, tears streaming down both their faces. People were looking at them, but they remained unaware of everything and everyone.

'I knew you'd come,' he said. They reined back to look at each other and Angela saw an older, male version of herself staring back; the same large, brown eyes, the wild, untameable hair.

'I just knew you'd come, Leeona,' Marco repeated through his tears. He dabbed his eyes with a handkerchief from his breast pocket.

Arm in arm, they walked outside and found a stone bench in a quiet corner of the gardens. Angela pressed herself close to her father's sports jacket. Somehow it felt right to keep him close now that she'd found him. Neither of them knew where to begin.

'Where have you been, my Leeona?' he asked, clasping both her hands in his. 'Where have you been? We looked for you everywhere. Everywhere, my dear.' The tears began rolling down his cheeks again. 'Your mother almost went mad trying to find you. As soon as it was safe for us to return, we went back to Munich and scoured the city. But the apartment was bombed and there was no sign of you.'

Angela sniffed back her tears, too. 'I was there, all the while, Papa. The Nazis came and shot my grandmother.'

Marco's bottom jaw shot out. 'I know. Your mother was betrayed by the family's lodger,' he told her. 'We discovered later your grandmother died at the hands of a brute called Karl von Stockmar.'

Angela nodded. 'I read about it. He was found guilty of her murder by a war crimes tribunal at Nuremberg.'

Marco nodded. 'The dog died serving his sentence,' adding bitterly: 'It was too good a death for him.' He unfurled the handkerchief in his breast pocket again, dabbing his cheeks. 'Of course, he was originally charged with your murder, too. But they never found a body. That's what kept our hope alive. We refused to give up.'

Angela saw his pain. The memories of that time and of what Lilli and he both suffered, she could see, were still raw. 'Herr Grunfeld and his wife saved me and brought me up.'

Marco's jaw fell. 'The janitor?'

'Yes,' said Angela.

'All those years . . .' He looked into the distance.

'But you and my mother, you lived here?' She turned to gaze at the magnificent mansion.

Marco flattened his full mouth in a half smile. 'Yes. We escaped to New York from Lisbon, then after the war, Lilli bought this place.' His large eyes, swept over the honey-coloured stone of the manor house. 'We had thirty-five happy years here, but all those objects you see today filled the hole that you left in our lives. We never stopped missing you.'

Suddenly remembering something, Angela reached into her handbag.

'Look,' she said, holding up a silver hairbrush with the name *Leeona* engraved on it.

Marco's eyes lit up. He also reached into his breast pocket and brought out a matching silver comb. 'I wasn't going to let this go in the sale,' he said, shaking his head. It, too, was engraved with the name *Leeona*. He waved it gleefully in the air. 'I keep it next to my heart,' he cried, a tide of tears threatening to overwhelm him once more. 'A present from the Duchess of Windsor!'

'The Duchess of Windsor?' asked Angela, puzzled. 'I don't understand.'

Marco put his arm through his newfound daughter's as, away

from all the hustle of the house, they started to stroll in the grounds of the manor.

'There is much you need to be told,' he said. 'And I know just the person to tell you.'

Epilogue

Marco insisted Leeona – a name Angela was happy to take – stay with him at the manor for as long as she was in England. She accepted and after dinner that night, as they sat together in front of a log fire in the low-beamed drawing room when all the visitors had left, her father walked over to an oak bureau. From it he fetched a large leather-bound book. Leeona was curious. At first she thought it must be a photograph album, one that her father had rescued from the auction. But no. It was a notebook.

'Your mother wanted me to give you this, should we ever meet again,' Marco explained, handing it to her. 'Read it later, in a quiet place.'

Later that same night, alone in her room, Leeona opened the bound book with trembling hands just as Marco instructed. On the very first page she was reunited with her mother, Lilli Sternberg, for the first time in forty years, as she heard a voice from the distant past in her head.

My beloved Leeona,
If you are reading this, it will be because I am no longer here. But it will also be because you have found your father, or he has found you. You will be rejoicing together and, wherever

I am, I will be, too. I shall be with you in spirit, as I always have been. A mother knows when her child is alive and I have always known that you lived. That is why we never gave up searching for you, seeing your face wherever we went, hearing your little voice that tinkled like bells. Do you still have those wonderful curls? Do you still love animals?

Your father, I am sure, will do his best to tell you our story. It is an important one, about how we both played a part in standing up to evil and, helped conquer it, but I believe it is also important you hear about my own personal journey. I want you to know the truth.

I hope you have found love in your life, my precious Leeona, as I did with your father. Perhaps you have also been given the gift of children. If you have, cherish them.

Nevertheless, we all have our own pain to bear and we must dance through it in our own way. In the following pages you will see how I danced through mine. It was never easy and, without you by my side in my later years, it was made harder, but I hope learning about the person I was, and who you are, will help you find your own truth.

These are my words to you, my darling Leeona. And they come with enduring love.

Your mother,

Lilli Sternberg

Acknowledgements

This work of fiction has been a very long time in the making – thirty years, in fact. The story was first conceived back in 1990 when I read an article in the *Sunday Times* magazine about an unusual auction Sotheby's was holding at an English country house that was hailed as the 'sale of the century'. Up for grabs were not only vintage cars and items from Cartier and Fabergé, but several dozen fabulous evening gowns and pairs of shoes. Most intriguing of all was the identity of the mystery owner of all these luxurious objects. It was reported Dorothea Allen was a reclusive millionairess who died without leaving a will or any known next of kin, but even more tantalising was the fact that she had defaced all the existing photographs of herself in an effort, it was supposed, to disguise her past. On the back of one of these images was a written the particularly enigmatic inscription: *The Woman Who Danced with Fred Astaire.*

As you might suppose, my imagination was immediately fired by the story and the rumours that inevitably accompanied it at the time. Who was this woman? What did she have to hide? Was she a spy or perhaps a Jew who'd escaped Nazi Germany? In pre-Google times the press was full of speculation and the wild rumours rumbled on for years until the woman's real – and rather less exciting – background was revealed. Nevertheless, for me, the seed of a story was already sown and I was happy to run with my own more fanciful, but nonetheless, historically credible, version of events.

In so doing I uncovered a shady episode in history that, at the time, was largely hidden from general view. The completed manuscript was, however, left in a drawer for several years as a career and motherhood took priority. The story remained at the back of my mind and was reignited when, as a journalist, I was fortunate enough to meet the real-life Hollywood film star Leslie Caron who had partnered Fred Astaire in the classic films *Daddy Long Legs* and *Something's Gotta Give*. Her own story – a poor ballet student becomes a Hollywood star – contained uncanny echoes of the one I'd already written and I would highly recommend her autobiography *Thank Heavens*.

In the meantime, several previously secret documents were released to the public for the first time, and a number of historians and journalists were able to uncover the true extent of the right-wing sympathies of the former King Edward VIII and his wife Wallis Simpson. Among the huge cache of secret documents discovered by American troops in the Harz mountains and compiled in Marberg, Germany in 1945 was a set of documents that came to be known as the *Windsor Files*. One of the shocking revelations, found in a telegram contained in the files, stated that the *Duke believes with certainty that continued heavy bombing will make England ready for peace.* In other words, Edward was advocating the killing of his own people, his former subjects.

Yet perhaps the most extraordinary and outlandish revelation about the Duke and Duchess of Windsor – and there were several – was the uncovering of *Operation Willi*, a plan that included kidnapping the ducal couple while they were leaving Europe to travel to the Bahamas where Edward had just been named governor. Michael Bloch's excellent investigative history

Operation Willi: The Plot to Kidnap the Duke of Windsor, July 1940 is recommended for further reading, as is Andrew Morton's *17 Carnations.*

As with all episodes of this nature, conspiracy theories abound. When, in 1945, King George VI sent Anthony Blunt, the art historian to Friedrichshof Castle near Frankfurt, ostensibly to retrieve letters by Queen Victoria to her daughter, Empress Victoria, he may also have brought back other correspondence in which the Duke knowingly revealed Allied secrets to Hitler. There is another suggestion from respected author Martin Allen, in his book *Hidden Agenda,* that after the death of the Duchess in 1986, her secret papers may have been 'acquired' by agents of the Royal Archives at Windsor Castle, although this has been denied. We may never know the full extent of the collusion between the Windsors and the Third Reich, so, in the meantime, writers of fiction can always speculate.

For an excellent insight into the psyche of Wallis Simpson and indeed her husband, I would recommend Anne Sebba's *That Woman.* And for an account of what life was like from a German perspective, *Bounden Duty,* is the memoirs of Alexander Stahlberg, an army officer reluctantly obeying Hitler's regime.

On a lighter note, Tim Satchell's *Astaire, The Biography,* is another fascinating read about the legendary dancer's background and rise to fame in Hollywood. Robert Calder's biography of W. Somerset Maugham, *Willie,* also gives an interesting glimpse into a bygone era.

In the production of this novel I am most indebted to Belinda Toor, my editor at HQ Digital for singling out my story and believing in it. Without her it may never have resurfaced from its thirty-year period of purdah. My thanks, too, go to members of the production team, including Audrey Linton and Dushi Horti.

I would also like to thank the many Gloucestershire authors who have lent me their support including Mandy Robotham, Dinah Jefferies, Jane Bailey and Caroline Sanderson. Miriam Buck and the team at Hawkwood College have also been so generous to me. Finally, but not least, my thanks go to my husband, Simon, with his keen eye for detail, who has seen this novel evolve over the past three decades into what it has become today.

Dear Reader,

We hope you enjoyed reading this book. If you did, we'd be so appreciative if you left a review. It really helps us and the author to bring more books like this to you.

Here at HQ Digital we are dedicated to publishing fiction that will keep you turning the pages into the early hours. Don't want to miss a thing? To find out more about our books, promotions, discover exclusive content and enter competitions you can keep in touch in the following ways:

JOIN OUR COMMUNITY:

Sign up to our new email newsletter: hyperurl.co/hqnewsletter

Read our new blog www.hqstories.co.uk

https://twitter.com/HQStories

www.facebook.com/HQStories

BUDDING WRITER?

We're also looking for authors to join the HQ Digital family!
Find out more here:

https://www.hqstories.co.uk/want-to-write-for-us/

Thanks for reading, from the HQ Digital team

ONE PLACE. MANY STORIES

**If you enjoyed *Beneath a Starless Sky*,
then why not try another sweeping historical
novel from HQ Digital?**

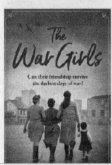